A NOVEL

DROPS

OF

CERULEAN

DAWN ADAMS COLE

GREENLEAF
BOOK GROUP PRESS

Published by Greenleaf Book Group Press
Austin, Texas
www.gbgpress.com

Copyright ©2019 Dawn Cole

All rights reserved.

Distributed by Greenleaf Book Group

For ordering information or special discounts for bulk purchases, please contact Greenleaf Book Group at PO Box 91869, Austin, TX 78709, 512.891.6100.

Design and composition by Greenleaf Book Group
Cover design by Greenleaf Book Group and Rachael Brandenburg

Cover credits: cumulus clouds ©iStockphoto.com/ojeol; Houston map ©alamy.com/nestign; natural background copyright vvoe, 2018. Used under license from Shutterstock.com

Publisher's Cataloging-in-Publication data is available.

Print ISBN: 978-1-62634-555-3

eBook ISBN: 978-1-62634-556-0

Part of the Tree Neutral® program, which offsets the number of trees consumed in the production and printing of this book by taking proactive steps, such as planting trees in direct proportion to the number of trees used: www.treeneutral.com

TreeNeutral

Printed in the United States of America on acid-free paper

18 19 20 21 22 23   10 9 8 7 6 5 4 3 2 1

First Edition

To Burton, who believed in me before I believed in myself. *Somnium Veram Evadit.*

To Caroline and Elizabeth, my splinters of the Universe, my reminders of the Divine.

It is the secret of the world that all things subsist and do not die, but only retire a little from sight and afterwards return again. Nothing is dead; men feign themselves dead, and endure mock funerals and mournful obituaries, and there they stand looking out of the window, sound and well, in some strange new disguise.

—RALPH WALDO EMERSON

PART
ONE

CADMUS

Autumn 2014

CADMUS ADMITTED HIS NEED FOR assistance, but his concession concluded with a staunch, "Surely that does not encompass every goddamn facet of my life!"

Somewhat obsequious in his treatment of wealthy residents, the director of The Oaks paused to give Clementine a look that implored her assistance. Taking the cue, she placed her hand on her mentor's shoulder with a gentle squeeze.

Cadmus looked down, a flush of embarrassment sweeping across his face. He could not fool Clementine; they knew his profanity was his way of summoning his late husband's resolve. The Dr. Doyle she knew rarely raised his voice or uttered a profane word. And with her gentle correction, he took a deep breath and attempted another plea, one using his normal voice.

"Please allow me to retain my car on your premises. I will only ride as a passenger, with your staff's assistance, of course," he corrected, reflecting his usual pleasant disposition.

"Dr. Doyle, please know it is our intention for you to feel that this is your home, not our premises. But even with that hope, our staff is not allowed to transport residents in their personal vehicles. They are authorized to drive you in The Oaks van. It is a luxury van, one that I believe you will find most comfortable and appealing."

Looking to Clementine, Cadmus whispered, "Please . . . I need to keep Robert's car. I will leave it here for you to drive us. Please."

"I believe Dr. Doyle's request is a fair one," Clementine replied confidently with a hint of a dare, the slight bite of her tone reminding Cadmus that she was a MacDougall. "The car will remain here with me as the only driver. I will take the keys. Thank you for helping us ease this transition. He is coming from one of the original George F. Barber houses, so you must understand how difficult it is for him to move from the only home he has known since 1935."

The director, smiling in resignation, extended his pen to Cadmus so he could add his signature to the new resident agreement. Cadmus forcefully shook his head while reaching into his interior breast pocket for his fountain pen, the Doyle Lumber engraving was long gone, as was the company itself, rubbed away from a lifetime of use. He cherished the opportunity to sign his name, knowing his time to do so was dwindling. Taking deliberate, cursive strokes with midnight blue ink, he slowly signed the contract: Cadmus Aleksander Doyle.

CADMUS DOYLE WAS A PARADOX of sorts, beginning with the name bestowed on him at birth. At first glance, his thick silver hair and surname conjured images of an Irish gentleman, and in less than a blink of an eye, a passerby could imagine him ruddy cheeked, holed up in a pub, animatedly regaling tales to entertain the patrons. People who knew their etymology, however, linked his first name to the founder of Thebes and grandson of Poseidon, the one heralded for delivering the first alphabet to the Greeks. And in the next blink, the observer glimpsed Cadmus' younger self—thick, wavy dark hair that complimented his full, dark brown eyes, a striking Greek gentleman whose elegance dwarfed his Irish surname. Two strong names—a juxtaposition that highlighted the opposing forces in his life, although his connection to his mother always prevailed.

Cadmus' third-floor room location gave away his condition. Third-floor residents suffered from varying forms of dementia, ranging from those in the early stages to others who were confined to their rooms, where loss of speech and movement rendered them virtually helpless, staring with hollowed pupils that searched for evidence that they were part of something greater than themselves. Cadmus knew he would eventually live in the west wing of skilled nursing, and with this understanding came a flood of contradictory emotions. He desperately wanted to retain his intellect and take solace in words, his faithful companion since he had been a child, yet he welcomed the final chapter that he hoped would unite him with his mother—although his predilection for Buddhism prevented him from fully vesting in the idea that he would see her as he had in this lifetime. Fifty-one years had passed since her death, but his advancing age only intensified his longing for her, an amalgam of love and guilt.

His first day at The Oaks, with Clementine assisting with the room setup, lent itself to the narrative of an ordinary, lonely widower adjusting to life in a new residence with a granddaughter by his side. No one knew that Cadmus, estranged from his extended family, relied on a former graduate student he once advised to help him come to terms with his growing medical needs, including the fact that he could no longer live alone. Clementine knew his story, and she knew when he asked her to adjust the framed photograph of the beautiful woman standing on Main Street in front of the University of Houston Downtown, formerly known as the Merchants and Manufacturers Building, that he was admiring his mother, the only person in his family who accepted that he had kissed a man when he was eighteen.

Clementine sorted through the last pile of books, setting aside the few that belonged on his nightstand and the others that would rest on the bookshelves. She paused at his tattered edition of E. E. Cummings poetry, knowing its rightful place was at the top of a short stack that fed his nightly ritual, his caressing of the yellowed, thin pages as much a part of the spiritual commune as the actual words, the most loved pages first showing wear when his mother marked them years ago when it rested at her own bedside.

A photograph fell from the book as she set it aside. Landing facedown, she could see the year 1940 written on the back. She bent down to pick up the photograph and turned it over to reveal a black-and-white print of Cadmus as a young boy seated atop his father's desk. Patrick's hand rested on his son's to guide the rotation of a compass.

"Wondering how we could be related?" Cadmus asked before offering a rueful chuckle as he entered the room.

"No, actually, I can see the resemblance. It's just that I don't remember ever seeing this one, which surprises me."

"I keep that one close to me."

Clementine raised the photograph to eye level, holding it up to the sunlight shining through the east window. After a few blinks, she commented, "You have his dimples."

She met his eyes with a tender smile, uncovering another layer of the mentor she thought she knew so well.

"But I don't use them as often as he did. He was an outgoing one, my father."

"Do you want me to frame this for you?"

Cadmus shook his head and turned back toward his bedroom.

"Dr. Doyle?" Clementine called, taking a few steps forward before handing the photograph to him.

Cadmus reached for it, his gaze falling on his wrinkled hand before moving to the idyllic image of father and son. He appreciated Clementine's tranquil nature, her cool blue eyes patient for a response, something she continued to wait for as he spoke less and less often.

"I am afraid to lose it all," Cadmus replied, turning around and continuing to his bedroom. "My memories are all I've had, all I've had for most of my life."

When he passed the threshold, he closed the door, thinking back to one of the handful of memories he held of Patrick, a rare occasion when his father's face was devoid of a smile. Cadmus remembered him gazing out the window facing The Boulevard, his flamboyant demeanor uncharacteristically subdued and reflective. He remembered peeking around the corner in the hallway, admiring his father's light skin tone and sandy hair. Even as a toddler, Cadmus intuitively felt different, something apart from his Greek features. He did not long to run, play tag, and shoot as his cousins. He did not long to command audiences with hearty laughter and drink in hand as his father. Cadmus longed to be a Doyle rather than the observant, reticent soul he already knew he was.

As he adjusted his weight to the other foot, the floor creaked, breaking his father from his thoughts and Cadmus from the study of his father. His father turned to him, paused, and offered a sympathetic smile that embarrassed Cadmus, their difference palpable and unspoken. His father walked across the hall and knelt beside him.

"Let's go for a walk in the garden," he whispered as he kissed Cadmus on the forehead.

ILONA

Spring 1930

ILONA CAREFULLY WROTE HER NAME at the top of her essay, taking extra care to proportion the loops of each cursive letter. Her nose tingled as she completed the date, May 14, 1930. Seventeen days until graduation. She was on borrowed time when it came to writing her name on lined school papers.

She held on to her work, scrutinizing her essay on John Keats. Her face flushed when reading his words intertwined with hers, confirming her thought that she really was a good student. After so much time spent dismissing compliments from teachers, she rationalized that her hard work was what garnered their adulation. It was her work ethic and intelligence in tandem that poised her as a worthy candidate for the teaching profession. It pained her that teacher's college was not an option.

Studying the classroom, Ilona embedded detail to memory. The wooden desks, so new only a few years ago, had softened, as if malleable from student caresses and bumps. She enjoyed sitting at her desk, which was a far cry from her usual position behind the counter at the café. While some kids nervously tapped the desk edge with a pencil while waiting for the teacher or even used the writing surface to raise themselves higher as they yelled across the room, Ilona sat in reverence, palms resting on the cool, dark surface. The desk did not constrain her. It was the vehicle that removed her from her everyday life.

"Ilona, reading es not bad thing, you know? Look the customers . . . smile. Head no belong book. It belong looking café with lovely face," her father "baba" said while removing the books she stashed under the counters, dog-eared novels stained with determination, sugar, and grease.

Students rushed to Miss Baker's desk at the sound of the bell, anxious to hand over their essays, one step closer to commencement. Springtime welcomed a flurry of engagements, many paths already chosen. It did not take long for the chatter to fill with wedding talk as the girls spilled into the hallway.

"Always the last to turn in, but the one I prefer to read first," Miss Baker said with a smile. "Have you given any more thought to talking to your father about teaching?"

Ilona shook her head. "After the new restaurant opens, after things get more settled, perhaps then will I speak to my father."

"A beautiful girl like you, Miss Ilona, will be married to a handsome Greek gentleman by that time," Miss Baker winked, swiping the essay from Ilona's hands.

Ilona nodded, offering a weak smile as she headed into the hallway to her locker. She thought about her baba, who was in the process of opening a second restaurant downtown, a bold move for the family in light of growing fears that the full devastation of the economy would soon reach Houston's doors, a fear many Houstonians continued to push to the recesses of their minds. Ilona would assume the role on Franklin Street that her mama played on Lawndale Street: greeter and cashier. Thoughts of wanting more flooded Ilona with equal doses of frustration and shame, seeing that the depression was ravaging so many other parts of the country.

"Your cousins in New York came home to loaf of bread! And seven in family!" her mama cried, shaking her head as she read the letter, a wrinkled scrap of paper revealing that they hoped to make it to Houston soon.

"Eucharistia. Be thankful," served as the stock response to most requests, and Ilona floundered to offer another possibility. Her sister, about to give birth to the family's first grandchild, was in no position to work at the restaurant, but Ilona surmised that Uncle Demetrius' sons could easily help. She could live with her family and even contribute her teaching salary, but she could not muster the courage to make the suggestion. And committing to teaching meant she was not committing to marrying, a thought that would leave her parents baffled.

The popular blondes huddled together near Ilona's locker with lowered heads. Millie, the pack's leader, held her proud head high as she posed her left hand midwaist.

"Excuse me," Ilona whispered, trying to nudge her way to her locker.

"Want to see my ring?" Millie called to Ilona over the heads of her friends.

Although Ilona did not know for certain, she had a hunch as to why Millie, a girl who had never spoken a word to her, now wanted to engage her in conversation. As shy as she was to admit it, Ilona knew that Millie's fiancé, Jody, was sweet on her. Seated one row over and two seats behind Ilona in Miss Baker's class, she frequently caught him staring. She recalled a recent poetry exam when she found her head nodding to a poem's cadence as she read it silently in her head. She giggled when she saw that Jody noticed it, too, and their gazes locked for a moment as a smile broke over his face. He chuckled, prompting Millie's attention from the far side of the room. Ilona knew he watched her out of the corner of his eye when she sharpened her pencil, and even though she was not attracted to him, his attention left her stomach in flutters.

Ilona did not believe she was beautiful, but she knew she had something, because she had heard Uncle Demetrius warn her baba when he did not think anyone could hear.

"Ilona es very pretty girl, Nikolas. Will be stunning woman . . . waiting come out shell. We need keep eye when she work downtown, you know. More Greek men downtown."

At Milby High School, however, Ilona was safely nestled in her shell. She played the role of the quiet soul, a diligent student and dutiful daughter. Her handful of school friends were just that, only casual friends at school. They sat together at lunch and supported one another, shoulder-to-shoulder, in an illusory stride down the hall. Ilona's group lived side-by-side in parallel relationships, unlike the intertwined, gossipy nature of the other social circles.

Ilona looked down at Millie's hand, tilting her head back as it neared her face.

"Yes . . . it is beautiful," Ilona stammered, recognizing it as the one she had seen in the Sears and Roebuck catalog a few months ago, sparkling chips set on a thin, gold band. Millie scored the engagement, but Ilona felt sorry for her, knowing that Millie had probably not scored his heart. "Congratulations."

"Of course, you don't get too excited about marrying, do you? I mean, your type arranges things like that, right?" Millie questioned, cocking her head to the side.

Quiet now, the other girls turned toward Ilona in anticipation. Other than formal responses in class, she rarely spoke.

Ilona's mind drifted to the café, to the way her baba approached her from behind when a respectable Greek family with an eligible son walked through the door. He would give her shoulders a squeeze before waving his right hand in the air. "Come, come meet my lovely daughter. Top of class at Milby!"

The sons were not always in tow. They did not need to be, since parents made the call on whether a formal introduction would follow. She wanted to fall in love and marry, but she regarded Greek men more as brothers than romantic interests. She could see her entire life before her: Marry a Greek man at the Greek Orthodox Church, and bring the next generation into the family business.

Ilona lowered her gaze, but her head remained high. She suspended her paralysis long enough to reply, "Perhaps not for me," in a tone bolder than intended, as she lifted her expressive eyes. Ilona did not intend for her words to provoke her, but they did. Millie's eyes widened, and Ilona realized that her response appeared a challenge.

Millie gave her one healthy nod backward while teasing, "Good luck with that!" as the coterie burst into giggles at Ilona's hope that things would be different for her. She opened her locker to trade her English book for history, and with a gentle nudge to the locker door, she hastened onto Broadway Street.

Ilona arrived at Lawndale Café, frustrated with herself for her reticence and for her inability to speak her mind on command. The power of her words came incidentally; she longed for a stronger constitution. Reaching for her apron in the storeroom, she caught sight of herself in the mirror, and unbeknownst to herself, she was mouthing the words *your type* in a most unattractive expression. It startled her to see her face contorted in such a fashion, and she could not help but giggle. In seventeen days, she would be rid of Millie and her friends. She would also be relegated to Lawndale Café for a while, but thoughts of her move downtown more than compensated— same restaurant setting but different people, more people, city people. She closed her eyes and tied the apron strings around her waist, praying for an openhanded gesture from God.

Pushing open the double doors from the kitchen, she scanned the restaurant. It was the normal crowd, a smattering of people at the counter and at the tables along the windows. Mrs. Jilufka's face perked up when she saw Ilona. Her elderly friend lifted her left hand from the countertop in a weak wave as she took a last bite of pineapple-coconut cake.

"Come talk to me, pretty girl," Mrs. Jilufka called from the far end of the counter in her shaky voice.

"Pink looks good on you, Mrs. Jilufka. Brings a glow to your cheeks."

"Not sure about that glow, but I'll take the compliment," she replied, using both hands to steady her coffee cup. Ilona grabbed the pot to refill the cup and a rag to wipe the counter. "I sure am jittery today," Mrs. Jilufka continued, shaking her head. "I'll miss you so when you head to the new place, but I imagine you're glad to have something new."

Ilona kept her eyes on the coffee to avoid looking her friend in the eye.

Lawndale Café was home, which was away from most other Greek families who settled closer to the heart of the city. Her baba selected their home based on a neighborhood in desperate need of a restaurant, but it was farther east.

"Find need and create!" he declared, pounding a fist onto the kitchen table that made the silverware skip, as her mama shook her head, unsettled to be so far away from her closest friends. He found a prime spot, ensconced in a charming, working-class neighborhood in need of "good, good food" to fill men and women on their way to factory work on the west and to the ship channel on the east. Uncle Demetrius' stake in the neighborhood was only due to her baba, who had encouraged his younger brother to serve as partner in the hopes of opening more restaurants around the city.

"Church where we see our people. We make money, move, see them all time when we have big house and have big party," he said. Ilona's connections were with the likes of the bohemians, the Novaks, the Rascheks, and the Jilufkas, God Bless Mr. Jilufka's soul.

Ilona offered a grin in acknowledgment before taking the seat at the far end of the counter, readying the salt and pepper shakers for refills. Chores would remain chores regardless of the downtown location or the new name, Franklin Street Diner. And the layout would remain the same even though the capacity would double: ten window tables and twenty counter seats to host city patrons. The most exciting difference was the foundation itself, with the windows poised north to face the Merchants and Manufacturers Building that opened a month prior. Ilona knew the M&M Building was one surefire way to keep her nose out of a book, her mind poised to weave the stories behind the countless windows of the building conceived at the seam of Buffalo and White Oak Bayous. As she secured the lids on the shakers, Ilona decided she would attempt to keep a journal alongside her books underneath the register counter. Perhaps she could put her musings to paper and experiment with writing.

For the past two years, conversations about the M&M circulated among the Lawndale patrons—men eager to work and prosper in Houston, a city well on its way to becoming an industrial power. She strained to hear bits and pieces as she cleared tables on those summer mornings, the cacophony of clanging utensils and sizzles from the grill teasing away her focus.

The city energy was palpable, and Ilona absorbed the excitement, methodically studying the construction from a distance, in awe of how something so seemingly impregnable appeared delicate at the same time: a copulation of glass, stone, and lumber that framed the burgeoning city. She looked at the M&M as a collective being, a marriage of hope and of what truly could be, with the dreams of Houstonians offering nourishment. She was not keen on continued work in a restaurant, but at least she had a front-row seat at the register one block away on Franklin Street, its ten windows facing the thousands of the M&M, a building now teaming with life.

Baba's use of the word *diner* for the restaurant was the result of a bit of fantasy on his part. Diners were common in New York, and although her cousins could not afford to experience them firsthand, Ilona knew from descriptions in their letters and her studies that he gratuitously used the term. Contractors created Franklin Street Diner in a space more generous than a prefabricated car arriving by rail as traditional diners were. She preferred the Greek blue script that would beckon customers from the façade of their new diner, but she knew it was very different from the steel exterior of the diners in the northeast. While Ilona knew most customers would not recognize the discrepancy, either out of ignorance or out of hunger, the naming still left her with a hesitation, making her wonder if she were more like her baba than she thought—someone who wanted to be something she was not meant to be.

The sound of the bells on the door signaled the arrival of her baba, jacket in hand and Homburg on head.

"Ilona, let's go Franklin. I check on new diner construction. We stop by Anthony's place and say hello," he announced as he entered.

A trip downtown was certainly enough to raise her spirits, even if it meant paying a visit to Anthony's Grocery. Anthony Senior, convinced that Ilona and his son were a match, was increasingly forceful in his approach, suggesting family dinners and outings so the children could get better acquainted. Images of Anthony Junior flipped through her mind, his elongated, bony face resembling a cursive V, from the dark curly lock that rested on his left temple to his pointy chin. She was not keen on a visit, but it was a quick jaunt, and his intentions were manageable in small doses.

"Nice young man, Anthony?"

"Yes, Baba. He is a nice man." Ilona watched out the window as their car moved in tandem with the streetcar heading into town along Harrisburg.

"The store es doing good, very good. They want new one, two stores even though times . . ." he tapered off, waving his right hand in a so-so gesture.

"That's wonderful, Baba."

"You will go supper with Anthony tonight? He take you home after."

"Baba, I have homework this evening. I need to study for my history exam. Maybe another night," she replied, her stomach becoming increasingly unsettled by the disturbance in her late-afternoon reverie.

"You good student. You make me proud. Now es time, Ilona, think about life after graduation. Time think about family, about business."

Ilona closed her eyes, deciding at the spur of the moment to take a chance. "Baba, I've been thinking about teaching. I think I'd be a good teacher, and of course I'll . . ."

"Nose in book make you better?"

"No, Baba, no . . . I am not better, just different. There is so much to learn, so many things I want to do."

"We need you, need your help, Ilona. Arianna married with own family. Your brother, God rest his soul, he would not let us down if he still here!"

Baba played the trump card, referencing her brother's passing. He had been the eldest child in the family and was poised to carry on the Petrarkis name had he not succumbed to tuberculosis at twelve years old. Ilona had but a handful of memories of Cadmus, the dearest when he drew hopscotch for her and her friends on the sidewalk in front of their house. His buddies impatiently yelling for him with baseball bat, balls, and gloves in hand, Cadmus shouted, "You can very well wait for a few minutes! Remember, one day I'll be pitchin' for the Buffalos." They groaned in frustration but did not protest, knowing that he, very well indeed, might play for the Buffalos. His death placed an indelible scar on her parents' souls.

Silence filled the car; Ilona surmised that her baba's thoughts, as hers, were turned toward her brother. As she offered a silent prayer and sent her love to the heavens, the car turned onto Franklin Street, the diner coming into view. As her baba pulled alongside the curb on the opposite side of the street and turned off the motor, Ilona's gaze locked on the M&M, and her thoughts filled with excitement that she, too, was now a downtown tenant.

She placed her hand on his shoulder and said, "Congratulations, Baba. You did it." And as she turned to face him, she saw his face beaming with pride.

ILONA

Autumn 1930

ILONA STOOD IN HER CLOSET, vacillating on what to wear while giving thanks for her good fortune—her baba was allowing her to tag along with her uncle to pay a bill to the glass company in the M&M. The new restaurant was faring quite well with a few hired hands, despite the "bad luck of the greedy ones in New York," but this did not relieve Ilona as a fixture at the register, where she alternated between greeting customers and stashing books under the counter. At least she would enjoy time off today after the lunch crowd dissipated, and it would be her first time in the M&M.

Uncle Demetrius and Ilona made their way over the bridge on Main Street. Eyes wide, she walked closest to the edge, paying careful attention to the M&M Building's ground floor dock off Buffalo Bayou, where a train pulled into the station, moments from fulfilling its delivery. The upper floors of the building housed offices and suites for an array of businesses, including the glass company her baba used for the restaurant. Ilona's interest resided on the third floor that rested at street level, home to an arcade of stores, including a hair salon, boutiques, a restaurant, and a lounge.

She smiled at the opportunity to shop at Morton's Millinery. Her niece was to be baptized in two weeks, and her baba, ecstatic at the mere mention of his first grandchild, found it difficult to say no to her request for a new hat, since he wanted his family smartly dressed for the occasion. Ilona knew something was afoot with the repeated mention of a certain attendee, a gentleman who owned a restaurant on Main Street and who had an eligible son. Baba had attended a ball game at Buff Stadium with this man the previous week. A part of her could not help but feel sorry for Anthony Junior, who had fallen out of favor after the introduction of this more prosperous family.

"I be on fourth floor, Suite 415, Sullivan Glass Company. I head to lounge after. Take your time, dear," Uncle Demetrius said. And with a wink, "I be awhile." Ilona knew he was happy to give her the opportunity to have time alone as an adult, something even the youngest of his three sons, a freshman at Milby, already enjoyed just because they were males.

As he disappeared from view, Ilona paused to take in the scene. A freckle-faced boy with red suspenders walked hand in hand with his mother into a confectionery, his eyes captivated by the canisters filled with candies that lined the walls. Only having heard the word *Morton's*, it took Ilona by surprise to see the name in print, an elegant elongated cursive script written in chocolate brown across a pale blue placard. The beautiful cascade of hats in the window confirmed it was the place, yet it still took her a moment to reconcile the abstract image she had in her mind with reality.

Throngs of people moved through the arcade, men in suits striding with purpose to the upper-floor offices while men in overalls scurried down to the railroad. Whether they had soft hands or grease-caked palms, everyone was searching for something. The energy left her light-headed, surrounded by spirits propelled to create, to forge something new. Her mind drifted to the Franklin Street Diner, to the patrons nourishing their bodies with food while sharing their dreams of Houston.

Ilona took only one step in the direction of Morton's when the freckle-faced boy raced past her, causing her to take a few steps backward to stop herself from falling. The boy's mother scurried after him, making apologies to those he bumped along the way. Wondering what could have happened in those few minutes they were in the candy store, Ilona watched the son and mother leave the building, shouldering past a handsome gentleman with sandy brown hair and gold-rimmed circular glasses.

"Easy there, buddy," he chuckled to the boy as he patted his back. As the man's gaze returned to the arcade, his eyes squinting in transition from the Houston sun now at his back, she instinctively returned the smile that he wore through his eyes. And Ilona Petrarkis had never met anyone who could do just quite that.

He walked right toward her with such assurance that she was sure he must know her from somewhere or have some news to deliver. She looked at the ground for a moment, her eyes darting as she tried to place how she knew him. He held out his hand, and as her eyes rose to meet his, he greeted her with, "Patrick Doyle, and you must say yes to having a drink with me in the lounge. It's close enough to cocktail hour, right?"

Ilona had yet to enjoy a drink, and she wondered where on earth he planned to order one given the law. She had only had a few sips of wine on graduation day months before when her baba offered a toast at the family's celebratory dinner; the wine came from a few bottles he had hidden in his closet. It was a thoughtful gesture: She knew her baba was proud, and she knew he loved her and wanted her to have a happy life. And although he was a believer that America and Texas, in particular, were fertile for making dreams a reality, his dreams were not her dreams. She wanted to learn, to teach, to meet new people, and to be part of city life sans family business.

She nodded subconsciously at the remark that *Gimlets are proof God wants us to be happy,* which he took as a yes, that she would love one. As they walked to the lounge, she scanned the arcade discreetly to confirm that she knew not a soul in sight. Her willingness to take a chance wakened the latent sentiment for adventure that she knew she possessed, and she relished the happenstance a moment could bring.

Her uneasiness grew as the waiter revealed a private room by opening a velvet curtain, a flimsy barrier that concealed a speakeasy. The other patrons, all men in fine suits and a couple of well-dressed women, all appeared at complete ease as they sipped cocktails in fine crystal glasses. This was definitely not one of the illicit, lowbrow bars around town she had heard her baba and uncle talk about late at night when they thought she was asleep. Patrick excused himself for a moment to shake hands with gentlemen at a nearby table, glancing back at her with his finger raised in the air, signaling he needed but a second more. Thankful for the moment to gather her thoughts, Ilona settled into the red leather booth and sorted through her catalog of memories once more; the affinity she felt surely meant she knew him from somewhere.

"What brings you to the M&M today?" Patrick asked as he took his seat, the waiter placing two cocktails on the table.

"Hope."

"Tell me more," he said, taking a healthy sip of his drink.

"I've watched this building from its conception, heard stories from the men in my parents' restaurant. It's giving people of Houston the opportunity to pursue their dreams. Exciting times for the city, and I hope for me."

She did not know how to regard his reaction, his gregarious personality now more subdued. At best, he was lost in thought, agreeing with her musings. At worst, he was considering how to extricate himself from such a queer young woman.

"And I have one more hope, a trivial matter but one that is important to me."

"Yes?" he asked, his lips pursed in the infancy of either a smile or a smirk.

"A new hat, for my niece's baptism."

His radiant smile reappeared, and, raising his glass, he toasted, "To our hopes and dreams. I do believe our paths were meant to cross."

As they sat and talked, she listened to stories about his family's lumber business, tons of lumber that had poured in from East Texas railroads at the turn of the century. The Doyles supplied the lumber for the M&M; Patrick was the building personified. Intoxicated with his sophistication and her growing confidence from the gin, she absorbed his spirit. No one had ever asked her so many questions about herself, not like this. Everyone she knew assumed they knew her, and as a result, the conversations remained at the surface level, pleasantries about the day and general interests. Why ask anything deeper when you knew the person, after all? She knew from her reading that people regard those they know well as flat and stagnant, that how they are is how they will always be. Strangers are afforded a more generous hand, one that honors their hopes with a reverence for the possibility of change.

She confided her love of literature and her desire to be closer to the pulse of the city, and he responded with his shared love of books and an invitation for her to see his collection at the library in his Heights home on The Boulevard. He had traveled and enjoyed his time away from the city immensely, but "Houston is a very special place . . . has an energy. Ripe for new things."

She did not realize the waiter had refreshed her gimlet at some point in the conversation, but she did realize the numbing of her chin. An older gentleman with a gold pocket watch hanging from the vest of his suit came over to shake Patrick's hand with hearty congratulations on a job well done with the M&M. At the man's first pause, Patrick confidently said, "Please allow me to introduce you to Ilona. Surely you have graced her family's new restaurant on Franklin?"

As the men chatted about the M&M construction, Ilona gave a word of thanks for the distraction. "*Eucharistia*," she giggled to herself. The room picked up its spin. She looked out the window to the bayou, attempting to still her eyes, but the windows and curtains remained slightly askew despite her deliberate blinks. Her mind drifted to her once imagined view of the glamorous people in the building, each pane framing a story. She was now one of the stories, gin-stocked and all. *A moment's decision*, her heart echoed, *can bring so many wonderful things*.

"And don't you worry one bit about the M&M occupancy. You got in at just the right time," Patrick assured.

The older gentleman replied, "Patrick, I'll take you at your word. And I suppose even last year's flood and the economic conditions of the north can't wash away all the dreams in here." The man then looked to her with approving eyes, gladly shaking her hand. "Absolutely charming, you two," he said nodding as if he was making the final determination whether they, indeed, complimented one another. "Yes, charming."

Ilona's eyes followed the gentleman as he opened the curtain to the main lounge. Elated with the man's conclusion, she turned her attention back to Patrick. His eyes intent on hers, he moved closer.

"Charming. Now that is really something. He's not an easy one to impress."

Ilona smiled demurely, surmising her best route at this point was to keep as still as possible in the hopes the room would follow suit. Her focus was shattered by the imposing figure standing at the curtain: Uncle Demetrius. After nodding a thank you to the waiter who pointed him in her direction, he made his way to the booth. He offered a quick glance to the cocktail glasses and then met her eyes with a raised brow before turning to Patrick.

"Demetrius Petrarkis, uncle of Ilona," he said with poise, after which Ilona whispered another *"Eucharistia"* under her breath.

"Patrick Doyle. I hope you do not mind that I stole your niece away for an early cocktail. It is a rarity to meet such an intelligent soul."

"Yes, she es our gem," he slowly nodded as he turned to face his niece, his eyes betraying the façade and revealing his utter bewilderment at her choices while he had been upstairs. "Ilona, time we head back."

He placed his hand on her back as a signal for her to follow; however, Ilona's legs took a cue from her chin and struggled to comply. Sensing her trouble, Uncle Demetrius wrapped one arm around her to help her from the booth, and Ilona gripped his arm as if they were walking down the aisle.

"Thank you for a lovely afternoon," she managed to mumble as she left the table.

"Yes, you're quite welcome," Patrick stammered, rising from his seat. "And may I . . ." he attempted to continue as her uncle ushered her away into the main lounge, leaving with a look that signaled to Patrick that he should leave Ilona alone.

CADMUS

Autumn 2014

WHEN CADMUS ENTERED THE OAKS, he vowed to enjoy supper in the dining hall as often as his health would allow. He admired the strict dress code of jacket and nice slacks, not only because it mirrored how he had dressed most of his life, but also, more important, because he hoped it would delay the inevitable. He did not want to see his fellow residents in their dressing gowns and robes, propelling their wheelchairs forward with crusty, bare heels. Everyone would be in that condition soon enough.

Exhausted from moving in that day, he took his supper quietly in his room. Clementine, along with a few hired hands, decorated the apartment with his family's rugs, Robert's paintings, and of course, his books. She exercised special care in assembling his study—his ornate mahogany desk displaying the accoutrements of a life well lived, including photographs of Cadmus and Robert in New York, Paris, and Key West. She made certain to fill his stationery tray with a fresh, crisp stack of ivory paper, knowing full well that the likelihood he would compose one of his beautiful letters was becoming more and more remote. His inkwell was full of his signature deep blue tint, and she rested his fountain pens on their stands before dusting his other photograph of Ilona, which was lovingly housed in a gold-plated frame with a flowing bow positioned above the black-and-white profile shot. Cadmus never revealed the details regarding his falling out with his mother to Clementine, the secret shrouded in such shame and regret that it was only well into his relationship with Robert that he could bring himself to expose such vulnerability.

His first night alone brought waves of trepidation. Lying in bed, he studied his new bedroom, reconciling his personal belongings nestled in a new space. The fresh paint on the walls bore a stark contrast to the worn, sweet wood scent of his childhood home. He was never particularly fond of anything modern or seemingly brand new. Clementine had woven the two worlds as best she could.

As he attempted to absorb his new reality, a train whistle sounded in the distance. An initial, quick burst gave way to a full-fledged roar, emphatically transporting Cadmus back to where the railroad intersected his neighborhood, the image of The Doyle House suspended between Downtown Houston and the Texas countryside, as it once had been at the turn of the previous century, well before his birth, near the time the Doyles had built the family home. Acting as a lullaby, the train's whistles lulled him to sleep with images of his childhood and scents of rose from Ilona's bedtime caresses.

CADMUS PROUDLY BEGAN PREPARING FOR supper early that afternoon by laying out his navy suit and mustard-colored bow tie. Vacillating on whether to wear his owl pin, he finally decided to fasten it to his lapel. Perhaps it would serve as a good conversation starter. He could easily regale his table with stories about his time at Rice as a student and as a professor, a much better option than divulging his sexuality. He often found it ironic that his Heights neighborhood, once so rooted in Victorian etiquette, had blossomed into an accepting haven for diversity, with rainbow flags prominently displayed in stores along Nineteenth Street. His family history and his lifestyle had been eagerly embraced in the mid-nineties, with he and

Robert even opening The Doyle House to The Heights Spring Home Tour. He strongly suspected that residents at The Oaks would not be as welcoming, because most people his age were not.

Cadmus made his way to the dining hall, standing at the entrance for a moment to get his bearings. The room was exquisitely set, draped in soft whites with large windows that framed the setting sun. The china, fresh cut flowers thoughtfully displayed, and long white candles in silver candelabras confirmed that he was getting his money's worth. He knew he was lucky that he never had to worry about money, even more so with his inheritance from Robert, but he also knew that the expense of receiving this luxury was too great a price. He had no one.

"Good evening, Dr. Doyle, and welcome to The Oaks," smiled a woman well dressed in a crisp white blouse and long black skirt. "My name is Josephine." Just as she said her name, Cadmus noticed the gold metal nameplate attached to her collar.

"It is a pleasure to meet you," he replied, making sure to extend a strong handshake and noting the tag once again, *Josephine.*

"Tonight, I reserved a seat for you at a special table, one that we reserve for new residents. A few veteran residents from the welcome committee serve as hosts of the table, which offers an introduction of sorts to help you meet your neighbors."

"What a lovely notion! Thank you for the consideration," he replied, very pleased to have one less thing to vex over, noting the many tables from which to choose. It was impossible not to notice the looks he had received during his brief time in the lobby and dining hall. Clementine had warned him that the women residents would be quite eager to meet him, seeing that he was still quite handsome, even at seventy-eight. Oilmen, doctors, and lawyers were all common at The Oaks. A professor, or, more important, a wealthy professor, was a fine catch, indeed.

As Josephine escorted him to his table, he rehearsed his lines to himself: *Although I have been a widower for nearly a year, it pains me greatly to speak of my spouse, even more so now that I had to leave our home.* He would say it in a manner and tone that would certainly, he hoped, dissuade further questions.

"Mr. and Mrs. Frazier, please allow me to introduce you to Dr. Cadmus Doyle, Professor Emeritus of Rice University," Josephine announced as they arrived at the table.

Mr. Frazier rose from his seat, offering his hand, "Nice to meet you. Please call me Robert, and this is my wife, Ernestine."

Cadmus responded with an incredulous smile when he heard their names, figuring the universe was sending him a sign that he was in the right place.

A new female resident, along with two others from the welcome committee, rounded out his remaining supper companions. Aside from Robert and Ernestine, he could not recall their names, but thankfully, his wits allowed him to navigate skillfully through the first course without making direct references.

"Doyle. Not a common name, but I did once know two men, two brothers, by the name of Doyle. Benjamin and Andrew—fine men with whom I collaborated to build a series of shopping centers along Westheimer Road. It was farmland not so long ago! Doyle & Dunn Construction. What a great venture that turned out to be! Any relation, by chance?" Robert asked.

Cadmus took a sip of his coffee, buying time before offering a weak smile and shaking his head, "No, sir. I am but an old professor of literature. No relation."

"Yes, well, I suppose Houston is quite a large city now, a far cry from when I was born."

"I'm from Dallas," piped in the other new resident. "My husband passed away several months ago, and I moved here to be closer to my children. Dallas is critical of Houston, but I admit I've always favored it. I do believe it's much more sophisticated than they realize."

"I'm sorry for your loss," offered Ernestine.

"Thank you. I throw myself a good pity party every now and then, but then I remember I had him for sixty-four years. It was a beautiful marriage."

"How long were you married, Doctor?" Ernestine asked.

Cadmus stared at Ernestine, stupefied by the question.

"I'm sorry. I shouldn't have asked."

"It's fine," he replied, his heart racing at the potential threads of conversation. "Thirty-nine years."

"Ah, you married later in life. Was she in education, as well?" Robert asked.

"No. H . . . She . . . she was . . ." Eloquence lost, Cadmus looked down into his lap, struggling with how to respond. Changing the pronoun left him feeling stripped of his fidelity to Robert. The thought of fabricating his spouse's profession made him feel even more sickened, but women their age were not lawyers. A litany of questions would accompany this answer.

"Forgive me for asking, Dr. Doyle. Sometimes I am too nosey for my own good."

"I second that declaration!" Robert replied.

A round of laughter punctured the weight suspended above the table as the attendant arrived with dessert.

Cadmus returned to his room, his thoughts heavy with his life's composite of shame. Those few lines uttered in the dining hall tapped into his rawest sense of self, beginning from his failure as a son and heir. Had he been stronger, he would have forged more memories with his father, and as a stakeholder in Doyle & Dunn, he would have never had a reason to usher his mother's death. The confluence of thoughts elicited even more consternation, for had they come to fruition he would have never met Robert. Thoughts of his life taking a traditional trajectory prompted him to feel as if he were forsaking his soul mate for the second time that evening.

He felt a fool to think he could create a façade from which to project during meals at The Oaks. Underneath his sophisticated veneer, Cadmus was an unexceptional gay man who paid a high price for his sexuality, as so many had before him and even more would continue to do after him, despite the changing times. As he returned his owl pin to its box, he sighed in resignation that he had yet to pay off his debt. He would not return to the dining hall, to the place where the residents shared their life stories, an opportunity to assess their life's accomplishments with other diners. To participate in such an exchange would call for him to disavow Robert, the one person other than his mother and Dear Ernestine who had loved him unconditionally. Perhaps he would have a change of heart, but for now, he would remain in his room, spending his days in restitution.

ILONA

Autumn 1930

ILONA DID NOT RECALL LEAVING the M&M. She awoke to find herself in the car with her uncle heading down Harrisburg, the sound of the streetcar's horn jarring her awake.

"No, dear, you might be sick. Leave down. No sick in car," Uncle Demetrius said as she fumbled to roll up the passenger window.

"I must get back to the diner. Baba is expecting me to run the supper shift."

"You no go diner. You go home."

"I'm sorry, Uncle. I . . . I . . ."

"Now you know danger of the drink. Be careful of men who want you drink, Ilona. You pretty young woman," her Uncle Demetrius warned.

"Baba will be so upset, so very, very upset," Ilona cried.

"He no need know everything. You get sick. People get sick, eat things that go bad. I take you home, put you in bed."

"Thank you, Uncle," Ilona said, brushing her hair away from her face, the strands blown about from the rush of the outside air. She turned to look out the window, her eyes having trouble following the moving streetcar that was also heading east, away from downtown. She smelled Patrick's cologne on her hands as she wiped her eyes. It had been barely over an hour, but the time she had spent with Patrick, the stories shared and hands held, confirmed her belief that she could change the trajectory of her life.

ILONA AWOKE, WELL BEFORE DAWN, to the sound of the whistle from the train signaling twice. Her head pounding, she reached over to her nightstand to turn on the light. A bottle of aspirin and a glass of water greeted her, as did a trash can thoughtfully placed next to her bed. Uncle Demetrius had served her well. Ilona took two pills and drank the entire glass of water. She could not recall a time she had ever been so parched.

She looked around her room, coming to terms with how different she felt now versus just the previous morning. She felt more mature, as if she no longer needed her high school diploma and certificates of achievement that lined the walls, former indicators of her worth. Ilona had never felt the want for a man, and now she was overwhelmed with physical desire for Patrick, a man she barely knew. Being with him was like removing a veil, revealing a womanly soul ready to take on new experiences. She feared she would sleep with him if she saw him again: no questions asked, no promises needed.

Needing another glass of water but fearful of waking her family, she tip-toed to the bathroom rather than the kitchen to refill her glass. Fragmented memories from the night before slowly unfolded, from their auspicious arrival home to an empty house to her uncle gently tapping on the door to her room, asking how she was coming along with her nightgown. She remembered him sitting on the edge of her bed and kissing her forehead while muttering a profane word about the Irish.

After brushing her teeth and splashing cold water on her face, she studied her reflection. She saw herself as a latent soul, someone on the verge of blooming. Patrick's attention, however, prompted her to see herself as something else. Her hair, usually tied in a low chignon, gave her a homely look. Closing her eyes and thinking of Patrick, she ran her fingers through her dark, thick hair, moving carefully at her temples that still throbbed from the gin. Raising her hair in a higher fashion, she turned from side to side, admiring the profile of a very different soul emerging. Smiling to herself, she made her way back to her room and curled into bed, fantasizing about the man who made her feel like a woman.

ASIDE FROM FEELING AS IF she was in a bit of a trance, Ilona thought she felt better when she awoke later that morning. Grateful for the dose of aspirin, she bathed and prepared herself for work, carefully arranging her hair higher, rather than at the base of her neck. She also added a bit of red lipstick, which left her mama staring, frying pan motionless in hand, when Ilona entered the kitchen.

"Your baba thinks you fell ill yesterday," Mama said, slamming a glass of orange juice on the table in front of her, before turning back to the stove. "You break baba's heart if know truth."

Ilona sat at the kitchen table, searching for feelings of regret she thought she should feel. Truthfully, if she had the chance to do it over, she would do it again. The independence was invigorating. She took a few sips of juice and watched her mama at the stove, where steam from the fried eggs wafted into the air. Mama shook her head, pausing on one side, her expression bearing more questions than upset. Before she had the opportunity to continue, her baba entered the kitchen, with his keys jingling in his hands.

"You feel better, dear? I worry," he greeted Ilona, offering a kiss to her forehead, before sitting down at the table. "I so sorry you no find hat."

"Yes, Baba, I feel better. Must have been a stomach bug," Ilona said quietly, avoiding his eyes as her lie became palpable, infiltrating the room. She stared down at her juice and took another sip, waiting for him to sense her betrayal. Her stomach began to burn, the scent of the fried eggs summoning her queasiness.

"You need stay home today?" he asked, noticing her closed eyes and flaring nostrils.

"No!" Ilona said with such immediacy and force that it prompted both of her parents to look at one another and then back at her. "Pardon me. I want to go to work. I'm fine, really I am."

Mama saw through her words, knowing her daughter wanted to make it back to Franklin, back to downtown.

"You work at Lawndale today. Close to home if you sick again."

"No, Baba, I am fine. I feel fine. Please, please let me go to Franklin. The customers expect me."

"Lawndale customers get treat see you again. They always ask how 'city girl' doing. You stay near home today," he commanded while placing a napkin on his lap, before eating his eggs and toast. "We drop you off, and then I take your mama downtown. Good for her see new things, too, you know?"

"Pardon me. I need a minute," Ilona answered, barely making it to the bathroom before she fell ill. She was foolish to think she had avoided this part of the hangover—the Monday morning virus, or for her, the Friday morning virus, she had witnessed firsthand from cooks and busboys over the years. "The drink, the drink," her baba would say after he had fired a worker for repeated tardiness or for attempting to arrive at work in such a haggard state.

Ilona propped her back against the wall, seated on the floor in front of the toilet. She had never seen the room from this vantage point. Looking up, she noted the etchings on the ceiling fixture that took a back seat to the light from the sconces that graced the sides of the mirror. Simple and pretty, yet a far cry from the fixtures she had seen yesterday in the lounge.

Her eyes welled with tears at the thought of Lawndale. Patrick knew her name and the general vicinity of the Franklin Street Diner, but would he try to contact her? She confided her hopes, even reciting lines from Keats during their time together, but she failed to give him her number. Did he even ask? She could not remember. She covered her face with her hands, feeling her cheeks flush equally from her condition as from a wave of embarrassment. The drink certainly had a way of lasting, slowly dispensing bits of memories that one must slowly weave together, revealing both merriment and follies.

Good Lord in Heaven, why did I recite that poem? I'm such a fool, an afternoon distraction. She envisioned Patrick at the lounge again today, meeting over drinks about the next project, another, worldlier woman in tow, who could hold her liquor and who was not escorted by an uncle.

Gripping the side of the bathtub, she pressed herself to her feet. Her hair was a fright, bobby pins dangling from the ends. She brushed out her thick, silky hair. The updo, albeit short-lived, gave her a lovely wave, a small token for which she was thankful. She reapplied the red lipstick. It offered a nice contrast, brightening her face. It was also a more modest upgrade to her appearance. There was no reason to shock the diners with a novice attempt at modernity, even more so considering her day was to be spent with the likes of Mrs. Jilufka and friends.

ILONA KNEW HER BABA WAS prone to exaggeration with his common affections:

My daughters, loveliest girls!

Our food, best in city!

Your grandfather, best working honest man all time!

One instance that he proved to be correct, however, was in her reception from the Lawndale patrons:

Ilona! My child, you are a woman now!

City work agrees with you, pretty girl!

Trade places with me for just one day! You take my shift at Nabisco!

With the early morning hours came a lift of her spirits, and she felt the seedlings of confidence as she strolled between the register and the counter, refilling cups of coffee and listening to updates from the patrons about relatives and friends, people she knew only through the stories of others, but this detail not making her interest insincere. She realized she was wiser and more compassionate than she thought, a solemn observer into the windows of so many lives. The diner only had a fraction of the windows of the M&M, but that did not make the stories they housed any less significant.

She cleared counters, thinking of how Patrick shared the death of his parents, from his father's sudden heart attack to the cancer that claimed his mother's life the previous year. Tragedy served as an odd elixir for his spirit, a call to relish each day with fervor. He hoped his father was proud of the transition from Doyle Lumber into Doyle Lumber & Construction, a necessary move as the lumber business dwindled. He followed his heart with the transition, drawing on his thirst to develop Houston, to be part of the inevitable expansion. While her heart was with the M&M, his rested a few blocks away at the Niels Esperson Building, home to the general offices. Doyle Lumber & Construction kept a temporary office at the M&M pending the resolution of the final construction items, especially after the flood from the previous year. His brother, Michael, spent his time finalizing the project while Patrick returned to the main office, eager for the next venture. Her heart grew heavy with the revelation that his office was farther away than she originally thought.

Ilona's confidence from the morning began to dissipate along with the lunch crowd. She was left at the register alone with her thoughts, which continued to drift back to the day before at the M&M. It was Friday afternoon, and she would not return downtown until Monday. Hopes dwindling, she did not favor the odds of crossing his path three days later—three days for his interest to wane, three days for another soul to charm him.

She took solace in the inclination that memory often bears a fair-weathered quality when one wants it the most, convincing herself that he was probably not as handsome as her memory painted. During her sophomore year, she pined after a junior, admiring the handsome upperclassman as she passed him in the hall. Her meekness had only afforded her a peek at him from the corner of her eye, and she had never managed a healthy observation until that following summer when his family popped into the café for lunch. Her heart pounding, she eagerly approached their table with menus in hand. He smiled at her, saying, "You go to Milby, right?" As she nodded, she was able to get a closer look at her crush and at the yellowed buckteeth she did not know he had. She also noticed a heck of a cowlick from likely a week of not washing his hair. Her infatuation evaporated in an instant. Returning to the counter, she wondered how she could have ever thought otherwise. Perhaps Patrick was the same, and she added another layer of convincing by remembering the power of the gin—it most certainly could color anything lovely.

With a healthy sigh, she pulled out her book. At least she had more time to read at Lawndale, especially at this hour. She tucked herself into the far corner of the cashier's booth: *Nose in book*, her baba's voice echoed in her mind.

The bells on the door jingled, but Ilona kept her head down, frantically reading the last lines of the chapter. Tucked so far into the corner and not readily visible, she took advantage of the opportunity to read for a few seconds more. She sensed a figure staring toward the counter, standing several feet in front of the register, which people often did when deciding where to sit. As she finished the last line and lifted her eyes to offer a greeting, she released the grip on her book. It was Patrick. Her book fell to the floor, the heavy thud prompting him to turn around to face her.

He stared her gin-soaked memory in the face and won. He was even more handsome than she remembered. Breaking into the same smile that he wore the day before, he made his way to her at the register.

"You are not an easy lady to find, Miss Ilona."

"I didn't know you were looking," she replied, silently patting herself on the back for the quick, witty reply, confidence replenishing her spirits.

"How could I not? You left me so abruptly yesterday, with not even a chance to get your number or give apologies."

"Apologies?"

"The first apology to your Uncle Demetrius, for failing to make a . . . um . . . how shall I say it . . . a less-than-stellar first impression. I hope he will enjoy these as much as I do," Patrick offered as he took two cigars from his interior left breast pocket, wrapped in rich brown paper with a heavy seal.

"And the second apology, the more important one, is to you. For not taking you on a proper date, which I hope to remedy in the very near future."

Mirroring his smile, she replied, "Yes, I am sure that can be arranged."

"Good," he said, nodding and biting his lower lip. "Now, what do you recommend for lunch? I'm starved. Driving all over East Houston looking for an enchanting woman has left me famished."

She walked him to the counter and recommended the patty melt, a very good remedy after a night of revelry. His hearty laugh led her to wonder what it was about her that he liked. She wanted to make sure she continued doing it. The thinning crowd at Lawndale made it possible to talk, and it made Ilona thankful for her work assignment. Had she been at Franklin, they would not have had this time.

"How were things at the M&M today?" She asked as she made her way to the other side of the counter.

"Good question, but one to which I do not have the answer. I worked in the main office this morning. Needed to give Michael his space."

"How much longer will the other office remain open?"

"Not much longer, I am sad to say, and Michael prefers to wrap things up on his own. It's been good for him."

Her countenance bore her question.

"Michael means well, and he is smart as hell."

"But?" she asked.

"He's not comfortable in his skin. He's an excellent manager, though. His time alone at the M&M has allowed him to meet people on his own, which is a good thing."

The bell at the kitchen window sounded, signaling that his lunch was ready. From the corner of her eye, she saw him nod and offer a "good afternoon" to the two elderly ladies at the far end of the counter. She tried to contain her grin when she saw the looks on their faces, whispering to one another as they sneaked glances his way. People who looked like Patrick did not often grace her end of town.

As he enjoyed his lunch, she continued to share her love of literature, figuring a way to reference yesterday's poetry recitation as legitimate rather than as a result of drunkenness. Placing his hand over hers, he shared that her ability to connect literature and life was incredibly alluring, commenting how so many women put on superficial airs to woo men. He agreed with her assessment that her reticent soul served her well, poising her for rich reflection, but with a coy smile, he added, "Yes, indeed, you would make a wonderful teacher, but wouldn't that interfere with your role as a wife and mother, societal obligations considering?"

Mrs. Jilufka arrived midafternoon for her coffee and pastry, her stride taking on an extra pep when she saw Ilona behind the counter.

"Pretty girl! Back for a visit," she quivered as she made her way to the counter. Ilona pardoned herself from Patrick to offer a hug, her tall, thin frame a contrast to her elderly friend's wide girth.

"It's so good to see you! I've missed you. Please tell me, how is your nephew?" Ilona greeted her warmly.

She walked Mrs. Jilufka to her usual seat at the far end of the counter as her friend rattled a quick report, offering herself as a cane to steady the elderly woman's gait, all the while knowing she had the attention of Mr. Doyle. Noting his steady gaze, Mrs. Jilufka looked to her and whispered, "Now, *he* is a handsome devil."

"Well, please allow me to introduce you," Ilona replied boldly, much to her friend's surprise. "Mrs. Jilufka, please meet Patrick Doyle."

Patrick rose to greet her, cupping Mrs. Jilufka's right hand with both of his. "I am very pleased to meet you, Mrs. Jilufka." She peered up at him through her black, horned-rimmed glasses, squinting her eyes to get a good look at his face.

"And it is nice to meet you, too," she replied. "My, my, you are a handsome fella."

THEIR FIRST SEMIOFFICIAL DATE WAS made to resemble happenstance, because a date with an older, Irish gentleman would not have been welcomed by the Petrarkis household. The Houston Fall Festival was set to begin over the weekend at Buff Stadium with a production of *The Last Days of Pompeii*. Ilona confided to her sister, Arianna, who excitedly agreed to join her, this opportunity allowing her to live vicariously as she was still acclimating to her role as a mother.

Part of their time that night was spent watching the show, but their energies were mostly spent gauging one another—glancing from the corners of their eyes at each other, acting in cue with the *ooohs* and *ahhhs*, and slipping whispered comments when they could think of something as quick and clever as the setting would allow. It was two hours of everything and nothing, two hours of relishing in the deceptively simple offerings of life—the starlit sky, the mélange of a diversifying Houston, and the seemingly casual brush of hands. When the elaborate fireworks display marked the end of the show, they eagerly stood in ovation with Patrick looking down into her eyes, placing a moment's kiss to her lips when Arianna looked away.

Ilona knew this was the man she hoped to marry: Patrick Doyle, heir to Doyle Lumber and founder of Doyle Lumber & Construction, the son of a pioneer who transported timber from East Texas to Houston, the man who helped build the M&M and who would continue to shape the Houston skyline.

To the delight of her baba, Patrick began frequenting the Franklin Diner. Not knowing Patrick was there to see Ilona, he was thrilled that someone of Patrick's ilk would dine at his restaurant. Patrick's suit and pocket watch reflected his prominence, but the confidence and enthusiasm he carried truly set him apart from others. It did not take long for her baba to introduce himself to his new regular. Patrick and Ilona, sneaking glances and knowing smiles, enjoyed the sport of the pursuit. They became more and more brazen with one another when Patrick dined: winking, once-overs, and her slipping handwritten lines of poetry into his palm when she was dispensing change at the register. In hindsight, a fly on the wall would have noticed that her chignon grew higher and tighter, and her lipstick darker, with each visit. Uncle Demetrius remained guarded with the new patron, but he did offer a hearty handshake with a murmur of thanks for the cigars when his brother was not looking.

One day after many consecutive weekdays of visits, her baba noticed Patrick's absence. Commenting that he "hope everything okay with Mr. Doyle," Ilona offered a prayer for Dear Ernestine as she refilled the candy jar next to the register. Patrick was taking his former nanny, now housekeeper, to the doctor for a persistent cough. The Doyle House held but two souls in 1930: Patrick and Dear Ernestine, forever coined by his term of endearment.

The following day, Patrick returned in good spirits, sharing with Ilona that all was well with his Dear Ernestine, except for the doctor chastising him for not bringing her in sooner. Patrick's stories cultivated in Ilona a fondness for his family. She longed to meet Dear Ernestine, and her heart grew partial to Michael and his struggles, knowing that most anyone paled in comparison to Patrick.

Patrick often told Ilona how she was different from other women he knew. He admired her earnest approach to life and how she knew who she was, which she found puzzling since she pondered the question frequently. She often heard her mama say, "He is who he is. God love him. She is who she is. God love her." She never regarded it as a positive statement, but now she surmised that the more she was herself, the more she attracted him. She realized that she had never truly been herself with anyone; she had always done what she was expected to do.

He provided her fair warning that he would ask her father permission to take her on an official date. This was one occasion that challenged her calm demeanor.

"Not yet! Please, give it more time!"

"It's time. He will approve either now or never. Aren't you ready to be with me?"

She did not know if his reference was an official date or something more, but she was overdue for either. Making her baba privy to their intentions, however, would lead to a change one way or another, and the uncertainty gave her pause.

Patrick waited for the lunch crowd to thin, all the while appealing to his audience that they should remain optimistic despite the economic forecast.

"Oil. Port of Houston. The spirit of this city can't be beat!" Ilona heard him declare as she looked out the window at the M&M, nibbling her lip and feeling her stomach full of knots.

Baba circled the diner, checking in with each table, before retiring to his usual spot at the counter at the end of the lunch hour. Patrick strategically selected his seat, knowing her baba would eventually sit next to him.

"Lunch good?" he asked, holding out one hand to shake while the other patted Patrick's shoulder.

"Of course, delicious as usual! I wouldn't expect anything less."

"And Rusk project . . . good?"

"Still in the proposal stage, but yes, it is progressing as well as it can at this point," Patrick replied.

Her baba nodded, taking a sip of coffee and enjoying his small part in the exchange over downtown construction.

"I do have another proposal in mind, if you would be kind enough to oblige."

He turned to Patrick, picking up on his playful tone and curious about what he would say next.

"May I have your blessing to take Ilona on a date?"

He stared at Patrick, coffee cup suspended midair. Turning toward the register, he saw his daughter quickly look back into her book. Noting her made-up appearance—new earrings and a more fitted dress—his face flushed with the realization of his ignorance. Their flirtation had been right in front of him the entire time.

"She grown woman. She decide herself," her baba said, standing after a long minute. He turned one last time to Patrick and held out his hand. "I wish you good afternoon, Mr. Doyle," he said before heading back to the kitchen.

PATRICK ARRIVED AT HER HOME off South Wayside with a bouquet of white roses in hand. Her baba, usually jovial and assured at the diner, offered nothing other than a nod and handshake when Patrick entered their home. The Franklin Street Diner, new and gleaming, might offer some degree of speculation at how the family lived. A restaurant owner would not have a fancy house, but there was room to advance from where they currently resided. Their humble roots confirmed; the façade lifted. Ilona knew this reality. This, and the fact that Ilona's suitor was not Greek, left her baba troubled. It would have been much easier had he not known the gentleman, but she knew he liked Patrick. She knew he admired Patrick's spirit and success, but she also knew he had never imagined him as his daughter's suitor.

Her nerves settled when she saw the way Patrick's face lit up as she made her way down the hall. He smiled and nodded, rocking back and forth on his heels. It made her wonder if he was nervous, too. They had waited for weeks to be alone, and then she realized that being unavailable might very well have added to her allure.

"Thank you, Mr. Petrarkis, for entrusting your daughter to me this evening. I promise to have her home at an early hour."

"Early for Irish or early for Greek, hmm?"

Patrick's sincere burst of laughter quickly relieved Ilona, whose eyes had widened from embarrassment.

"Fair question, sir. Early for Greeks. Is 9:00 too late?"

And with that, the gentlemen shook hands with Mr. and Mrs. Petrarkis conceding the most modest of grins.

Ilona's pleas for a clue as to where they were going garnered only his dimples, making her wonder how even his profile could be hypnotic. Although it was their first official date, they had shared countless conversations over the past three weeks, albeit punctuated with requests for meat loaf, apple pie, and Coca-Cola. This evening marked the first period alone, time for uninterrupted conversation, among other things. The Houston sun acquiesced to its inevitable descent, and shades of orange and pink chalk colored the sky. Patrick took the long way to The Heights, deliberately steering his convertible toward the M&M, declaring, "We must pay homage to the masterpiece that brought us together—where all things are possible," with a raised fist to the air. Ilona released her hand that shielded her hair from the wind, and she, too, raised both arms to the sky.

Ilona had been to The Heights a few times, with her parents driving their family along The Boulevard in their roadster. She studied the streetcar as it offered greetings to the Victorian homes that lined the street. The realization that she was on the edge of the city, a stone's throw from the sprawling Texas countryside, filled her with excitement, as if she, too, were on the verge of creating something new.

As Patrick stopped the car at an intersection, he gestured to The Doyle House, the roses he once referenced framing the picket fence and brick paths throughout the yard.

"I prepared dinner," he said after a lull of silence, keeping his eyes a second longer on his home before turning back to her. "Well, I had help from Dear Ernestine, and perhaps quite a bit of help." He turned back to the house. "This is a first for me, Ilona."

Patrick turned at the intersection and pulled into the back driveway. She noted a light in the garage apartment, Dear Ernestine's quarters. Ilona felt a wave of nerves; it was like meeting his mother, which she had not been antic-ipating. Patrick came around to open her car door, gingerly taking her hand to help her to the brick sidewalk that meandered around the grounds. They walked through the garden to the front of the house and up the pristinely polished wooden steps.

"Welcome to my home," he said as he opened the stained-glass door.

Even though she had prepared herself mentally, its beauty left her in wonder—the polished wooden paneling, ornate rugs, and crystal chande-liers. All these beautiful items together in one place left her in awe. What most captured her attention, however, was the curious face peeking from what she presumed to be the kitchen. Ilona welcomed the face with a smile, instinctively taking a few steps in that direction, arms opening. Patrick, fol-lowing her gaze, bellowed, "My Dear Ernestine, please come meet Ilona!"

Dear Ernestine slowly made her way down the hall to the couple, her freshly pressed uniform certainly not resembling that of someone who had spent time in the kitchen this evening. She must have freshened up for the special guest.

Ilona opened her arms to offer an embrace. Retreating a step, Dear Ernestine looked at her intently, seemingly unaccustomed to such displays of affection.

"It is a most sincere pleasure to meet you, Dear Ernestine. Please forgive my presumed familiarity, but I feel I know you, considering all the lovely stories Patrick has shared," Ilona said.

"Pleasure's mine, Miss, truly it is. It's so very, very nice to meet you," Dear Ernestine replied before returning the embrace, her hands lowering to cup Ilona's in a final touch, her face breaking out into a smile before she returned to the kitchen.

They made their way to the sitting room, where two gold-rimmed champagne glasses rested on a table. "You would not believe how difficult it is to procure champagne!" Patrick declared as he reached for the bottle.

He popped the cork, and Ilona's jolt brought a round of laughter from them both.

He began the tour of the house with a toast and an introduction to his late father, Patrick Doyle, who austerely studied the couple from his ornate gold frame housed above the mantle. Patrick shared his father's prominent role in the development of The Heights, including ownership of another home several blocks north on Harvard Street, where his brother's family lived. His brother had taken a few pieces of furniture and art when he established his own household shortly before their mother died, but most of the heirlooms remained, waiting for the first-born son to "find a most charming and suitable young woman to marry and carry on the family name."

They toured the library, where Patrick highlighted the scores of books but admitted to a slight exaggeration on the number. The library faced the north garden with a sitting nook in a bay window that provided just enough room for two souls to sip tea, or as was more appropriate with the likes of Patrick, a heartier beverage, while reading, musing, and admiring.

They only walked past the master bedroom, Patrick explaining that he still resided upstairs. He hoped, one day, to move into this room when he found a bride with whom to share it. She could not tell if his continued references to marriage were deliberate or a natural byproduct of the tour, but the potency of the notion charmed her regardless of his intent.

"I do hope you like flounder with shrimp, thank heavens for the Gulf's delicacies. And we have baby potatoes and Dear Ernestine's famed green bean casserole," he said as they made their way back downstairs after viewing the second and third floors.

Dear Ernestine served supper before retreating to the kitchen. She returned twice, once to check on the meal and the second time to offer dessert, coffee, and her goodnight wishes. Patrick refreshed his champagne on a few occasions, noting that Ilona's glass "must be magical—the nectar remains!" She did not plan on duplicating the imprudence of their first encounter.

With but a few bites of raspberry trifle remaining, her mind turned to his expectations for the evening. For the past month, the idea of intimacy with Patrick had saturated her reveries both day and night. Consumed by fantasies, she was curious how his energy would manifest physically, the speculation literally leaving her in a trance.

"Ilona! Focus work!" Her baba had shouted when, after more than one occasion, customers had turned at the sound of a plate or coffee cup shattering on the floor. Now that the time and location were prime, her mind raced with practical matters, including the fact that she had never been truly kissed. She felt nauseated thinking about the gamut of considerations she had failed to take into account.

"Let's take a walk in the garden," he said as she finished the last bite. "It's a beautiful night."

The cool air ushered a much-needed moment of clarity. He wrapped her ivory stole around her shoulders, leaving his arm around her as they walked along the brick sidewalks that meandered through the yard. She noticed a stone bench near the pecan tree in the far northeast corner. He did not say a word as they made their way to the seat and sat facing the house now bathed in moonlight. A light in the garage apartment snapped off where Dear Ernestine was heading to bed.

"I love you, Ilona," he said after several minutes of silence. Continuing to look straight ahead, he added, "And I've never loved anyone." He turned to her, open palm to her cheek.

"And I love you, Patrick."

She had her first real kiss that evening, under the pecan tree at the house on The Boulevard.

ILONA TOOK SOLACE IN THE fact that no one she knew disowned their children. Greek friends and cousins teased with the claim, but it was more to grandstand, to challenge one another on who would make the most audacious move. She also reluctantly admitted to herself that no one she knew tested the waters as much as she had lately, but she managed to bury this morsel. Greeks called a good game, but in the end, their lives followed suit: They married the people they were supposed to marry, and they fulfilled the vocation set by their family.

She arrived back at South Wayside at a respectable hour, her mama listening to the radio while her baba read the paper, both parents making their best attempt to disguise their concern.

"You have nice time, dear?" Mama asked, returning her needlework to her lap.

"Oh, Mama, it was a lovely time. Patrick is a gentleman," she said clearly, making certain her baba would hear. His only offering: a grunt accompanied by a furrowed brow as he turned the page of his newspaper. Ilona gingerly walked over to kiss him on the cheek, but he remained unmoved, his eyes focused on the article, much to her disappointment. She turned to go to her bedroom, tears forming as she made eye contact with her mama, who returned the look with unspoken sympathy before glancing at her husband.

Aside from her first kiss and declaration of her first love, that late October night gave rise to another first: She heard her parents arguing. She lay awake, watching the moonlight shine through the eyelet curtains as it created a pattern on the wall that resembled a distorted sphere of vibrating stars. She thought about how the moon bathed both The Heights and South Wayside; they were not so far away from one another as it seemed.

"What you expect, Nikolas! You tell girls create! Dream! Ilona dream . . . dream different!"

"Yes . . . dream! But no pull from family. Family es good!"

The night trains approached South Wayside, whistles piercing the tension in the air, muffling their shouts. Ilona pulled the covers over her head and indulged in another first, reaching her hand down and reminiscing on her first love.

ILONA WAS DELIGHTED THAT PATRICK enjoyed lunch at Franklin every day during the week. Her baba gave him a nod and a handshake but nothing more. And this was more than he offered his daughter, which could be described only as indifference as he watched them from his seat at the counter.

"Give him time. Es new to us, Ilona. He no see you as woman of Patrick's kind. He see you as young, proper Greek lady," Mama said, zipping her daughter's dress for a Saturday dinner date before turning to leave the room.

"Mama?" Ilona called, both daughter and mother turning to face one another, Ilona a good foot higher than her mama in her heels.

"My dear?"

"Mama, I've fallen in love with him."

After a pause, her mama nodded her head in resignation, "Yes. That es new to us, too. Not love, my dear. *Falling* in love." She turned back around at the sound of a knock at the front door.

"You take your time. I go answer door," Mama said as she left the room, giving Ilona pause to look in the mirror at her transition that was well underway.

Tonight she would meet Patrick's brother Michael and Michael's wife, Sybil. And although Michael was younger, she thought of him as the elder of the two brothers, serious and brooding, as if he was the one saddled with the pressure of the Doyle legacy.

She studied her reflection in the mirror, her unease over meeting his family tempered by her growing confidence. Her years of earnest study in books and in work, along with her life spent alone all the while surrounded by others, set her apart in school, yet these things had conditioned her as a compassionate soul. It was not that she doubted Patrick's assessment. His criticisms of Michael were filtered through a lens of understanding and even longing for a better connection with his brother. She knew that winning over Michael would be a challenge, but she believed it was one for which she was well suited. She had the potential to bridge their relationship and forge a relationship with Sybil.

Patrick caressed her cheek when they settled in the car.

"I'm so glad to have you with me," he said, turning the key in the ignition. "It has been a trying afternoon. I am hoping you can work some magic with my brother."

"I share that same hope," she offered with a wink.

"We had quite a row today. Michael insisted we need to partner with Dunn on the Rusk proposal."

"And you remain confident you can do it on your own?"

"Our *father* would have wanted us to do it on our own. Look what he and Grandfather Doyle created, for Christ's sake," Patrick replied.

Turning away from her with his eyes back on the road ahead, he took a breath and conceded, "A joint venture would help. I want to do more than provide lumber. I want to shape the skyline."

"But not with Dunn?" Ilona asked.

"He can't be trusted. He'd sell his soul for the right price, the arrogant bastard. Father would have never consorted with him."

"Then kindly hold firm, my love," she replied, touching his cheek. "Let's see what tonight will bring."

They were walking hand in hand in the garden when Michael and Sybil pulled into the driveway. The confidence she felt earlier withered when she saw their countenance. Even from across the grounds, Michael appeared tense, walking toward them without waiting for his wife. She was not sure if she realized the misstep on his own or if Sybil had called to him, but he stopped midstride and turned back toward her, extending his arm for her to catch up to him.

"Sybil, so lovely to see you. It's been too long," Patrick greeted, offering his sister-in-law a kiss on the cheek. Ilona wondered how it could be so long when they lived but a few blocks away. Patrick shook his brother's hand before turning to Ilona.

"Ilona, my love, I am very pleased to introduce my sister-in-law, Sybil, and my brother, Michael." Michael remained unmoved, eyeing her carefully before extending his hand in a formal handshake.

Sybil's edge seemed to stem more from fear rather than a sentiment of her own. Ilona detected a hint of enthusiasm underneath Sybil's shell, her eyes a bit brighter in the hopes that, perhaps, a friendship was on the horizon. Sybil leaned in toward her as Ilona began to extend her hand to mirror Michael's greeting. They both switched stances to match the other: Ilona then reached for an embrace as Sybil extended her hand.

"Oh, for Christ's sake, give one another a hug!" Patrick chuckled.

As the women burst into giggles and embraced, Ilona noted Michael's expressionless face staring at his wife in disapproval. Her challenge would be more difficult than she thought. She turned to Michael, who, in turn, remained still. Her hopes for an embrace dashed, she took it upon herself to offer a warm smile. She wanted him to know that he could rest his defenses. On paper, he shared Patrick's features, albeit in a thicker frame. His eyes, however, fell flat, casting a shadow over his appearance that made the brothers appear incongruent, disparate souls united only by bloodline.

"Well now, let's head into the house for supper. I hear beef wellington is on the menu," Michael said, turning to make his way into his childhood home.

"GOOD EVENING, MR. AND MRS. Doyle," greeted Dear Ernestine, standing at attention, as they entered the house.

"Ernestine, it's good to see you, and supper smells absolutely wonderful," Michael said.

"Thank you, sir," she replied, causing Ilona to note the formality between the two, which was quite a contrast from the relationship she shared with Patrick.

"Mr. Doyle," she said as she turned to Patrick, "are you having drinks in the library?"

"No, Ernestine, we will not," Michael interrupted. "Unfortunately, we must make this an early evening. We wanted to wait to make our announcement until we were far enough along. I can now gladly report that we are expecting."

"What wonderful news! Congratulations!" Ilona offered to an uncomfortable-looking Sybil.

"Sybil, dear, I am so very happy for you. My heartfelt good wishes. *This is the time,*" Patrick shared as he embraced her.

"Thank you," she whispered, choking back tears. "Michael is worried about me staying out too late. He takes such good care of me, saying I need to rest."

"Of course you do. You are carrying the next generation of Doyles!" Patrick cheered, giving his brother a hearty handshake and slap to the shoulder.

Ilona's preparations of planning dinner conversation topics were for naught given that the men dominated the conversation with talk of work. Patrick encouraged Michael to "tell Ilona about the people you've met at the M&M, so many fascinating people." Michael took the bait and carried on with tales of his new acquaintances, as well as with the list of final items for the building and an update on their efforts to increase the number of tenants. Ilona nodded and offered murmurs of approval and amusement, but Michael never once looked her in the eye, choosing to focus on his brother and Sybil. Dear Ernestine dashed through dinner more briskly than Ilona had ever seen, causing her to wonder how much was due to Michael's request and how much was due to her own desire for them to leave.

"And what I've come to appreciate the most is becoming so well acquainted with Timothy Dunn. Innovative. A risk taker. And a hell of chunk of capital. I think he'd give you a run for your money, dear brother." Michael said.

"Well, what a shame that dinner is coming to an end. It certainly would have been a terrific turn in conversation," Patrick replied, resting his fork as he finished a pecan tart.

"Come now, Patrick. I talked to Tim earlier today, and I do want to share a few ideas we had."

"Let's do that in the library over a drink."

Sybil looked to her husband in concern, slightly shaking her head.

"Just one drink. Then we will head home for you to rest," Michael replied as he made his way from the room.

"I'm sorry we are a bit of a bore this evening. I suppose this pregnancy is riling our nerves," Sybil said as she took a sip of tea. Her lack of eye contact signaled that, while the apology was sincere, the reasoning was not. Ilona surmised it was her way of apologizing for her husband.

"I can imagine. And one day I hope to say I understand," Ilona teased.

"Oh, I have a feeling you will. You know, I couldn't be happier with Patrick's choice," she confided, her eyes lighting up with a hint of what Ilona had detected in the garden.

"Excuse me?" Ilona questioned, steadying her cup on its saucer.

"Patrick is not bound by convention; surely you've seen it. He's a maverick . . . a bit of a wild one. One who would remain alone rather than settle for a woman who was less than a match."

"Well, he's not quite settled down," Ilona replied, humbled that she did not have a ring on her finger yet.

"No, but he will. And you are his match. Michael doesn't tell me much, but even he knows his brother has found his wife."

Ilona greeted her new friend with a warm smile.

"Here's to sisterhood," Sybil said, raising her teacup in a toast.

DEAR ERNESTINE CARRIED THE SILVER teapot to refresh her cup for the last time before heading to bed, leaving the library with a gentle sway, moving in rhythm to Duke Ellington's voice on the radio. The sound of the back door locking served as the cue for Patrick to make his way closer, coming up behind her as her eyes scanned the bookcase.

Ilona placed her cup on the table with his first kiss to her neck. Placing her arms over his as he wrapped them around her waist, she could feel his warmth pulsing through her body. She did not know how much longer she could wait, figuring that even a proposal still meant months longer before an actual wedding date.

A knock in the kitchen interrupted their kissing, Patrick pulled away sharply to call out, "Dear Ernestine? Do you need something?" As he left the room, he tried to appear casual. Ilona straightened her dress before wiping her chin for smudged lipstick.

"I guess some things just go bump in the night," he said as they made their way to the sofa, Ilona nestling under his arm.

"I'm sorry for my brother's behavior," Patrick said after a few minutes of silence.

"It's not your fault, love. No need to apologize," Ilona replied.

"Perhaps having his own child will allow him to open up more to me. It's just him and me, after all."

"Children do have a way of working magic."

"Yes, they do. And I believe even I am ready for some of that magic," Patrick replied, kissing her neck. "I want to be with you, Ilona. Do you want to be with me?"

"You know I do, Patrick," she replied, running her fingers through the hair on the back of his head.

"Dear Ernestine is staying with her sister next weekend. The house will be empty," he said, pausing to look her in the eyes.

Ilona sat paralyzed, dumbstruck on how to respond, her desire to marry

Patrick, coupled with her intense physical longing, playing tug of war with her guilt and fears of fornication and pregnancy.

"I promise we will always be together, Ilona, but you know it will take some more time."

"Yes, Patrick. Yes," she answered, passionately returning his kiss and wondering why it would take more time.

"Next Saturday, then? I'll take care of everything," he said with kisses to her neck. She was too embarrassed to ask what "everything" meant, but she figured she had a week to figure it out.

"THANK YOU FOR THE RIDE, Uncle Demetrius," Ilona said as the car came to a stop in front of the Niels Esperson Building the following week.

"You are quite welcome," he returned with a smile.

"We've come a long way from that day at the M&M, Patrick and I."

"That true! Don't tell your baba . . . I like him. Look good together."

Ilona kissed her uncle on the cheek before opening the car door. She waved goodbye from the sidewalk before heading into the building to Patrick's office, wondering if he would still say that if he knew what the following night would entail at The Doyle House.

She looked up to the top of the Niels Esperson, the cupola barely in sight. The newness of the M&M that captured her heart paled in comparison with the building a few blocks south. As the white-gloved attendant pressed the button for floor 16, Ilona straightened her gloves and rubbed a stray mark from her handbag as the elevator made its way to the top. She loved the idea of meeting Patrick at his office, marveling at how this regal building could be but a few blocks from the diner. She nodded to the attendant as she left the elevator, making her way down the long corridor to Patrick's office.

"You could have married for love! Why in the hell do you care who I marry?" Patrick's shouts carried down the hall.

"Goddamn you! I found a way to do both! Love and family!"

"Love? Yours is not the same as mine, and you know it," Patrick smugly replied.

"You're right about that one, Patrick. I married a well-bred Irish woman. You are marrying into a poor family who lives in a kitchen!"

Ilona stood in front of the closed office door, uncertain what to do, staring at her amorphous reflection in the Doyle Lumber & Construction brass placard on the wall.

"And she will soon wear mother's ring, Michael."

Ilona tiptoed back toward the elevator, the excitement over the impending proposal tempered by humiliation over Michael's remarks. She knew her parents needed time to accept their relationship, and perhaps they never would. She did not realize that Patrick felt it on his end. She had assumed that his parents' deaths absolved him from family expectations. Perhaps Michael would have felt different had he been the first born, married in The Doyle House with his Irish wife and child on the way. With a more prominent place in the family, it would be easier to excuse a younger brother's unorthodox choices. But Patrick was the patriarch, both in lineage and reputation. It was clear to everyone that Patrick and Ilona were both taking a risk that others were afraid to take, and Patrick's charisma would quite possibly carry it off.

She walked around the area in front of the elevators, waiting for one of them to exit or for enough time to pass before she approached again. Patrick knew to expect her, as they had supper reservations at the Rice Hotel. Her mind drifted to the following night, the night she would give herself to Patrick. Knowing he loved her, knowing the proposal was imminent, made it all the easier to take the risk.

The forceful sound of an office door opening shifted her attention down the hall. Her eyes met Michael's, and for a moment, she caught a glimpse of his humanity, of the little boy vying to be as good as his older brother. He met her sympathetic smile with acrimony, but she held her gaze steady as they walked toward one another down the hallway.

"Hello, Michael."

"Ilona."

"Good to see you," she said, stopping to chat.

"Likewise," he replied, continuing to the elevator without looking back.

He stood in front of the elevator, his agitation palpable with each punch of the down button. She watched him until the elevator doors opened, hoping he would look toward her but once. He entered the elevator without a glance, the silence at the closing of the doors like a slap to the face.

She took the last few steps to the office door. Her soon-to-be-husband on the other side, she could not help but smile as she gave it a few knocks before opening the door, the vulnerability she had overheard endearing him to her even more.

Patrick stood looking out the window behind his desk, a smile of relief breaking out across his face when their eyes met.

"Come here. I want you to see the view," he said, opening his arms and making his way around the desk to take her into a full embrace.

Holding her hand, he led her to the other side of his desk. He wrapped his arms around her from behind, and they stood in silence, taking in the 180-degree view of the east side of the city.

"It's an exciting time to be in Houston," he said in a low voice. "The city is changing; times are changing."

"Changing for the better. It's good to try new things," she replied, giving his arms a squeeze.

CADMUS

Autumn 2014

JANINE REMINDED HIM OF DEAR Ernestine, which made for a nice consolation after he decided to spend most of the time in his room. Not overly saccharine in her speech, she radiated calm, an authenticity that put him at ease. He did not doubt that the other attendants meant well with their ebullient approach, but he found it demeaning. When Janine spoke to him, her words and tone evoked the belief that he remained a beautiful person still capable of many beautiful things.

"I picked this up for you today, Dr. Doyle," she said, handing him a copy of Paulo Coelho's *The Alchemist*. "A friend of mine just finished it and loved it. I hope you don't mind a second-hand copy."

"Thank you, Dear Ern . . . I'm sorry. Thank you, Janine," he said as he caressed the textured cover of the book. "It is very kind of you to think of me."

"You are quite welcome, sir. May I prepare another cup of tea for you before I leave?"

"No, thank you. Have a nice evening, and please send my congratulations to your daughter on her mathematics exam. I'm glad to hear she scored so well."

With the final click of the door, Cadmus took in a long, deep breath. Another exhausting night of recollection lay ahead, his nocturnal routine assuming its customary form. His gaze rested on the photograph of Robert that graced his nightstand, a candid shot snapped at his fiftieth birthday celebration, a lively night marked with a handful of dear friends and flowing cocktails at The Doyle House. And although the night invoked a most lovely memory of a life well lived, a life that had found its way despite the odds rolled against it, his next thought was always that Ilona's life had ended when she was that age.

Cadmus turned back to the book in his lap, longing for the prose to douse the haunting guilt that consumed his nights. He made it a few sentences down the page before losing his place. He returned to the first few sentences and then read them again and yet again. It took him nearly ten minutes to read one paragraph. Closing the book in frustration, he turned off his lamp, regretting not asking Clementine to bring him a bottle of whiskey to help him sleep. Perhaps it was not too late for him to become his father's son.

That night, the train cried at 2:19 a.m., waking Cadmus from his sleep. His eyes opened to the sight of his hands gripping his pillow, blue veins bulging. Moments before, it had been 1963 in The Doyle House—his arms were outstretched, and he was clawing for his mother, who lay on the ground next to the staircase, her body strewn in irises.

"Mom!" he cried, pushing himself up in bed, struggling in the sheets to race to her side. He burst into tears at the realization that it was but a dream. She had been within arm's reach.

His guilt ebbed and flowed over the years, never fully abating but maintaining a steady undercurrent throughout his life. Coupled with the dementia consuming his mind, it was logical that his emotions ran high. Attempting to grab hold of these facts intellectually, with what mind he had left, he also knew something else for a fact: Ilona was near. Clementine told him that agitation was normal; his body was responding to his deteriorating mind. And regardless of her logical assessment, he countered her at every turn: His mother was looking for him, truly she was. He believed his agitation meant she was close.

He lay awake, thinking of the sudden deaths endured by those close to him. Cadmus believed it was his destiny to die a slow death, alone. The universe vaporized almost everyone he had ever truly loved, whisking them to the heavens. His transition, however, assumed the form of a slow decay, and he knew he was in store for a gradual metamorphosis, one soaked in remorse. He not only bore the stigma of homosexuality, but he also betrayed one of the only people who had loved him unconditionally. And regardless of what the doctors said, he knew he had ushered her death. Thinking of his mother's smile, warm tears flowed from his eyes as he looked out the window into the night sky, his paper-skinned hands wiping his cheeks.

"Mom, I'm here," Cadmus called out, falling into slumber and dreaming of her in a yellow dress holding a bouquet of irises.

CADMUS PULLED A CHAIR UP to the small table near the dining hall's entrance, straining his head to peer into the lobby. Josephine's attempts to persuade him to a normal seat had fallen flat, with Cadmus insisting he had to sit at the table that housed the pitchers of water and juice at the entrance, because he was on the lookout for Ilona. She planned to join him for breakfast that morning, and he did not want to miss her.

Josephine nodded her head in understanding, motioning for another member of the wait staff to relocate the pitchers. Smiling confidently as she surveyed the room, Josephine noted a full house of residents savoring their breakfast. She excused herself for a moment to speak with the front desk before returning to arrange the place setting at his new table, laying fresh linen and flowers while humming a pleasant tune.

"And please don't forget to set one for my mother. She'll be here any minute," Cadmus beamed with excitement.

Josephine smiled sympathetically and arranged Ilona's place at the small table, while Cadmus fidgeted with his cuticles and began to rock back and forth as the morning unfolded.

She refilled his coffee many times, nodding at his remarks.

"I don't know what's taking her so long! I hope she is okay!"

He angrily pushed away a bowl of oatmeal and fruit, shouting at the waiter, "Can't you see she is not here yet? I need to wait for her!"

Thankful that the room was beginning to thin out, Josephine removed the dishes and moved to the side to monitor his agitation level from a short distance, while nodding and offering "good day" as the residents sauntered out to enjoy the morning. The nurse and an attendant arrived when the last guest left, aiming for as much discretion and dignity as the situation would allow.

"Dr. Doyle, it's time to return to your room," the nurse soothed.

"I can't! She's supposed to meet me!" he yelled.

"When Mrs. Doyle arrives, we will escort her to your room. There is no need for you to wait here," she kindly replied with conviction, extending her hand to him for balance.

"I don't understand. I thought she'd come. There's so much to say," he wept, his hands covering his eyes as the attendant inched forward with a wheelchair. "So very, very much to say."

Cadmus' weeping turned to wails as they wheeled him to the service elevator. The attendant shrouded him in a blanket and looked above as if making a personal plea to spare her from the fate of a long life and a maddening mind.

ILONA

Winter 1930

"SO WHAT DOES MY LOVELY lady plan to wear to the Port of Houston Dinner? With only a few weeks remaining, surely you have something picked out?" Patrick asked as they strolled through the M&M arcade, holding hands and making their way to the private lounge. Today marked two months from the day they had met. She was not certain if Patrick knew this detail when he suggested stopping at the M&M in route to his home, but she could not think of a better way to mark the occasion, even if only to herself. She was hesitant to mention the significance of the date out of fear it might be taken as pressure to marry.

"Yes, I found something quite nice, but I want to surprise you," Ilona coyly replied, thinking of the dress she had found at Foley Brothers just this past week. Her baba had balked at the price, refusing to pay the full amount. After much cajoling, her sister Arianna had agreed to lend her the difference, even though she, too, expressed disapproval of Ilona's relationship with Patrick and of such extravagance. It would take Ilona a good while to fulfill the debt, but she knew it was worth it. When she got the dress home, panic set in when she thought about the other gowns she would need to purchase should their courtship continue.

One dress at a time, Ilona, she thought as she held the dress up to herself in the mirror, admiring it with a turn of her head, held high in a glamorous pose. She had never been to the Crystal Ballroom at the Rice Hotel for a formal society event with Patrick.

"And jewelry, have you thought about jewelry? You know these society women, always hankering to display a disgustingly gaudy show of gems despite the times," Patrick asked.

"Well, I cannot compete in that arena, but I am borrowing a lovely pair of costume earrings from my aunt. And while they are, indeed, faux, I do find them very beautiful and fitting for the occasion," she replied, her tone a bit forcefully upbeat. She took her seat in the red leather booth, the very one they sat in when she tasted her first gimlet. Looking out the window, she thought about how much she had changed over the past two months. She was now a woman of the city, who drank cocktails and enjoyed an intimate relationship with a man. There were words for women who did things like that, but her recent life experience prompted her to question those names. Just as in her readings, there was always another layer to the story.

Sitting in the posh lounge with the moneyed people of the city no longer gave her nearly the unease it once had, but his comments about the jewelry rattled her more than she cared to admit. She looked over at a woman in a fine navy dress with perfectly coiffed hair and painted lips. Surely she owned a decent set of jewelry. She could not understand why he would suggest such a thread of conversation, knowing full well the modest stock from which she came.

"I trust they will be lovely. I *was* thinking, perhaps, that this bauble might make a nice accompaniment to your ensemble."

She turned back from the window to see a black velvet box resting on the table. Her heart rapidly picking up its beat, she watched him rise from his seat and place one knee to the ground, the lady in the navy dress offering an endearing smile as she nudged the gentleman accompanying her to admire the impending proposal.

"I know I must ask your father's permission, but before I do so, I thought it fitting I ask you first. We are in more modern times, are we not? We need not share this trivial detail of today," he said as he opened the box to reveal a ring set with an enormous oval diamond resting between smaller diamonds on each side.

"I have never thought much about marrying. I knew I would, but only as the fulfillment of an expectation. I never thought I would *want* to marry. Until I met you. Your spirit, your intelligence—you are the most beautiful soul I know. I am a better person with you by my side. Will you marry me, Ilona?"

Eyes filled with tears, she whispered, "Yes. Oh, my love, yes . . .yes . . .yes." The tears now formed a steady stream down her cheeks.

"This ring belonged to my mother. She passed it to me as the first son, asking me to carry on our family name and traditions. I know with all certainty that she is beaming down at us from heaven, filled with joy that she could not have asked for a more perfect match for me."

Ilona enjoyed her gimlet while looking at her ring, humbled by its perfection, in awe that he had chosen her to be his wife. She curled up even closer to her fiancé, the man with whom she would soon spend her life. They kissed lightly, and as he raised his glass to take a sip of whiskey, she turned, gazing out at the image of this moment beautifully framed in one of the many thousands of windows.

SEEKING HER BABA'S PERMISSION WAS another matter—one Ilona and Patrick talked about as they lay in bed, her head on his chest while she twirled the ring around her finger. It would be difficult to leave the ring behind when she went home for the night, but she would have it soon enough. She was giddy with the notion that soon she would reside in The Doyle House with Patrick, being able to fall asleep in his arms until the morning. She was also relieved to curtail her life of living in sin, worries of pregnancy consuming her more often than she cared to acknowledge.

"I'd like to have Patrick over for supper on Saturday," Ilona said from the back seat of the car as they drove home from church the following day. She was thankful she could look out the window instead of meeting their eyes, although her baba did take a quick peek at her from the rearview mirror.

Mama turned her head to look at him before craning her neck to the back seat.

"Our home?" she asked.

"Yes. You don't need to worry about a thing," Ilona continued. "I will prepare lamb and potatoes. Patrick offered to bring dessert."

"He's *cooking?*" her baba asked, as her mama gestured for him to return his eyes to road.

"Of course not!" Ilona chuckled. "Dear Ernestine will bake an apple upside-down cake. It's one of his grandmother's recipes."

"Dear who?" Mama asked.

"Her name is Ernestine. She has worked for the family since he was a baby."

Her baba nodded in affirmation, glancing at his wife who was turned toward the window.

Later that evening, Mama came into Ilona's room to kiss her good night as she lay in bed reading.

"Patrick a nice man, very handsome and has where it counts," she said, pointing her index finger to her head. Ilona smiled without saying a word, wondering what her mama planned to say next. She rarely initiated questions regarding Patrick.

"I glad he coming over . . . good to talk more since I no see him when at Lawndale."

"Yes, Mama, I agree. And I do believe you will like him even more, really you will."

"I hope so, Ilona, hope so. Now tell me, you have other plans for Saturday? Hmmm? Things no seem right. Don't surprise your baba, now."

"I'm not sure what you mean, Mama," Ilona replied, looking down at her book to mark the page.

"Help me, help you, eh?"

After a minute of biting her lip, Ilona whispered, "Patrick wants to marry me, Mama. Marry me, *me*. Can you believe it?"

Cupping her daughter's face into her palms, her mama lowered her eyes to her meet her daughter's, their noses barely brushing. "Yes, dear. Of course I believe," she said, closing her eyes, forehead to forehead, with her youngest daughter.

Ilona spent the night wrapped in nostalgia, her heart weaving a chrysalis in preparation for her new life. She was on borrowed time, and as was the case when her days as a pupil had been ending, her senses began to review the blueprint of her life as a Petrarkis. Although she was ready for new experiences, she was thankful for the foundation her parents had provided. She was grounded, thoughtful, and hard working—all qualities she learned at the restaurants, qualities that helped mold her constitution, a constitution that captured the heart of a sophisticated man like Patrick.

She took in the scent of the cast-iron gas heater, the weighty sweetness giving form to the warmth, dancing blue and orange flames, that emanated through the ornate lattice. She knew she would miss her ceiling tiles, creamy with the slightest swirl imprint that bore a faint constellation of glitter. Her room at night was tranquil, the moonlight and glow from the heater coating the room in soft pink. After the train signaled its obligatory good night, Ilona heard the door to her parents' room open and shut, followed by footsteps heading to the kitchen. She would not have thought much of it had she not heard a muffled sob. Her baba knew.

PATRICK, ARMED WITH HIS CUSTOMARY charm, brought an enormous bouquet of roses for her mama, who, in turn, had to cover her mouth after gasping quite loudly. She could not help but laugh at her own reaction, which helped ease the tension for everyone. Ilona had considered inviting her sister's family but had decided against it, considering the intention behind the visit. Had they attended, Baby Agatha most certainly would have served as a conversation piece throughout the evening. Now, Ilona worried that her mama's humorous reaction might be the only laugh of the night.

"So, please do tell me how the restaurants are faring. Based on what I see on Franklin Street, it certainly looks like you are well on your way to a third location," Patrick offered as they sat down at the dining table.

"Yes, yes. My business is still good." Her baba's slow and clear reply stung her heart, because she knew how much effort he exerted to fold in small words that most people took for granted. She noted his hands squeezing his utensils; he needed to focus his mind. And although she surmised he was uncomfortable, Ilona was impressed at how well he held eye contact, nodding and assuming his best attempt at ease.

After a painfully silent few seconds of glancing around the room, Patrick delved into his family story, starting with his grandfather who immigrated to Texas from Ireland with but a few coins in his pocket. He had made his way to East Texas and found work cutting timber—saving every cent possible, working harder than every other dreamer. His grandfather eventually bought into the sawmill where he worked, and before he knew it, he had bought out the other two owners. Patrick's father, mirroring his family's work ethic, continued in his father's footsteps: hard working and adventurous, willing to roll the dice. He channeled his father's East Texas riches to the bayou city, determining the Doyle family's destiny—to provide high quality lumber for the city primed for growth after the hurricane of 1900.

Patrick's story gave depth to his character and supported his regalia. The car, the pocket watch, the fine-tailored suit were all results of his family's sweat. Ilona remained skeptical to the extent of her baba's conversion, but she knew that he felt admiration for Patrick, at least in the abstract sense. Patrick segued to the nuptials with the concept of "creating something new and beautiful in this uncharted world, bridging seemingly disparate objects together to forge a most exquisite creation."

Her baba's nods stopped just short of the declaration of his thesis, prompting Patrick to realize that his final request was past due.

"Mr. Petrarkis, I know I am not what you envisioned for Ilona. I'm Irish, I'm Catholic, and I do not have much living family to show for. What I do have, however, is a love for her that I have had for no other and a family name that will bring her great respect. I humbly ask for your permission to marry."

Her mama's eyes filled with tears and remained fixed on Patrick. Her baba looked down for a moment and then over to his wife. Taking a swallow and a deep breath, he stood and faced his daughter's suitor. Patrick rose to his feet, in kind.

He extended his hand and, looking up to meet Patrick's eye, replied, "Welcome to our family."

After supper, Ilona took Patrick for a walk through her neighborhood. The homes, although modest, were pristine, the families filled with pride over owning a home. They meandered to the park where Ilona's brother, Cadmus, once ruled over the baseball diamond. He commanded attention yet had always been benevolent and kind, never taking for granted his natural position as head of the neighborhood pecking order. After hearing a litany of stories about her brother, Patrick declared that they seemed to share the same disposition, "a charming man of many talents, indeed." Patrick then suggested that Cadmus would be a fine name for their firstborn son. Perhaps this offering would help temper her baba's reaction to her more-than-likely decision to convert to Catholicism, although she knew that he would have a most difficult time reconciling this piece regardless of how generous Patrick was with the selection of Petrarkis family names.

HER GOWN FROM FOLEY BROTHERS, more sophisticated and form fitting than anything else she had ever owned, boosted her self-esteem. When Patrick arrived to pick her up with the engagement ring sized, it rose substantially more. And when he pulled out another box that housed his mother's diamond and pearl earrings, she was over-the-moon confident that she could assume the role of his wife. She knew the evening was significant. It was the first time she would attend a society event and meet many of Patrick's friends and business acquaintances. Her nerves got the best of her for most of the day, but the family heirlooms acted like armor. She was ready.

Throngs of people filled the lobby of the Rice Hotel, introductions launching from the moment they stepped inside. Ilona's mind swirled, trying to remember the bevy of names. She had given thought as to how to give a good handshake, and her practice served her well. She had not anticipated, however, the number of times people would embrace her upon the first introduction, welcoming her into their world and wanting to know about this new woman who had captured the heart of the charismatic Patrick Doyle.

Ilona turned to see a blonde woman making a beeline toward her, her striking red dress and diamonds setting her apart even from the most well-dressed guests.

"You must be Ilona," the woman declared with a smile, impressing Ilona with her confidence.

"I am," Ilona replied, uncertain of the woman's intentions.

"I am Margaret. My husband, Phillip, is the silver-haired one over there.

Don't let it fool you . . . prematurely gray. Isn't it unfair how men look better as they age?"

"Fair point, one I couldn't agree with more. It's called a longer shelf life . . . at least that is the term my father uses when he talks about food."

Margaret howled with laughter and placed her hands on Ilona's shoulders.

"You are exactly how I'd hoped you'd be!" Margaret said with a wink. "With Patrick's zest for life? I knew he would eventually settle down with a sharp woman. I am very glad to meet you, Ilona. And please know you can count on me as you navigate these social circles. Don't let the smiles around here fool you for a moment. These ladies are not always what they seem."

Patrick turned to the ladies after finishing his conversation. He looked at Margaret with raised brows and a grin.

"Of course, I approve! Ilona was worth waiting for," she exclaimed.

Ilona entered the Crystal Ballroom thinking about her conversation with Margaret while taking joy in how the kaleidoscopic lights bounced off her ring—with light shimmering from chandeliers, candelabras, and the city peering through the windows. Even though she knew Patrick was worldly, hearing the words "eventually settle down" left her slightly disconcerted. Given his deftness from alcohol to sex, she figured he had earned his fair share of experiences. But with her doubt came her remembrance that he had chosen her to be his wife. And so she raised her hand upon request so others could admire the enormous diamond, thankful for another opportunity to study it for reassurance.

"Patrick! So good to see you!"

Ilona turned around to see a handsome couple heading toward them, the tall gentleman grinning widely, extending his hand even though he had a few steps to go.

"Gavin! Always a pleasure," Patrick replied, returning the handshake with an additional pat to Gavin's right shoulder but not making eye contact with the woman accompanying his friend.

"Rumor has it there is an engagement to celebrate this evening," Gavin said, looking to Ilona with an approving smile.

"For once, I am glad to report that a rumor about me is true. Gavin and Maureen, I am honored to introduce you to my fiancée, Ilona Petrarkis."

Gavin opened his arms wide, embracing Ilona in hearty congratulations. She looked over his shoulder to see his wife, Maureen, studying her with a stone face.

"Well, my dear, you have accomplished quite a feat, taming this one," Gavin joked, wagging his finger at Patrick.

Ilona turned to Maureen, who promptly held out her hand for a formal handshake.

"Pleased to meet you," Ilona said, summoning the handshake she had worked at perfecting over the week, the one she had not used often that night.

"The pleasure is mine," Maureen replied in a monotone voice, catching herself as her eyes darted down toward Ilona's left hand.

"Where are you seated? We are at table 2," Patrick quickly said, prompting Ilona to wonder if he registered the tension.

"Of course you are right in front; high flyers usually are. We are at table 12," replied Gavin before turning back to Ilona. "It was a most sincere pleasure to meet you, Ilona. A handsome couple, indeed, don't you agree, Maureen?"

Maureen gave a weak nod as she turned to make her way to her seat, linking her arm through her husband's.

"That was a bit odd," Ilona said to Patrick as they walked hand in hand to the front.

"Ilona, steer clear of Maureen Sullivan," he stated emphatically. "She is a troubled soul."

ILONA

Spring 1931

ILONA WOULD COME TO MARK the day of her final fitting for her wedding dress as the first time she felt unsettled over her soon-to-be life, the first time she truly tasted her new role as an outsider. Ilona knew her decision to marry Patrick would alter her life trajectory, but she took for granted a presumed level of consistency, that many parts of her life would remain the same.

Her mama wanted to join her, as she had on the other meetings with the seamstress, but she needed to stay behind, since the café was short a server. She helped Ilona select the fabric—ivory satin and crocheted lace for the bodice. Her mama attempted to dissuade her from a short-sleeved gown, waxing unexpectedly poetic at how the tiniest of buttons along her forearm would make a lovely adornment, but she nodded in resignation when Ilona reminded her of the reception in the rose garden: Ilona wanted to enjoy the event without concern over discomfort in the Houston heat. A Roman Catholic wedding, a reception at The Doyle House that would certainly limit the number of guests, a modern-cut dress—Ilona did not fully appreciate it at the time, but each decision inched her farther away from her family.

Arianna would have accompanied Ilona had she asked a second time, but she knew her sister disapproved over her choice in a husband. They were never particularly close, but they were always kind to one another, something Ilona had thought was enough to jumpstart an adult relationship at the right time. She surmised that her sister's hesitation stemmed from her belief that the choice of Patrick was a statement against Arianna's own marriage and family. Arianna had enjoyed her participation in Ilona's secret meeting with Patrick at Buff Stadium, but she never once thought Ilona would marry him.

Ilona made her way down Main Street, hoping she would find her baba in good spirits despite her late arrival. Ever since the afternoon that Patrick asked permission to take Ilona on a date and especially after the proposal, her baba had remained guarded with her. On good days, she saw wistfulness in his eyes, as if he were longing for the days she meandered around Lawndale barely reaching the height of the counter to the days she graced the aisles from the kitchen to the tables. Other days, however, brought a melancholy that made her wonder if he was anxious over how the next chapters would unfold and whether his nephews would turn their backs as his daughter Ilona had. Last night marked another quarrel over the upcoming union after Ilona made a comment about lighting candles in front of the Virgin Mary and Baby Jesus.

"You want worship statues? Worship the Pope! What es wrong? Where I go wrong?"

"Baba, that's simply not true. Catholics do not worship the Pope, and the talk about the statues is just plain silly."

"You no call me silly! They say Pope make no mistake. Pope always right. Crazy!"

"Baba, Patrick and I will live in his house in The Heights . . . you know this! Holy Family was his parents' church . . . He grew up there, and Michael's family are members, as well. And it is only a few blocks away from the house. It makes sense, Baba."

"Your church? Your people?"

"And what about Patrick's people? My family's life will be The Heights, Baba. My family will worship at Holy Family."

His eyes filled with tears as he shook his head.

"We are praying to the same God, Baba, Catholic or Orthodox. That I do believe . . . I believe it with all of my heart," Ilona declared.

She turned the corner onto Franklin before hurrying into the diner to find her cousin, Demi, positioned at her station at the register. He was all smiles, entertaining her baba and another gentleman she had yet to meet. They had moved two counter stools to the side of the register, allowing the three men to talk while patrons paid their bills. She was unsettled to see her baba so jovial at the register, knowing his usual place was on a stool at the counter away from his daughter.

"Ilona! Back so soon!" Demi cried, raising his hands in the air. All three men met her with smiles, but the air was different.

"Yes, I wanted to return as soon as I could. You know how busy it is at lunchtime," she said, walking toward the men and noticing the magazines that had displaced her candy jars at the far end of the counter.

"Frederick, please meet my daughter, Ilona. She no be here much longer, marry and be society woman soon," her baba said with a blend of sarcasm and pride as the man rose to shake her hand.

"Congratulations, Miss. What a shame I will not see you more around the diner. I've heard many good things about you."

"Well, I'm not gone yet, and I can still pitch in after the wedding, after all," Ilona retorted with slightly more defensiveness than she intended.

"Ilona, you are heading to the altar with a wealthy Irishman! Your focus will be on your new family!" Demi chuckled.

"Ahhh! Good for you, Miss Ilona! It's a new world here in Houston!" Frederick replied.

CADMUS

Winter 2014

"GOOD MORNING, DR. DOYLE," CHIRPED the nurse who entered his new room in the west wing. "It's so nice to see you awake this morning."

He offered his best nod, but it did not matter. She would offer a perky response regardless of what she saw or heard. He missed Janine.

In his few short weeks as resident on the third-floor's west wing, he assumed his neighbors stared out with barren minds. But now he knew the vacant stare of the aged was born from reviewing their life's film, one that would garner a few tears and a few smiles, one that would elicit rapt attention as the reel played from the earliest memories. The countenance of the viewer remained flat, but it was merely a contrast to the vivid scenes replaying in the mind.

The well-intentioned greetings of the staff, the attempts to uphold their end of the conversation in the hopes of creating normalcy, was but for the caregivers themselves. His soul was transitioning; his words were becoming fewer and fewer as his energies gravitated to reflection of his soul's journey during this lifetime.

CADMUS

Winter 1940

"MERRY CHRISTMAS, MR. DOYLE!" BELLOWED the doorman as Patrick entered the Niels Esperson with his son. "And a very special Christmas to you, too, *Mr. Doyle*," he added, bowing down to meet Cadmus' eyes.

Cadmus nodded shyly, Patrick gave his hand a squeeze. He looked up into his father's light brown eyes, golden spectacles bearing down on him with a raised brow. Cadmus mustered the courage and offered his hand.

"Merry Christmas," he whispered, the doorman shaking his hand.

"Now, now, son. You can do better than that!" Patrick chided.

"Merry Christmas," Cadmus attempted again, the effort to raise his voice a notch not commensurate with the final result.

"Thank you, *Mr. Doyle*," the doorman smiled, giving the little hand an extra pump.

Cadmus did not go to the office with his father frequently, but he went often enough to form a routine. He stepped into the elevator, the operator smiling down at him with a finger to his lips. "Shhhhh . . . It's our secret," he whispered as he gestured to the buttons, allowing Cadmus to press 16 himself after an exaggerated scan around the car to see if anyone was watching.

His father doled out a few sheets of stationery—Doyle Lumber & Construction embossed at the top of the creamy thick paper. It was a nice indulgence, the textured paper resting between his forefinger and thumb. Cadmus settled into the secretary's desk chair, and his father reassured him that the office would remain empty seeing that it was so near the holiday.

Cadmus began writing a story about Christmas Eve, an imbalance of words spelled phonetically with a sprinkling of correct ones. The sweetness from the cigar smoke wafted from his father's office, the scent finding its way into the narrative Cadmus wrote about a family waiting for Santa.

The opening of the office door jarred Cadmus from his reverie. The red-headed woman did not even notice him curled up in the chair. Her gaze was fixed on his father's office door.

"Now were you going to forget to wish me a Merry Christmas?" she teased, raising her right hand to rest high on the doorframe. Her dress was very snug, far tighter than his mother would wear.

His father appeared at his office door, his eyes intent on finding Cadmus rather than meeting hers. She followed Patrick's gaze and jumped back, startled to see a pair of chocolate brown eyes staring back at her.

"Well, pardon me," she apologized, her eyes zeroing in on his face. "My, my. You are most certainly your mother's son," she said wryly.

"He's *my* son. *Our* son," Patrick said before turning to Cadmus. "Give us a minute alone, Caddie. Just need to wrap up an issue."

Patrick closed the door to his office, and Cadmus waited a few seconds before slinking to the door and pressing his ear against the cool, dark wood.

"What in the hell are you doing here?" Patrick questioned.

"I missed you," she purred, her heels clicking on the floor, which Cadmus guessed was drawing her closer to his father.

"It was a mistake. A terrible mistake," he protested.

"Shhh . . . want the little one ratting you out, my love?"

"I'm not your love, Maureen. And you are not mine. You are one big fucking mistake that needs to go away for good," he seethed.

"And does my money need to go with me? Sure would be a shame for Gavin to continue on without the Doyle Brothers."

"Maureen, please don't do this. You know I was drunk. If you care about me at all, you will leave me the hell alone."

"And if you didn't care for me at all, you would have never allowed it to happen again."

Hearing the high heels cross his father's office prompted Cadmus to dart back into the seat. He grabbed the pencil and stared at the paper, willing his heart to quiet and fearing that the sound of its thumping would give him away for certain.

A minute later, the door opened. Maureen held her head high as she stared at him, studying his features. He was not accustomed to adults examining him. After an endearing smile or a pat on the head, they returned to their own world. He intrigued the red-haired woman.

"Merry Christmas," she said as she made her way out of the office.

Cadmus stared at his father positioned at his office door, Patrick uncharacteristically vexed. He returned to his office to gather their coats and hats, motioning for Cadmus to rise from the chair. His father knelt down to button his son's coat, their faces inches from one another. Cadmus noted a flatness in his father's spirit, a sharp contrast to the lighted trees and music that filled the city streets just sixteen floors down.

"Now, we have one stop to make. I have a Christmas surprise for your mother waiting to be picked up . . . a most beautiful diamond bracelet that I know she will love."

ALTHOUGH COUNTER TO THE ACTUAL chronology, what Cadmus perceived as his earliest memory of his father's death was walking along The Boulevard toward Nineteenth Street, Dear Ernestine's hand holding his, as if she was protecting him from an unknown force. It left him searching the esplanade, looking for people lurking.

Callista walked a few paces in front, her hair uncharacteristically tangled and greasy, draping over her downward tilted head. He remembered looking at the sun as it rose to its zenith and how the humidity sprinkled across his face even though it was February, as the black birds crowed with the chimes of the church bells. The spire from the Cooley mansion contrasted sharply against the blue sky, and it made him wonder if it had been metal from the car that pierced his father in such a way as to summon death.

His memory shifted to his mother's sequined gown, how the elegant glimmer of the previous night morphed into a jarring flash, now draped haphazardly over the chaise as his mother lay in bed staring at the wall wide-eyed, her mascara flaked under her eyes and her stained coral lipstick smudged as she whispered, *"Patrick, Patrick,"* under her breath.

He remembered the evening before when he was curled up in the Cogsdale chair in his mother's boudoir, tracing his forefinger along the gold leaf prints that were embossed on the pale pink silk of the armrest. And he remembered her sitting at her vanity, the delicate silver sequins from her gown playing off the light from the chandelier. He knew his memory exaggerated the light, the golds and silvers shimmering around the room, her eyes and the evening star, but the imagery had become part of the tender narrative of the night when his world irrevocably shifted.

Ilona applied a coral shade of lipstick, a hint of sadness in her eyes as she met Cadmus' gaze through the reflection in the mirror. She paused, lowered the lipstick, and with moist eyes mouthed the words, *I love you, sweet boy,* as his sister skipped into the room, dispelling the solitude between mother and son as she gregariously wrapped her arms around her mother.

"You are a princess going to a ball! Where is your prince?" asked Callista.

"Here at your service, Princess Callista," chimed his father as he sauntered into the room, not missing a beat as he swung his arm into his tuxedo jacket, light glinting from his gold-framed eyeglasses.

Ilona blinked her eyes dry and rose to meet her husband, and playing the dutiful part for the children, they reached for one another's hands and began humming the tune "And We Danced All Night," as they waltzed around the room. Callista, arms raised as if holding an imaginary dance partner, twirled around them giggling and collapsing to the ground from dizziness, only to get up and twirl again.

Cadmus and Ilona were the only ones not caught in the fantasy of the happy family, Cadmus not knowing why he felt an emptiness. His mother was a quiet soul, so many people never noted the subtle change, but Cadmus did. He followed his mother with his eyes, observing how her eyelids appeared heavier and how every seventh breath extended a bit deeper in resignation.

Cadmus observed the evening's scene with trepidation, as if he knew at five years old that the Doyles were on the precipice of a climactic family event. His parents dancing in tuxedo and sequins; Callista giving way to bursts of giggles in her white cotton ruffled nightgown; Dear Ernestine coming into the room to announce the driver was waiting; and only his mother's eyes betraying her stunning façade. His father patted his head and gave a wink, his palm resting for a moment longer on his cheek. His mother knelt down and offered a deliberate kiss to his forehead and a playful kiss to his nose. His parents were off to a party at Shadyside.

Ilona arrived at home at half past midnight, the grandfather clock marking the time as the key slipped into the door. Cadmus ran a hand through his wavy dark hair before sliding out of bed in his footed pajamas and creeping like a snake into the hallway. He pretended he was a predator looking for prey, gripping the bottom of the stairwell banister and peering through the railing to spy his parents. His fantasy of startling them dissipated after several minutes of waiting. He wondered what was taking them so long, and then he realized that he had heard only one person enter the home.

He knew it was Ilona, noting the sound of her high heels slowly making their way across the wooden floor. But then, silence. She must have taken a seat. He saw Dear Ernestine walking down the hallway, passing the bottom of the stairs to the sitting room with two cups of hot tea in hand. Her countenance suggested that she was upset; perhaps she was frustrated at having to make a cup of hot tea at that hour when she should have been in bed herself.

He took a few cautious steps downstairs, his arm outstretched high along the wall to help him balance as he arched his body to the right for a glimpse of what was unfolding below. After taking another step, a growing viscidity in the air stopped Cadmus from going forward. He paused for a breath, struggling to understand why he was uneasy.

A teacup clinked to its saucer, breaking the tension he registered. His mother said what he thought was "Patrick" on cue with another clink that muffled the subsequent words. Did they know he was there trying to listen? Where was his father? Then he thought the word could have been "party" or "park." Perhaps his father was parking the car, or maybe his mother thought Dear Ernestine would want to hear details of the party. He found it strange for them to have such a discussion at this hour, but then again he did not know what adults did after he fell asleep.

Several minutes passed without another word; there were only a few clinks to punctuate the silence. He heard his mother gasp, trying to muffle her sobs. Dear Ernestine rose from her chair and sat next to Ilona in the loveseat, stretching her arms around his mother. He blinked several times in disbelief to check whether he was dreaming. His mother rested her head on his nanny's breast, her fragile hands covering her face as she wept. Dear Ernestine patted her head, gently rocking her back and forth with her eyes closed. That was what it looked like when she comforted him after a scrape, after tears from a bad day on the school playground. The vulnerability of his mother in pain was unnerving. Looking back as an adult, this was the moment he realized that parents were not bastions, unflappable forces capable of keeping misfortune at bay.

Although he was not particularly close to his father as his friends and boy cousins were with theirs, an intense longing for Patrick swept over him. Suddenly, he knew intuitively that they would never again hunt for doves or talk of the railroads and lumber, things that never held the faintest interest for him in the first place. He knew that the time had passed for the smell of whiskey and cigars on his father's jacket. Cadmus' eyes filled with tears, his gaze fixed on the front door, willing Patrick to come in and give familiar form to the pain and uncertainty that was downstairs.

At a loss for what to do, Cadmus climbed upstairs backward, his eyes locked on his mother's wedding rings, before tiptoeing into Callista's room. He curled into bed behind her and buried his head in a pillow. If in the morning all was well with the world, he would do everything in his power to become a dutiful son.

EVERY PEW AT HOLY FAMILY was filled for his father's funeral mass. Although only a few candles were lit, the scent of melted wax from over the years permeated the walls, emitting a hallowed sweetness in the air. Cadmus recalled the dark hair of the Greeks blending in with their black apparel, the numbers so great as to create the effect of a shadow or a wave rising on the left side of the church. He, Callista, and his mother sat in the first pew on the right along with Uncle Michael and his family. Throngs of Irish friends, with their pale skin and a palette of hair spanning red to sandy brown, filled the entire right side of the church.

Uncle Michael's sons, Benjamin and Andrew, whispered to one another and giggled in between reprimands. Cadmus had never felt close to them, and now that Patrick was gone he did not see how that would change. The teachers at Harvard Elementary were surprised that the Doyle boys were cousins, not only because of their physical differences, but also because they did not play together at recess and barely acknowledged one another in passing. No animosity, no fighting. There was simply no interest shared. Cadmus preferred to walk the school grounds collecting twigs and rocks while narrating fictional tales in his head. The sandy-haired Doyle cousins were masters of sport, assuming a natural command of the playground that was a precursor to their future positions as prominent Houston businessmen and philanthropists.

Cadmus heard the word sorry so many times that day that the sounding of the word itself became peculiar. Repetition stripped away its meaning, leaving him reciting the pronunciation of the word over and over in his head.

I'm sorry for your loss.

I'm sorry your father passed away.

I'm so sorry, Cadmus.

You will be the man of the house for your mother.

Sorry, sorry, sorry.

A soft, innocuous "s" followed by a hard "r" and concluding with whimsy. The word even looked odd, written on the scores of cards sent to their home in the weeks following—the slopes of the *s* and the arches of the *r*'s. He wondered how a simple word had come to represent such a complexity of emotions.

The other inescapable word he kept hearing after the horrific event was the whispered "she."

She is a harlot, the way she dyes her hair flaming red.

She better not dare show her face here.

She should have been the one killed.

She killed Patrick.

Even as a young boy, Cadmus was confounded by the supposed allure of women, of their power. Last year, Callista so carefully culled over the valentine choices from the box Ilona purchased at the variety store. She wanted to select the perfect card for Edward, whom she was lucky enough to sit behind in Miss Smith's class. Cadmus had overheard boys on the playground teasing Edward about his interest in another girl, but Cadmus did not have the heart to share this news with his sister. When Callista asked his opinion between two valentine selections, he found himself eager to assist. Cadmus did not feel an attraction to any particular girl, but he did experience an odd feeling whenever he thought of Edward.

Cadmus welcomed the silence that descended on the house after Patrick died. He felt guilty for his appreciation of the stillness, of the solitude, but his remorse dulled as he indulged more and more often in his own reflective world. His father was known for his boisterous personality and charm, qualities that no doubt helped strengthen Doyle Lumber & Construction as a presence in Houston industry. It was the Doyle's wealth that allowed them to remain in their house on The Boulevard. When Patrick was alive, Cadmus had been assumed to be next in line as the primary heir to lead the business with the next generation. Men at the lumberyard had greeted him as "Our Greek Boss" and "The Greek Doyle," as they offered him broad smiles and pats on the back.

Cadmus remembered visiting the lumberyard one summer, his father animatedly discussing the timetable for a particular job. The Houston humidity glazed his skin, and the moisture from his scalp formed droplets of sweat that tickled down to the middle of his back. He envisioned the beads as tributaries forming across his body, commanding this image to cool his temperature and still his dizziness from the sweltering heat.

Cadmus pulled the handkerchief his mother had given him from his shorts pocket and wiped his brow. Sitting on a small pile of freshly cut lumber, catching his breath and caressing the smooth wood, he thought about his teacher's explanation that paper was made of wood and how much more appealing it would be if his father had been a publisher instead. He broke from his daydream after hearing the word "delicate" and glanced up to see a few of the men looking at him, shaking their heads, before turning away to resume their work.

Early one morning well before dawn a few months after his father died, Cadmus crept downstairs and out the back door so he could observe the deep violet of the night. Unable to denote the differences between the leaves and the sky, he lay still under the pecan tree, intently watching, waiting for the sky's subtle transformation to daybreak. He dozed off after several minutes only to be awakened later by a sudden gust of wind.

The energy around him breathed a vivacious life into the tree, limbs swaying and leaves rustling, a sharp contrast from the moments before he had fallen asleep. The violet sky's transition was well under way to a lighter hue, the color flickering behind the rapid movement of the leaves. In that moment, Cadmus overwhelmingly felt Patrick's presence, his eyes brimming with tears at the thought that his father was near. His mind raced for a way to embrace him, to force his spirit to return to physical form so he could apologize for being a disappointment, for being delicate. As Cadmus haphazardly leapt upright with flailing arms, the connection weakened. Every subsequent attempt to catch the spirit caused further retreat, yet he continued to circle the tree with hope. The screeching sound of a train's wheels in the distance sliced through the twilight, as if releasing the force from the wind and settling the leaves.

Cadmus returned to his seat on the ground, resting his back against the deep ridges of the tree's bark and catching his breath. He slowly caressed the protruding roots of the tree with his left hand, gently stroking each vein and thinking of the life force that silently willed it to live. He thought about the life force within himself that willed him to live, as well as the lasciviousness that thrust it from his father that winter night. After tracing his way along each root, Cadmus opened his palm to the sky. He told his father he loved him and then accepted his father's apology, all of which was exchanged in silence and with unquestionable certainty.

ILONA

Summer 1931

PATRICK'S KISS TO HER FOREHEAD woke Ilona from her sleep. Her eyes opened to find him seated at the edge of the bed, fully dressed for work and running two fingers through her hair and down her cheek. She had not intended their night routine to be what it had become, projections of their future life taking the form of artificial snapshots: preparing meals in the kitchen, enjoying uninterrupted time together after sex, welcoming babies. Not fully appreciating Dear Ernestine's role beforehand, Ilona now understood that she never had to cook or clean, a fact that continued to dismay her mother and Arianna, who shook their heads in disapproval when they asked what she made her husband for supper.

Dear Ernestine prepared a lovely meal for the couple every evening, which was followed by their walk in the garden before retreating to the library. Ilona assumed her spot in the nook with a book in hand, sneaking glances at her husband as he poured over papers at his desk. A crank of the numbers, a positioning of the straightedge and compass on a grid of the city with a furrowed brow and disheveled hair: Patrick's mind and heart remained set on developing downtown Houston, despite the city's economic struggles that could no longer be overlooked.

She was not a teacher, but she had found something quite unexpected: a husband who provided her a life of sheer learning that allowed her curiosity, enthusiasm, and hope to fuel his own. She had become his muse. His wealth provided security and the ability to keep dreaming, albeit in a suspended state, and she hoped it would carry them through to more prosperous times when he could bring his dreams to fruition.

As the evenings drew to a close, he asked her to see his work. She reviewed the nuts and bolts of proposals and commented on sketches while seated on his lap. Swirling the last of his drink, he turned off his desk lamp. They walked hand in hand to their bedroom, closing the door tightly to keep their privacy from Dear Ernestine, who would return to the house shortly after dawn to commence the morning routine.

Ilona had not anticipated making love well over once a night, each encounter suspended between pockets of sleep, musings, and admiration of the moonlight's projection on their bedroom walls. She had not anticipated taking long baths with her husband, washing his back and massaging his shoulders as he did for her, sharing tales about their days and hopes of what was to come as the trains wailed through the city. She had not anticipated how often she would fall asleep without her nightgown, sleeping late from a night spent shrouded in intimacy. She had not anticipated that her husband would be equally a passionate lover and her best friend.

"I'm heading to work, my love." he whispered, kissing her lips once as she lay half asleep in bed. "And what does your day have in store?"

"Margaret is helping me plan my first tea. I am due for my foray into the women's social circle."

"Yes, well, she is a fine resource to help," he replied. "Just keep her away from my whiskey," he teased as he headed out the door.

Margaret arrived at the house at half past two, thick book in tow.

"What's that?" Ilona asked, gesturing to the book that had a few errant pages peeking haphazardly from the edges.

"My family's recipe book," Margaret replied, grasping the handrail and making her way up the front porch stairs. "Now, please do not misunderstand me. Ernestine is a damn fine cook, but my grandmother's lemon scones will leave the ladies speechless. And that is something that is hard to do with this bunch."

Margaret and Ilona entered the home to find Dear Ernestine setting out tea and biscuits in the sitting room. Ilona smiled and rested her hand on Dear Ernestine's shoulder as a thank you. She wondered if she would ever become accustomed to a life free from domestic duties. Her time in the diner had gifted her with a humility that bonded the two women. Dear Ernestine looked to her with a wink, a gesture Ilona could not imagine her doing had Patrick married someone who had never swept floors.

"I started working on the guest list, but I confess I found it more complicated than I thought it would be," Ilona began. Margaret shook her head and raised her eyebrows in an *I told you so* manner as she placed her handbag on the hallway table before joining Ilona in the sitting room.

"Let me have a look," Margaret said as the ladies took their seats. "Hmmm . . . yes, yes, yes, of course," she said, offering an affirmation for each name. "Interesting connection, but yes, I can see it. Not sure about this one, but okay."

Ilona studied her friend's reactions, a bit nervous as if she were in class with Miss Baker reviewing an essay. Margaret seemed to approve of Ilona's list. However, Margaret paused when she came to the end, her head jerking back.

"Maureen S.?" she asked.

"She's a friend of Sybil's. Surely you know her?"

"*Friend?* Ilona, Maureen Sullivan does not know how to be a friend to any woman."

"Maureen Smithly? She and Sybil have been friends for years," Ilona defended.

"Ahh! Pardon my error. Yes, Mrs. Smithly is a fine lady," Margaret agreed, relieved at the revelation. "And I do think it is good for Sybil to have someone in her corner, so to speak."

"Patrick warned me to stay away from the other Maureen," Ilona stated.

Margaret only stared at her, which kindled even more curiosity in Ilona, considering it came from a garrulous soul.

"Margaret, tell me," Ilona pleaded.

"She just wants what she wants when she wants it," Margaret said, the initial satisfaction with the simplicity of her response waning a moment later. "Like we all do, I suppose. But then again, it's *not at all* like we all do."

Ilona took a sip of tea, deciding to wait out the belabored response.

"She's ruthless and doesn't mind who she steps on to get her way. Let's leave it at that. She will not be of any significance until her father dies, and then we are all in trouble."

"How so?"

"Oil money. Dallas. She doesn't have nearly as much as she wants now, but when the windfall comes, she will be in our face. Now, on to other things . . ." Margaret said as she reached for a biscuit.

"I saw Michael at The Warwick having lunch last week," she continued, changing the subject.

"And how was he?" Ilona asked, knowing it was a strange question given he lived only a few blocks away.

"His usual stiff self, but he did say something rather crass," Margaret replied, carrying it out a bit longer for effect. "His response to my expressed congratulations with respect to Katherine Grace? 'Yes, well I suppose the race for an heir is still on.' Who the hell says things like that after the birth of your first child nearly killed your wife? And in public at The Warwick, for Christ's sake?!"

"Yes, comments like that should not dare be uttered at *The Warwick*," Ilona teased, her mind scanning the calendar to recall when she should expect her period, or not.

ILONA

Summer 1932

ILONA'S BRIGHT SMILE AND WAVE did little to change the blank countenance of the tiny face that peered at her from the front window. While the reaction did not surprise Ilona, her niece's passivity over her arrival was still a disappointment.

"She's two years old, love," Patrick said, sensing her unease.

"I know. But I also know I don't see her very often. She doesn't really know me," Ilona replied.

"You are making up for it today," he said, opening his car door and coming around to help Ilona. He opened her door and held his hand out for hers.

"Good Lord, I do not know how much longer I will fit into the car, seeing how large I am already," Ilona said, taking a deep breath as she stepped out and steadied herself with one hand in Patrick's and the other on the open car door.

"Yes, well, as far as I'm concerned, you can keep on getting larger. It's a sign of a strong, healthy baby!" Patrick declared, his eyes sparking with pride.

Her mama answered the door with a raised index finger to her lips followed by palms together in prayer resting against her cheek to gesture sleep. Patrick and Ilona slipped into Arianna's home, where Ilona placed her handbag on the table near the door. Arianna stepped out of her bedroom, gently closing the door and offering a formal smile to her sister as she came over to greet them.

"From Dear Ernestine," Patrick whispered as he handed her a pecan pie.

"Ah! Please send her my thanks. She was kind enough to share her recipe, but I can't seem to do it right. Mine is too goopy," Arianna laughed. "Come, have a slice with us."

"I would like nothing more than to visit with three lovely," Patrick began before noticing the little face now peeking from behind the sofa. "Pardon me. *Four* lovely ladies, but I need to run to the office for a spell of paperwork that cannot wait until Monday. Sweet Agatha, won't you please give your Uncle Patrick a hug before I go?"

A shy smile broke out over Agatha's face as she hobbled over and sat on Patrick's bent knee.

"Now, let me take a look in my pocket, because I do think there might be something in there for you," he teased, reaching into the interior breast pocket of his jacket and pulling out a new pack of crayons. Her smile opened as she gave him a hug, shuffling off to her room with her gift in hand.

"I'll be back in a few. Enjoy your time, ladies," he said as he headed out the door.

Ilona and her mama made their way to the kitchenette table while Arianna gathered utensils and plates.

"Only a small slice for me. It's for you to enjoy," Ilona said.

"Yes, I am sure she prepared one just for you . . . waiting on The Boulevard," Arianna replied, much to Ilona's resignation. She had not thought the digs would start so soon.

"Dear Ernestine so wants to see the baby. Perhaps after the baptism, you can bring him and Agatha by the house."

"I am anxious for the forty days to be over, that is for certain. But I don't know if I can muster a drive as far as The Heights," Arianna replied. After seeing the sadness in her sister's eyes, she attempted a recovery. "But for another pecan pie? Well, maybe that can be arranged!"

Ilona accepted the comment as an apology, albeit a weak one. She knew Arianna continued to struggle with the differences in their lives.

"Perhaps that would be a good time to bring the baptismal gown. I can't believe two Petrarkis babies will wear it in the same year!" Ilona offered, attempting to bridge a connection with her sister.

"That's true," Arianna replied, lifting her fork from the plate. "Have you and Patrick decided on godparents?"

"I'm afraid we are in the same predicament as you and Aleksander. We must have Roman Catholic godparents, so we asked Michael and Sybil."

Her mama and Arianna nodded, their eyes remaining downcast.

"Surely you understand, as I know you asked Aleksander's family to serve for the baby," Ilona replied, sensing the tension.

"Yes, we asked his cousins," Arianna said. "It's just odd now that you are Catholic, seeing as you committed to serving as Agatha's godmother when you were Orthodox."

"I hadn't thought about it like that, Arianna. I'm sorr—"

"Honestly, Ilona, sometimes it's like you only think of yourself. I feel as if my daughter's been cheated."

"Oh, no, Arianna! I'm so sorry! I know I have not been by often, but I'll do better," Ilona pleaded, looking to her mama for support.

Her mama's eyes remained downcast, signaling her allegiance to Arianna. Ilona paused, cleared her throat, and decided to offer an apology once more.

"I'm sorry I hurt you both," Ilona said. "It was never my intention."

"I know you sorry, Ilona," her mama said, reaching for her hand. "You just living life . . . different life."

"I love you both very much," Ilona said.

Ilona looked over at Arianna, but her sister kept her eyes on her plate. She could not tell whether Arianna felt bad for the remarks or embarrassed over her open expression of envy.

Mama collected the plates and took them to the kitchen sink, and Ilona meandered into Agatha's room to find her niece coloring in her window seat. Ilona picked up a book of nursery rhymes and took a seat next to Agatha, a grin breaking out over her niece's delicate face.

"Want to go on a journey with me?" Ilona asked, opening the book to a well-loved page she was certain Agatha would recognize.

Agatha curled up next to her, Ilona's stomach not allowing her lap to serve as a perch. She looked into her aunt's eyes and then at her ears, noting the sparkles that highlighted her lobes.

"Can I tell you a secret?" Ilona asked.

Agatha nodded, her eyes widening in anticipation.

"If I have a little girl, I want her to be just like you," Ilona said, her finger delicately tapping the tip of her niece's nose.

"And her name will be Callista," she whispered, offering a *shhhhhh* before continuing, "a name that means beautiful in Greek. And I do hope you two will be dear friends."

"LET'S GO WITH THE IVY pattern," Ilona said to Dear Ernestine, who was entering the dining room where Ilona was studying the family's china.

"Mmmmm . . . hmmmm," she responded, her eyes fixed on Ilona.

"What? It's a lovely pattern. Simple. Perfect for the occasion."

"Perfect for the christening of your first child?" Dear Ernestine pressed.

Ilona returned her questioning with a stare, dumbfounded that Dear Ernestine would contradict her so boldly.

"Look, Mrs. Doyle, please pardon me. But I know what you are thinking. You don't want to be highfalutin with your people."

Ilona looked away, a wave of embarrassment sweeping across her face.

"I get it. My sister tells me I'm highfalutin! Can you believe it? All because I tell her how to do things better thanks to what I've seen here at The Doyle House?"

Ilona watched, mesmerized at the life force radiating from Dear Ernestine's customary calm demeanor.

"Mrs. Doyle, I love my Paty."

"Paty?"

"Paty is like my son. I've been taking care of him since he was three. His daddy was a good man who worked hard for this life. You and Callista are now Paty's people, and he's making a beautiful family," Dear Ernestine said, making her way from the dining room back into the hallway before calling out, "And we are using the rose china! With the gold trim! Fancy for Miss Callista Aislinn Doyle!"

HER PARENTS WERE THE FIRST to arrive at the house after the baptism at Holy Family with Arianna, Aleksander, Agatha, and baby Christos in tow. Dear Ernestine took Agatha's hand to escort her to the sitting room, where dolls and a tea set awaited her. Patrick poured lemonade into crystal glasses as they chatted in the library; Ilona was relieved at the ease in the room.

"Aleksander, tell me about the plans for the new store," Patrick said with genuine interest. "You know I love talking about making a dream a reality."

"Yes, we certainly have that in common!" Aleksander said, with Mr. Petrarkis nodding in agreement. "Instead of building anew, I am considering making Anthony Senior an offer to buy one of his stores, the one closer to Preston. With his son's untimely death, it's a struggle for him to keep up with two places."

Ilona's mind turned to Anthony, the young man so eager to win her heart. At least she had been kind the night he had taken her to supper. In retrospect, it was Millie's attack that afternoon after school that had emboldened Ilona's confidence to create a different life for herself, even though she did not know how it would happen at the time. She remembered reaching for Anthony Junior's hand and telling him how much she enjoyed his friendship. She had assured him that he would find a lovely girl to marry, which he had. And now that girl was a widow, a thought that made Ilona visibly shudder.

Michael and his family's grand entrance changed the tenor, Sybil parading Katherine in the most exquisite brocade dress, one that caused sweet Agatha's simple frock to pale in comparison. Dear Ernestine welcomed the little girl, and Sybil took care to straighten Katherine's dress as she ambled to the sitting room to join her Greek cousin.

"Now where is my beautiful goddaughter, Callie?" Michael bellowed down the hall, which Ilona surmised was to hold court with her family.

Callista—Ilona and Patrick loved the duality. Callista was a strong Greek name, but one that easily beget the nickname Callie, which was Irish for "from the forest." It was a name that served both of their heritages, a symbol of the new life they continued to forge together.

"Callista is sleeping, Michael. Worn out, no doubt, from her debut," Patrick said, pouring his brother a glass of lemonade. "And Sybil, how are you feeling, my dear?"

"Tired," her comment and subsequent healthy plop onto the sofa garnering a hearty round of laughter from the room.

"Yes, you bringing new life into world! Exciting!" Mrs. Petrarkis cheered.

Ilona smiled, offering thanks as her eyes rested on each guest. The room was not free of tension, but a fabric of commonality bared its threads as the conversation unfolded.

"It *is* exciting," Sybil whispered with a grin. "I need to focus more on the excitement rather than the fear that something will go wrong."

Patrick walked over and handed her a glass of lemonade.

"On that note, let's offer a toast. To the next generation—may we continue to welcome more children into the fold!"

CADMUS

Winter 2014

CADMUS LOVED TEXAS THUNDERSTORMS, ESPECIALLY the ones that came during the day, with the sky cloaked in charcoal and navy hues as if it were midnight. The nurse positioned his wheelchair to face the window, not that she would notice his excitement growing at the great storm that was upon them.

He thought back to his childhood ritual, remembering how he had cocooned in the third-floor garret window with a blanket, curled in amazement as he watched The Boulevard trees start with a shimmy before giving way to full-fledged fanatical sways, overcome by the spirit of the storm—the spirit that was alive the night he came into the world. He often recalled the story of his birth that was shared so many times that he had all but convinced himself he remembered it firsthand.

When the rain started on December 6, 1935, Ilona was not alarmed, knowing well that Texas storms often made a grand entrance only to leave a short while later. His mother counted her blessings: It was a Friday, and his father would be home for the weekend.

"A week overdue—as if you were having second thoughts!" she said with a laugh, shaking her head with each and every rendition.

The tapping turned to pelting, and Ilona rose from her bed after the clock struck one in the morning. She paced the house with her hands over her belly, feeling a maternal instinct to protect her baby from the storm. Patrick had left his desk light on in the library, and she remembered seeing plans on his desk, his ideas fluctuating between having a proposal ready for an investor in need of a construction company and having himself as an investor, with others joining him, to build on their own.

It left Cadmus crestfallen when he thought of how life turned out for his family. His father continued dreaming despite the Great Depression, excited that his second baby would help continue the legacy. It was a time of unbridled enthusiasm and hope, yet the decline was soon to come. And it came even sooner for his Grandfather Petrarkis when floodwaters devastated the Franklin Street Diner. It was not until the start of World War II that the economy picked up its fast pace again—the year his father lost his life.

At dawn on Saturday morning, the rain continued its torrent, and Patrick received word that downtown was flooded, the bayou running well over into the streets. It was impossible to make it to St. Joseph's Maternity Hospital should the baby decide it was time.

His mother often shared how scared she had been to deliver at home, even knowing that Dear Ernestine had delivered many babies in her family. Ilona knew a stay at the maternity hospital was a luxury that eluded many women, but that was the only experience she knew, the nuns taking such good care of her with Callista.

As he watched the rain form rivulets on the window, Cadmus imagined his mother in labor, beads of sweat along her temples, mirroring the drops that pelted her bedroom window late that Saturday night. He could hear her wails as the crown of his head seared her body, as if purifying his soul's return to earth. His father had not been present during Callista's birth, the nuns seeing to it that he was comfortably settled in the father's waiting area, far from the reality of childbirth. But with Cadmus' birth, he held Ilona's hand as they felt the new life traverse worlds, her body tearing with the release. Dear Ernestine told Patrick to stay with Ilona, but he shook his head as if in a trance, moving to the foot of the bed to witness the birth of his son.

Ilona always concluded the story with watery eyes, recalling it was the only time she ever saw her husband cry. He scooped up his son from her chest where Dear Ernestine laid him to sever the umbilical cord. Cadmus shrieked as Patrick studied him in wonder, and Ilona committed their profiles to memory.

Cadmus cherished the story, knowing that no one or nothing, not even the fact that he was a disappointment, could take away the moment he and his father shared the night he was born.

ILONA

Summer 1936

ILONA'S FINGERS GRACED HER BABY'S cheek, gentle at first, hoping that a soft touch would be all Cadmus would need to awake. She pressed her fingers to his supple lips, cueing him to continue nursing, his mouth instinctively returning to her breast. Despite his propensity to doze while feeding, he had an easier time nursing than Callista. The struggle to get her daughter to nurse had left Ilona feeling deficient as a mother and sadness over a missed opportunity to bond.

The rocking chair creaked lightly, the only other sound in the room coming from the wooden blocks Callista attempted to stack as she sat on the rug in the library. Ilona knew it was an idyllic moment, and closing her eyes in a prayer of thanks, she committed it to memory, as the scent of apple pie wafted from the oven. She ended her prayer at the ringing of the phone, knowing Dear Ernestine would be there soon to relay a message.

"Mr. Doyle won't be home for supper. Something's come up."

"Thank you, Dear Ernestine," Ilona replied, her spirits dashed that he would miss another meal with the family.

Ilona knew the weight Patrick faced at the office, his efforts to advance Doyle Lumber & Construction's position consuming his time both physically and emotionally. The Great Flood of 1935, as that fateful weekend had come to be known, had ravaged downtown. Patrick's dreams for significant development had been put on hold again, just as they had after the Flood of 1929. And while he continued to garner a meager income, the lion's share of the money pouring in from the past seven years was from reconstructing what had been, not from stunning projects of what could be. The M&M, the last accomplishment up to his standards, was fading quickly, with more and more tenants vacating the building as the Depression continued.

She looked out the window, rocking Cadmus and weighing options on how she could help. They were well-to-do, but now that she was part of the other world, she knew firsthand the gradations of the rich. It would take Patrick's charisma, with a heavy dose of his family's pedigree, to charm the right investors to place him at the helm of a major construction project. This fact was something her well-intentioned family did not understand as they recommended Patrick's services to other Greek families needing to construct their businesses. And he never, not once, told them no, even going so far as to invite many families turned clients to The Boulevard home for drinks to talk about how they envisioned the floor plans. It spread his resources thin, but he could not look away once he looked someone's dream in the eye.

Ilona motioned for Dear Ernestine to put Cadmus down for a nap, his lips breaking into the slightest smile, belly full and diaper in need of changing. Buttoning her blouse, she returned to her bedroom to rest. Cadmus was nearing eight months old, but she still had yet to recover fully from his birth.

She hoped Patrick would not be too late or too drunk when he arrived home later that summer night. She missed him, missed the passion, and she was ready to resume where they had left off months before Cadmus' birth. While they had been together many times in the past few months, she had yet to fully abandon herself as she had before her pregnancy. She lay in bed, looking out the window to the garden, knowing she was ready for Patrick. Ilona also knew the renewed physical connection would help her husband. It made them stronger, as if their physical energies coalesced, each one giving rise to the other. They made a powerful team.

Later that night after supper, Ilona drew a warm rose-scented bath before slipping on a new ivory silk nightgown. Her heart quivered when she heard the back door open, prompting her to walk to the bedroom door, ready to greet him when he entered the hallway. He stopped the moment he saw her, a knowing smile breaking over their faces after a moment's stare. He walked over to her and took her hand, escorting her into the bedroom and closing the door behind them.

ILONA

Autumn 1939

"OF COURSE, I'D LOVE TO dine at the Empire Room on Saturday," Ilona offered in response to Patrick's suggestion.

"Then what's with the baffling look on your face?" he asked as they watched Callista and Cadmus, both with heads bent over a rosebush, looking for bugs.

"Because it's with Gavin and Maureen. You've never wanted us to socialize with them before now."

Patrick, lips pursed and unable to speak, kept his stare on the children. Ilona's concern grew as the seconds elapsed, knowing her husband was rarely at a loss for words.

"I need Gavin's help. I need more capital to place a competitive bid."

"Are you changing your mind on a partnership?" Ilona asked.

"Not a merger, not a partnership," he retorted, breaking his stare to look at his wife. "A joint venture, but one that will strengthen our legacy. I don't want to build shopping centers, at least not just yet. We could do those projects with ease, but a new downtown building... Well, that is a different story altogether."

Ilona reached for his hand. She understood, and she loved him for it. His passions, like hers, remained in the city, in downtown. Houston's expansion tempted neither of them; their desire rested in playing an intimate role in the changing skyline. The M&M, now so fallen from grace with a smattering of occupants, no longer held clout. Building something substantial would strengthen the Doyle name.

Callista screamed as a ladybug landed on her shoulder. She galloped in circles to prompt it to fly away, much to Cadmus' delight.

"Ladybugs are our friends," Ilona soothed, walking over to the children. "Did you know they help our garden?"

"How?" Callista cried, her neck tilted as far from her outstretched left arm as possible.

"They eat other bugs that hurt our plants," Ilona explained as she gently tapped the ladybug to flight.

"Ewww!" Callista shrieked, running back to the porch with Cadmus trotting behind her.

As she turned back toward Patrick, who was still seated at the bench, Ilona saw his face downcast, staring at the brick sidewalk. She could not help but wonder if he was vexed over the proposal or over something to do with the mysterious Maureen.

"It will be a great venture," she replied, looking down at him and grabbing his hand for a squeeze. She winked and turned back toward the house.

"Where are you going?" Patrick called.

"To make an appointment at the salon for Saturday afternoon. I can't grace the Empire Room without help from Vivian," Ilona replied.

She had only seen Maureen a handful of times since the day she had first met her at the Crystal Ballroom shortly after their engagement, the last time being in the lobby of the Esperson. Ilona had entered the building to find Patrick talking with Maureen and her husband, Gavin. "You remember Gavin Sullivan, Darling, of Sullivan Glass? The Doyles and Sullivans are building this city!" Patrick reminded her. And although Patrick and Gavin did all the talking, she could not help but notice how Maureen's gaze rested on Patrick's lips every time her gaze shifted his way in the exchange between the two gentlemen.

Ilona's attempts to engage Maureen in side chat were futile. Maureen neglected to offer Ilona even a cursory glance, not even a speck of acknowledgment that could offer a bridge for conversation. The only acknowledgment came at the end of the exchange. Maureen could no longer avoid Ilona's eyes when Gavin suggested that his wife invite Ilona to the upcoming tea she planned to host for the Irish Women's Group. The women's eyes locked, Ilona noting Maureen's overly arched eyebrows and her nostrils taking in more air than normal.

"Of course, I'll call you next week," Maureen coolly replied with a forced smile.

"Well, it's all set! The Irish Women's Group will welcome its first non-Irish member!" Gavin declared.

Maureen and Ilona held one another's gaze for a second longer, confirming Ilona's suspicions that she had a rival. On the occasions when Ilona saw Maureen, all made up and naturally red hair dyed an even more vibrant shade with loose curls cascading down her shoulders, Maureen looked as if she were out on a night on the town rather than visiting an office building. She was a beautiful woman, quite striking from a distance. Yet when she got closer to her, Ilona could see that Maureen was trying very hard, assuming a false confidence with the layers of makeup and heavy fragrance.

Aside from the Milby blondes, Ilona had a remarkable ability to connect with everyone, from elderly Czech diners to high society friends to the men in the lumberyard. Maureen, however, remained elusive, reminding Ilona of her high school days from so long ago.

Maureen never called about the tea, which brought Ilona relief. Maureen seemed a little too interested in Patrick.

"TELL ME MORE ABOUT MAUREEN Sullivan."

Ilona's question was met with silence, prompting her to wonder whether

Margaret had heard her from across the aisle. She walked over to see her friend studying crystal champagne flutes with narrowed eyes.

"Do you think the blue is tacky?" Margaret asked, with her head cocked to the side.

"No, not at all. It's a light hue. Delicate."

"I'll take twelve," Margaret said, looking over at the saleslady. "I'll also need them gift wrapped. Wedding gift."

The saleslady smiled before heading to the stockroom, Margaret's eyes remaining fixed on the crystal display.

"Margaret, tell me more about . . ." Ilona attempted again.

"I heard you the first time," she snapped.

"We had dinner with Gavin and Maureen last Saturday night at the Empire Room."

Margaret turned to face Ilona, an uncharacteristically serious look on her face.

"Why?"

"Patrick and Gavin are pooling their resources together for a new venture."

The saleslady returned for Margaret's signature before taking the flutes to the gift-wrapping station.

"Margaret?" Ilona said, growing impatient with her friend's reticence.

"Before he met you, Patrick was involved with Maureen."

"You mean they dated?"

"No, I certainly wouldn't call it that."

Ilona felt sickened, thinking of how experienced Patrick had been when they were first together.

"Why didn't you ever tell me? We talked about her when I planned that tea," Ilona questioned, puzzled over the omission.

"Ilona, it was a long time ago. There was no reason to share something like that seeing that you had just married."

"She still has feelings for him. It is written all over her face."

"I am sure she does. But those feelings were never returned."

"Well, he had something," Ilona replied.

"All men do, my dear. Don't confuse that with love."

"Does Gavin know?"

"I imagine not, considering the venture. You know, Gavin only came to Houston after his cousin started Sullivan Glass. He was not around here at the time. And I do believe that Maureen threw herself at Gavin in the hopes of making Patrick jealous of the new man in town. She got herself so damned wrapped up with Gavin, fawning all over him at events. I don't think she ever thought she'd marry him, but what else could she do when she found herself in a delicate condition. Supposedly, she miscarried after they married."

"It makes me feel sorry for Gavin," Ilona murmured, struggling to absorb the details. "And still no children?"

"Well, either she can't have them or doesn't want them, and I do think it could very well be the latter. She has not been faithful to her husband."

"Then she would cheat with mine if given the opportunity."

"Ilona, I've known Patrick for a very, very long time. Yes, he once lived a colorful life, but now . . ." Margaret said, reaching for her hand, "he loves you."

"They are joining forces for a new building," Ilona offered. "It's Patrick's dream."

"Hmmm . . . and the money from Gavin's end is Maureen's money. Her father died several months ago. Gavin has more than a few dollars of his own, but it's not enough to pool together with Patrick on a project of this scale."

"And Patrick knows it's her money?" Ilona asked, her naïveté brought to life at hearing her words aloud.

"It's not about *her*. It's about finding a way to his dream," Margaret replied. "That said, you just need to know that she will find a way to make it about herself. Be careful, Ilona."

That night, Patrick did not arrive home until half past one in the morning, with the sour stench of alcohol on his breath. He slept late, waking once to ask Ilona to bring him aspirin. When she heard the running water from the bath later in the morning, she asked Dear Ernestine to take the children for a walk along The Boulevard, her stomach aflutter over how to best approach the subject of Maureen.

"Feeling better?" Ilona asked as Patrick entered the dining room, and she poured him a cup of coffee.

"Starting to," Patrick said, his eyes swiftly turning away from her and to his coffee cup. "I'm sorry."

"I know," she said, placing her hands on his arms, attempting to get him to raise his eyes to hers to see whether his apologies extended beyond his delay in arriving home.

"I am late to a morning meeting. I'll be home for supper tonight. I promise," he said, placing the cup on the dining table.

He planted a heavy kiss on her forehead before heading out the back door, her concerns over the previous night exponentially increasing with his abrupt departure.

Ilona thought back to the day she had met Patrick, his spirit drawing her in like a magnet. The spirit that made him a successful businessman also made him appealing to women—appealing to Maureen.

Thankful for the Holy Family Women's Group luncheon she was hosting later that afternoon, she retreated to the library to review her agenda item on bazaar booths, which included her report on the profits from the doll booth she chaired last month. Based on the participation, it looked like she scored a winner of an idea.

She headed to the garden with a basket and a pair of sheers to cut fresh roses for the table, saying her morning prayers for her husband and their family and counting down the hours until he would come home.

Patrick arrived home in time for supper, his eyes bright and fully recovered from the previous night.

"Cadmus Doyle! Now pay close attention, son!" Patrick commanded in a playful tone while Ilona and the children waited in excited anticipation.

Callista squealed with delight when Patrick handed her a bouquet of pink carnations with baby's breath after presenting Ilona with her own enormous bouquet of irises.

"Ladies love flowers, Cadmus. You should always find ways to surprise the ladies in your life!"

Cadmus smiled and nodded, taking in the scene. Patrick knelt beside his son and asked, "Guess which hand?"

Cadmus studied his father's left side and then his right; both of his father's arms were tucked behind his back. He tapped the left one, to which Patrick cheered, "Correct, indeed!" before handing him a bag of brightly colored licorice.

While elated over Patrick's mood, Ilona knew his zeal was rather exceptional, even for him. She accepted his actions as an apology, noting the remorse in his eyes as she looked up and placed a gentle kiss on his lips.

ILONA

Winter 1941

THE EXCITEMENT OVER THE INVITATION to William Miller's party at his Shadyside home was tempered by Ilona's realization that the Sullivans would undoubtedly be in attendance. She found an exquisite gown at Sakowitz Brothers, a traditional cut that was attentively tailored, one that accentuated her figure in such a way that she no longer resembled a mother of two children. She had never seen sequins that tiny, and the way they were delicately layered over every inch of the material reminded her of moonlight cast on the ocean. For once, she knew she looked beautiful, and she knew it would be an enchanted evening, one in which her presence would declare that she was, indeed, Mrs. Patrick Doyle. The diamond bracelet Patrick surprised her with at Christmas, the one he claimed "would even blow my mother away," would be a fitting accessory. Its extravagance, an indulgence from the predicted profits with Gavin, along with his unusually wistful tone as he made the comment, gave her room for pause. The bracelet came with an additional price.

Thoughts of Maureen continued to haunt her, and Ilona cursed herself for her inability to address the matter with Patrick, her incapacitation stemming from fear of knowing more; turning thoughts into words made abstractions a reality. Silence was a preferred option, for with it came an ignorance that left her with the hope that her marriage was immune from an affair.

Ilona weighed the balance of evidence, taking solace that there was no smoking gun pointing to an indiscretion. Patrick demurred from her most recent intimate advances, but he assured her it was due to stress from work, as every waking hour at work was spent on the proposal. He had no energy for anything else.

She recalled Michael's visit earlier in the week. He had stopped to deliver papers that Patrick needed to review before the next morning. She stood in the hallway, eavesdropping on their conversation in the library, wondering what Michael meant by his comment, "Enjoying the supplemental benefit from working with the Sullivans, aren't you?" Given his tone and Patrick's response to "fuck off," Ilona knew it was a jab, but she convinced herself there was still no proof. She began to will the proposal to fail, although losing the bid for the new building would be Patrick's first real failure as a businessman.

More and more late nights spent at work and at business dinners left her paranoid. She was filled with questions, wondering if he was with Maureen. The week prior, he had arrived home in the early hours of the morning, the latest he had ever come home. Her fears as to his whereabouts were put at ease a few days later when she ran into William Miller at Kaplan's, when William thanked her for lending her husband to their planning meeting at his home. Despite the significant consumption of scotch and cigars, the night was a "roaring success thanks in no small part to Patrick's ingenious ideas." Patrick was where he said he was, and she felt guilty for having doubted him.

The conversation with William Miller fed her hope, and she headed to the hair salon the day of the party on a high that her fears were unfounded. She eagerly entered the salon with eyes searching for Vivian. She had a few ideas in mind, and she even brought the dress to show how the neckline generously swept a tad below her shoulder, a bold fashion choice given her normal wardrobe selections.

As she scanned the salon, her gaze caught on the back of a red head, with curls flowing down as the stylist gave the do a final spray. Ilona heard Maureen say Patrick's name followed by a few disjointed fragments about something being unfair and about them falling in love with one another, cackling loudly with a remark about marriage. For a moment, Ilona was unable to move, unable to hear the salon receptionist beckoning her to the check-in. And she had always thought the idea of paralysis in the face of adversity was hyperbole.

With the third calling of, "Mrs. Doyle?" she gathered her resolve. Summoning every morsel of courage, she took thoughtful, intentional steps toward Maureen. *She* was Mrs. Doyle, wife of Patrick and mother of Callista and Cadmus. Maureen met Ilona's eyes in the mirror, prompting her to cut off her thread of conversation mid sentence. The stylist looked up to see the reason for the pause. Her eyes widened and then darted back toward Maureen's curls, as she nervously nibbled her lower lip while applying more layers of hair spray.

"Good afternoon, Maureen," Ilona stated, her natural dulcet tone marking yet another contrast between Ilona and her loud-mouthed rival. Ilona was moments from another comment, although she did not quite yet know what it would be. Maureen, however, did not give the conversation a chance to continue, as she abruptly waved the aerosol from her face while feigning a coughing fit. She waved goodbye to her stylist and Ilona before heading out the door, the stylist offering an awkward smile to Ilona, confirming her complicity.

Oddly enough, a sense of empowerment overtook her, a welcome surprise to befriend her sorrow. The events further supported that her fear was a reality, and yet she found solace that she possessed power over Maureen, something she had not realized. Patrick often told her he was the lucky one, to have found someone as enchanting as her, a woman both beautiful and intelligent. He sometimes offered these compliments in a jovial, self-deprecating manner in the company of friends, but he also asserted his love, eyes closed and with unquestionable solemnity, on countless occasions. It crossed her mind that his transgressions may have been the impetus for his affirmations, and although he was a charmer, she did not doubt Patrick's sincerity when he professed these feelings. They shared a rare intimacy—at least they had at one time. The best answer she could hope for was that he had succumbed to Maureen's wiles while drunk, nothing more.

Vivian approached her from behind with a half embrace, the intensity of her expression and squeeze of her arm indicating that she knew what transpired. Ilona nonchalantly put the dress away, understanding the importance of establishing a sense of normalcy. The customer's stares darting from underneath hair dryers and curlers returned to their normal gaze—to cups of tea and then to their own reflections in the mirror, their eyes serving as a humble reminder that they, too, were not immune from suffering, odors of ammonia and burnt hair revealing the vulnerability ladies attempt to hide with perfectly coiffed hair and couture. Now it was Ilona's turn to create the façade, as she sat in the salon chair and willed herself to remain composed, with her head held high and her shoulders back.

ILONA RETURNED HOME FROM THE salon to find Dear Ernestine preparing supper for the children, the aromas of pot roast and potatoes welcoming her at the door. She stood still in the hallway and wondered how she had gotten to where she was, an ordinary Greek girl as the lady of The Doyle House. She looked at the Persian rug resting below her feet and the teacups from Ireland on display in the sitting room. She knew she needed to start getting dressed; the late afternoon sun was shining through the stained-glass octagon, fragments of light oscillating on the wooden floor.

She took a few steps toward the library, the sanctuary she and Patrick had once shared. Her grandmother's antique doll "from the old country," stood upright in the bookcase, beckoning her forward as she entered the room. Ilona ran her hand along the spines, books of poetry and art slowly filling up the bookcases, each additional tome gradually displacing another Doyle family porcelain figurine to the sitting room. The north library window faced the garden, and she smiled as she saw the rosebushes gently swaying in the breeze. The Doyles may have planted the rosebushes, but it was Ilona who had nurtured them to be as luscious and bountiful as they became in 1941. She wished she could take a stroll around the garden, but even her heartbreak was not enough to shake her vanity. The weather would certainly ruin her hair, and she was not about to arrive at Shadyside looking a fright. She sat on the sofa, recalling the nights she and Patrick had spent there when they dated, with Patrick's hands caressing her body and Dear Ernestine ensconced in her garage apartment.

Clunky steps down the stairs broke her reverie; then a pause was soon followed by "Mommy! You're home!" Callista barreled down the remaining stairs, swinging along the bannister to catapult herself into the library. "Your hair is gorgeous! Isn't it time for you to get ready? Can I help you? Can I pick out your jewelry?"

Ilona knelt and embraced her daughter for a second or two longer to blink back the tears. She opened her eyes only to meet those of Cadmus, who was kneeling on the third to the last step and peering at her through the railings. Cadmus was a gentle one, "a keen observer," she always told him. She was exposed.

The kitchen door swung open, sounding throughout the house. Patrick kissed her hand when he entered the library before heading to the liquor cabinet for a whiskey. Ilona knew the moment was ill timed for a confrontation, but the event at the salon signaled to her that she could no longer look the other way and hope for the best. She would do so on Sunday, fully knowing that Saturday would be spent nursing tonight's indulgences. If history was any indicator, the day after the hangover was best suited for discussion. The major aches having subsided, Patrick would assume more humility, more vulnerability. This was her best chance for resolution.

ILONA APPRECIATED HER EVENING COUNTENANCE, her face numbed after a hearty cry. It provided a shield to face whatever else might follow, and whatever would follow at the party would be weak in comparison to what she had planned for Sunday. She felt foolish, the way she entered the salon with the gown in tow, beaming about the night ahead, her tendency for reticence and reflectivity cast aside. She suffered a stinging reminder that she could not get away with acting boldly, with overt confidence. It did not suit Ilona as it did some women—as it did Maureen.

As Coleman shut the car door and made his way around to the driver's side, Patrick reached over to caress her hand. Although the scent of whiskey filled the air, she did not doubt his sincerity when he whispered, "You are a beautiful one, my dearest Ilona." The back of his fingers stroked her right cheek, and he told her, again, how much he loved her. He felt guilty. Blinking to mask her tears, she turned to look out the window as the car headed south down The Boulevard.

Patrick was the only person she knew who liked to regale drivers with tales rather than enjoy the comfort and luxury of a peaceful ride. "Can you believe they had the audacity to protest our rates? After everything they pulled along the way?"

Coleman smiled, chuckling and shaking his head, "Man, oh, man . . . hmmm . . . hmm . . . hmmm."

"I know! Unbelievable." Patrick smiled and said, "There is a lot of opportunity in Houston, Coleman, lots of opportunity, and with opportunity comes people who will take advantage and rob you blind."

Her heart began to race as the car neared Shadyside. Maureen's arched eyebrows flashed through her mind—the right brow lifting upward in an exaggerated gesture, sending the message that yes, she has had Patrick.

Ilona found it frustrating that even her own fantasies taunted her. She could not lose her stoic countenance; her earlier cry had cost her too much.

She fixated on the address of the corner house at the intersection, 219. She noted the curves of the 2 and the 9, proportioned nicely between the simplicity of the 1, anything to distract herself from the welling emotions that threatened to break through the pristine package she had diligently worked to assemble.

As the car made its final turn onto Longfellow, the illuminated windows of the Miller's Georgian-style house came into view, a view that was in stark contrast to the cozy familiarity of their own Victorian home in The Heights.

Coleman drove the car into queue with the others, the sound of seashells cracking as the tires rolled along the driveway next to the newly planted trees. Ilona watched the ladies being escorted from their cars and elegantly strolling the long sidewalk leading to the front door. Patrick squeezed her hand, distracting her from the societal parade, and as she met his eyes, she remembered the day she met him in the arcade of the M&M. She had known then that he was not like any other man she had ever met. His eyes sparkled, illuminated from the sun that glinted from his gold-rimmed eyeglasses. The smile in his eyes that evening let her know that he wanted so much to be the man he was not, the man he knew he could never fully be.

In that moment, she saw his purity, his soul, his zest for life that was all too suddenly clouded by the covetous desire that settles over so many men. She asked herself if she could reconcile the two, knowing she had a remarkable man haunted by other desires. Her thoughts turned to Callista. Is this what she would want for her daughter? And Cadmus. Would he be a faithful husband? She struggled to picture him married, but then, he was only five.

Warm air enveloped her as she stepped from the car. The February breeze did not offer much of a respite, and the Houstonians remained on the lookout for winter. Patrick patted his tousled hair and wrapped his arm around her as they made their way to the entrance. Their grounds paled in comparison to the Millers', as the sidewalk was flanked by over an acre of perfectly manicured grass. It looked as if the Millers had draped green carpet over their yard.

From the corner of her eye, she saw their car pull away. She briefly entertained the thought of beckoning Coleman back to take them home. She questioned why she had to wear a brave face and conceal the truth. She longed to wrap her arms around Patrick and take them back to the times they had been at ease, enjoying cocktails in the lounge of the M&M, fully enraptured with plans for their up-and-coming cosmopolitan life. *Sunday*, she reminded herself. She would engage in an honest conversation with Patrick on Sunday.

The front door gave way to the sound of "One Dozen Roses," the jazz quartet's station in the back gardens not interfering with the beautiful music making its way through the home. Ilona was taken aback by the scores of people in the house sipping champagne and engaged in lively conversation. She knew the party would be the biggest event of the season, but the sheer beauty of the people, the flowers, and the candlelight took her by surprise. She accepted a glass of champagne from the butler, taking in a sizeable sip to soothe her nerves.

She cast glances around the room, looking for signs of Maureen. After scanning the house for a minute, Ilona remembered to still her mind. She wanted to exude confidence, which would be difficult to do with nervous glances. After closing her eyes for a few seconds, she reacquainted herself with the room, facing forward in the receiving line.

"Patrick! We are thrilled you and Ilona could join us this evening," Mr. Miller greeted. Mrs. Miller embraced Ilona with an extra squeeze, echoing her husband's sentiments. They were only a few years older than the Doyles, but their opulence graced them with an aura of wisdom and sophistication.

The champagne began to warm Ilona's insides as they made their way into the east room. She looked down at her glass, which, to her surprise, was nearly empty. Patrick swooped another two glasses from a server, offering Ilona a wink of approval. She could not help but giggle as her chin began to tingle, and droplets of champagne fell from her lips onto her chest. Ilona could count on one hand how many times she had been drunk, and those times were all with Patrick. She once heard that Maureen enjoyed a good scotch. Perhaps loosening up a bit more was something Ilona could work toward.

For an average girl, she had transitioned very easily into her role as matriarch of The Doyle House. Her reticence and tendency for introspection suggested a regal appearance that at times masked her insecurities. Patrick certainly had his faults, but there were areas where Ilona could improve, as well. She could strengthen her sense of self, become more assertive in her feelings and opinions.

Smiling, Patrick brushed the drops of champagne off her chest. Ilona wrapped her free arm around his waist, pulling him closer. She wanted to be at his side tonight, not as a fixture but as a confident, engaging participant. She wanted him to remember how wonderful she was, how wonderful she could be, to look at her as an active choice rather than as a shackle. She looked at his lips with a sultry smile, the champagne affording her confidence. Patrick reciprocated her mood and locked his gaze with hers. They still had it. It could be rebuilt. Sunday.

"Ilona, darling! It's about damn time you arrived."

Ilona turned to see Margaret heading toward her. She appreciated Margaret's brashness, the way she commanded a room. She encouraged Ilona to come out of her shell just as Ilona cautioned her to be more judicious, jokingly suggesting, "Say only every third thing that pops into your mind." This phrase became their signature line with Margaret playfully announcing from time to time, "I'm letting thought number one pass. Oh, that was a good one. Aren't you a little bit sad to miss it?"

"Patrick, I see you are as dapper as ever. Now run along with the boys in the library so us ladies can enjoy a little sport of our own."

"Always a pleasure to see you, Margaret," Patrick playfully retorted as he kissed Ilona on the cheek. "Don't have too much fun without us."

Ilona held her grip on his hand as he turned to walk toward the library, causing Patrick to stumble.

"I'll not be far away, my love," Patrick whispered in Ilona's ear as he walked to the west side of the house.

The confidence summoned by the champagne slowly dissipated in Patrick's absence. The discussion turned from food to families to fashion, with Margaret throwing the occasional barb. They talked about the continued development of River Oaks and what was happening on the west side of town. Ilona's inquiries about the river garnered a few laughs.

"What is the difference between a bayou and a river, anyway? It's the South's goddamn way of reminding us how time barely moves in good ole Texas, that's what. Even the water is a goddamn dolt!"

Noticing the wary eyes of the new acquaintances, Margaret self-deprecatingly continued, "My family's biggest regret is that their privilege begets an unyielding confidence that challenges the traditional definition of a well-bred woman."

While she was aware that Margaret unapologetically narrated for effect, Ilona knew her well enough to recognize that alcohol oiled Margaret's speech. She took the opportunity of the pause to excuse herself to the powder room, making her way from the garden back into the house, smiling and nodding as she brushed past the guests. An embrace here, a kiss to the cheek there, her gaze darted around the rooms, looking for a head of bright red curls.

The nocturnal version of the Miller home, seared in a crapulous haze, bore little resemblance to the gracefulness Ilona experienced at their twilight arrival. Booze permeated the air, painting a glaze over many an eye. Ilona realized most of the men, the inner circle rather, remained tucked in the library. Cigar smoke seeped from under the library doors into the other rooms of the house, giving form to the simmering energy of aggression that seemed to fill the air. Noticing that the downstairs powder room was occupied, she made her way up the curved staircase, head held high and shoulders back. Several women dotted the stairs and second floor—a trip to the other powder room serving as a guise to catch a glimpse of the Millers' more private quarters. Perhaps Maureen was among the gossiping pockets of women.

The tranquility of the upstairs gave Ilona a well-needed break. She released her neck and cast her face downward; her tension slowly peeling away with each deep breath. By her estimates, it must be approaching midnight, and she had yet to see the Sullivans. It then occurred to her that perhaps, just perhaps, the episode at the salon had humbled Maureen into staying away from the party. While it would be unusual for her to skip out on an opportunity to outshine other women, perhaps she also knew that it would be a dreadful mistake to make a misstep with Patrick at an event of this caliber.

The half-moon met Ilona's gaze as she raised her head. It looked like a coin slitting into the dark violet sky. The soft moonlight revealed a faint, feathered imprint on the window. Wondering if the bird had survived its encounter with the glass, Ilona smiled at how the mind, from moment to moment, could string one subject to the next.

She looked in the mirror before reaching into her clutch for lipstick, stopping the touch-up midair when Margaret barreled into the powder room.

"Good Lord in Heaven, Margaret! My heart just about stopped!" Ilona shrieked.

She felt a sinking sensation as she looked at Margaret reflected in the mirror. Her furrowed brow, the steely look in her blue eyes; Ilona could not bear to turn around and face her directly. The mirror provided detachment.

"Ilona, it's . . . it's . . ." Margaret stumbled. She was unaccustomed to seeing her friend struggle for words. Ilona's nose began to sting, not over her assumption that it had to do with Patrick but over the heartfelt love that radiated from her friend.

"Please, Margaret. Please. Say it," Ilona stated with such a forthright tone that even she was somewhat surprised.

"Maureen is in the library. Patrick is, too. They . . . she . . ."

Ilona nodded once as she returned the lipstick to her clutch. She took a long breath and looked again at the feathered imprint before returning her gaze to her own reflection in the mirror. Her mind turned to Callista and Cadmus sleeping soundly in their beds where the same moon was casting its glow over the rose garden and through their bedroom windows. She could not control her husband's behavior, but she could control her response, and for once, she was determined to stand up for herself. And knowing that all eyes would be on her, she reached down deep, once more, for her final trace of resolve to close this unbelievably taxing day.

Ilona made her way down the stairs with a strong, determined gait. It was as if Margaret's grit and impertinence moved to another energy source more like its own. The role reversal fueled Ilona's confidence as she made her way to the west side of the house. The other ladies realized that some sort of story was unfolding, and they quickly followed, their lips pursing with eagerness at the turn of events.

The right library door remained closed, but the left one was ajar, revealing the backs of several men turned toward the bookcases with cigar smoke snaking around their heads. Ilona walked to the entrance and placed her palm on the engraved paneling that marked the left door. As she gently pushed it open, she saw the object of the men's attention: Maureen, along with another woman, wearing a shockingly form fitting Kelly green gown, sitting atop a table, cigars in hand. It was abundantly clear they were all quite inebriated, and fits of laughter punctuated Patrick's regalement of one of his usual tales. Maureen was the first to notice Ilona's arrival. With a smug smile, she hopped down from the table and made her way over to Patrick, who was turned away talking to another group of men. Although it was jarring to see them in the same room in that condition, Ilona initially wondered why the scene was such a big deal, seeing that they were in different circles.

Maureen smiled at Ilona before running her bright red fingernails through Patrick's hair and down his cheek as she bit her lip in a drunken grin. Ilona's heart sank at Patrick's response: He looked back to see who was touching him and then nodded at her with a casual smile and wink before returning to his conversation, as if Maureen's behavior was something to which he was accustomed.

The scene's bold colors were striking—black jacket, green dress, and bright red hair and nails among the neutral hues of the library. It was mesmerizing, such unabashed illicitness on display. She cursed herself for flirting with the notion that Maureen had shied away from the party because of her. Patrick had not left the library since their arrival, and by the looks of it, the other occupants shared his tenure. They had been drinking for hours.

Ilona was only there for a minute more before one of Patrick's colleagues caught a glimpse of her as he gave his scotch a swirl. Eyes widening, she saw him cross over to Patrick, his back shielding the couple from view. When he stepped back, Ilona and Patrick's eyes met. The room fell silent, which Ilona found impressive given their state. Maureen stood behind Ilona's husband, drunk and smiling in victory.

"Ilona! No, Ilona! Wait!" Patrick shouted as she turned toward the front door. She was not more than a few steps away before Gavin Sullivan stormed down the hall toward the library, his face contorted in anger and ruddy from the night's revelries.

"I'm going to kill that son of a bitch!" Gavin shouted as he violently shrugged off the other men who attempted to stop him. He made it into the library, heading straight to Patrick with a raised fist in the air. With one hand on the front doorknob, Ilona turned back to see Patrick reach his right arm out to her as he screamed her name once again. He appeared sober for a moment, the moment he realized his two worlds had collided. She turned away and stormed out the front door down the sidewalk, the muffled noises of shattered glass and fists sounding from within the Millers' home.

Coleman brought the car around, and to his credit, he read her face well and did not ask about her husband. As Coleman pulled away, she looked once more at the Miller home; lights streamed from every window, illuminating the block. It was a new feeling, taking control and taking decisive action. Coleman turned left onto Sunset and then left again to head home.

"Sorry, ma'am," Coleman offered. At first, she thought his apologies stemmed from the events that had transpired at the Millers', but with the comment, "Give me a second to head back to the main way," she realized his comment was related to his failure to yield in the roundabout. The car drove around the Sam Houston monument, and Ilona looked out at the reflection pool and moonlight glittering on the surface of the water. It was the same light she had noticed in the Millers' powder room, the same glow she had imagined washing the roof above her children's heads as they slept. She thought that would make a good story, following a few beams of light to the earth, detailing each distinct ray's focus, zeroing in on the different stories life begets, all happening concurrently.

As the car returned to its place on the main road, it crossed her mind to ask Coleman to circle back to the Millers'. Patrick screaming her name reverberated through her mind. She had never heard him yell as he had in that moment.

She firmly shook her head. *No*, she could not return to the home where he had so terribly disgraced her and their family. She felt like a fool, having doubted herself for her speculations and honestly believing but a few hours ago that they could have worked through the affair. And perhaps they could have had it remained a private matter, but how could they possibly move forward from this turn of events? A brawl at Shadyside? She closed her eyes in humiliation, but with the physical pain she felt in her heart, her tears started. She loved him.

SHE MISSED THE WAY HE woke her up during the night, placing his hand on the small of her back before slipping it under her ivory silk gown. Her propensity for whites, for beiges, and all-buttery colors appealed to him. It was elegant, seemingly predictable, but her spontaneity never disappointed, which was a secret that only he knew.

Ilona believed that Patrick continued to visit her right after his death. She lay in bed every day, weeping and half awake, screaming for Dear Ernestine to "let down the drapes for Christ's sake!" With nightfall, she bathed and adorned herself in creams before slipping into a new nightgown delivered from Sakowitz Brothers, much to the puzzlement of Margaret, now a temporary fixture in the home. Well after the children were fast asleep, Ilona would lie in bed waiting for him, for his touch on her back, signaling he was ready to be with her again, as the warm tears contoured her cheeks.

She cherished those nights when she left the windows and drapes open, with humidity rustling through the pecan tree and carrying scents of roses into their bedroom. And then he would come, Patrick's soul was with her; she knew it without a doubt. Lulled into fantasy and sleep, she awoke the next morning with Dear Ernestine letting down the drapes, shaking out her covers, and bringing her morning tea. Twelve hours until their next encounter.

The month after Patrick's death followed the same pattern, broken only when she was called to the Esperson for a reading of his will. She refused to get out of bed, but Dear Ernestine urged, "Love, for the children. Please, please, let's get ready for this day. Callie and Caddie need you!"

Ilona had not seen the children in days. She vaguely recalled Cadmus napping next to her, absentmindedly running her hand through his hair, but it could have very well been a dream. She sat in the library sipping tea from the Doyle family china that had a dainty green vine circling the rim. Making her way to the rose garden in her robe, she slowly walked down the brick sidewalks that circled the grounds, taking intentional, careful steps. She made it to the far end of the yard and sat on the stone bench and remembered the first time he had told her he loved her, the first time she had been kissed. It was still unfathomable that he had been carrying on with Maureen, yet she cried because of the guilt she felt for having left him. She did not know whether she would ever forgive herself for causing his death. She knew he loved her, that she was the one, and she betrayed him by leaving him at Shadyside.

She faced the north side of the home, noting the library's bay window, where she often sat. Her eyes looked up to the second floor, where she saw Callista staring down at her from her bedroom window, with her hand pressed against the glass. She knew she had to find strength for the sake of her children, but she was at a loss on where to start.

"ILONA, YOU ARE NOT WELL enough to do this by yourself! Please let me go with you," Margaret pleaded when she learned that Coleman would drive Ilona downtown alone.

Ilona dismissed her friend's offer, optimistic that Patrick would join her on the drive as he did during the night. Shaking her head, Ilona knew she would not be alone.

After Dear Ernestine eased her into a warm bath, she laid out an elegant black dress along with Mrs. Doyle's pearl and diamond earrings. Looking back, Ilona knew it was Dear Ernestine's attempt to help her feel confident and powerful, as she suspected Michael sensed an opportunity now that the cards were stacked in his favor.

She stepped out onto 808 Travis, staring at the ornate doors and running her gaze all the way up the thirty-two floors of the skyscraper. She was alone, with not even the faintest detection of Patrick's spirit. Breaking her concentration, the doorman to the building tipped his hat, saying, "Good afternoon, Mrs. Doyle. Please accept my heartfelt condolences on your loss."

Ilona offered an obligatory nod of appreciation as she entered the foyer. She corrected his instruction to the elevator operator, "No, I must stop on floor sixteen before heading to twenty-six, thank you, kindly."

Walking down the corridor of floor sixteen, she slowly and deliberately placed each step in the hope Patrick would catch up to her. She stopped at Suite 1615, closing her eyes as she turned to face the engraved brass business plaque: Doyle Lumber & Construction. Removing her glove, she raised her right index finger to trace the lettering, whispering, "I am so very sorry I left you that night. Please come back to me. Please, please, my love."

She stood there for quite some time, and a security guard stopped to offer, "Doyle Offices are temporarily closed, ma'am. May I be of assistance?"

"No. I'm on my way to floor twenty-six. Law Offices of Lehane and MacDougall, please."

Ilona had been to Lehane and MacDougall on several occasions, from the writing of their wills to celebrations of business ventures, but this visit would not end with a drink atop the building.

She could hear the laughter from Mr. Lehane's office as she stepped from the elevator. She surmised Mr. Lehane must not be in there, and it seemed Michael was most certainly running late.

"Good afternoon, Mrs. Doyle," the receptionist warmly greeted as she rose to embrace Ilona. "Please accept my sympathies. Mr. Doyle was such a kind, jovial man. He is missed in the building."

There was another burst of laughter with a vehement roar, "Exactly!" followed by a series of utterings Ilona could not quite decipher. The receptionist, discomfort creeping into her face, stammered, "Please allow me to show you to the library. May I bring you a cup of tea?" She had taken several steps past the staircase and into the library before she realized that instead of following her, Ilona had turned right in the foyer and was opening the door to Mr. Lehane's office.

Mr. Lehane, along with Michael and another man, stood near the bookcase, scotch-laced tongues wagging as if they were discussing a new venture, which she was beginning to realize they were.

"My dear, Ilona, please pardon our most vulgar indiscretion," Mr. Lehane calmly asserted as he noticed her in the doorway, not meaning to slam his highball as hard as he did onto one of the shelves. The unknown gentlemen looked down and then out the window, uneasy at the quick turn of events. As the man placed his glass on the desk, she noticed he wore a gold ring with a malachite stone. She was not accustomed to a man wearing such garish jewelry.

Michael, the only one who continued to hold his drink, walked over to his sister-in-law, offering a half hug, the only option one free hand allowed. His gaze focused on her ear after he kissed her cheek. It took a moment before she realized that he was staring at his mother's diamond and pearl earring, nestled gently on her lobe.

"May we get something for you, dear? Tea, coffee?" Mr. Lehane offered as Ilona shook her head just as Michael closed the door to the office. "Well, I suppose it is time to finalize Patrick's estate."

Michael placed his scotch on the table and helped Ilona into her seat. She closed her eyes, attempting to settle her thoughts. She presumed this piece was a formality, understanding that the inheritance was for her, Callista, and Cadmus. The Doyle House would remain with the three of them with appropriate funds for Ilona and the children. Callista and Cadmus would inherit their father's half of the business, with Cadmus stipulated to take the helm in his father's place when he became of age.

Mr. Lehane placed a leather-bound folder in front of Ilona before disseminating copies to the others seated at the table. She wondered about the man with the ring, but she did not have the energy to ask. She closed her eyes for a few moments to still her mind only to rejoin the group with Mr. Lehane staring intently at her. He opened his leather-bound folder and began the reading of the will.

Her eyes followed the text while her mind and heart searched for Patrick's spirit. Surely he would not leave her now. She longed for nightfall, to be curled in her bed waiting for his visit.

"I hereby do bequeath to Callista Aislinn Doyle and Cadmus Aleksander Doyle . . ."

Hearing the sterile reading of her children's full names reminded her that there should have been one more name read, the middle child she miscarried. Early in the pregnancy, she had not favored an announcement, but

Patrick, with his usual zest, had beamed with pride that he would soon become a father again.

"Please, darling, please, let us tell Michael and Sybil. My legacy, our legacy!" After much hesitation, she acquiesced, allowing Patrick to share the news with his brother's family at Easter brunch at The Doyle House. He offered a most beautiful toast to Ilona and his unborn child, weaving in Michael's family and Callista, "to the next generation of Doyles!" Consumed by his own joy, Patrick failed to note the feigned felicitations of his brother, wary for his own children's interests, especially considering his infant twin sons.

Not more than a week later, Ilona had awoken to a scarlet-stained bed, her stomach warm and cramping from the passing of a soul. She had feared, perhaps, that God was punishing her for having been intimate before her marriage. On more than one occasion before they wed, she stayed up all night, praying for her period and waves of cramps, lest she be rejected even further by her family with a child out of wedlock. *Three. There should have been three.* Her mind wondered if Patrick had now met their baby, the soul of a boy or girl.

"Patrick's last will and testament is very clear, Ilona. Michael, however, wishes to offer a counter proposal in the settlement of his late brother's estate."

Ilona's eyes widened, suddenly turning her head to Michael, who then looked to Mr. Lehane nervously, as if needing reassurance. Mr. Lehane must have given him just what he needed in that look, for when he returned his gaze to Ilona, his eyes had resolve.

"I want to buy your share of the business."

"It is not mine to sell, Michael. It belongs to the children."

"The children? No, Ilona. It is yours until they are of age. You are welcome to sell it if you see fit, as stipulated in the will."

"Michael, what . . . what is 'fit' at this point?" she stumbled, struggling to piece together her words, "Patrick . . . he . . . um . . . Patrick . . ."

"Is dead," Michael finished, coldly.

Ilona felt the air become still, noting that her brother-in-law was now on the brink of being unhinged, with anger seeping through his eyes. How had she missed this before? He rose from the table and walked to the window, looking out west over the city.

"I have been very patient with my brother over the years, Ilona, very patient. As a good son, I accepted my role as the younger one, not the first prize as my one and only brother was and continued to be for his entire life."

"Patrick loved you so, Michael, so very, very much! You must know that, you must have felt that!"

He placed his right hand over his eyes, ostensibly to wipe tears. A minute passed, and her heart started to settle, daring to hope it was evidence that he was regaining his constitution.

"Patrick loved me as much as Patrick was capable of loving. He was a selfish man, Ilona, selfish enough to risk his family name, his business, his wife, and his children to romp around with a whore."

Maureen floated through her mind many times over the past month, but the lion's share of her energies was spent in disbelief and sheer grief over Patrick's gruesome death. The body, too battered for an open casket, from Gavin's blows and then the horrific crash, left her mind spinning with the physical anguish that consumed Patrick's final moments. This was the one time she prayed the drink had done what it was intended to do—that it had numbed the agony Patrick's soul faced during its final exit. Hearing the most emboldened reference to Maureen was, in some ways, the first scratch on the surface of Ilona's anger, although her grief never quite made it to that stage.

"Michael, we don't know . . ." Ilona attempted to counter, placing her right palm on the cold surface of the table to steady the room.

"Yes, we do know! Honestly, Ilona, I do not know if your devotion is commendable or laughable. Of course, that *is* one of the reasons, perhaps *the* reason, he was so endeared to you, heralding him like the Only Son of God the Almighty. Even Maureen called him on his bullshit!"

"Michael," Mr. Lehane warned, eyebrows raised. He looked to the gentleman with the ring, who then brought Ilona a glass of water. She did not realize until she took a sip that beads of perspiration dotted her upper lip.

"Let's return to matters of the estate. Ilona, Michael is prepared to offer you a cash buyout of Callista and Cadmus' share of the business. Given that you and the children are, indeed, family and will no doubt continue to suffer through this terrible loss, he offers this additional amount to the fair share with the stipulation that neither you nor the children will ever attempt to regain control of the business and will never speak a word that it was Michael who initiated the offer," Mr. Lehane stated as he placed the offer in front of her.

Ilona looked up from the document to see Mr. Lehane and the other gentleman staring at her, waiting for her reaction. Michael had turned back to the window.

"Where is this money coming from, Michael? You are offering a sizeable amount," Ilona asked.

He nodded and turned to her smugly, "Yes, Ilona. You will be even wealthier, and the children will be well taken care of for the rest of their lives should you be a good steward of the funds."

"I do not care about the money, not for me at least. I want to know how you are coming by this money. And why the secrecy?" she demanded.

"Both questions are none of your concern. I have the money, and it is legal, as evidenced by the blessings of Lehane and MacDougall," Michael replied with a firm nod from Mr. Lehane.

"I need time. I don't understand, Michael. I need to think about Callista and Cadmus, their future, and what Patrick wanted for them."

"Ilona, be realistic. Do you really see your children successfully assuming the reins of a construction company?"

"Michael, they are children! How can you say that? How do you know whether your children will want to do it either?"

"Want is different from can't. And my children want to do it, because they are different from Callista and Cadmus, and you know it. The business is in their blood, Irish blood; the boys are already strong and determined."

"Cadmus is only five years old, Michael!"

"Cadmus is a faggot, Ilona. You can already tell he is not like the other boys his age, and the men in the lumberyard know it, as well. The Doyle gene skipped a generation with him . . . he doesn't even look like one of us and most certainly does not sound like one of us with that ridiculous name!

"And your daughter, quite lovely, will no doubt marry well given the Doyle pedigree and wealth, her saving grace given what you have to offer her."

Ilona sat up from her chair, barely managing the words to excuse herself. The receptionist must have overheard the exchange, because she was standing at the door when Ilona burst through into the foyer. Instinctively, she wrapped an arm around Ilona, asking if she wanted to go upstairs for fresh air.

Ilona made it up to the cupola alone. Her hand resting on a north-facing column, she looked out at the city, her face paralyzed with shock. The M&M Building, once so ambitious and proud, stood in a feigned show of strength. It made sense that she met Patrick there. It was the place where energies manifested to bring her what she wanted. Now its life mirrored hers and Patrick's again, its slow demise leaving Ilona crestfallen, her early memories of downtown and of her life dreams anchored to its creation. To have witnessed the tenants lose hope in its potential filled her with a maternal sorrow, as if someone were hurting one of her children.

A part of her understood Michael's feelings of inadequacy. Patrick was a rarity, a man who had been able to harness a spirit that won over even the most reluctant of souls. There had been no point in challenging Patrick; he was someone with whom to align and hope that your energies would coalesce and take you to where you wanted to go. She knew Michael was envious; she did not realize the depths of his resentment. He was thirsty to command the ship and wanted to secure a prominent position for his sons.

She circled the cupola, her mind vacillating between the city she knew and the city Houston was becoming, between Patrick's will and Michael's offer, and between who Cadmus was expected to be and who he truly was. She absorbed all views of the city, taking mental panoramic snapshots of the landscape, doing her best to imprint it to memory. New construction was taking place at a rapid pace, the Mellie Esperson Building adjacent to that of the Niels nearing completion. Her Houston was changing, and this time Patrick would not witness the evolution.

The irony of her location at this moment did not escape her. Mellie Esperson was a Houston legend, who channeled grief over her husband's unexpected death by assuming his role in business, including erecting the very building in his honor that heralded the cupola upon which Ilona now stood. Mellie continued her husband's legacy in a way that was uncommon for women. And here she was, Ilona Doyle, a lost soul, still filled with hope that her unfaithful, deceased husband would join her at any moment.

Mrs. Esperson was a pillar of strength, a woman who carved her own way, continuing to achieve notable goals in the face of grief and uncertainty. What had Ilona accomplished? She had chosen to marry a man whose scandalous death would forever link them to his mistress. Materially, she was well adorned in her diamonds and pearls, but she had fallen short of her life's dream.

Michael's words echoed, piercing her thoughts: *selfish, whore, faggot, ridiculous.* She closed her eyes and took a seat. Hearing her son's presumed sexuality verbalized in such a manner jolted her. She knew Cadmus was different, preferring to draw and tell stories. He desperately wanted to read and had been making good progress, having already learned his letters and written words far in advance of other children his age. Being an intellect was not what singled him out particularly, rather it was his apathy, almost distaste, for playing games. If not alone at recess walking the playground's edge, he was partial to chatting with the girls under a tree. He watched boys roughhousing as an observer, as if he was studying another species. Ilona, curious to draw her own conclusions, had taken many a walk around Harvard Elementary during recess to see for herself.

She thought back to how she would prod him to join Patrick on his visits to the lumberyard. Michael's sons clamored to go, running and jumping on stacks of freshly cut wood, fictionalizing games of war with each stack serving as a blockade. Cadmus countered that the lumberyard was dirty and humid, and he preferred jaunts to the Esperson instead. His expressive face studied the ornate designs while his mind constructed stories as he made his way through the lobby to the engraved elevator doors.

Michael was correct about Callista. She would be more than fine, regardless of her actual stake in the company. And while Ilona took vehement exception to his profane description of her son, she painfully conceded to herself that she could not envision Cadmus happily leading the company. He was an outsider; they all were now that Patrick was dead, and perhaps they had always been, with Patrick's magnetism sanitizing the disdain Michael had felt for his brother's family over the past ten years. If Cadmus were to succeed, he would need to want it with every fiber of his being. Michael and his sons would do everything in their power to exclude him. She could not bear to see Cadmus in that position; instead, her maternal instinct welled up to protect and nurture him to be who he wanted to be. She did not want family expectations to shackle him as they almost did her.

Nearing a full revolution of the cupola, she found herself facing The Heights. She looked out, imagining Callista and Cadmus in The Doyle House with Dear Ernestine, anxiously awaiting her return. They would enjoy lemon-roasted chicken, mashed potatoes, and asparagus with almonds on the family china. She would enter the home, holding her head high, focusing her energies on raising her two children.

ILONA DID NOT FREQUENT MANY places right after Patrick's death, her outings centering on the children's school, where she would meet them for walks home. Other than that, she had only ventured out a handful of times with Dear Ernestine next to her. Her first outing on her own was to the post office, an attempted trip that fell short after she noticed the number of stares she garnered while waiting in line to buy stamps for the scores of thank-you notes she needed to write for flowers, favors, and other tangible condolences that, although well intended, made not one dent in assuaging her grief.

Some ladies sharply turned away when they saw her, perhaps fearful that tragedy was contagious, their families made vulnerable if they got too close. Others held fast to their stares, endeavoring to express a sympathetic smile and nod, which made her wonder how much of their pity stemmed from sympathy over Patrick's infidelity more than over his death. While everyone politely expressed their condolences, remarks on his love for her were glaringly absent, as if they did not dare express a presumed sentiment given his demise.

They could not say he was a good man; they could not say he was a loving husband. And even though the events spoke for themselves, Ilona knew the truth. Her husband was a beautifully flawed man who had loved her, even though it may not have been enough to counter what haunted him—fears of inadequacy and of not being able to live up to the standards of success set by his father and grandfather.

The line at the post office that day was as long as the temperature was hot. Ilona abruptly left, figuring it best to exit before fainting from the heat, which would be yet another subject of fodder for the Doyle name. In her haste to search her handbag for her keys, she literally ran into Sybil in front of her car. The two women shared an instinctive fondness for one another, despite Michael's attempts to maintain the most formal of family ties. Ilona did not necessarily assume that Michael had been so blatant as to forbid his wife from forming a strong relationship with her sister-in-law, but she speculated that Sybil was afraid of him, knowing his stance and his resentment when it came to Patrick's family.

"Ilona, I . . . I've been thinking about you. I should have called," Sybil said in a rueful tone. She had not spoken to Ilona in over a month, right before the estate settlement. Ilona surmised that Sybil was not privy to her husband's handling of Doyle Lumber & Construction, probably thinking that they had done her a favor by taking the weight of the children's interests off her shoulders.

"It's okay, really, it is. I spend most days in bed, so I probably would not have been available anyway," Ilona replied, attempting a graceful transition.

"Well, I know Michael is planning on calling soon about Easter."

Easter brunch at The Doyle House. She closed her eyes as memories flooded through her mind, echoes of laughter swirling around images of the children hunting for colored eggs. It was Patrick who woke up early to orchestrate the event, his dimples revealing the sheer delight he took in the choreography of the early dawn hours, nestling eggs throughout the grounds and tucking variety store delights he had bought himself in the vines and branches. No one would have believed it was he who made the event as spectacular as it was, and his desire for anonymity left Ilona even more endeared, albeit with an ounce of guilt. The ladies, and even the gentlemen, lavished praise on her as the hostess, and her temptation to tell the truth was tempered by Patrick's wink as he raised his glass in a toast to his wife and their family.

"I haven't given it much thought," Ilona replied, shock over Patrick's death chilling her face.

"Oh, my goodness, of course, not! Please do not fret one bit. We figured it best to have it at our home. It will make things easier on you, and it also will be nice to have it at our place at least once before we move."

"Move?"

"To River Oaks. We are moving at the end of the year. I thought you knew?"

Ilona shook her head, not quite grasping how she would have known.

They were moving to the newer upscale neighborhood, a beautiful family of five with a husband who was alive. She wondered how they could make such a purchase so soon after the sizeable amount she received from the buyout. The Doyles must be wealthier than she originally thought.

Hours later, the doorbell woke Ilona from her nap. Dear Ernestine knocked on her door a minute or two later to inform her that Michael was there to see her. Ilona's mind played back the earlier events with Sybil, and it left her wondering what prompted his visit. She had not seen him since that day at the Esperson.

She entered the sitting room to see him staring at the oil painting of his father. He had not heard her approach despite the sound of the heels down the hallway, his gaze fixated on the former patriarch.

"Good afternoon, Michael," Ilona greeted him.

"Good afternoon? My dear, it's early evening," he replied before turning around to face her.

She offered neither word nor expression, placidly matching his stare. She might have said it was because she was toughened, but she knew, however, that it was really because she was newly awake. It was the countenance that mattered, and he would not know the truth.

"Mind if I take that painting with me to River Oaks? I think it will serve my family quite well in appreciating their Heights roots."

"Why in the hell are you here, Michael?"

"Now, now, Ilona. Easter is around the corner. Sybil tells me she mentioned it to you today. I came here to extend an invitation to you and my niece and nephew."

She continued to eye him, not saying a word.

"My current home may not be as grand as yours. It is not *the* Doyle House, but it is still *a* Doyle House. Let's continue our Doyle Easter brunch."

"And my family? You know they join our celebration."

"Yes, but as I said before, my house is not as grand as yours. Unfortunately, there is not enough room for the Petrarkis clan. I'm sure you can call on them for supper, or perhaps Thanksgiving will be their holiday."

Ilona shook her head, incredulous as to his continued antipathy.

"Why are you doing this, Michael? You got what you wanted!"

His countenance softened, a small smile broke out over his face, and for a moment, she saw his brother in his eyes.

"Dear Callie, such a beautiful lass. Come give your Uncle Michael a hug," he replied to the little girl peeking from around the corner.

Her daughter ran, eager for his embrace, a touch most similar to that of her father.

Kneeling down beside her, Michael held her hands and said, "You, Cadmus, and your mother are invited to our home for Easter. I know Katherine Grace, Benjamin, and Andrew are very eager to see you all, as is your Aunt Sybil."

"What fun!" Callista cried, looking back at her mother for confirmation.

ILONA

Autumn 1941

ILONA SORTED THROUGH THE STACK of mail as she made her way through the foyer, coming to an abrupt stop when she saw *Maureen Sullivan* written in the upper left-hand corner of an envelope. Her heart beating rapidly and her mouth salivating, she slammed the mail onto the hallway table and bolted to the restroom half expecting to vomit. Her mind raced in befuddlement as to why Maureen would contact her after so long, seeing that she had never once reached out to her after the accident. She knew Maureen and Gavin had moved to Dallas in the months after Patrick's death, but she knew little else. Her friends were careful to avoid mention of the couple.

Ilona retreated to the kitchen for a glass of water and looked out at the leaves of the trees swaying in the wind against the overcast sky. Whatever was in the letter would no doubt offer another lasting imprint on her mind and heart. During the year since Patrick's death, Ilona spent innumerable hours carefully curating each layer: examining, reflecting, and praying on each piece of her life and their marriage that had brought her to where she was today. She was unsettled at the thought of a new layer from Maureen, for it would more than likely be of significance. She took the letter to the rose garden, making her way to the bench and begging God for strength.

Dear Ilona,

It is with heavy trepidation and unspeakable regret that I write this letter, as we approach the anniversary of Patrick's death. Composing words on paper certainly removes any speculation. Although the circumstances are widely presumed, nothing was fully substantiated, and I imagine there is some degree of solace when unpleasant rumors escape final confirmation. I suppose I now should apologize for this indulgence. By writing, I am confirming. I do believe, however, that the reason for my letter will bring more comfort than it will take away.

Ilona, Patrick loved you. He truly and unequivocally loved you. Our first involvement began well before you two met, and while for quite some time I attempted to convince myself otherwise, the truth is we were nothing more than passing distractions to one another, becoming available only when at our worst, a misshapen pair. This is the last I will write about him and me as a "we," because there never was a "we," not in the truest sense, and I am filled with remorse that my attempts to create something of the kind resulted in the most cataclysmic of circumstances.

Patrick was a good man. As odd as this may sound, you were his main topic of conversation. He admired your caring nature, your intelligence, and your spirit. He said on countless occasions that you made him a better man, and he cursed himself for his shortcomings. He had been attempting to extricate himself from me completely for a good while. I manipulated him, which was not difficult to do when he drank. I threatened to take away the investment money, threatened to tell Gavin, which would ruin his business interests. Patrick was tormented with how to resolve the affair, and I know this contributed even more so to his alcoholic tendencies.

I do not expect you to understand my temperament, for you are not privy to the circumstances that prompt me to view the world as I do. I hold earnest hope that one day you will accept my most heartfelt apologies for the pain I brought to you and your family. My actions altered our paths in ways I struggle to reconcile, and perhaps will continue to for the rest of my life.

With continued deepest regret,

Maureen Sullivan

Two days after receiving the letter, Ilona received a phone call from Margaret. Maureen was dead, having shot herself in the head at her Dallas home.

THE CLINK OF A TEACUP being set upon her nightstand broke Ilona from her dream. She opened her eyes to see Dear Ernestine pulling back the drapes.

"Quarter after nine, Mrs. Doyle."

"The children . . . are they . . ."

"Well at school, no need to worry about that."

"Thank you," Ilona whispered. She'd had a good stride going, rising before dawn, dressing herself nicely and then joining Callista and Cadmus for breakfast. She had held their hands en route to school and enjoyed a slower walk home on The Boulevard. Maureen's letter and suicide had shaken Ilona, fracturing the fragile shell she had managed to piece together.

She thought back to her dream, where she had been but moments ago. She was alone in the car as it sat in front of the Millers'. She stared at the house; it was nighttime with lights streaming from all the windows. Patrick stood in the far left window upstairs, looking down at her, his hands pressed to the glass. Maureen stood next to him, staring down at her, arms by her side, wearing the gown she had worn to the Port of Houston Dinner at the Rice Hotel the first night they met. As the car began to pull from the curb, Ilona asked Coleman to stop. Her request unanswered, she spoke louder and louder and then screamed at the realization that the car was driving itself and picking up speed.

"I killed them," Ilona said aloud, staring out the window.

Dear Ernestine paused in her routine, her gaze suspended. After a few seconds of thought, she pulled a chair next to Ilona's bed, cupping her palms over Ilona's hands.

"Paty was my son," she began after several minutes, snagging Ilona's attention. "Friendly to everyone with a good heart, ever since he was yay high," she continued, her eyes remaining downcast, palm facing down a few feet above the floor. "He had a good heart, but a restless heart . . . we all have it. Some hide it just fine; some just can't. Paty had trouble with it. Mrs. Doyle, I loved that boy, so very much I did," she paused to choke back the tears, managing to whisper, "but *he* is the reason for *his*, and *she* is the reason for *hers*."

Squeezing Ilona's hands together in prayer, Dear Ernestine looked into her eyes, tears flowing down her face, "It's not your fault, ma'am. No, no, no. Sweet Jesus, no . . . it's not your fault."

CADMUS

Summer 1941

THE YEAR AFTER HIS FATHER'S death, Cadmus remembered Ilona spending her time in the library nook, staring into the rose garden. Her days were spent in silence; the room's stillness fractured only by endless tears streaming down her cheeks and occasional whispers, "I'm so sorry, my love" in between her litanies of "my fault, my fault." Cadmus passed many of those days curled up in the chair beside her, with crayons and coloring book in hand to pass the time.

Without the pressure to be a boy, Cadmus spent more time in the garden, lazing about under the majestic pecan tree in the far corner of the grounds and paying homage to the sky's variations throughout the day, his vantage point framed by tree limbs and leaves moving ever so slightly in the breeze. He recalled seeing his mother in the window as he leaned against the bark, her countenance and posture so still he feared that life was abandoning her.

"I'm heading over to Uncle Michael's and Aunt Sybil's," Callista said as she offered Ilona an obligatory kiss on the cheek.

"Why not stay home this evening?" Ilona asked, her resignation evident in her tone despite the words.

"Katherine and I have a lot to talk about, Mom. They will be in River Oaks before we know it. I can't imagine school next year without her."

Cadmus recalled the talk about new Houston and the upset it stirred in Callista to think of the world unfolding west. She was more of a Doyle. River Oaks held little charm for him, and he struggled to understand her reverence for the uncle who showed him so much disdain.

As the front door closed and after Callista made her way down the steps, Dear Ernestine came into the library with Ilona's early evening tea.

"Just you and Caddie for supper?" she asked, pouring a steaming cup of Earl Grey.

Ilona paused and turned to her son with a weak smile.

"Yes, thank you, Dear Ernestine. Just me and my boy," she said, her choked tears stealing the speck of light that had shown itself for but a moment.

Cadmus missed his mother's beauty; he missed her smile, which radiated her zest for life, a spirit eviscerated by guilt in the wake of his father's death. He knew his mother was not what you would call a knockout, not the type of woman the redheaded one had tried to be. Ilona held her beauty like a secret, which only those who really knew her appreciated; the longer you looked, the more her beauty revealed itself, making observers wonder how they could have missed it in the first place.

Upon first glance, Ilona's medium frame and thick black hair camouflaged her as an average woman; yet as it sometimes does, the universe tinkered with the design and made the features of her wide brown eyes, upturned nose, and toothy smile something of exquisite proportion. Cadmus longed for the mother he once knew, perhaps more than he longed for the father he never did. Ilona doled out her smiles begrudgingly after she became a widow, her countenance signaling approval relegated to barely a grin.

It made him wonder when his father had first seen her smile. It also made him wonder if a man would ever see her again the way his father had. He knew one man already did. Regardless of his outward disdain, Cadmus knew that Uncle Michael was attracted to his mother. At family gatherings, Uncle Michael's gaze fell on places it should not fall when he thought no one was looking, but Cadmus was always looking.

A sharp set of raps to the front door woke Cadmus from his slumber. The second round prompted him out of bed to see who would come to the house at that hour. He peeked downstairs to see Uncle Michael standing in the doorway next to his mother in her ivory silk robe.

"I expected you much earlier," Ilona stated, her tone harsher than normal. "Is everything alright with Callista?"

"Callie? Yes, of course," Michael said in an unusually pleasant tone. "She and Katherine Grace enjoyed a milkshake at Ward's this afternoon with Sybil. Thank you for letting her sleep over tonight."

"I found the papers you asked about," Ilona said, turning to head into the library as Michael's eyes scanned down her backside when she turned away.

Cadmus tiptoed down the stairs and knelt next to the wall in the hallway. Watching with one eye, he saw his mother at his father's desk staring at a folder she pulled out earlier. Uncle Michael helped himself to a whiskey from his father's liquor cabinet, downing the highball as he made his way over to the desk.

"These are the plans Patrick worked on with Gavin. Gavin certainly does not need or want them now."

"Thank you, Ilona," Michael said. "May I make you a drink?"

His mother stared at his uncle in silence, her constitution stoic. It was her post-Patrick look, the stare of a widow who had suffered tragedies and could not easily be rattled. Cadmus could not see his uncle's face, but he knew they were looking one another in the eye, as if playing a game of who would look away first.

"No, thank you," she replied, holding his gaze.

"There is another subject I wish to broach if you don't mind," Michael said.

"What is it, Michael? What more do you want?" Ilona said, making her way to the sofa, her defensives beginning to settle.

"An interesting question," he replied, following her to the sofa but pausing to refill his glass along the way. He sat down on the sofa, watching her intently as he swirled the liquid in his glass.

"Yes?" she asked, her impatience growing.

"Sybil is a wonderful mother. I couldn't have asked for better," he began. "But . . . but she just can't seem to meet all of my needs."

His mother stared at Uncle Michael with a furrowed brow and her right hand now splayed over her mouth.

"And . . . I am sure you have needs that are no longer being met," Uncle Michael continued in a matter-of-fact tone, taking another sip of his whiskey. "I've always found you very attractive, Ilona. Perhaps that is another reason I begrudged my brother so. He had something I still want. Passion with an exotic woman. I heard you two once, before you were married. Thinking the house was empty, I let myself in to leave a few papers."

Ilona made an effort to bolt from the sofa, but he pulled her back down, slamming his highball on the table.

"No!" she shouted, causing Cadmus to fall backward at the sound of her raised voice.

"You know you want me," he said as he moved on top of her, gliding one hand underneath her robe and nightgown while he placed the other over her mouth.

After several seconds with his one hand still making its way around her body, he removed his other from her mouth and kissed her. Ilona momentarily stopped resisting, as if she wanted to see whether he tasted like his brother. She attempted to push Uncle Michael off, but his weight overcame her. He pinned her down with one hand while he reached for his belt with the other. Cadmus saw his mother struggling to get loose, her hands beating against his uncle's back to no avail, begging, "No, no, please Michael, please don't do this!"

Cadmus rose from his crouched position.

"Mommy!" he shouted, and Uncle Michael jerked back.

He ran to his mother, who had by now extricated herself from the sofa, leaving his uncle to buckle his belt and tuck in his shirt. They returned to the hallway, his mother standing tall while Cadmus stood in front of her, his head barely at her waist. Ilona opened the front door, where both she and Cadmus stood staring at Michael, waiting for him to leave. He remembered the effort he exercised in glaring at his uncle. He mustered his best menacing look to make certain Uncle Michael knew that he was her defender.

Uncle Michael did not look at Ilona, but he held his nephew's stare as he exited The Doyle House for what would be the last time. Years later, Uncle Michael would attend Ilona's funeral, but he did not dare enter Cadmus' home for the reception.

ILONA

Spring 1952

AS LOATH AS ILONA WAS to admit it, Callista's departure to the University of Texas brought peace to the house. She had not been around that often when she had attended Heights High School, spending most of her time with friends or with Katherine. Her frustration with Cadmus intensified as they entered their teens; Ilona surmised it was because he was coming more fully into what he was supposed to be.

She thought back to a conversation they had during Callista's senior year.

"Callista, please invite your brother to the game. I bet he would love to attend, but he needs a ride from someone other than his mother," Ilona had pleaded.

"I doubt he wants to go, Mom. Sports are not his thing, you know."

"Well, perhaps not to play, but cheering the team on is another matter, sweetheart."

"Mom, look, I can't bring him with my friends. I just can't," Callista said shaking her head as she made her way from the kitchen into the hallway.

"Callista, your brother is such a nice person! How can anyone not like him?"

"Because he's too nice. And he's . . . well, you know."

"What?"

Callista stopped and turned around to face her mother, who followed close behind. "I don't think he likes girls."

Ilona remained stricken, not sure how to respond.

"Mom, I'm sorry. It's hard on me, you know. What people say . . . so many gir in his class find him handsome, but he doesn't care . . . just wants to read an hang out with the boys from Chess Club."

"I hope you defend your brother, Callista. He focuses on his studies and not girls, and for that I'm thankful. The others could learn from him," Ilona replied.

"Are you saying I need to learn, too?" Callista questioned, sensing the growing rivalry with her brother. "I'm a good student, maybe not perfect like Cadmus, but at least I have lots of friends!" she shouted heading to the second floor.

"Callista, I'm sorry! I didn't mean it that way!" Ilona called after her, following her up the stairs. "I just want the best for you both. You are smart and lovely, with so many friends. You are so far ahead of where I was at your age . . . so full of confidence! I want the same for Cadmus, too. Please help him."

"He needs to help himself, Mom," Callista replied, shaking her head. "I'm sorry, but I can't help," she said as she shut the door to her room.

Anyone who truly knew Patrick could easily recognize his spirit in both children. The trouble was that no one knew Patrick as Ilona had known him, and as such, Callista received the most comparisons to her late father. She demonstrated his charisma, his moxie. Her involvement in extracurricular activities at Heights High School; her time with Michael and Sybil in Houston Society from the time she was in junior high; her initiative to leave home for the University of Texas: These were all things foreign to Ilona when she was her daughter's age. She was proud to see her daughter's achievements. She only wished it all came with a dose of humility.

Ilona acknowledged the irony that, as it had been with his father, she was the only one who truly knew Cadmus, the introspective young man who, by no direct choice of his own, had been thrust into the shadows of the legendary Doyles. He mirrored the innate part of Patrick's spirit, the raw purity and hope of what could be. It was this essence that fueled the magnetism that most people regarded as pure ambition. Physically, Cadmus was assuming more and more of his father's appearance: chiseled bone structure and consummate handsomeness, albeit in a more beautiful form.

Callista's comments that day had prompted Ilona to realize the increasing difficultly Cadmus would have blending in with others if he continued to reject female interest, something she would hold at bay as best she could from the vantage point that he was focused on his primary goal to graduate at the top of his class and attend Rice University, both of which were true.

"Hellooo? Anyone home?"

"Callista!" Ilona called out from the top of the stairs, holding on to the railing as she hurried down to her daughter. She reached for an embrace, and much to her delight, her daughter returned the squeeze in equal measure.

They held one another's gaze a second longer after the embrace, Ilona hoping her daughter would notice the effort she had put forth for her visit— her new, fashionable dress and brighter lipstick. She vowed to make her best effort to smile a bit wider, to try to be more of the mother Callista wanted her to be. Callista did not come home often, using her breaks to travel or spend time with friends at their homes and ranches around Texas. Her times in Houston were often spent with Katherine, dining at the River Oaks Country Club and hobnobbing with the elite.

Seeing how the past two years had unfolded when Callista was away led Ilona to the conclusion that Callista would come home more often if she wanted to come home. Before she left for college, Callista had no choice but to reside with her mother and brother. But now she had a choice, and she received more of what she needed from others in her life. Ilona knew she could not keep up with that lifestyle, in large part because she had no interest, even though she had more money than her children realized. Margaret's attempts to woo her to the society scene were for naught. To assume such a role based on Patrick's money and name only left Ilona sickened with remorse.

What she could do, however, was breathe a little more life into The Doyle House. Perhaps the past few visits, with Dear Ernestine preparing her favorite meals, a nice chardonnay with supper alongside an invitation for Katherine and other friends, and the fresh roses in her room were taking effect. It was Easter weekend, and although she would attend brunch at Michael and Sybil's on Sunday, Callista agreed to arrive home early to attend awards night at Heights High School the Wednesday before the holiday, with Cadmus slated to receive more than a fair share of awards to mark his junior year.

"You look good, Mom. You really do," Callista said with a curious smile.

"Well, that's because I have both children under one roof tonight!" Ilona replied, sneaking in another hug.

"Is Ya Ya here? It smells wonderful," Callista asked, peeking down the hall.

"Ya Ya?" the voice called from the kitchen. "Now don't you think I learned how to cook some Greek food by now?"

Callista broke into an even bigger smile as she made her way down the hall.

"Dear Ernestine!" Callista cried as she enveloped her in an embrace, Ilona and Dear Ernestine giving one another an "I can't believe it, either" smile over Callista's shoulder.

"It's so good to see you."

Dear Ernestine, cupping her face, replied, "So nice to have you home, Miss Callie!"

"Where's Cadmus?" she asked, much to their continued surprise.

"He should be home soon. We didn't expect you so early," Ilona said.

Callista clasped her hands together with a smile, "I was hoping to arrive early so you and I could talk."

"Of course," Ilona replied in her best attempt to sound confident. "Cadmus should be home in about half an hour. Your grandparents will be over for supper around 5:00, before we head to the school."

"Give me a few minutes to freshen up," Callista said as she hurried up the stairs with her suitcase in tow.

Ilona made her way to the rose garden to soothe her nerves for the conversation. She had not the faintest idea what her daughter would say, but she knew it was strong enough to temper her spirit. She meandered along the sidewalks, reminding herself that her normal flat countenance suggested a stronger constitution than the one she had.

The thwack of the kitchen screen door brought Ilona's attention back to the house. Callista walked toward her smiling with her head held high. Ilona wondered whether she had ever embodied such confidence. Callista linked her arm through her mother's and steered them over to the bench.

Callista pursed her lips, looking at the uneven bricks. "Do you ever wonder where to begin a story?"

Ilona laughed, giving her hand a pat, "All the time."

Callista smiled, raising her brows with a nod as if to say *of course you do.*

"I met someone. Well, I've known him for a quite a while, but things have become more romantic."

"Oh, my! That is news, indeed!" Ilona exclaimed. "Who is this young man who has stolen your heart?"

"William Dunn," Callista said, raising her downcast eyes to meet those of her mother. "You know his father, Timothy Dunn, the man who became Uncle Michael's partner after Dad died."

Ilona did not need to worry about a stoic expression; the shock offered a strong shield.

"Mom, as excited as I am, I realize my relationship might bring you more pain. It's another reminder of Dad and what we lost as a family."

"What do you mean?"

"I know Dad's will gave the business interests to Uncle Michael. I mean, I know we received some money, but had Dad not made that decision, then the Dunns would not be involved with our family."

Ilona sat in silence, knowing she had to be careful with her words. She had never discussed what happened that day at the Niels Esperson, and she did not plan to at this point. She spent the past eleven years glossing over the details, allowing the children to make their own assumptions. Although she took solace in the fact that she never lied outright, she knew she was dangerously close to crossing that line.

"Tell me about William," Ilona said.

"William? He's smart, handsome, so full of spirit. He reminds me of Dad," Callista said, making Ilona's nose begin to tingle. "He's graduating from UT this year. He will return to Houston and join the ranks at Doyle & Dunn. I know this sounds crazy, but in a way, I feel like Dad brought us together."

Ilona could not confide to her daughter that her father would not have wanted that to be true. She could not tell her now that she first met Timothy Dunn at the reading of her father's will, where he had been complicit in Michael's bullying tactics that changed the course of their lives. She could not tell her daughter that nothing Michael demonstrated over the past eleven years made her regret the decision to extricate her children from the dysfunction of the family business, and now her daughter was choosing it. Ilona could only cry tears that let Callista believe her mother only felt pure sadness over Patrick, which was in large part true.

"Mom, I know I am asking a lot. But I have another request, please," Callista said, holding her mother's hands. "William will be in Houston for Easter brunch. The Dunns are joining Uncle Michael and Aunt Sybil for brunch at their home. Please come. With Cadmus."

Ilona looked at her daughter, dumbstruck at how to respond. She had not seen Michael since that dreadful night he attempted to take advantage of her. They politely maneuvered their way to avoid one another on the rare occasions their paths might intersect, as she was almost certain that he had feigned illness on Callista's graduation day from Heights High, the flower arrangement and diamond earrings he sent more than compensating for his absence.

He knew how to keep his niece and goddaughter close, and Ilona knew she had to figure a way to insert herself into this developing latticework.

"Hey, Callista!" Cadmus called out from across the grounds, removing the momentary need for Ilona to answer.

"Dear God. He's almost a man," Callista gasped in disbelief. "He looks like Dad. Well, a Greek version of Dad."

THEY DROVE TO RIVER OAKS in silence, as if they needed to conserve their energy for the image to uphold in the face of adversity. The previous evening, Cadmus mustered the courage to ask about the night Uncle Michael visited his mother after his father's death. A few months previous, Cadmus read a book in The Heights Library, a book not welcome on the shelves of Heights High School. It detailed a rape. It was only when he read it that he realized the magnitude of his uncle's transgressions so many years ago.

Ilona stared at him in disbelief, unable to say anything other than, "It was a very long time ago, Cadmus. Never mention it again," before she returned to her room, supper left untouched, to prepare for Easter brunch the following day.

As ill-timed as it was, on the eve of seeing the other Doyles, Ilona knew Cadmus was a good son; he was only attempting to arm himself with the knowledge necessary in the event tensions should surface again.

"Ilona and Cadmus! So glad you could join us!" Sybil said when she answered the door.

"It's always nice to see you, Sybil." Ilona said as they kissed one another on the cheek. "You have a beautiful home."

"Thank you. It is much more to manage than I ever realized! Please, join the madness," she cried as the trio made their way down the hall to an over-sized living room with windows facing a sizeable lawn, where bright pink azaleas were cascading throughout the grounds.

Ilona saw a bevy of young people bunched together, champagne filling the hubris of the next generation of Doyles and Dunns. She recognized Katherine and Callista talking to a girl she did not know, as well as Benjamin and Andrew playfully arguing with two other young men, one of whom she presumed was William.

"Mother! Cadmus!" Callista called out, placing her champagne flute on the mantle. "I'm so glad you are here. I want to introduce you!"

Ilona and Cadmus looked at one another, surprised by the flowing alcohol given the hour and the occasion. Callista made her way over, pulling the young man Ilona suspected was William over to her family.

"Mother, please allow me to introduce you to William Dunn," Callista said, as William extended his arm for an embrace.

"Mrs. Doyle, it is an honor to meet you. I've heard so much about you," William said, the informality of his half embrace taking Ilona by surprise.

"And please meet my brother, Cadmus," Callista said, lifting her arms in a playful gesture toward her brother.

"You're quite tall for a high school junior! I'm sure you play basketball," William greeted.

"Um, no. But I do play a mean game of chess," Cadmus teased, much to William's amusement.

"We need to bring you each a glass of champagne," William said, motioning to the help.

"Yes, I hear a celebration is in order," Ilona replied with a smile, causing William's green eyes to open a bit wider before he turned to Callista.

"You already told her?" he asked in an attempted whisper that was much louder no doubt due to the champagne.

Callista wrinkled her forehead in confusion as she looked at her mother.

"Graduation. I understand you are graduating next month from the University of Texas."

"Ahhh! Yes, ma'am," William said, nodding his head in relief. "I am graduating with a degree in business and with honors."

"What a wonderful achievement," Ilona replied, curious now as to the other announcement.

Cadmus demurred from the champagne offered, but Ilona surprised herself by taking a healthy sip from her glass. "The young man talking to Ben and Andrew is my younger brother, Richard, also a Longhorn. He will graduate in two more years with Callista, and over there is my sister, Helen. She graduated last year and will marry this summer. The Dunns bleed burnt orange!"

Ilona nodded as she took another sip before turning toward the footsteps coming from the hall. Her eyes landed squarely on Michael, her mind attempting to reconcile her memory with the man she saw in front of her. Age and success had served him well; his appearance was lighter, full of confidence as he made his way toward her. Taking advantage of the full court, he extended his arms to embrace his sister-in-law, and given the eyes watching, she knew she could not refuse.

"Ilona, I am so glad to welcome you to my home," he said, drawing her in a tight embrace. Timothy Dunn now came into view as he made his way down the hall, the malachite ring still prominent on his right hand.

"And Cadmus . . . my, my, you are becoming a young man," Michael said, extending his hand in a firm handshake, studying his nephew's features for traces of Patrick before gesturing ahead. "Please, join us in the family room. It looks like Nancy just put out a few hors d'oeuvres."

"We'll be there in just a second. I need to steal Mrs. Doyle away for a moment," William replied, which caused Michael to raise a brow. "I know how much you enjoy the flowers in your own garden. May I show you the azaleas?"

"Yes, please do," Ilona replied, Callista looking on with a smile.

Making their way to the veranda door, William introduced Ilona to the other Dunn children and refreshed her glass while she offered hugs to her niece and nephews. As she got older, Katherine had grown increasingly reserved toward Ilona, a probable result of the confidences she and Callista shared, but Ben and Andrew made up for that distance with their warm embraces. Ilona could not help but stare a few seconds longer; they took after their Uncle Patrick.

William led Ilona to the veranda and to the swimming pool at the west end of the grounds. He shared his plans to return to Houston in June and delve into his role at Doyle & Dunn. He admitted his initial doubt, daunted at the thought of being the first of the next generation to continue the legacy; however, he harnessed that energy into enthusiasm, knowing that his brother, as well as Ben and Andrew, were not far behind to join him.

She recognized his sincerity, his purity; he possessed a propensity for kindness similar to Patrick's. And while her heart admired his vulnerability and conviction, she also felt a weight from his honest omission of Cadmus' place. She questioned which action resulted in more pain: deliberate or blind exclusion? William's benevolent indifference toward Cadmus brought her an even deeper pain than Michael's and Timothy's intentional acts.

"I am ready to take the next steps for my future, and a very important step in that journey involves Callista."

William and Ilona took a seat at a table near the pool, Ilona noting the cabana and outdoor bar. She wondered if she and Patrick would have followed suit and moved to River Oaks, her mind whirling at how much Houston had changed without her knowing, because her life centered in The Heights and the occasional trip to Lawndale Café or a department store downtown.

"I love your daughter, Mrs. Doyle. I know she and I will have a happy life together. May I have your blessing to marry her?"

"She's only a sophomore, William."

"Yes, about to be a junior. We will not marry until her senior year at the earliest, maybe even after she graduates, but we do believe an engagement will help me better establish myself in the eyes of our clients, show them that I am more than just a young bachelor, and," he continued with a laugh, "and it is inevitable anyway . . . We are in love."

Although his eyes resonated sincerity, Ilona surmised the families had done their fair share of maneuvering to help him reach this conclusion. She knew any level of protest would label her unreasonably contrary, a woman upset that she had drawn a pitiful hand.

"You have my blessings for a happy, long life together, William," Ilona replied, placing her hand over his as she prayed for the continuation of his kindness.

NEXT TO ILONA'S PLACE CARD was a glass of chardonnay. *What the hell*, she thought, as she took her seat in between William and Cadmus. Michael offered an Easter blessing, Ilona opening her eyes and lifting her head a second before the others to notice Michael eyeing her from the head of the table. Sybil noticed her husband's glance as well, and her gaze darted rapidly between the two.

William took the collective *Amen* as his cue to rise, glass of wine in hand.

"I'd like to take a moment if I may to share some joyous news." He looked over to Callista, Ilona recognizing the wide smile that was once her own. Her daughter made her way over to William, her gaze fixed adoringly, waiting for him to continue. "I am honored to share that Callista Aislinn Doyle will be my wife."

Everyone burst into applause even though Ilona surmised this proclamation was far from unexpected. William lifted Callista's hand to reveal a stunning solitaire, a ring quite fitting for a Doyle-Dunn. Another round of cheers accompanied their kiss, with Michael then raising his glass to toast the happy couple. Ilona rose from her seat to offer hugs and congratulations to her daughter and William, blinking away the tears welling in her eyes.

Conversation naturally centered on wedding preparations, Helen sharing thoughts on the process since her own wedding was in but a few months.

Her fiancé was in Dallas with his grandparents, and Helen wondered aloud how they would divvy holidays after the nuptials.

True to form, talk of business surfaced, with the younger generation piping in with comments of their own. Cadmus remained true to himself as the quiet one, the announcement of his intent to study literature at Rice University not offering a viable path for follow-up questions with this particular bunch.

Ilona was thankful when Ben rose from his seat at the end of the meal, beckoning the other young ones to change into their suits for a swim. Cadmus accepted the offer to borrow a suit from his cousins. Although the efforts warmed her heart, she was hoping for an early departure. She took advantage of the flurry, taking her refreshed chardonnay to the library she noticed when they first entered the home.

The library was impressive, oak-paneled walls lined with books and photographs of Michael's family. She grazed her hands along the spines, doubting that anyone in the house ever cracked one open. She knew the wine conjured more emotions as she scanned the photographs, noting the milestones of the happy family of five and their physical resemblance to Patrick.

She cast her attention to the oil portrait of Patrick Doyle, Sr. that once graced her home, his steely eyes taunting her from the mantle, as if to say *You could have had all of this with Patrick.*

"Here you are."

She turned around to see Michael coming toward her, another drink in hand.

"I really am glad you came today, Ilona. I think about you more than you might realize."

"I can't imagine why," she snapped.

"I like that fire. I always knew you had it somewhere." He smiled, tone softening. "How have you been?"

"Not much different than before. My life has remained largely the same," she acquiesced, knowing her world had been so very still since Patrick died.

She accepted Michael's motion for them to sit, dizziness from the morning of wine in effect. The sun shone through the front window, the breeze fluttering the azaleas that colored the windowpane pink.

"How can you have so many azaleas?" she asked, realizing the foolishness of her question as soon as it escaped her lips.

He looked out the window and laughed, "I guess it was my way of establishing a new tradition apart from roses. But roses always remind me of you."

She looked at Michael, her mind flashing to the morning spent with Benjamin and Andrew, Timothy, Richard, and William, now her daughter's fiancé. Overwhelmed by the semblances to Patrick and to the life she might have had, she lost her resolve and let a few tears make their way down her cheeks.

"It's not too late for us to spend time together, Ilona," Michael said, mistaking her tears for receptivity and placing a hand on her thigh. "I'm a successful man, but there is something, or I should say someone, who continues to elude me."

She looked up at him, frustrated by her naiveté and by her belief that he could have changed.

"I have found ways to address Sybil's continued deficiency in that area, but I do believe you could address them best."

Ilona jumped to her feet, confounded that he would proposition her after so many years and with his entire family but a few walls away.

"You are a disgusting son of a bitch, Michael Doyle! I can't believe you could be anything worse than you once were, but your success includes becoming an even bigger asshole than Patrick could have ever imagined!"

She rose to leave the library, her chardonnay splashing her and the Persian rug. As she brushed it from her dress, her gaze met those of William, Callista, and Katherine, standing at the door stupefied.

Ilona brushed past them to look for Cadmus, the walls appearing like a fun house, tilting as she stumbled to the veranda. She motioned Cadmus from the pool, and Sybil and Anne Dunn asked if everything was okay. Ilona walked over to talk to Cadmus privately, sharing that she would wait next to the car.

In those few moments with her son, a makeshift group assembled that included the victim, Michael, along with his wife and the witnesses to what would become known as her "drunken assault," something that Ilona's friend Margaret later heralded as a "fine and most overdue achievement," even though it obliterated any opportunity for Ilona to enjoy a full relationship with her daughter's family.

ILONA'S ASSUMPTIONS ABOUT HER SON'S sexuality were confirmed the summer after his graduation from Heights High School. He had a friend, Paul, with whom he hung around in the neighborhood, often grabbing a burger at Sander's before heading home to study. Dear Ernestine gladly prepared an abundance at suppertime, encouraging Cadmus to bring friends home. Paul and Cadmus talked about girls and poked jokes about teachers, which made Ilona wonder what students would have said about her had she ever become a teacher. She idealized her would-be role in the classroom, but her lofty ideas may very well have subjected her to ridicule from the students.

Paul's frequent visits prompted Dear Ernestine to set a place for him regularly, which Ilona did not mind. She liked Paul as a person, but she also liked that he grounded her son. One of four children who lived in a neighboring bungalow, Paul was accustomed to doing more with less. His father, an accountant, was a kind man with a strong work ethic, using every opportunity to teach his children the value of a dollar. Paul's mother took in mending for extra money, and although Ilona and Dear Ernestine were quite nimble with a needle and thread, Ilona sent a few garments her way here and there.

She knew Paul was just the right person to hire and work alongside Cadmus to paint Dear Ernestine's guest quarters while she was away at her sister's house for a few days. The extent of Cadmus' laboring resided in his studies. Intellectually curious, Cadmus always matched the academic challenges presented by the faculty. Physically, however, he rarely broke a sweat. The work would be good for him.

Ilona prepared fresh lemonade for the boys, carefully slicing an extra lemon into slices to float in the glass pitcher. She found comfort in the intentionality of cutting the thinnest of slices, of feeling the bumps and texture on the peel and hearing the fleshy sound made by the knife. She sliced each round and, for the first time, gave the lemon its due, counting twelve distinct geometric shapes that formed the circumference.

Walking up the steps to the garage apartment with tray in hand and cuticles burning from the juice, she paused to look over the grounds from the outdoor staircase, a vantage point rarely enjoyed. She imagined a middle-aged Patrick walking through the garden, gray hair peppered throughout his sandy brown. Would he have still favored gold-rimmed glasses, or would he have donned a more modern look? If only she would have replied in kind that night, extending her hand to meet his in the Millers' library. Things would be different.

Patrick would have walked Callista down the aisle last month rather than Michael. And Callista would have welcomed a wedding shower at her family home had her mother not shot off her mouth at her uncle, the only father Callista knew. Ilona was thankful the wedding was over, after too much time tiptoeing, of seeking forgiveness, and of finding her place in the pecking order of the new family design.

Michael and Sybil assumed the lead, considering the Doyle & Dunns' membership to the River Oaks Country Club offered the gateway to the reception, and even though the event bore the stamp of business interests, as evidenced by the extensive guest list, Ilona conceded that it was a beautiful wedding. Given the need for airs, Michael and Sybil greeted her and

Cadmus properly, which suited her just fine. She had no desire to share with Sybil, Callista, and Katherine that Michael, their rock, was a philanderer and bully, and their formal behavior allowed everyone to continue superficially without digging into the reasons for the discord.

Taking a full breath, she resumed her flight upstairs with the lemonade, thankful for the peace at home with her son. Noting the door was open but a crack, she turned her back to nudge it open from behind. The smell of wet paint welcomed her senses: good progress made. And as she turned around to greet the boys, she saw her son in a most passionate kiss, with his shirt falling to the ground.

ILONA

Autumn 1962

ILONA'S EYEBROWS ROSE AS SHE looked at each contestant with great anticipation.

"Are you ready?" she called out with her wide, toothy smile.

She received mostly eager nods from young girls, too shy to answer with a resounding yes.

"Oh. I don't think you're *really* ready," she replied, shaking her head, eyes downcast, putting on a show of false dejection. She continued to shake her head, pacing around the flattened grass from inside the booth.

"We are!" piped a squeaky voice on the far left end, tapping her washer on a string that was placed smack dab in the middle of her number—3.

"Okay, lucky number 3, then help me!" Ilona enthusiastically called out, slapping her hands on her thighs. "Let's try it again! Are you ready?"

"YES!" the chorus of girls shouted, jumping up and down in front of their respective squares.

"Then let's see who our winner is!" she shouted as she turned the number wheel. She stepped back to observe the little girl's eyes excitedly following the wheel, attempting to see where their numbers would fall as the wheel made its quick rotations.

Ilona delighted in chairing the doll booth at the annual church bazaar. She and Dear Ernestine prepared dolls throughout the year: sewing, crocheting, and knitting an array of ensembles to adorn their small figures. These were the times that brought them closer as women, sharing stories and thoughts as if they were background music. With their attention on the dolls, sharing stories became easier, more natural without eye contact, and with no worry over when to nod or gesture, no concern to fill every moment with speech when there was another task to be done.

Ilona's volunteer service made her wistful for Callista at that age, seeing the heartfelt, earnest look in the girls' eyes as the wheel turned, willing their numbers to land under the arrow. She longed for a redo, a chance to build a stronger relationship with the adult daughter who regarded her with frustration and resentment. Feeling kindness and love from the little ones, albeit fleeting, filled a void.

She also relished the theatrics she brought into the game, cajoling little ones to play and then good-naturedly teasing them during the games. She wondered how much of this part of her personality would have manifested in the classroom had she the opportunity.

"Hey, Mom. Ready to break for lunch?" Cadmus asked as he approached the booth. There were times she could not believe this handsome young man was her son, the same baby born twenty-six years before, now in graduate studies at Rice University.

"Soon, my dear, as soon as the other volunteer relieves me," Ilona replied.

"I'll try my luck at the cake booth," he said, gesturing to the booth a few stalls down the row. "Maybe I will win Dear Ernestine's apple upside-down cake!"

"You mean your great-grandmother's, right? It's her recipe!"

He smiled and nodded as he walked away toward the booth. Although his dark hair and brown eyes were from Ilona, his profile was unmistakably Patrick's. Her nose tingled at the sight of his dimple, as he smiled and waved to a friend. Her heart still ached for her husband, and not a day passed that she did not pray for him. She had even drawn from the well of compassion and prayed for Maureen. She, too, would still be alive had Ilona stayed behind that night.

Cadmus was a good soul. She knew full well he wanted to spend time with Thomas, but he knew what the bazaar meant to his mother, seeing her work on the project in the library throughout the year. He had yet to confide explicitly that Thomas was his boyfriend, and she knew perhaps he never would. It was an unspoken understanding, evidenced by her tone when she asked about Thomas and by her warm greeting when she saw him.

After the barbecue lunch, Cadmus and Ilona strolled around the bazaar, chatting with other parishioners and playing a few games. A good number of parishioners knew their circumstances, but time healed the awkwardness that had been in place in the early years after the accident, especially after she started attending the Women's Club. It was a formal group, and the routine of meetings and volunteering served her well. Ilona kissed Cadmus on the cheek and thanked him for a lovely lunch date. She scurried to the ladies' room before returning to her booth.

"I can't *believe* you didn't know," accused Bernadine in a shrill voice as she entered the ladies' room. Ilona rolled her eyes in the stall. Bernadine was at it again with her gossip. Ilona chastised herself for not placing her own name on the ballot for president of the Women's Club. Bernadine had a powerful platform from which to spew.

"How could I? I've only been here a few months," said the other woman in her defense.

"Yes, it was awful, poor thing, to be cheated on so, and then have him die in such a horrific, public manner."

Ilona's heart sank. It had been so many years. Why on earth would Bernadine do this to her?

"It *is* a shame. Well, now I do not envy her as I once did!" the other woman said with a forced laugh for effect. "Can you believe she looks as good as she does? How old do you think she is?"

"Nearly fifty, I'm sure. Too old to find love. And what's even more regrettable is that she attends mass every day, probably praying for her husband

and son. Her husband is already in hell, and her son . . . Well, he has a one-way ticket there, since he sleeps with men."

"No! Oh God, poor Ilona. He does seem effeminate come to think of it, like he's too pretty to be a man."

"We all feel sorry for her, so pathetic in that big house alone all day and then coming to Sunday mass with her gay son."

Ilona unlocked the door and stepped out to the sink, looking straight into the mirror, straight into the wide eyes of Bernadine, a woman she thought was a friend, and the new parishioner. Their positioning and the mirror reminded Ilona of the night Margaret shared the news about Patrick and Maureen in the Millers' powder room, where the mirrors made the moment even more surreal.

Nudging the two ladies out of the way, Ilona confidently washed her hands while they stood there, speechless, eyeing one another, trying to determine who should speak first.

"Ilona, we are so . . ." the new woman stammered, flashes of scarlet wrapping her face.

"Save your apologies. And be careful. There may be two more spots in hell waiting for the both of you," Ilona retorted, for once able to respond boldly on command, as she exited to resume her shift at the booth.

THE ARGUMENT WITH HER BABA over her conversion, held so many years ago, reverberated throughout her mind as she completed what would turn out to be her last stint as chair of the doll booth. She absentmindedly collected money for washers and spun the wheel with unusual force, as she silently cursed herself for taking solace in her fellow parishioners' kindness over the past seventeen years. How many people were lying, their kind actions either stemming from pity or from a morbid curiosity to be so close to death or to another's illicit behavior? And although it was only two women, there were probably more. A tongue speaking that freely had been bolstered by years of support.

Ilona felt a fool, converting to a religion that had such resolute views on eternal damnation and then continuing its practice considering her family's circumstances. No wonder Callista never wanted to attend mass with them at her childhood parish, even on holy days, preferring to remain at her own parish in River Oaks.

Patrick can't be in hell, can't . . . she said to herself. *He had so much good, so much good,* she continued as mothers, noting that Ilona was slightly unhinged, ushered their daughters past the doll booth. *Cadmus, so kind and sweet. Never hurt anyone. My sweet boy,* she thought pacing around the interior of the booth, brushing blown leaves from the counters.

As soon as the six o'clock tower chimes rang out, she packed up the remaining two dolls, returned the cash pouch to the church office, and made a beeline down Fifth Street to The Boulevard to head home. She was not going to stay for two more spins; the bazaar was officially over. The leftover dolls were returning to The Doyle House, one for her and one for Dear Ernestine. The irony was not lost on her that the dolls donned traditional Greek dress, always the outcasts, the ones no one wanted.

The rose garden served as church the week following the bazaar. Rising before dawn each day, Ilona threw on her robe and slippers, reaching for her rosary on the nightstand before tiptoeing downstairs. A student of the night sky on scores of sleepless nights, she was accustomed to its dark hue, tempered by glass and framed by curtains. She spent those nights riddled by the guilt she assigned herself for killing Patrick and Maureen. She knew they had made terrible decisions, but she made the last one that set the final thread of events in motion. She could have been stronger, could have taken it one more time.

Standing outside in the early morning air, she offered a prayer of thanks to the heavens, the indigo sky protecting her under its dome. The din of crickets and frogs greeted her from the rosebushes, nestled in among the soil moistened from the dew. She took a full, deep breath, lifted the rosary from her robe pocket, and began the recitation, making deliberate steps on the sidewalk that circled the garden.

She wove Our Fathers, Hail Marys, and Glory Bes into the fourth movement of the nocturnal symphony. As the sky turned to lapis and cerulean, she found herself seated on the bench, the formality of prayer complete. Feeling quelling words, she placed her left hand on her heart with her right palm up. She sent love and peace to Patrick in heaven and to her son in his bedroom upstairs.

ILONA MADE ONE ATTEMPT TO return to Holy Family. After a week at her garden church, she found the resolve to face the situation for what it was, hoping, perhaps, that the opinion expressed in the ladies' room was that of a minority. She entered church the following Sunday, arm linked with Cadmus. As they made their way to their usual spot in the fourth pew, she attempted to convince herself that the stares were figments of her imagination, nothing more than a natural place a face may fall when looking around the nave.

As they knelt in prayer, Cadmus whispered, "What is going on?"

Ilona kept her eyes closed, only raising her prayer hands over her lips as a signal for him to be quiet. She was filled with shame that she had brought him back to the church, back to the parishioners who denigrated him in private. She knew there were those who did not fall into this camp, but she doubted they could muster the courage to defend her family, especially when the church viewed Cadmus' sexuality as a mortal sin. That was when she realized that no one, not one soul, had reached out to her the week after the bazaar, and she figured the happenings in the ladies' room were mentioned to at least a few if not the entire Women's Club.

She knew this was the last time she would set foot in Holy Family. Stand, sit, kneel, stand, sit, kneel: She responded and gestured on cue, while using the time to take in her surroundings for the last time. This would be the last time she would see the altar where she had taken her vows with Patrick.

At the end of mass, Cadmus exited to the aisle and held out his arm for Ilona. She smiled, held her head high, and linked her arm in his. Cold stares returned her smiles and nods, the final confirmation coming from a group of women huddled in the corner. Well out of earshot of Father Joseph, one of the voices said loudly, "Maybe it's time she found another church. Why be a part of ours when there are spots in hell waiting for us?"

Cadmus did not hear the remarks. Ilona only heard them because she knew to tune her ears in that direction. They enjoyed the walk home, Cadmus telling her about his hope to join the Rice faculty and her nodding, looking away when she needed to wipe a tear. *My dear, sweet boy*, she said to herself over and over on the walk home. *Kindest soul . . . always thoughtful, not a mean utterance, ever.*

The next morning, Ilona rose to ordain the garden as her new church, her sanctuary of peace. She found herself bowing to the indigo sky as she began her rosary procession.

"MAY I TAKE YOU TO lunch after mass next Sunday?" Cadmus asked as he placed his books in his bag for school. "I need to make reservations."

"Yes to lunch but no to mass," Ilona replied.

"Why?" Cadmus asked, a puzzled look on his face.

"I'm just having a hard time lately, thinking of your father," she lied. "It's hard to see so many happy couples, you know?"

She looked away, returning to her book as she sat in the nook.

"Mom, what's going on?" he asked, taking a seat next to her.

Ilona looked at her son, his eyes full of concern for her. She could not bring herself to tell him about the cruelty she overheard.

"I can't attend mass at Holy Family anymore, Cadmus. I've rescinded our membership," she replied. "Please do not ask any more questions."

He nodded his head, giving her the space she needed. She knew she was not off the hook. He would attempt to raise the subject again another time, and until then, she would work on enriching her fib.

A doctor's appointment that day framed the first day of the week, and on Tuesday, she headed to Kaplan's to buy a baptismal gift for Callista's newborn, Baby Timothy. With Wednesday came no official marker. Morning prayer in the rose garden completed shortly after dawn; the day stretched out in front of her. No children for whom to cook; no trips to the notion store for cloth, thread, silk yarns to create fashion for dolls; no weekday mass or prayer group; no Women's Club activities. She passed her time reading. She placed a phone call to Margaret, who was not available for lunch until the following week because her "cur-sed cousins" were in town from Oklahoma.

While serving breakfast on Thursday, Dear Ernestine asked about the menu for the weekly rose garden lunch for the Women's Group on Friday, to which Ilona replied in the same words she had said to Cadmus. The exact wording, coupled with the force of her response from someone who was usually much more modulated, prompted Dear Ernestine and Cadmus to exchange a silent look, with Cadmus' eyebrows messaging, *See, I told you something was wrong.*

Dear Ernestine followed Cadmus' lead, nodding in befuddlement with "mmmmm . . . hmmmm," before heading back to kitchen, where Cadmus casually joined her for a consultation.

That evening, Ilona slowly retreated upstairs, wondering what tomorrow would bring. She pinned her hair up as hot water filled the tub, catching the profile of her eighteen-year-old self rather than the fifty-year-old reality in front of her.

She looked down at her naked body, reminiscing the passion she once shared with Patrick, the way he had awakened her womanhood, electrifying her in that first afternoon discourse at the M&M, now an almost derelict building. References to sex among women were increasingly common and generally at the expense of the man. She laughed uncomfortably in response. Her only option was to tell the truth, that she and her husband shared the most intense physical experience for most of their relationship, even after their second child, with the exception of the tapering off after his mistress came into the picture. If she had known she was destined to reach pariah status regardless, she may very well have let loose on her tongue. She wondered if it were possible to feel that way again. Patrick flipped a switch she had not known she had, and she wondered if another man could do the same.

She felt her skin thinning from a difficult life, but one well lived nonetheless. She caressed the stretch marks from her pregnancies, hands resting over her belly that once insulated those precious souls. One good thing came from overhearing the conversation that set her new trajectory: The women thought she looked good. As vain and fleeting as it was, it was something for God's sake. It wasn't something she earned or deserved, but it was a small token. Perhaps she could find love, or at the very least companionship, now that her social circle narrowed once again.

She held the secret of the financial settlement for so many years to protect Cadmus, and now there was another reckoning for the unconditional love of her son. She vowed not to leave him as she had his father, regardless of the circumstances. She would always defend her son and make certain he was protected. Her heart ached when she thought of the continued challenges ahead, as she could not envision a full personal life for him given his sexuality.

Callista did not share her brother's vulnerabilities. Recalling Michael's crass reference many moons ago about *the Doyle gene*, she knew Callista inherited it, as strong-willed as she was. She would be fine, and she was fine, living as a Dunn in River Oaks.

As Ilona eased into the hot bath, she began to think about her life as a continuum rather than as a daily schedule. Preoccupied with filling her days, she lifted her mind to a bird's-eye view, studying the landscape. Her early memories were like snapshots, the same images developing when she let her mind reflect on her time in East Houston. Even the memories of her brother's death were fragmented, fitting together like a collage with her other childhood moments, some pieces larger, others more like specks that came together to present an overall image.

Ilona wondered how long she would live, envisioning herself as an elderly lady in The Doyle House alone, with Dear Ernestine long passed. She imagined the next twenty-five years in snapshots, adding to the growing collage of her life that she was reflecting upon in this moment. Knowing she would not remember most of her daily events and interactions, she wondered which ones would make the cut. What would the subject of the photographs be?

CADMUS

Autumn 1962

"I'M NOT ASKING FOR A lot, Callista."

"I know you don't think it's a lot, but you don't know what it's like to have household responsibilities and raise three children . . . one a newborn at that," she countered.

"You are right. I don't know what it's like, but I do know our mother needs support," Cadmus replied, taking deep breaths to steady his frustration.

Several seconds passed without either of them speaking, Cadmus tightly gripping the receiver while he sat at his father's desk.

"What happened at Holy Family?" she asked.

"She won't tell me. She just says she's been thinking a lot about Dad and that church makes her sad."

"Well, perhaps Timothy's birth has something to do with it. Maybe it reminds her that he will not know his grandfather," Callista offered. "She could be telling the truth."

"If it were true, she would at least be receiving calls from her church friends. Callista, no one is calling."

"What do you want me to do, Cadmus? I can't be her sitter. I have enough to do on my own."

"Yes, with a full-time housekeeper and a nanny. You do have enough!"

Cadmus countered. Callista's antipathy toward Ilona was the one thing that brought him the most frustration.

"And what about you, hmmm? Dear Ernestine still cooking for you while you spend all day reading and thinking? Must be nice!"

Silence again. He knew he had a privileged life. In the end, it did not matter that he used his inheritance to further his education. He chose a profession that would allow him to read and learn, all the while remaining comfortably in a historic mansion with help to cater to his needs. He knew he should not begrudge her for enjoying the same luxuries, albeit in River Oaks.

"I don't want to argue. All I ask is that you call her more often. Invite her over to see her grandchildren, perhaps over for tea. Please, Callista."

"I will," Callista replied after several seconds. "I need to go, Cadmus. See you in a few weeks at the baptism."

Cadmus sat at his father's mahogany desk, his index finger tracing the ornate wooden detailing along the edges. He wondered what their relationship would have been like had his father lived, whether he would be working alongside Benjamin and Andrew. It was a challenge to visualize five Doyle men in the office, his father and Uncle Michael still leading the charge. No one had ever told him explicitly of the tension between his father and uncle, but the few memories he held, coupled with action and inaction from over the years, substantiated his theory of a major conflict.

He accepted Callista's propensity to default to their father's side, just as his inclination bent toward his mother. What he struggled to reconcile, however, was the degree of allegiance Callista held for Michael and Sybil, a much stronger connection than he could ever recall her holding for Ilona. It was a natural fit, his sister and William. She spent so much time with her aunt and uncle, especially after they moved to River Oaks. Tennis, swimming, dining— so many memories at the country club that became a natural part of her childhood. She was a Doyle, and her name granted her access on her own, despite the fact that her membership was tied to her uncle and aunt.

It was understood why her mother never came around given her outburst at Easter, along with Ilona's propensity for reflection that became even more pronounced once she became a widow. Ilona was reserved with most people after his father's death. The people who had come to know her after she became a widow, however, attributed at least part of her constitution to the fact that she was a lady of means with an air about her, which could not have been further from the truth. Although church became Ilona's world, she was a quiet participant, with her reserved smile and a good set of hands to work, preparing a luncheon at her home, baking goods to sell, or assembling dolls for the booth throughout the year.

He sensed that Ilona struggled with Callista's adult life, and although Callista did not know what he knew, Cadmus believed that she should be able to piece together more than she did, at least enough to give Ilona the occasional benefit of the doubt. He believed she should be a greater part of her mother's life, especially now that Ilona had never been more alone.

ILONA

Autumn 1962

ILONA COULD NOT RECALL THE last time she had driven so far by herself. Turning on the ignition, she checked her fuel, adjusted the mirrors, and took a deep breath. She had not been to Lawndale in almost a year.

Nerves getting the best of her, she pulled the car over in front of Robert Cage Elementary. She watched the gaggle of students crowding the fountains on the side of the building. She could not help but laugh aloud seeing one little boy, the tiniest of the bunch, jumping up and down to gauge how many were in front of him while a young teacher tried desperately to create order.

Another teacher appeared at the door and blew a whistle, which appeared to do the trick. The students lined up quickly—four rows, one in front of each fountain. At first glance, all of them looked the same, roughly the same height, same types of clothes, even the same general colors. Ilona thought about the unique souls inhabiting their little bodies, hoping the teacher was nourishing their individuality, giving them strength to be who they were meant to be. She hoped the teacher thoughtfully exercised her authority in word and deed, thinking back to how one of Cadmus' teachers at Heights High had discouraged him from studying literature, telling him to "man up and learn how to play ball."

After the students returned to the schoolhouse, she resumed the drive. Save the crumbly patches of brick here and there, it was the same place, the dulled sheen of the navy blue cursive Lawndale Café lettering offering a greeting. She could not make her way from her car for the longest time, scanning the façade, knowing that something else was different. Newer car models were a given, but there was something else she could not quite shake. It looked smaller than she remembered.

Scents of bell peppers and tomatoes greeted her as she opened the door, breaking her unease. Patrick enjoyed a great many things, but stuffed bell peppers were not one of them. She smiled knowing that was what she would order. Perhaps she would even introduce them at The Doyle House, although the potential for feeding people other than herself was rapidly dwindling.

Only a few seconds passed before her mama looked up from the register and saw her, but the universe can reveal much in even the smallest particle of time. Her tight silver-haired bun and neat periwinkle dress spoke regally while resting on a shrunken frame. Ilona knew her placid mien had been curated by a lifetime of happiness and hardships, perhaps more on the hardship side, but more important, it was in how her mama navigated the two. Ilona had inherited her mama's restraint, her ability to remain calm and observe. As she smiled in gratitude, her mama raised her eyes to meet her daughter's. The wrinkled forehead prompted Ilona's stomach to take a turn; she had not intended for her presence to cause upset. But not more than a moment later, Ilona realized the expression was an attempt to stop the tears that fell from her eyes, her mama rising to meet her, cupping her hands around her daughter's face as she broke into a smile.

Ilona had been at the cafe for almost an hour, resting in Mrs. Jilufka's old seat while savoring the last few bites of stuffed bell peppers over rice. Her mama was walking back and forth to the counter from the register as often as customers would allow while her baba quietly read the paper at the other end. After catching up on neighborhood news and old church friends, there was not much more to say; the breaks in conversation served them well.

Ilona began to realize how little she talked to her parents, even her sister, for that matter. She made an occasional visit to the restaurants, first to

Franklin and then to Lawndale after the downtown location closed because of the flood. But her life had taken such a different trajectory the day she visited the M&M with Uncle Demetrius. After her marriage to Patrick, she assumed the role of lady of the house, hosting parties and volunteering at Holy Family. And then they welcomed the children, precious souls who brought her immense joy, but their dependency bound her to The Heights even more so, especially since she counted on Dear Ernestine for help. Her family bore the burden of travel since she had assumed life as a Doyle, enduring the jaunt from East Houston to The Heights, the days before the interstate.

"You had a nice lunch crowd, Mama."

"Yes, it steady . . . it good," she replied, nodding and moving her hand side to side, palm down.

"And Uncle Demetrius and the boys are still doing well, right?"

"Yes, it funny how things work out. Expanding again! Make it three fancy restaurants in Houston. Can you believe it?"

"I know. It's wonderful. It's wonderful to see a dream become reality," Ilona said, thinking of Patrick as she folded her napkin, looking toward her baba hunched over the paper and reaching for his coffee. Closing Franklin Diner was such a huge disappointment, but he could not afford to rebuild during the Great Depression.

"And now, what your dream, eh?"

"That's a good question. I'm working on it, Mama," Ilona conceded.

"It okay to search . . . We all search. Go back to heart," she said, left hand gesturing to her chest. "What do you really want?"

Ilona looked down at her hands, her engagement ring maintaining its prominent role despite Patrick's death. She caught a look at herself in a mirror against the far wall, her painted face, pearls, and posture distinguishing her from the other patrons. Such a subtle transformation over many years, she had not realized how far she was from her life in Lawndale. In her eyes, she would always be the girl from East Houston, although she was the only one who held that opinion. She was the reason the cafe was different.

"Eh? Time es moving, love," her mama said, nudging her arm. "What you want?"

Ilona looked to the family in the corner window booth. One child counted sugar packets while another moved a toy car underneath the table.

"I want to teach, Mama," Ilona replied with a grin, feeling a bit like the teenager who had cleaned the counters and refilled coffee cups.

"Then do it . . . find way, and do it."

ILONA AND CADMUS ENTERED THE church, eyes looking to the front, where the other family members were already gathered. Anne Dunn stood near the baptismal font, holding Lillian in her arms, swaying her back and forth while whispering in her granddaughter's ear. Michael and Timothy stood together in the main aisle, Timothy animatedly moving his hands, the malachite stone visible even at that distance. Michael gave a hearty laugh in response to his business partner and in-law, striking a sharp contrast to the sanctity of the church.

"Cadmus, please leave me a moment. Let me light a votive. Please go ahead, greet your family."

Cadmus embraced her before heading down the aisle, where Michael and William turned to greet him with formal handshakes. Ilona counted it a blessing that they were polite to her son. They were never warm or affectionate as they were with Callista, but their societal status would never permit them to be anything but gracious in public. She was certain Cadmus' pursuits at Rice also contributed to their reception, knowing he held virtually no interest in Doyle & Dunn, a name that now spanned Houston, interlocking Ds on signs in front of many construction sites throughout the city that continued to expand west. The city's rapid ascent might have humbled even Patrick's vision.

"My dear Patrick, I'm so sorry, so very, very sorry," Ilona whispered, tears filling her eyes as she knelt in front of the Virgin Mary holding Baby Jesus, her tears clouding her view of Mary's beatific expression. The irony not lost on Ilona, she turned to see her son, the kindest soul she knew, attempting to make his way into conversation with his brother-in-law, William, the one who had taken his place at the table. She prayed for forgiveness, that her decision to spare him the battle would be worth the cost of the war. She wanted him to have a happy, fulfilled life.

"Sweet, Sweet Cadmus," she murmured while doubting he would have a life as enchanted as his sister's. What was Patrick thinking as he looked down upon them? She looked at Baby Timothy, another male destined to carry on the legacy, society already placing more expectations on him than on Grace or Lillian.

Timothy greeted her with more warmth than Michael had. She knew with distance came a gift of understanding, but Michael was too leery to be called out, even all these years later, to offer anything more that the most rudimentary welcome. Ilona managed her most placid expression that covered even the declaration of godparents: Cousin Thomas and his wife. Cadmus was left out once again.

"Honestly, Mother. You really think Cadmus is an acceptable role model for the Catholic faith?"

Callista's words, said before Timothy's birth, echoed through Ilona's mind, an overlay to the images of the chosen godparents, who unabashedly showed their disposition at the Dunn holiday party, drunkenly shouting their achievements and New Year's plan for the construction of a new mall. Ilona made a silent vow to continue shopping downtown, and she did not care one bit if her neighborhood had fallen so far out of favor. She loved its history, and there was always hope for a comeback.

Ilona could barely attend the brunch at Callista's home, overcome with emotion on the christening of a grandson. It was as if she had lifted a stone in the garden, noting the creatures that teamed with life underneath. If she had remained with Patrick that night, he would have lived. His very life, however, would have taken the family on another course, one in which the grandchildren, Grace, Lillian, and Timothy, may not have manifested. Cadmus would have had a real chance at the business, perhaps as an architect rather than networking. With his father by his side as a mentor, Cadmus' intelligence and prudence could have fashioned Doyle Construction, a company that needed only one D—a D strong enough to stand on its own.

Ilona took a seat on the bench in Callista's front yard until Cadmus could pull the car around, the thoughts too much for her to bear. Her misfortune resulted in good—good for her daughter and good for Doyle & Dunn. She returned to The Doyle House with a throbbing headache and a slice of cake for Dear Ernestine, vowing to make more sense of things during her walk in the garden the following morning.

THE TEXTURE OF THE BRICKS was smoother than she thought it would be, and the coolness they emanated from a night of slumber made for soothing steps. Ilona had lived in the house for thirty years and not once had she taken off her shoes in the rose garden. She could not remember the last time she had taken off her shoes anywhere other than in her bedroom, come to think of it. The novelty brought her joy.

She continued along the path, her fingers caressing each rosary bead as she made her way through the Joyful Mysteries. As she came to the path near the pecan tree, she noted the bricks raised from the growing roots. Countless walks in the garden, yet this was the first time she had noticed this change.

Several weeks passed since she first visited her mama at the diner, but she had yet to act on anything related to teaching. She felt most confident, most limitless at night, when she opened the window with the curtain gently moving in the breeze, and in the garden before dawn, when she meandered down the paths, noting the tiny veins that ran through the petal of a rose. Anything seemed possible in those moments of stillness. Her retreat to the library to engage in any real constructive planning, however, left her at a loss.

She began to visit Lawndale more and more often. Breaking bread with her parents was slowly chipping away at the distance built up over the years. She had always admired her parents' strength, but she realized it was something she took for granted, assuming it was a God-given gift rather than the result of years of toil. The same line of thought carried over to her mama's detached expression, a trait she now realized had been assumed after her brother's death. Intellectually, Ilona knew this causation, but she had buried its relevancy, consumed for years in her own grief and guilt.

Her sprinkling of memories when they were a family of five included a bright, summer day in the backyard. Her mama bellowed with laughter as she removed the clean laundry from the clothesline while Ilona, Cadmus, and Arianna wore the sheets like ghosts, shrieking and spinning around the yard, Ilona falling to the ground after bumping into the chain-link fence. Her baba opened the back door, yelling, "What you doing? Ss-eets clean!" Mama waved him away before placing a sheet over her own head and howling "boooooo" as her children laughed at her uncharacteristic rebuff to their baba.

At Lawndale, her mama sat next to Ilona at the counter, motioning for the waitress to bring her a cup of coffee. Her baba was at the register reading the paper. Ilona thought she had fallen asleep for moment, as her mama's eyes remained closed for several seconds longer than normal. Ilona wondered how long she would be able to work at Lawndale as she glanced at the old photograph of her baba and uncle that hung behind the register.

"Callista like the baby blanket I knit, yes?" Mama asked, taking a sip of coffee.

"I believe so, I . . ."

"Coffee es burnt! Old from morning . . . Make fresh pot!" Her mama yelled out to the waitress, pushing her cup to the side in disgust. "Hard find good help these days," she continued, shaking her head, eyes bearing down on the countertop in front of her.

Ilona waited several seconds more before attempting a return to the conversation, glancing at the waitress, who came to retrieve the cup as she glared at her mama in frustration.

"As I was saying, yes, I am sure she loved it. I have not spoken to her since the christening. I was not there when she opened the gifts."

Ilona prayed Callista would write her ya ya a thank-you note, especially since she had more than likely already sent one to every Irish family member and friend who attended Timothy's baptism.

Mama's eyes rose to meet hers, signaling she had something to say. She reached for her daughter's hand, causing Ilona's stomach to swirl, because her mama was not prone to physical displays of affection.

"Ilona, I glad you visit me here. My heart full when I see you come home."

"And I am so happy to be here, Mama, I . . ." her mama waved her index finger in the air to silence her.

"I say with love . . . you need find your way and way *not* in café. Home will be your home but not home in same way, you know?"

Ilona knew she was right, but it left her crestfallen and even a bit shocked. Her mama was kicking her out of the café, at least as a frequent visitor as she had become over the past few weeks. She was back to the drawing board.

"HEY, MOM, I'VE BEEN THINKING," Cadmus shared as they made their way through Kaplan's.

"Of course you have been thinking . . . That is all you seem to do!" Ilona playfully replied, giving him a wink as she linked her arm through his.

"I'm serious, Mom," Cadmus replied, stopping and turning to face her directly.

"I think you need to go to Heights High School to inquire about a job."

"A job? I'm not qualified to teach."

"You are qualified in the purest sense of the word, but you are correct in terms of hiring."

Her heart picked up a beat, knowing he had an idea in mind—an idea that just might be viable.

"I think you would make a wonderful tutor, someone to help the students who are struggling, and I can tell you, there are plenty who struggle."

"You really think they would hire me to tutor?"

"Well, maybe not hire for pay, but perhaps as a volunteer."

Ilona beamed, excited by a viable possibility.

"DO YOU HAVE AN APPOINTMENT, Mrs. Doyle?"

"No, but I do know Mr. Murray. My children attended Heights; my son was valedictorian many years ago."

"Mr. Murray retired, along with *his* secretary. Mr. Pennington and *I* have been here now five years," the assistant crossly retorted. "He is available tomorrow at 9:30 a.m. for fifteen minutes."

"Thank you, and I do apologize for the imposition," Ilona replied, baffled by the rude reception.

She walked back to the school the next day, and while she awoke with a clear head and bolstered confidence from stillness gained in the rose garden before dawn, the thought of the brusque secretary allowed anxiety to creep back in not more than a block away from her house. She was early, and rather than head straight to the principal's office, she impulsively turned right after entering the main doors and walked confidently down the hall with purpose. She did not know where she was going, but she needed time to gather her thoughts.

Noticing a group of students entering the auditorium, she fell in queue. She ducked away to a seat in the far right corner as the procession made its way to the front of the stage. Throngs of students began entering from all three sets of doors by the time she sat down, the noise acting as a cloak, attention drawn to settling the students for the assembly.

She often saw students walking through the neighborhood after school hours, never more than a handful together, their energy spent from a day of studies. Aside from Callista's and Cadmus' respective graduations, this occasion marked the first time she was part of a mass gathering, the rowdiness leaving her somewhat stupefied. She surmised the children could easily take over the adults had they but desire and leadership. Tutoring one-on-one would suit Ilona just fine. Perhaps she missed the window for teaching, too much time spent alone on The Boulevard left her stiff.

1930, 40, 50 . . . she tapped her thumb to each finger, marking the decades to herself even though the counting was simple. *It couldn't be,* she thought, as she confirmed the number. *Thirty-two years* since her graduation from Milby, which had but one year on Heights High, the building erected in 1928. She thought about the countless souls who had graced the halls and classrooms during that time. How many students had sat in her very seat in the auditorium, with their hands on the armrests, palms down, warm from the blood pumping through their veins, providing the opportunity to fulfill their dreams through the gift of life.

Thirty-two years but my blood is still pumping! she silently cheered, playfully pounding her fist on the armrest. Glad to find her resolve, she quietly sat up in her chair just as a handsome, dark-haired gentleman walked on stage, eyeing her all the way in the back as he greeted the students over the microphone. Keeping her head down, she made her way out of the auditorium, tiptoeing and carefully squeezing through a door that was slightly ajar.

When she entered the school office, Ilona received a curt nod in exchange for her best smile.

"He will be with you shortly," the secretary said, waiting to reply until after her gaze returned to the typewriter.

A good ten minutes passed before Ilona heard a back door open and shut. She recalled then that the principal had another entrance to his office. The secretary's ears perked up, and glancing at Ilona, she made her way back.

Although muffled, she clearly heard the words, "The old Doyle widow is here to see you."

The crude description stabbed at Ilona's heart. She stared intently at the floor, hoping that her legs would move as soon as she was called.

"Mrs. Doyle?"

Ilona looked up to see the man from the stage. His dark hair peppered with a healthy sprinkling of gray up close, he offered her an apologetic smile, seeming to know that his secretary uttered her comments loud enough to be overheard.

"I am Mr. Pennington, and I am so sorry to have kept you waiting," he said, shaking her hand and walking her back to his office.

Any nerves she had been feeling evaporated when she sat down in his office, their conversation beginning so naturally and escalating at such a rate that she took a pause, realizing the extent of her loneliness. She shared how her dreams of teaching had taken a turn when she met Patrick, and while she knew her skills were a bit dull at fifty years old, she hoped she could be of service to the students at Heights High.

He shared that she was a young one at fifty; he was fifty-two. He asked her to tell him a favorite piece of literature, to which she easily replied, "E.E. Cummings . . . 'somewhere I have travelled, gladly beyond.' He published it the year I married Patrick, although I only discovered it in the past few years."

They talked for nearly an hour in his office before he suggested a brief tour of the building, his secretary staring them down as they made their way out of the office. Ilona attempted to say goodbye, offering a kind nod and thinking it would be reciprocated once the secretary had seen that Mr. Pennington accepted her. Turning her head back one last time, Ilona noticed the

Holy Family calendar posted next to the woman's typewriter. She realized then that her reputation might very well have preceded her.

"I believe you'd be a wonderful addition to our staff," Mr. Pennington beamed as he walked her to the front entrance after the tour. "I need but a day or two to get the teachers on board. If you'd kindly share your number, I'll call when we are ready to move forward."

ILONA'S FACE BROKE INTO A grin as she read Helen's essay on *Of Mice and Men*. A painfully shy student who had recently moved to the school, Helen was well on her way to repeating her sophomore year. The principal and Helen's English teacher figured they did not have much to lose when the "old Doyle widow" arrived at the school, offering to volunteer as a tutor. Seeing the red-inked A– written at the top of the paper filled Ilona's heart with joy, as if she had written the essay herself. It was kind of the teacher to allow Ilona a first peek at the grade, and it was even more generous that she asked Ilona if she wanted to be the one to share the news, knowing how much time she had spent working with Helen in the library during lunch and after school.

The teachers from the social committee entered the library with holiday decorations and trays of food for the afternoon faculty Christmas party. Ilona returned the essay to a folder and began packing up her bag.

"Ilona! Please say you are staying for the party," one of the teachers asked.

"I would love to attend, but I don't want to impose, since I am a volunteer."

"Volunteer-shmolunteer! We are thrilled to have you here. And the work you are doing, well . . . let me put it this way . . . you *are* a teacher."

Ilona did feel like one of them. Aside from the prickly secretary, nearly every other person on campus could not have been kinder. The English and history teachers were among the most welcoming, thankful for her assistance in helping the reluctant learners.

Ilona arrived at Heights High thirsty for purpose, and once there, she fully realized how thirsty she had been for company, for the invitation to be part of something. The school community filled her with joy, even the students extending invitations to her for basketball games and concerts. One of the most endearing gifts came with their use of her name: Ilona. Mrs. Doyle, her moniker for so long, was first based on marriage and then wealth, and now as a natural consequence of age. Hearing the faculty and staff call her Ilona made her feel young, more of an individual. She found herself coming out of the carefully constructed shell she had nurtured for so long.

She and Mr. Pennington had also become quite friendly, their countenance to one another garnering the attention of the faculty. He could not help but wink as he playfully referred to her by the name his secretary uttered but a month ago. He later confessed his astonishment the moment he realized *the old Doyle widow* was the beautiful lady he first spotted in the back of the auditorium when introducing the speaker.

He asked her to the Yale Diner for lunch over the Christmas holiday. When he ordered a patty melt, she looked around to see if Patrick was watching. Mr. Pennington must have sensed her emotion, asking whether he had said something wrong, but she just smiled, offering a simple, "Sorry, I'm a little new to this," which garnered her a sympathetic nod. He had not been on a great many dates since his wife died, but he had a "bit more familiarity" in the arena. He could not say it gets easier with time, but he learned to anticipate the chain of emotions, and over time, his initial feeling of guilt changed to a feeling of curiosity over whether his wife would approve.

"And?" Ilona lightheartedly asked, waving her hand around her head.

"A standing ovation," Mr. Pennington replied, with a wide smile and watery eyes. "May I escort you to a dance at the SPJST Lodge on Saturday?"

CADMUS

Spring 1963

A FEW WEEKS BEFORE HIS mother died, Cadmus quietly let himself into the house, thinking his mother might be asleep. Gingerly opening the back kitchen door, "I Fall to Pieces" drifted from the library. He heard her giggling, followed by an apology for stepping on Mr. Pennington's foot. He had never stayed over this late. Cadmus figured his best option was to attempt discretion and tiptoe upstairs to avoid an interruption.

As he made his way down the hall, his mother appeared for a brief second, the twirl and swish of her skirt taking a peek into the hallway as she returned to her dance partner. It was the first time Cadmus had seen her dance; her joy was magnetic. He was at the door for several seconds before they noticed him, giving him time to count the empty Lone Stars resting on the table.

She screamed when she saw his figure standing in the doorway, and the rapid change of her expression from joy to fear caused Cadmus to burst into laughter. "Caddie! You scared me to death!" she gasped, hand over her heart, laughing.

"Looks like you have had quite a night!" he replied, his eyes looking to the beer bottles.

"Yes," she giggled, knocking one of the bottles to the floor as she tried to collect them. "I guess there is a first time for everything."

Mr. Pennington darted over to Cadmus, bearing the expression of an apologetic teenager who had been caught.

"I hope you know it was never my intention for your mother to become tipsy," he implored, looking into Cadmus' eyes. "I had no idea it only took two beers. She seemed fine after the first one."

"Mr. Pennington, it's fine, really it is. It is wonderful to see her so happy."

As Cadmus made his way upstairs, he realized that he could see his mother marrying this man. Perhaps not in the near future, but somewhere down the road, so long as she could continue working out the knots surrounding his father. Cadmus had seen her from the window the other morning, walking the rose garden paths, her lips moving but no rosary in hand.

"Who were you talking to out there?" he asked.

"Your father, of course," she responded quietly, her right index finger caressing her engagement ring. "I miss him every day, and every day I tell him how much I love him and how sorry I am."

"But you like Mr. Pennington?"

"Mark?" She looked at her son, her cheeks blushing and lips breaking into a girlish smile. "Oh, yes. I do like him so very, very much," she whispered.

CADMUS GREETED MR. PENNINGTON AT the front door, his hands extended to take the irises nestled in a white box tied with a white, satin ribbon that he had bought for Ilona.

"Thank you, Cadmus, but I do take such pleasure in giving them to her myself," he replied. "I'm enchanted."

Cadmus smiled, not knowing what to say.

"I'm sorry if I embarrassed you. Tell me about your studies. How are things progressing?"

"Coming along quite well. I am still on target to finish my dissertation."

"Terrific! Perhaps you and Thomas can join us next weekend at the art museum. Lunch afterward? I'd love to hear more about it."

"Thanks for the invitation," Cadmus replied, his stomach fluttering at hearing him say his boyfriend's name aloud, something very few people did. Mr. Pennington had met him a few months before as they were leaving the house for a movie. Uneasy at first with the initial introduction, Mr. Pennington could not have made his approval clearer with his warm handshake with one hand and his other arm patting Thomas' shoulder.

"I am so pleased to meet you, Thomas," he had said with sincerity and enthusiasm that left them marveling, thinking this is how heterosexual couples are treated. A week later, Ilona hosted a Sunday brunch for the four of them at The Doyle House, a wonderful afternoon of intellectual conversation. Callista politely declined the invitation. She did not approve of what she considered to be Cadmus'"choices," and the fact that her mother's only interest since her father's death was with a high school principal left Callista less than enthused.

"Please make yourself at home in the library. I'll tell my mother you are here."

He walked into his mother's room to find her dabbing perfume behind her ears and wrists. She met her son's eyes with a wide, toothy smile, looking beautiful in her new pale yellow A-line dress, with its wide collar wrapping around her shoulders.

"He's here," Cadmus said, not knowing why his nose began tingling. "You look beautiful, Mother."

"I feel beautiful. I am happy," she said, walking over and raising her palms to cup his face, teasing, "Now when did you get to be so tall?"

Cadmus only smiled and, placing his hands over hers, bent down to kiss her forehead. As he lifted his hands from hers, he noticed she was not wearing her wedding rings.

The banging at the front door jarred them from the moment. They ran into the hallway to find Mr. Pennington standing at the front door with Callista pushing past him, screaming for her mother.

"What in the hell are you doing?" Cadmus demanded.

"Oh, I'll tell you what I am *not* doing. I am not putting up with Mother's bullshit any longer!" Callista shouted.

Mr. Pennington placed the flower box on the hallway table and walked toward Ilona, an instinctive action to protect.

"Callista, what on earth has happened?" Ilona shrieked.

"I know the truth, Mother," she fumed.

"Truth?" Ilona responded, brows down in confusion.

"Having a son certainly frames things differently, does it not?"

"I'm sorry, I do not know what you mean," Ilona replied, still confused.

"William and I talked to Uncle Michael and his father about our wills, Mother. Revisions for the inclusion of Timothy. It was a very informative conversation, indeed."

Ilona gripped the banister, feeling the air leaving the room.

"Callista, no! Let's talk in private. You don't . . ."

"No, let's talk here and now! Cadmus should know the truth!"

"What in God's name are you talking about, Callista? This is ridiculous!" Cadmus shouted.

"What is ridiculous is that our mother sold us out, sold our shares in Doyle Lumber & Construction to Uncle Michael after he offered her a healthy profit."

"No, the business went to Michael's family after Dad's death, the will . . ."

"No! Mom sold it to them, because you are weak. She knew it then as we all know it now. She knew a faggot could not carry on in Dad's name! Uncle Michael made her an offer!"

Ilona could do nothing more than shake her head, unable to let go of the banister and dumbfounded as to why Michael would do such a thing after all these years.

"You are lying, Callista! Why are you doing this?" Cadmus shouted to his sister before looking to his mother.

"Oh yeah? You think *I'm* lying? Ask her," Callista said, lifting her chin in defiance.

"Mom?" Cadmus whispered.

"It's not as it sounds! Michael was awful, he is awful . . . a bully . . . he . . ."

"Was I supposed to . . ." Cadmus began, wide-eyed in disbelief. "Did he make you an offer to cut me out?"

"Yes, yes . . . but it was never for me!" Ilona screamed. "I wanted you to be free!"

"And the condition of the offer was that we would be out. Out for good!" she shouted. "Thank God I married a Dunn and have my share. Poor Cadmus . . . with no part of what I have now, which I can assure you is a hell of a lot more than this place!"

"Why are you doing this to us?" Ilona pleaded.

"Because you changed the course of our lives for your own ease! Your decision made me spend my life fighting for my place, and Cadmus has nothing to do with our business because of you. And tell him why you stopped going to Holy Family. Might as well let it all out."

"Oh, God!" Ilona cried, falling to her knees.

"They made fun of you, Cadmus, had been making fun of you for years. And for her, too, for being so damn devout after Dad's deplorable behavior and knowing you are a queer."

"Why didn't you tell me the truth?" Cadmus shouted. "How could you have kept this secret for so long?"

"I have always tried to protect you, my son! I always had the best of intentions!" Ilona wailed, struggling to get up to make her way to Cadmus.

"Who the hell are you? What do you have for me? Love or pity?" Cadmus screamed, pushing away her outstretched arms and storming out the door, with Callista not far behind.

ILONA

Spring 1963

MARK WALKED TO THE FRONT door, hoping to catch Cadmus' eye to beg his return. Cadmus looked back only once at his mother, anger savagely animating his face, revealing in a second how he might have looked had life played out differently. He could easily have been mistaken for a wayward young man.

After locking the front door, Mark gently picked Ilona up from the floor and carried her to her bedroom, resembling a husband carrying his wife over the threshold. Her cries for him to leave her alone were met with silence.

Her yellow dress thrown in a ball onto the bathroom floor, she curled into bed in her robe, sobbing uncontrollably. Mark lovingly hung her dress on a hanger, taking in the scent of her perfume as he hung it in the closet. He brought her a hand towel soaked in hot water to wash her face, the heat bringing relief to the tenderness of her swelling cheeks. He removed his jacket and shoes before crawling into bed next to her, drawing her close as she wept with her head on his chest.

"I lost my husband. I lost my children. I lost my son," she whispered through chokes. "I'm to blame."

"Give it time, Ilona. Time has a way of working things out," he said, kissing her firmly on the forehead and pulling her closer.

The following morning, he asked her if she wanted him to call Dear

Ernestine, who had been spending weekends with her sister. Ilona assured him she would be fine and to let Dear Ernestine have her well-deserved time off. She would learn of the events soon enough. He offered to stay and even to come back later, but she maintained that the time alone would serve her well. He gave her aspirin for her headache and kissed her goodbye, saying he looked forward to seeing her tomorrow at school and for her to call if she needed anything at any hour.

There was no sign of Cadmus, but she surmised he was with Thomas, which gave her a degree of comfort. Surely Thomas would help talk sense into him. She returned to bed after Mark left with her headache worsening, sleeping until half past noon.

The sound of the phone ringing woke her from her nap. Her heart racing, she ran to the phone in the library, knowing it had to be Cadmus calling.

"Hello?" she called loudly into the phone, gripping the receiver with both hands. "No, you have the wrong number," she softly replied, crestfallen. She took a seat in the nook, her heart still racing from the hope that had sprung to life in those few seconds.

She picked up the phone and quickly dialed Thomas' apartment.

"Thomas! Please put Cadmus on the phone. He's there, isn't he?"

"He doesn't want to speak to you," Thomas replied bluntly.

"Please, Thomas, please, for the love of God, please put Caddie on the phone!"

"As I said, Mrs. Doyle, he doesn't want to talk to you, and quite frankly neither do I."

"Please, please, let me talk to my son," she implored.

"What part of Thomas' words do you not understand, Mother? Leave me the fuck alone!" Cadmus shouted before hanging up the phone.

Ilona stared absentmindedly out the window and into the garden, the receiver still lodged in her limp hand, her temple pulsing. His words and tone marked a sharp dissonance from the son she knew, a man whose reflective capacity and natural stillness had marked him as a compassionate soul since the day he was born. She knew even people with strong constitutions bear moments of restlessness, and her actions unearthed a layer of vulnerability. She had been his rock since birth, since he knew he was gay, and now he doubted her character.

Returning the phone receiver to its cradle, she turned her eyes to the framed photograph of her wedding day resting on the table—she and Patrick looking at one another, smiling in the rose garden at the reception. A candid shot, it was by far one of their favorites. Only they knew the words exchanged just seconds before the shot was taken: *We did it our way!*

With Patrick's parents deceased and her parents marginalized, she and Patrick had the luxury of planning a wedding on their terms. The traditional Catholic service was a given, but the reception was one area for freedom. They decided the rose garden was the most fitting for the occasion, a space large enough to host a respectable crowd while offering natural limitations on the guest list. Dear Ernestine attended as a guest and sat at the family table. Perhaps more important, however, it served as a benediction, a time to honor the next evolution of The Doyle House. She now questioned *her way.* What had she done to their family?

Ilona opened the desk drawer, fingering the fountain pens, pencils, rulers, and compass—relics from their early marriage that had not been touched in years. She thought about Patrick's hands gripping the instruments, knowing they once reverberated with his love for Houston and wondering if they still bore even his slightest fingerprint.

She spread out an old map of the city, the frayed edges a sign that it had been useful at one time. Ilona squinted, hand to her temple, looking for Franklin and Main. Her eyes then wandered east, scanning to locate Lawndale, before heading west to find where she sat now on The Boulevard. She picked up Patrick's compass, and placing the needle on the M&M and the pencil on Lawndale, she drew a circle. It perfectly intersected The Doyle House on Heights Boulevard as it made its revolution. Her life looked so small, the points of the three locations following a perfect 180-degree line, a circle of eight millimeters. Life looked simple from the bird's-eye view, but she had done more than her fair share of ruining her family, from her rejection of the Petrarkises and her failure as a Doyle.

Ilona walked outside to the rose garden in her robe, barefoot and hair disheveled, disregarding the numbers of people along The Boulevard. She came up empty handed when she reached into her pocket for her rosary, realizing it must still be under her pillow. Taking a deep breath, she began her walk, counting each step and taking in the texture of the bricks under her feet.

The images came rapidly, Patrick appearing on the bench, looking at her with his high-voltage smile, waving her to come over and take a seat. "Give me a minute, my love," she whispered as she made another revolution, hand rubbing her temple as the wind picked up its force.

Her eyes teared at the sight of Callista picking a flower for her hair and twirling in the lawn barefoot, hands outstretched for her mother to join her in a dance. "Not your time, sweetheart," she smiled, efforts to tuck her hair behind her ear at odds with the strong breezes. A storm from the Gulf was on its way.

Cadmus walked along the perimeter of the grounds, his left hand tapping every other picket and mouthing words to a story, his eyebrows moving with the telling of the tale. He stopped at the front gate and turned to Ilona, embarrassed, with a you-caught-me smile. She blew him a kiss and waved, "Keep telling your stories, sweet boy!"

As she headed back toward the pecan tree, she saw her brother sitting next to Patrick, both men talking for a moment more before noticing her approach. Her brother stood when he saw her, a warm smile breaking across his face and his head tilted to the side. Patrick followed suit and walked toward her, extending his hand.

"It's time, my love."

CADMUS

Spring 1963

CADMUS DID NOT RETURN HOME until Tuesday, and he would have stayed away longer had he not needed his papers for class. Pulling into the driveway, he noticed Callista's car parked in front.

What in the hell is she doing here? he wondered as he gave his car door an extra-hard slam to let his mother know he was still upset.

Dear Ernestine threw open the back door screaming, "Where've you been, Caddie? We've been looking all over for you!"

Knees weak, he placed his right hand on the car hood. Something was terribly wrong. He kept his eyes on hers, mentally preparing for what was about to be said as she scurried down the stairs, wrapping her arms around him.

"Your mama's gone, Caddie," she cried. "She passed on Sunday."

Cadmus looked up to see Callista's tearstained face staring at him from the doorway as a rush of wind made its way through the trees.

The moisture from the rainfall saturated his pants, but Cadmus remained rooted under the pecan tree, the same location he had rested the night he said goodbye to his father.

"It would have been nice to know how to contact you, Cadmus," Callista's reprimand echoed through his mind. "Two damn days of being in this hell alone!"

Other than Ilona, no one knew much about Thomas. Other than Ilona, no one truly accepted him, Callista's rebuffs growing stronger over time, especially after her children came into the world. What was he supposed to do? Give his boyfriend's number in case of an emergency to his sister, who was disgusted by him? Or maybe it would have been better to give it to his seventy-something-year-old grandparents he rarely saw?

He looked at the stone bench on his right, broken in two pieces like bookends, the weight and jostling of the paramedics' equipment fracturing it in half. Later, the neighbors from across the street had hesitated to share too many details, but they gave in to his pleas, "I must know what you saw in her final moments, please."

The neighbor leaned on her broom, her eyes filling with tears. "I'm sorry, I've never seen someone die," she choked, the screen door slamming behind her as she left her husband to explain.

It was Sunday afternoon, moments before the storm rolled into town. He and his wife had been planting annuals, trying to hurry as the first drops started to fall. Just as she stood to brush the soil from her pants, they heard the scream, a bloodcurdling scream from across the esplanade. They ran across the street to see Ilona's body splayed in the rose garden.

"But where, where in the garden?" Cadmus asked.

"Next to the bench."

The ambulance arrived a short time later, the paramedics doing their best to revive her, but she was gone, rain pelting her body as they lifted her on the stretcher.

"I never knew you could tell like that, tell the difference between sleepin' and dyin', but you can," the man said, almost like he was convincing himself, still in shock at having come so close to death.

FATHER JOSEPH AGREED TO SPEAK at the funeral even though it would take place at a funeral parlor rather than a church. Callista put up a valiant fight to have it at her parish, but in the end, even her priest conceded it made more sense to have it at another location given the circumstances of her falling out with Holy Family and with the Church in general.

"The humiliation continues!" she raged, slamming the door to The Doyle House and speeding away down The Boulevard.

Cadmus believed his mother's death would elicit a softer side in his sister, bring her back to the Callista who had opened her room as a sanctuary when his nightmares loomed. And while he did see glimpses of her regret, of her love for her mother, what took front seat was Callista's anger over the skeletons brought to light.

How many tragedies can befall one family?

Poor Doyles, God love 'em! Maureen cursed that family. Remember her?

Cadmus? Alone in that house with a man? That house was made for a real family!

Cadmus used reason to suffer through the funeral planning with Callista. He reached into the well of compassion, as Ilona would have wanted, and deduced that anger was Callista's way of dealing with her mother's death. Surely she would come to her senses in time.

"I don't feel right about leaving you, Caddie. I can stay in the apartment and only come out if you need me."

"Please, Dear Ernestine, please," Cadmus said, gripping both of her hands. "I need to be alone. I am a grown man."

"Look here now, you'll always be my baby. I delivered you! And I raised Paty since he was three, and he's still my Paty even though he passed," she said, breaking down in tears. "And your mother was a fine lady, kind lady."

Cadmus embraced her as she wept, her head falling at his chest. He envied her ability to cry, something he desperately needed to do.

THE DAY CADMUS DISCOVERED HIS mother had been dead for two days, Thomas wanted to come over immediately to be by his side. Cadmus told him the time was not right; he and Callista were pouring over details for the funeral, which was partially true. He wanted to be alone, needing to absorb the initial shock of the loss. After some time in the rose garden, he spent the night alone in the home with the spirits of his deceased parents, studying the home as he had never done before. It looked different, death casting its shadow on the Doyle family objects that now belonged to him and his sister.

Thomas insisted on attending the funeral and reception. With so many people from an array of social pockets—Irish, Greek, Houston society, Heights High School, and even Holy Family—he could easily blend in without notice.

"But I want to be by your side," he urged.

"It's not the appropriate time," Cadmus emphatically retorted. "If you attend, then you must keep a distance from me."

Cadmus stood at the front of The Doyle House, greeting the floods of people who continued to pour through the door. His brain ping-ponged to place how he or his mother knew them, darting between her varied worlds. The visitors from Holy Family made him even more apprehensive, leaving him to wonder whether they might be the ones whose sharp tongue caused his family even more pain.

In the few times he turned his head to scan the room, he found Thomas staring at him oddly. Despite their time together, he could not register the emotion, which left Cadmus unsettled. He looked as if he were heading toward him at one point. When Cadmus firmly shook his head "no," Thomas stopped suddenly before darting off to another part of the house.

After a few minutes had passed without another person opening the door, Cadmus took advantage of this pause and headed down the hall only to see Callista bawling, surrounded by a group of Irish women, who were consoling her over the loss of her mother. For Ilona's sake, Cadmus did not want to question her sincerity, but it pushed him to head out to the rose garden in disgust nonetheless.

"Cadmus! Over here!" called his cousin, Benjamin, who was standing next to his twin, Andrew.

Cadmus' heart picked up a beat, sensing that his cousins bore a genuine look of interest in their greeting. Hope found him in the few seconds it took to cross over to them, stationed in front of the birdbath. He knew tragedy had the potential to bring people together as much as it could tear them apart. Perhaps they could attempt to forge a relationship.

"I'm so sorry," Andrew said, reaching for an embrace. "Your mother was always so kind to us. What a tragedy."

Cadmus turned when he felt another hand on his shoulder, presuming it was Benjamin. He turned around to meet the eyes of Thomas, staring at him blankly.

"Cadmus, I've been looking for you to make sure you are okay," he said, touching his arm before turning to the brothers. "Hello, I'm Thomas, Cadmus' *good friend.*"

Benjamin and Andrew tensed, their disposition retreating to its more formal nature. They politely shook his hand before heading away to talk to the other members of the family.

Cadmus stormed to the side of Dear Ernestine's garage apartment, with Thomas following him closely.

"What in the hell are you doing?" Cadmus shouted.

"I'm tired of being ignored. Ilona would have wanted me here."

"Yes, but only on her son's terms! And you will still refer to her as Mrs. Doyle, understood?"

"I'll be moving in soon anyway. What difference does it make who sees us together?"

"How on earth did you come up with that idea?"

"You in this big house all alone? Surely, you are not going to be selfish, Cadmus. You know I struggle."

Cadmus stared at Thomas in disbelief, wondering how he could have misjudged his character. He had never thought of himself as a rich man, often comparing his station to Callista and William's success. But wealth is relative, and he and Ilona were wealthy compared to most people. They simply did not flaunt it as others did.

"We are over," Cadmus said, turning away to head back in the house.

HIS GRANDPARENTS AND AUNT ARIANNA tried their best to reach out to him after Ilona died. He accepted a few invitations to Lawndale Café, sitting with Ya Ya at the counter, drinking strong coffee and staring into the kitchen. And while he did not doubt their sincerity to support him, the time he spent next to them left him feeling emptier than if he had stayed home.

He held fond memories of the café of long ago, of his grandfather bellowing, "Ah! My boy!" when he walked through the doors, the grand welcome and glittering eyes of his grandfather popping a towel to polish the best counter seat for him to sit. He ran as fast as his buckled dress shoes could take him, giving a preemptive leap in the final stretch, his grandfather lifting him high to swing him into the seat. He had looked back to see his mother and Callista making their way back to him, his grandfather's greeting to Callista loving but more reserved, as if he did not quite know how to greet his green-eyed granddaughter.

"Biggest piece of apple pie for my grandchildren! You hear me? Biggest, I say!" he demanded, heads of the other patrons turning toward them, some wistful as they viewed the familiarity of the scene through the lens of their own lives while others grinned and scraped the plates with the sides of their forks.

"Yes, and young Cadmus know his letters and numbers . . . even know how spell . . ." His grandfather bragged, looking over to him, hand cueing him to speak.

"Petrarkis. P-E-T-R-A-R-K-I-S." Cadmus enunciated with pride, carefully sounding out each letter.

"Now that hard word for boy who five!" he pronounced as Callista bent her head down to tuck her hair behind her ears, her eyes rolling.

"My Callista, now she write story . . . beautiful story . . . best of grade," he said, gesturing his coffee cup over to her for confirmation.

"*Poetry* contest. *Second* place," she corrected.

"Yes . . . that what I mean . . . po-eh-tree. Fine job!" he said with a sharp nod to the head, oblivious to her annoyance.

His grandfather continued, bragging on his grandchildren. Whereas Callista often felt embarrassed or annoyed, Cadmus watched the narration of his life in fascination as it was told in exclamatory terms. It prompted him to think his life was much more exciting than he realized. As an adult, he wondered how often this routine occurred, questioning if it were only that one memory that bore such an impression as to have heralded it as one of the cherished from childhood that made its way to the gallery.

He remembered his mother sipping her coffee, with her painted lips, shoulders back, and pearls resting against her smooth skin. He wondered how she had ever wiped the counters.

"Sixty percent, you say?" She asked, incredulous with her eyes watery over the occupancy of the M&M.

"Good we no rebuild Franklin. And going down every day. Building empty before you know it."

"Perhaps it can still make a comeback . . . it's such a lovely building. It's never too late for a second chance, at least it shouldn't be," she had said, choked up and shaking her head with thoughts of how its impending demise mirrored her marriage.

"Yes, my dear. Hope," her baba replied, placing his hand over his daughter's. "Always hope."

Hope. Cadmus figured it was still an option. He could hope to forge a relationship now, although it would be difficult. Lawndale Café was ten miles away, but it might as well have been on the other side of the earth. The limited time spent together during his childhood, coupled with the stark differences between their worlds, left few topics for conversation and a reminder of the family he really did not know. He also surmised that they did not approve of his sexuality, but he could not say it for a fact. Cadmus often caught his grandfather staring at him from the corner of his eye, like he was studying how they could be related or how Cadmus could do what he did.

He decided to take side roads back to The Heights, just as his mother would have when she worked on Franklin, taking in the developing city. The Houston skyline was beginning a wave of transformation: The Humble Building was now open, the first skyscraper in over twenty years. He and his mother had planned to visit it to honor Patrick, and now she would never experience it. He drove down Franklin, noticing the building where the family diner once stood, abandoned and boarded. His cousins' new chain across Houston boasted a success for the Petrarkis family, although it was not directly from his grandfather's line.

He thought about what his life would have been had his mother married a Greek man, had he been raised as his cousins. Would he have fallen in love with a woman? One chance day at the M&M to pay a bill, the boy in red suspenders running past her, what if she had arrived one minute later? Would she have met Patrick?

Now that his mother was dead, Cadmus did not have a family in the real sense. Callista and William did not accept him, saying to him in the months following, "If you decide to make other choices in your life, you are welcome to join us. Cadmus, if you had children, you would understand what we mean. You make decisions in their interest and not your own."

Callista's station in River Oaks certainly gave her the appearance of surpassing the Doyle standards of wealth, but even she was surprised at the reading of the will. Her mother had not touched a penny of what had been left to the children, which was a sizeable amount. Ilona left a remainder of her portion to Dear Ernestine and left The Doyle House to Cadmus, since he would live alone on a professor's salary. Even without the Doyle & Dunn money Callista enjoyed, they were very well-to-do. It sickened Cadmus to see the dollar signs behind his name, Callista having made him doubt his mother's intention with the settlement of his father's estate, not to mention jarring him to the core when she had so vulgarly enunciated his sexuality.

Cadmus knew who Uncle Michael was, yet he entertained the possibility that his mother had pitied him over loving him. He was still overwhelmed with disappointment that she never told him the truth, but he should not have rejected her. She had only done it out of love.

Pulling alongside the curb, Cadmus looked at The Doyle House, his house. Despite his tendency for stillness and reflection, his early thoughts of living here alone unnerved him, leaving him feeling as if he had robbed his parents of their due. Their untimely deaths, so tragic and unexpected, how could he possibly carry on the family legacy alone? What was the legacy of a man destined not to marry?

The reason old souls enjoy spending time alone is because they never really are.

—AUTHOR UNKNOWN

PART

TWO

DELPHINA

Autumn 1973

"DELPHINA," PATRICIA ANSWERED WHEN THE nurse asked for the name of her baby, who was born on the eleventh of October 1973.

"Come again?" the nurse asked with a quizzical gaze, suggesting a misunderstanding.

"Delphina Ann Cizek," Benny emphasized, his protective fatherly instincts kicking into gear.

Patricia decided to name her daughter Delphina long before her birthdate, the decision rendered during the 1963–64 school year when she was in the sixth grade. The essence for the name dawned the summer before the school year started, the summer Patricia spent alone in her room, draped perpendicularly across her bed, arm's-length from the battered record player that rested on her nightstand, so she could reset the needle for a continuous running of "Pintor" by The Pharos. The melodic rhythms of the guitar, punctuated by crisp claps of the maracas, took her to another place, and the fact that there were no words—only sheer instrumental musings—offered an invitation to create her own romantic narrative of a life that bore little resemblance to the current one she held as the second youngest of the six Vizcek children.

Only three children remained at home, and since she was the only daughter left in the house, it was agreed she would have a room to herself while her two brothers shared another. And even though she had her privacy, the thin walls gave way to her brothers pounding, "Knock it off with the cha-cha stuff. Cain't ya play somethin' else?"

But she could not play something else. The song was a muse for the life she would one day inhabit, and starting junior high was as good of a time as any to start the transition. Her best friend's mother not only read *Vogue*, but she also had an actual subscription, a fact that pushed her to the top of the ranks as far as mothers were concerned. Patricia could not believe her luck when Mrs. Spilka had asked her if she wanted her April issue because she planned on throwing it away.

Patricia carried the magazine home right-side up, as if she were carrying a three-layer cake. Jean Shrimpton stared into her eyes, saying, *I know what you want, and I promise you it is as wonderful as you imagine.* She painstakingly studied Jean, and with her chipped plastic hand mirror, she practiced what she hoped to be her default expression: aloof, yet inquisitive eyes; a barely there smile; and excellent posture with a slight tilt of the head to elongate her neck.

One day during the summer holiday, Patricia went to Cloth World to rifle through discounted fabrics—some so outdated they carried a coat of dust and others being nicer remnants considered treasures for those lucky enough to have a smaller frame. Patricia, cloudy from the buzz of a morning spent daydreaming about white sands, drinks with umbrellas, and an olive-skinned gentleman, stopped when she came across a fabric dotted with tropical trees and squiggly lines meant to resemble birds. It was a tacky print at first glance, shades of orange and yellow printed on cotton so durable you might mistake it for drapery. She saw it as something created by the *Pintor* from her favorite song, and it made her think of a place she would live when she was older, where she would wear coral lipstick and take those mysterious vitamins from the disc, like her sister did when she thought no one was looking.

Patricia's efforts to channel Jeanie, as she had affectionately dubbed Jean after hours of bonding and primping, fell to the wayside on the first day of school. Her palm tree frock provided hearty fodder for the Havlik twins, who claimed it was the same material their grandmother had used to make a tablecloth over the summer. Attempting to muster the pleasant, low-key smile perfected over the course of countless hours in her bedroom, she excessively tensed her cheek muscles trying to avoid tears. The boys then taunted, "Patricia ate a lemon from her lemon tree dress!" Try as she did to remain composed, she shouted, "Shut up!" before stomping down the hall.

Walking down the hall to history class, she decided all was not lost. It was only fourth period. She had another class to regain her composure. Miss Matthews was a new teacher and new to Granger, and even though Patricia had known the other kids since birth, this new class presented an opportunity as new classes do. The same faces give way to a new matrix that could tilt the balance of social circles. She knew she might be able to pull it off in that class at least.

Unfortunately, her effort to look elegantly effortless followed suit, falling completely to the wayside when Miss Matthews combined and mispronounced Louis Sassa's name as "Loose Ass" during roll call. Patricia's attempt to stifle her chuckle resulted in a most tragic snort that opened a gateway of laughter. It did not matter that the entire class roared—her reaction was among the first registered, which led her to wonder how much of the laughter was directed to Miss Matthews, to red-cheeked Louis, or to her failed attempt at elegance.

Patricia soon lapsed into her old self, or what could more appropriately be described as her true self. Her gig had been short-lived, but for a few periods, she tasted the new persona she idealized. While her desire to transform did not dissolve, it was certainly dulled. Truth be told, she found it too damn exhausting to change her entire way of being, especially living in Granger without a catalyst to return her to reverie. The inspiration elicited from "Pintor" faded into little more than a nostalgic reminder of the summer before junior high.

She was in Miss Matthews' class on November 22, 1963 when the principal announced that President Kennedy had been assassinated. And while the gasps and screams could be heard from all directions of the school, she would always remember Miss Matthews sitting quietly at her desk, with mousy hair draped evenly around her bowed head like a curtain, while tears dripped steadily to form a small pool on her open history textbook.

JFK's death consumed the nation, but its impact on Texas carried an additional weight, and selfishly Patricia found it equally horrifying and humiliating. On a cold, dreary day the following February, she awoke to Jeanie's eyes peeking at her from under the bed as she rose to get ready for school. She had thrown the magazine under the bed over the holidays, feeling overwhelmed with shame for daring to want something new when so many others simply wanted what they once had. Now it was as if Jeanie was taunting her: *You still want it.* Kicking the magazine back under the bed with her heel, Patricia hopped back into bed and buried herself under the covers.

With May came a sense of relief that the end of the school year was in sight, the summer days ahead filled with new fantasies of what could be. They were learning about Ancient Greece, a topic that made the fifty-minute period drag to a standstill. Acropolis, Sparta, Pericles . . . but then her ears perked at a term that reminded her of last summer's romance—*Delphi.*

While Miss Matthews droned on about the ancient capital, Patricia's mind meandered to the forty-five turning on her record player—the Del-fi label of "Pintor" upon which she gazed as it made revolutions in time to the island sounds. Perhaps the summer of 1964 would offer a new chance for reinvention, or at the very least an opportunity to yet again indulge in an intoxicating fantasy sans interruptions from the humdrum daily routine of school.

Later that month, when her brother received the Sacrament of Confirmation, she heard Annette Kopecky's chosen saint name, Delphina, when she approached the altar. Enchanted by the beautiful resemblance to the record label that once nourished her dream, Patricia decided that she would also select this name when her time came for Confirmation, not knowing that Saint Delphina took vows of chastity and poverty, which was far from the life Patricia envisioned.

By the time July rolled around and "The Girl from Ipanema" became the rage, Patricia indulged in an exotic fantasy once again, this time with another foreign sound that called to mind a faraway place, a place where she would fall in love with an olive-skinned man and have a daughter they would christen Delphina.

CADMUS

Winter 2014

"I DON'T KNOW HOW MUCH longer I can work here," murmured a voice from behind the nurses' station.

"You get used to it. You can learn a lot from being here," a woman with a throaty voice responded while shuffling papers into an even stack before paper clipping them together.

"Yeah, like learning it's hell getting old," the first one said with a rueful laugh.

"Don't you think it's better than the alternative?" she said, rising to file the papers in a cabinet behind the desk.

"Well, that depends."

"On?"

"On if you're alone. I can't imagine doing it alone," she answered, nodding her head in the direction of Cadmus seated in his wheelchair, legs wrapped tightly in the blanket, catatonic in the sitting area near the window.

"Be careful. You do not know what he is thinking. Hearing is the last sense to go, and he may very well be listening."

CADMUS

Autumn 1973

TURQUOISE FLECKS PEPPERED HIS BOOTS, an odd addition to the worn, brown leather that carried a story within each dusty crease. Cadmus, kneeling and looking through different sizes of sketchbooks on the bottom shelf, kept his eyes downcast while his ears attended to the conversation overhead.

"I understand the cotton canvas is primed and ready, but I want to prepare the linen myself," Robert enunciated slowly, attentive to every syllable and annoyed by the clerk's questions. "Yes, I will gladly pay more coin in advance of the order. Please forgive the perceived lunacy of such an extravagance. There certainly must be a benefit to my day job of practicing law."

The faint Texas twang, discretely nestled within a calm, deep tone, elicited the spontaneous smile that spread across Cadmus' face. He looked up to meet Robert's eyes, and, unbeknownst to himself, he had been nodding in agreement.

"You know what I am talking about, don't you, brown eyes?"

They spent over two hours casing the art supplies, Robert explaining in detail the varietals of paints he favored for different pieces: oil, watercolor, and gouache. As a litigator, he loved winning arguments with his intellect. He supposed this was because of all the times he had been bullied and beaten in the trailer park by strangers and family alike. Robert spent long hours at work downtown but equally loved to come home to his bungalow and lose himself in the art studio he had fashioned from the living area and second bedroom.

A wave of heat seared across Cadmus' face as he heard the word *bedroom*. He followed Robert's words, nodding and smiling in his usual reticent fashion, completely captivated by this rugged man: a hybrid of cowboy, attorney, and artist. Cadmus remained a pace behind Robert, wanting to be closer but not knowing for certain if Robert felt the same way.

Cadmus shared with Robert that his love for art came second to literature, although he considered himself a man of humanities in general. He wove in that he lived alone in The Heights to see if Robert's disposition changed, while following it with the fact that he enjoyed time in museums apart from his work at Rice University. He enjoyed sketching and was interested in formal study, but he had yet to find the time. He was currently busy working on a collection of poems and short stories.

They made it back to the canvas section, Robert detailing the canvases, palms open, gliding across the textures. When he began talking about the viscose, he grabbed Cadmus' hand, and laying it squarely on the fabric, he placed his hand on top, explaining how the "delicate canvas is not as common, but you know when it is right."

Later that evening with Robert fast asleep, Cadmus gently peeled himself from the embrace and headed into Robert's studio. One piece spanned the entire wall, abstract shapes like a jigsaw, coming together to create a mélange of hues juxtaposed to elicit pure emotion, a sea of blues and greens cascading across the canvas. Cadmus sat on the hardwood floor, hypnotized by the piece, his heart beginning to race and eyes filling with tears as he felt his mother's presence settle in around him. It had been ten years since her death, and his regret was still a noose that continued to entrap him even in the home of a new lover.

Cadmus knew his mother had been supportive of who he was, a fact that amazed him more and more as he aged. He was convinced that he had robbed her of life, prompting her early death. And as a recipient of his mother's unconditional love and compassion, he wanted to serve as a good steward of her blessings. He wanted to live a life that would have made her proud, a life that was rich both professionally and personally. He had known Robert for less than a day, but this was the first time Cadmus could envision the real possibility of sharing his life with someone.

His eyes absorbed Robert's piece, its serenity giving a moment's respite to his pain, as if Ilona brought them together, giving her blessing to the union. He whispered, "I love you, Mom," and returned to the bedroom. Raising Robert's arm and resting his head on his breast, he stared at the diagonal lines formed by the neighbor's porch light that streamed through the gap in the curtain, amazed by his developing accomplishment of spending a full night alone with someone.

CADMUS WAS ENDEARED BY THE way Robert touched him on the cheek. Even after their most intimate nights making love—and it was only with Robert that he first and ever used those words to describe sex—it was the gentle stroke to his face that invigorated Cadmus with the most intense feelings of intimacy.

They had just finished lunch on a Saturday in October, meandering through the streets to return to Robert's craftsman bungalow. Heady from the chardonnay, Cadmus knew what the afternoon had in store. It was a windy, brisk day for early autumn, a retreat from the summer that notoriously overstayed its welcome. The day was a gift, an unexpected pocket of time that had been unfathomable only a few weeks ago when Cadmus first met Robert at the art supply. With its gentle hands, the wind spiraled the fallen, yellow leaves that lay in front of Robert's home. They laughed in disbelief at the enchantment of the moment, pausing beneath the limbs of the oaks that formed an arch like ballerina arms, so high overhead.

Robert turned to Cadmus, having to look up into his eyes ever so slightly, gently caressing his temple with the backs of his fingers, dark brown waves of hair falling on his hand, and then following the path down Cadmus' cheek. He jerked his head away after a few seconds, realizing that someone might see them. Robert smiled reassuringly and whispered, "We are safe in this neighborhood," as he pulled Cadmus to him, gently kissing him on the lips. Cadmus reciprocated, and as the seconds passed and intensity strengthened, he could feel his inhibitions beginning to evaporate. It was the first time he had ever kissed a man in public.

The green and gold of Robert's eyes even more brightly illuminated in the afternoon sun, coupled with the contrast of his callused thumb softly brushing his delicate face, prompted Cadmus to think of his father. An exaggerated image of Patrick's face seared through Cadmus' mind like a camera flash. He held a sprinkling of memories of his father, but he clearly recalled the sense of longing he had felt as a child, yearning for the desire to connect with someone with whom he had no connection. Cadmus often heard people referring to family as blood: Blood is thicker than water; blood binds families together. Never regarding it as an intimate description, he viewed it as clinical, sterile—a dissonance. And now he had fallen in love with a man who resembled a worker from the lumberyard, like the distant cousins and recent immigrants his father and uncle had hired to do the laboring. Cadmus smiled, holding Robert's stare, as they joined hands and stumbled up the sidewalk to his house.

CADMUS' VISIT WITH MR. PENNINGTON the following day would be his last, and perhaps he would not even know Cadmus was there, seeing that he had been moved to acute hospice care. The two men only visited once a year over the holidays, but the infrequency was not an indicator of the bond held. Aside from Callista and God, Mr. Pennington was the only person who witnessed Cadmus' vitriolic reaction toward his mother, the evening he misunderstood her deep love for pity and doubt. His humiliation and regret initially kept him from accepting Mr. Pennington's request for a visit all those years ago, but one day Mr. Pennington appeared at Cadmus' door unannounced, pleading to indulge him in just one visit. That one visit beget a friendship, but not one of traditional standards. They were bonded in tragedy and love, both fiercely loving the same person.

Attempting to hypothesize his parents as an elderly couple left Cadmus at an impasse. Whether it was because he held few memories of his father or if it was because his parents seemed so different, he did not know. Alcohol held a presence in his early childhood as if it were another member of the family, like an invisible coating that distanced his parents.

Mr. Pennington, on the other hand, joined his mother for tea in the library, the couple spending evenings reading and talking, whether it was about literature, music, current events, or the birds in the garden. Cadmus once saw them kiss before he left home for the night, a passion so delicate and full of wonder, perhaps the effect of already having lost a love, understanding impermanence firsthand. He knew his mother had found a new love, and Mr. Pennington had adored her as she deserved to be adored.

Silence met his taps at the door. Cadmus opened it slowly and crept into the room to find Mr. Pennington asleep, breath rattling. He pulled a seat next to him, studying his wrinkles and gray hair. Had his mother lived, she would have been the one by his side, a widow for the second time. He felt a wave of jealousy at the possibility that Mr. Pennington and Ilona would soon be face-to-face in the heavens.

"Pardon me," the nurse said, startling him from Cadmus thoughts. "I need to check his vitals."

"Certainly. Has he been awake today?" Cadmus asked.

"No, he's been asleep since yesterday morning."

"Will he wake up again?"

"Can't say for sure. Souls tend to do their own thing when the time comes to transition," she replied with a gentle smile. "But based on his signs, I would venture not. He can still hear you though, you know."

After she exited the room, Cadmus reached for Mr. Pennington's hand.

"I'm sorry I did not come sooner," he choked. "I have important news to tell you, news that I want you to pass on to my mother. I think I've fallen in love. He's a wonderful man, someone I know you and my mother would have liked."

His lips parted wider, as if he wanted to say something, but his breath continued to rattle.

"I'm so sorry I cheated you from your time with my mother. Knowing what it feels like to fall in love . . . I'm sorry, Mr. Pennington, so very, very sorry. Please forgive me," Cadmus said as he caressed his hand.

ROBERT MARKED THE FIRST, OF what would become the only, romantic relationship Cadmus welcomed into his home. It was true that he thought of his home as a sanctuary, considering it was where his soul entered the world and his mother's exited, but its sanctity was not the only reason behind his reluctance.

Cadmus maintained clear boundaries, because he knew visiting The Doyle House begged questions, from the design itself to the contents and from the photographs of his family to the gardens that pristinely graced multiple lots. He found the vulnerability and stamina needed to answer the questions unnerving. His encounters, albeit few in number, had taken place at the apartments of his past lovers, with him leaving before the next morning.

"Goddamn, this place must have some stories," Robert said as he meandered through the rooms on the first floor.

"That is certainly one way to put it," Cadmus nodded, steadying his breaths in preparation for the questions to follow.

"The trailer has stories, too. Just not draped as pretty as these," Robert said and after another second added, "Everything does, you know?"

"Yes, I do know," Cadmus said with a knowing smile.

They made their way into the library, Cadmus walking to the cabinet to prepare drinks. Robert liked a good whiskey, straight up. Cadmus chuckled at the thought of his father enjoying a drink with his boyfriend, a vision he could barely imagine. Cadmus turned to see Robert studying a photograph of Ilona and Patrick, champagne glasses toasting on top of a building that overlooked downtown.

"Are they at the Niels Esperson Building?" Robert asked, incredulously.

"Yes, how can you tell?" Cadmus wondered.

"You can see the column from the cupola right there," he replied, pointing to the left edge of the photograph. "I know the building well . . . that's where my office is located, twenty-sixth floor."

"They were toasting the groundbreaking of a project on Main. It was taken before I was born."

"Well, I can tell you no one is toasting up there now. They closed off the observatory long ago."

Cadmus walked over to the bookcase to pick up the brass Doyle Lumber & Construction nameplate that rested on an easel.

"This was my family's original business."

"Holy shit! Doyle & Dunn are our clients . . . been so well before my time."

"You know them?"

"I talk to them in passing, but I've never worked directly for them. Ben is the one I see most often."

"My cousin. My estranged cousin," Cadmus nodded, returning the placard to the easel.

"Damn. It's a small world," Robert said, shaking his head. "How in the hell could you be mistaken for an Irishman?"

"Doesn't happen that often, trust me," Cadmus laughed.

"I'd love to take a walk out there," Robert said, his eyes cast out Ilona's bay window to the garden.

"Maybe another time," Cadmus demurred. His heart warmed at Robert's gentle smile, grateful that with age came maturity that there was time to understand the serpentine threads of their lives.

Cadmus' mind swelled with thoughts of the Esperson and Robert and of the new direction his life was taking. He never thought he would have a spouse, not only because marriage was not a legal option but also because he could not envision himself falling in love. He was a private, quiet soul reluctant to expose his own vulnerability despite the thoughtfulness he radiated to others. And now, he had not only fallen in love, but he had fallen in love with someone who worked in the Esperson—someone whose firm represented his family. He thought, perhaps, Ilona had a hand in this match, as if she were sending him signs that she approved of, what he hoped would be, her son-in-law.

He had not stepped foot inside the Esperson since the Christmas before his father died—December 23, 1940 to be exact. That was the only time he came face-to-face with the woman who caused his father's death. He knew he could not visit Robert at work right away. He could possibly bump into his cousins, or someone from the firm might even link them as a couple given Cadmus' mannerisms. Robert had worked for the firm for many years and was on the verge of partnership. He could not risk anyone confirming his sexuality at this particular time.

"I bring in more money that any of those good ol' boys; that's for sure," he once said. And although he was correct in terms of the bottom line, he knew things would be different should any wonderings be verified.

Cadmus also knew he needed time to prepare to visit the building again, the building that was intended to house his life's purpose to lead a company to develop Houston. Cadmus knew that one day, perhaps even in the near future, Robert would take him to his office after hours, after the Doyles and Dunns were long gone for the day.

"I'M TRUSTING YOU," ROBERT SAID as his car turned onto Post Oak Boulevard.

"Of course you can trust me. She will love you, and remember, she's the only person in my life who will," Cadmus said.

"I trust you on that one. I'm talking about trusting the restaurant she chose. After striking down the Petroleum Club for said reasons, I figured for certain she would select something more discrete. Lord knows who will be lunching there today. Might be the goddamn Queen of Sheba."

"Yes, well, then you would be in luck. What use does the Queen of Sheba have with a Houston attorney?"

"I'm serious, Cadmus. I need to be discrete about us for now."

"She knows, Robert. And trust me, someone with as much money as her always needs an attorney or two in her pocket. Just a lunch meeting with a prospective client, if anyone asks," Cadmus assured.

Robert straightened his tie in the rearview mirror while waiting in line for the valet. No one would take him for a gay man; his demeanor and disposition were overly masculine and daunting. Cadmus had inherited his father's chiseled face, but he was often referred to as beautiful in a tone that embodied the feminine. He had to work harder to conceal his sexuality.

"Genesee, party of three," Cadmus said.

"Yes, Mrs. Genesee is here. Right this way," the maître d' replied as he led them into the dining room.

"Cadmus!" she exclaimed, drips from her martini glass making their way to the white cloth as the table shook from her efforts to rise.

"Aunt Margaret, stunning, as always," Cadmus said, pulling her into an embrace that was much tighter than intended. She held on a second longer, whispering in his ear, "It's going to be fine. I promise you."

She turned to Robert, and Cadmus knew she was fighting the urge to wrap him in one of her signature hugs, knowing his reservations to meet at such a high society place with his boyfriend.

Smiling, she extended her diamond-clad hand and in her most genteel, Southern drawl whispered, "It is an absolute pleasure to meet the man who has made my godson so very, very happy." And with a wink, they took a seat, Margaret gesturing the waiter to bring two more martinis.

Cadmus wanted Aunt Margaret to meet Robert. He regarded her as Ilona's proxy; she was someone who had loved his mother for who she was and who accepted him unconditionally. He also knew the lunch would be a hit; the martinis that oiled the conversation certainly made it livelier than he predicted. And while he was eager for the introduction, he knew another outcome: His mother would be brought to light.

His guilt over Ilona acted as an undercurrent, always present but taking full force when he least expected. Enjoying a lively class discussion; holding Robert as they talked about what a union would look like given their circumstances; watching the sunrise from the garden bench as the rose petals opened to the warmth of the sky: These were the kinds of moments his mother had been destined to enjoy for many more years had he not vulgarly rebuked her.

"Now, are you planning on introducing Robert here to Callista?" Margaret asked, nibbling on her olive.

"Margaret, you know she is not open to our *lifestyle*, as she calls it," Cadmus replied, his fingers in air quotes.

"Yes, well, I didn't say it would happen. I just asked if you planned on it . . . at least to offer. Cadmus, trust me . . . time will give the paddle to fit her fanny!"

"Margaret, if I were a straight man, I would be after you in a heartbeat!" Robert chuckled, taking the last sip of his martini.

"And I would gladly accept your advances, handsome and smart as you are," she retorted before continuing. "But in all seriousness, Robert, Ilona would have given you the stamp of approval. She was the dearest, kindest soul I have ever known. I am sure Cadmus has told you."

"He hasn't said much at all," Robert replied, challenging Cadmus from across the table.

"In due time," Cadmus said, motioning for another round of drinks.

"Now, I highly recommend the calamari. Can't find anything like it in Houston," Margaret said working to diffuse the building tension.

"What a fine idea, Margaret," Robert said. "We are always ready for new things, isn't that right?"

"Be careful when you speak of new things. See that couple over there?" Cadmus and Robert glanced across the room at the corner table to see a young woman draping her arms over a man old enough to be her grandfather.

"Well, that is the third woman he has brought here this week. You should have seen the one from Monday night," Margaret entertained, taking another sip. "I'm dead serious. Ask the waiter."

"No, we do not need confirmation on that one," Cadmus assured.

"Look, my point is that your love story will not be a big deal one day. Too many other salacious happenings in this town. Mark my words: One day, you two will celebrate your union publicly and with approval!"

"I'll toast to that!" Robert said, the alcohol affording him the confidence to give Cadmus a wink at the swankiest place in town.

CADMUS FOUND HIMSELF IN HIS usual routine late that night, puttering around and making a pitiful attempt to write at his father's desk. As the clock struck a quarter past two, he returned to the bathroom for aspirin, cursing himself for ordering a third round of martinis. His low tolerance for alcohol served as another reminder of his deficiency as a Doyle.

Returning to the library, he grabbed his latest purchase from the bookstore, hoping the prose would carry him far from his worries. Regret, his companion for eleven years, remained steadfast by his side. He struggled to understand how it could manifest so acutely, even to the point of feeling his heart piercing—his thoughts of his row with Ilona center stage in his mind.

He heard the creaking of the stairs and opened the book, making the best attempt to disguise his night as an ordinary bout of insomnia. Robert walked up behind him, and placing his hand on Cadmus' shoulder, said, "Tell me the story of Patrick and Ilona."

The two men sat side by side, their reflections in the bay window stark against the night sky. Cadmus told the story as he knew it and as it had been told to him, from the day his parents met at the Merchants and Manufacturers Building to their Roman Catholic wedding in The Heights. He described his father's magnetism, how it attracted good fortune but also caused his ultimate demise, his imagined vision of his father's bloody, lifeless body wedged in the car that crashed into an oak tree along Montrose Boulevard in his attempt to race back to The Doyle House to reclaim his life with Ilona.

For the first time in his life, Cadmus spoke the words that his father's death freed him from a life he knew he could not have lived, and although he knew this truth when he was but a child, it did not impede the overwhelming rage he felt the evening he learned of his mother's actions that severed all business ties with the company. He now knew Uncle Michael's characterization that "she jumped at the opportunity to offer your shares" was inaccurate given her modest life as a widow.

He had already known his uncle was untrustworthy given the attempted rape and whatever had happened at Callista's engagement; he should have known better than to believe his sister. Although he had tried to convince her of Michael's intentions, she was already too entrenched in their way of life to see things differently. Callista remained scornful of her father's promiscuity, her mother's actions, and Cadmus' sexuality. Michael's side gave

her the image she wanted, and without a father, he became a natural sub-
stitution. He did not really know his nieces and nephew, although he sent
birthday and holiday cards in good faith.

He talked about his Greek cousins, now owners of a successful restaurant chain that spanned the city. They were polite when they saw him,
which was not very often, seeing that his childhood was spent largely in The
Heights, his mother cocooned in regret while he poured over his studies.

"Regret is part of the Doyle inheritance," he said with a rueful chuckle as
the early dawn broke the night sky, dissolving their images from the window
as he concluded with the last words he ever said to his mother, the words he
believed shattered her heart, ushering her ultimate demise. Ilona was never
more than a thought away anywhere and at any moment, and his desperate
hope would always be to see her but once more to make amends.

After several minutes in silence, Robert reached for his hand. They
walked outside to the rose garden, making their way throughout the
grounds. Cadmus, visibly exhausted from lack of sleep and shaken from
sharing his story, stared Robert in the face, half expecting him to get the
hell away from someone so broken. Robert caressed his cheek, and in a soft
tone markedly different from his accustomed demeanor, he told Cadmus he
wanted to spend the rest of his life with him.

CADMUS LOOKED UP AT ROBERT with a coy smile as he made
his way up the stairs to the third-floor landing, carrying three precari-
ously stacked boxes, the last of Robert's supplies for his new studio in The
Doyle House. He scanned the attic walls, knowing the light was perfect
for his husband's work. It was a bigger space than Robert had thought,
especially after Ilona's garment boxes had been removed. It did not take
much convincing, but Cadmus had to work harder than he had originally

thought when he initially suggested The Doyle House become their permanent residence.

"We can be ourselves here," Robert would repeat when they debated neighborhoods. And it was true. Montrose was a burgeoning community of artists, writers, gays, and activists. Although they were two gay men, they were remarkably boring by the neighborhood standards—an attorney and a professor. Their simple desire to hold hands over coffee was not worth noting compared to the homeless misfits and drag queens who filled the streets.

Montrose was a sign that the times were changing for the gay community, but Cadmus remained anchored to his history. Leaving would mean abandoning the place his family's souls had entered and exited earth's plane, and as such Cadmus chose The Heights despite its decline and its reputation as a dumpy neighborhood. Many historic homes had been razed because of dwindling funds and lack of interest in their upkeep, as prosperous families had moved west long ago. The Doyle House stood strong, roses cascading throughout the grounds with abundant funds that allowed them to create a fortress amid the shabbiness.

Although Cadmus was adamant about The Heights over Montrose, he had a difficult time making room for his husband. It had not occurred to him that they would take his parents' room; his face held a vacant stare when Robert suggested new bedroom furniture. They moved most of Ilona's belongings to the garage apartment, which was evolving into a makeshift shrine. Robert attempted to convince him to give the things away and start fresh, but he stopped short when he saw a flash in Cadmus' eyes.

"I'm sorry," Robert said, pulling him into an embrace. "Too much, too soon. At least consider paying Callista a call, or perhaps write her a letter. She may very well want some of your mother's belongings. Lord knows she has room for it. And don't you think she might be a little curious to know her little brother is in love?"

Cadmus vacillated on whether to contact Callista, a pit developing in his stomach at the thought of hearing her voice. They spoke twice per year on their birthdays. Even Christmas had been relegated to a card since her family traveled so often. Callista's greeting always arrived on extra heavy cardstock embossed in gold and silver. The phone calls were obligatory contacts, and they never met in person, although they lived only a few miles from one another. A quick, formal phone call with the same standard exchange: "And I do hope you are still working on your own writing? You are a keen observer, Caddie. I know you have more to share with the world." Well intended, but he found her comments infantilizing.

Callista had the dark locks of her mother, but her Irish ancestry shone through her sharp, green eyes. Her efforts after graduation from Heights High School to reintegrate herself into Houston society resulted in enormous success. She continued to invoke The Doyle House as a reference that she was worthy, a descendant of a prominent Houston family, deserved of her place in River Oaks.

One afternoon, Cadmus decided to place the call. He looked out the window at the intersection, remembering the streetcar that had run by his home so long ago. He forced himself to conjure a good memory of Callista, one that heralded her as a kind soul who did not seek to ingratiate herself to a better standing.

He recalled the sound of the strokes of the grandfather clock echoing through the stillness of the house, the aroma from the funeral flowers turning rancid, petals falling to the hardwoods. His mother sat in the library, draped in a blanket and staring out the window toward the garden.

"Here you go, Mrs. Doyle, fresh cup of Earl Grey tea, just as you like it." Dear Ernestine said as she placed the teacup and saucer next to Ilona on the end table. "Afternoon sun sure is rising. Let me lower the drapes a bit."

Cadmus made his way to the sitting room, where he found Callista reading a book. She looked at him, her eyes swollen from crying, and motioned for him to join her on the sofa. He rested next to her, placing his head on her thigh and his thumb in his mouth. She ran her fingers through his hair and caressed his back.

"Why does Dear Ernestine do that? Why does she keeping bringing Mommy tea she won't drink?"

"Hope. Because she hopes she will drink it, just as she hoped she would get out of bed, and she finally did. Dear Ernestine is trying to make things normal for us again."

"Normal?" Cadmus wondered, almost rhetorically, as he returned his thumb to his mouth.

"We must figure it out, together," whispered Callista, stifling her tears and assuming a brave front. "It will be fine. We will be fine. We will find our way, Caddie, you and I."

With this memory fresh in his mind, he picked up the phone and quickly dialed her number.

"Good afternoon, Dunn Residence."

"Yes, good afternoon. May I please speak with Callista Dunn?"

"May I ask who is calling?"

"Cadmus Doyle."

"One moment, please."

A good minute passed, and Cadmus wondered if the call disconnected.

"I'm sorry, but Mrs. Dunn cannot come to the phone. She will call you at her earliest convenience."

Cadmus hung up the phone and looked out the window to the rose garden as Robert entered the library with a box full of records.

"Well?"

"I think it's safe to say she's not interested," Cadmus replied, eyes intent on the garden.

DELPHINA

Summer 1978

THE STOPLIGHT CONTRASTED AGAINST THE early dawn sky, and Delphina wondered why her daddy obeyed the red signal knowing there was not another car in sight. She wondered if he already missed Granger, the shadow over his eyes visible in the dim light peering from the dashboard of the car.

"Houston, here we come!" her momma squealed as the light turned green, and Delphina fell back into slumber, wrapped in her blanket as her heavy eyes watched a star in the violet sky. She said a prayer that Houston would make her feel better, and she hoped that in the new city she could reinvent herself and not be known as the odd kid. Closing her eyes, Delphina dreamed of the life she was leaving behind, images of her skipping through the countryside and twirling with her head toward the heavens.

She jolted awake as their car hugged the edge of downtown, mid-morning sunlight showcasing the buildings, her attention drawn to the one closest to the interstate. It was not very tall as it was long, the countless number of windows framing her new city. They continued heading east, making their way to the industrial end of town. As Benny exited I-10, Delphina sat upright in her seat, watching the shopping centers give way to the newly planted trees that lined the neighborhood.

Their car inched along the street, Delphina taking note of the homes that dotted the way, so new compared to their old home in the country. Her momma stepped out of the car with a stretch, her legs stiff from the long drive. She looked across the street to see a neighbor kneeling down next to her flowerbed.

Patricia grabbed her pocketbook from the front seat, offering a "Wish me luck. I can't remember the last time I met a new friend."

"And you had plenty of friends back home," Benny teased as he removed his sunglasses, shaking his head with a rueful chuckle.

Delphina hopped out of the car, and taking her mother's hand, the two walked across the curbed street, a feature she had never given much thought.

"Good afternoon! We are your new neighbors. I'm Patricia, and this here is Delphina."

"Why, hello!" the blonde lady bellowed as she removed her soiled gardening gloves to offer a greeting. "It's nice to meet our new neighbors from Granger. I'm Bea."

"Now how did you know we were from Granger?" Patricia asked in surprise, offering her hand.

"I guess you could say our block is a small town of its own," Bea replied with a smile. "I'm known as the Queen Bea for a reason, I suppose! Pardon my hands—they are quite rough from all this weeding."

"Then I have something for you to try." Patricia replied with an eagerness to impress. "A little aloe vera does wonders."

Patricia handed her a small tube along with a most delicate handkerchief, the lilac cursive letter *P* discretely embroidered in the corner. Bea's attempts to dissuade her from soiling her beautiful handkerchief were for naught, as Patricia dished about the time she scored them at Battlestein's after-Christmas sale. Never able to keep a good deal secret, Patricia prattled on about the unbelievable price of the wicker bag she had in tow and how, "Yes, the style is from last season, but the lining is ever-so-delicate, and wicker bags, you know, are a staple after all."

Patricia charmed Queen Bea. She saw in Patricia what Benny noticed when he became smitten in high school, a time when the world seemed full of possibilities. She inspired him to believe they could move to Houston from Granger and harness the course of their lives. Her heartfelt belief, expressed in a tone and countenance of her fictional Jeanie, convinced them to dream that their newfound work, her as a secretary at the Maxwell Coffee Plant and his as a foreman at Arco, would take their lives in exciting new directions.

"Please join us for supper tonight," Bea offered as she then turned to Delphina. "My daughter, Stacy, will be so excited to have a friend her age who lives right across the street!"

DELPHINA'S LOVE AFFAIR WITH THE divine began when she noted the perfectly appointed seeds of a strawberry, a reprieve from the anxiety that never abated despite the move to Houston. She examined her snack carefully that day during first grade, where Mrs. Wallace had been unable to suppress frustration with Delphina's tendency to become fully engrossed in examining objects, from fruit to leaves to the designs that created a faux mosaic formation on the girls' bathroom tile.

"Delphina, focus! You should eat your food, not stare at it."

"But there is a pattern in things, Mrs. Wallace. Her apple has a star in the middle," Delphina protested, pointing at Kim.

Kim rolled her eyes, tossed her silky straight blonde hair, and took another bite of the apple, its juice spraying across her white velour unicorn blouse. It was a small victory for the unkind gesture that Kim directed toward Delphina, the tallest soul in the class with the odd name, frizzy hair, and warm hands. Delphina longed to be like the others: tiny girls who had nice, simple names like Kim and Amy, girls who had cold hands to mark their delicateness when you linked hands to play Ring Around the Rosie. But she was Delphina, Deli as her parents sometimes called her, the girl who spent recess alone studying the trees while the others jumped rope to chants about love, marriage, and children.

Delphina returned to her study of the strawberry—seeds, delicately positioned, each one resting with an intention that quietly spoke of the order of the universe. Everything had an intention, a purpose, a pattern. The seagulls that flew in formation along the shoreline, with each bird departing the front of the line one-by-one to take up the end; the symmetrical markings on a blue jay's wings; the blood that circulated through the body in an elaborate system of veins—how could anyone think of playing games or memorizing spelling lists when such amazing things existed?

"I'M SERIOUS, PATRICIA," BENNY SAID, TAKING a sip of coffee and watching his wife flatten the sausage patties with the spatula. "Worried 'bout her."

"Lord, Benny, the girl's fine. Bea said it's normal. Her kids get scared at night, too," Patricia replied, jiggling the spatula underneath the sausage patties to flip them to the other side.

"Now don't go tellin' Bea our business! Whole damn block'll know."

"So what if she sneaks into our room late at night to sleep? Before too long, she won't want anything to do with us. Might as well enjoy it."

"Patricia, last night I found her at the foot of our bed in a ball. Weepin' in her sleep with a hand grippin' my ankle," Benny said.

Delphina heard her momma rest the spatula on the countertop with a sigh. She hoped her momma believed him now. Perhaps she would finally think about it.

"What should we do?" she asked.

"I already done did somethin'. Stopped by the school on Monday."

"Benny! Without me? And you didn't even tell me!"

"Graveyard shift made it easier. Woke up around noon thinkin' 'bout it and decided then and there to talk to her teacher."

Delphina's stomach parachuted from the sky. She loved that her daddy wanted to help her—she wanted help, too. If only she could put her anxiety into words.

"What did she say?" Patricia asked, her chair screeching across the linoleum as she took a seat at the kitchenette table.

"That she's a kind young lady, smart as a whip, always thinkin' and askin' questions."

"And?"

"And . . . she's a bit of a lost soul," he replied. "At recess, she wanders around the yard rather than playin' with the other kids. Has a collection in her desk of rocks, snail shells, things like that . . . things from the school yard."

"She has those things on one of the shelves in her closet, too," Patricia acquiesced in a soft voice, stirring in another Sweet'n Low.

"Teacher said Delphina says those things show her God is real and everything'll be okay," Benny said, the final word choking from his mouth.

Knowing her momma would soon call her for breakfast, Delphina tiptoed back to her room so she would be ready to sashay into the kitchen as if she had not heard a word. She walked into her closet to admire her collection, taking special care to line up the rock she had found yesterday. It was so gray it looked purple, and as she began to wonder how it came to be like that, she heard her momma calling her.

"Hey, Lil' D," her daddy greeted as she bounced into the room. He lifted her into his lap. "How'd ya sleep?"

"Okay, I guess," Delphina lied, knowing full well she tossed and turned much of the night.

"Your momma and I were thinkin' it might be nice to drive on down to Galveston Saturday. Weather's good, and maybe we can stop and get ice cream at that fancy place on The Strand."

Delphina squeezed her daddy, burying her head in his shoulder to hide her watering eyes. And although she doubted ice cream would do the trick, she hugged him so tightly he uttered, "Hey, Lil' D, watch it there! Your daddy ain't no spring chicken!"

THE DRIVE TO GALVESTON WAS quiet, marked as their time together usually was with all three of them lost in thought. It was not difficult to surmise her momma's musings, seeing that she narrated her inner voice aloud every now and then while thumbing through magazines. Delphina knew she shared more of her daddy's soul, even if it was only out of their shared reticence. He focused on the drive, window rolled down with his left hand resting on the top, and only breaking his concentration to turn over the Don Williams cassette. Delphina rolled down her window, too, enjoying how the wind whipped up her hair to tickle her face as they made their way to the Gulf of Mexico.

Delphina looked out to the horizon as her father maneuvered a parallel park along the seawall. Her view looked like a painting, intense cerulean meeting Spanish blue at the horizon. She thought of how her art teacher, Miss Levey, spoke of colors as a collection.

"There is a gradient of hues," Miss Levey had said.

On that particular day, a boy in back moaned, "Blue is blue!" Delphina shushed him, charmed at the idea and wanting to learn the shades.

Miss Levey, undaunted and with a cryptic smile, retorted, "Hmmm? Blue is blue? Challenge accepted!"

Spanish, cerulean, indigo, navy, cobalt, periwinkle, sapphire, turquoise, sky: By the end of the next six weeks, Miss Levey's room looked like a sanctuary for celestial objects; drawings and paintings covering every conceivable place on the wall. It left Delphina's mind swirling, as she studied the colors she found and then sought their correlating spot on the wheel, demanding to know if they each had a unique name.

Delphina ran into the art room one day to find the walls bare, the sight like a punch to the stomach. Miss Levey, on a stepladder with a chalked azure Neptune in hand, turned to her at the door. Noting the shock in Delphina's face, she smiled brightly with the proclamation, "It's time for green!"

"C'mon, Deli! Now where'd your mind go?" her daddy teased, opening the car door and bringing Delphina back from her daydream.

"The horizon is beautiful. Cerulean meets Spanish!"

"And I see brown water on the shore. But I still love my Galveston," her momma added as she gathered her oversized straw bag, loaded with towels and magazines, and headed down the stone stairs to the beach.

After nestling the lawn chairs and settling the blanket over their patch of sand, Benny said, "We'll be right back, Patricia." With a wink in his eye, he held his daughter's hand and took her to the souvenir store on the seawall.

"Let's buy you a tube. Then I can take you far out into the water," her daddy suggested, pointing to whimsical tubes shaped like animals.

"What about a shovel and bucket set instead?" Her tone meek, she did not want to appear ungrateful, knowing money was tight. She set her gaze on the sifter, imagining how many discoveries would come into view as the granules of sand made their way back to earth.

"I say, let's take 'em both!" Benny cheered, his eyes lit up in a rare moment of levity. "And I say we buy the Dolphin! Sounds like my Delphina!"

Benny and Delphina made their way into the water, waves lapping against their ankles before splashing on their legs, signaling it was time to lift her onto the Dolphin tube.

"I'm scared, Daddy!" Delphina cried, turning back to see her momma becoming smaller and smaller in the lawn chair on the sand.

"Be strong, Lil' D," he said, his voice soothing and commanding all at once.

"It's too rough!" Delphina protested.

"Just you wait an' see," he replied. And then pausing to look her square in the eye, "Trust me."

As Benny shepherded her tube over the choppy waves, Delphina gripped the smiling dolphin's head, praying for the time to pass. She opened her eyes a minute later to calm water lapping through the middle. It gave her the courage to raise her gaze to the horizon where the cerulean met the Spanish, the scent of new plastic a contrast to the drops of salt water dotted along her lip. Her heart settled in the understanding that she was past the rough waters and now part of the peace she admired from the seawall.

"There's gonna be tough times, Delphina. And there's an awful lot to get scared of in this world. But you're part of somethin' much bigger. And that part, well, that part is real good," her daddy told her.

Delphina wondered what the seagulls flying above thought of her and her daddy—two souls floating in the Gulf, yearning to ebb back into the world from which they came.

That night after her bath, Delphina washed the shells she found along the shore. With her sun-kissed hands, she intentionally placed them among her other treasures. She pulled her pillow and blanket to the closet and fell asleep, taking delight in her shrine, illuminated in the soft glow of her nightlight.

CADMUS

Autumn 1982

"I NEED TO DANCE WITH my demons today, brown eyes," Robert said as he entered the kitchen to find Cadmus pouring himself a cup of coffee. Cadmus did not turn around to face Robert but nodded his head in understanding. Silence filled the space between them, and Cadmus turned, wondering if Robert was still in the room.

"Want to join me?" Robert asked.

"Join you? You sure? You usually . . ."

"Yes, well, perhaps I need to get over the whole alone thing," Robert interrupted. "Just be merciful in your judgment, please. Not all of us came from good stock."

"Are you referencing the good stock that cut me from Doyle Lumber & Construction and continues to disown me because I am . . . what is it they say . . . a faggot?" Cadmus retorted in his most academic tone as he stirred cream into his coffee.

"Hell, you know mine fucked me over. But at least yours were decent enough to provide something for you to forge a goddamn life of your own! I thank the Good Lord every day for blessing me with a good mind, but there are days I'm still pissed I grew up getting beaten in that trailer park." Quivering, Robert's voice retreated to a whisper, "At least you have your name, as shitty as it really is."

Cadmus quickly made his way around the kitchen table, never intending his cheeky response to be taken in such a way. He enveloped Robert in his arms. He had yet to meet a gay man who did not have demons, and despite Robert's well-earned success, Cadmus knew that his husband felt like a fraud on bad days. Had Robert not been gay and not been so smart, he probably would exist as his father and brothers did—in and out of work and drinking at the local watering hole. People from the trailer park came in and out of Robert's life. They were a revolving lot of stories, each person hoping that the latest trailer imprint would be the antidote for their restlessness.

"You better grab a jacket. I'm keeping the top down the entire time," Robert said with a wink, breaking free from his husband's arms as he turned to head to their bedroom to get ready for their drive. "The Pasadena air will be good for you . . . toughen you up."

Cadmus had a general idea of where Robert went on his drives. Robert had taken him on a tour of the part of town where he grew up a few months after they began dating.

"I clean up pretty well. And I want you to see where I came from, need you to see it. Then, perhaps, you will understand why I am so damned determined to take action and do something."

Cadmus had never been back after that first time. Once or twice per year, Robert would look at him with sorrowful eyes coated in a slight veil of tears, a signal that he needed time alone to indulge in a good cry and a few good shouts of furor, followed by quiet time to collect himself and draw upon the well of acceptance that he had so carefully nourished over the years. Robert demurred from Cadmus' offers to join him, and while Cadmus never doubted his fidelity, he was usually left feeling somewhat bereft by the omission.

He asked Robert to drive down Harrisburg on his way east, turning onto Broadway and then Lawndale. They stopped at Lawndale Café for a late breakfast, knowing it had changed ownership but appreciating it the same nonetheless. They sopped runny eggs and grits with white bread, doing their best to look like chums rather than spouses. Cadmus casually gave Robert his last slice of bacon, knowing he had been eyeing it on his plate. Cadmus rarely allowed bacon in the house, because Robert's family had a history of heart disease. No telling how much Robert would have weighed now had he not left his life in the trailer park.

Preservation instincts kicked in at certain times and places, which restrained Cadmus from his desire to reach for Robert's hand. He waved his hand for the check before excusing himself to the men's room, knowing he had to get hold of his emotions, his unresolved feelings over Ilona creeping into his heart. This day belonged to Robert; it was his day to reflect and mourn.

People often talked about giving others their time in the sun to enjoy the spotlight. Cadmus extended this thinking to suffering. Expressions of sympathy too often turned to the person expressing the feeling of consolation: well intended but denying the person in pain his right to self-expression. Both Cadmus and Robert knew how the day would end—an acceptance of how things came to be with a healthy dose of gratitude. What could have been was Robert never escaping the cycle of poverty in the trailer park and Cadmus doing a piss-poor job at the reins of Doyle Lumber & Construction, which would probably have gone out of business. What could have been was that they were born straight men, who may not have fallen so deeply in love with women as they had with one another. They could have lived a lie, hiding who they were to appease others, whether it was their family, society, or church. How life came to be was quite nice given the circumstances and the artificial rules of society.

As Cadmus washed his hands, turning the heavy, worn knobs, he wondered how this restaurant continued to pass inspection. The glimpses he caught of the kitchen when the doors swung open revealed a sea-green tile coated in film, prompting him to wonder if it had been cleaned since the day his grandparents died.

He had only seen his mother as a Doyle, at least in terms of status, thoughtfully made up and elegantly dressed, but she possessed a spark, an honest, humble way that drew others to her. He could imagine her donning an apron, taking orders, and checking on customers with the same grace she had held at social events.

Despite the conditions, there was still a charm to Lawndale, the ghosts of his family giving warmth through the scents of coffee and butter saturated into the walls. He offered a prayer to his grandparents, remembering how they suffered from strokes less than a year apart, most people attributing it to broken hearts over losing two children before their time. By the end of the sixties, Arianna had been the sole survivor of their Petrarkis strand. Cadmus had never been close to her. He knew his money made her uncomfortable, but his sexuality solidified the barrier.

It did not surprise Cadmus that he did not recognize the lady at the register, seeing that his visits to the café were few and far between. She must have been in her early twenties, raven-stained hair lacquered in wings. The anonymity proffered latitude for conversation, a chance to satisfy a curiosity. Robert went to start the car, while Cadmus stood in line at the register. When his turn came, he casually pointed to the framed black-and-white photograph of his grandfather and uncle, arms crossed with wide smiles, as if they had just conquered the world.

"Was that the original owner?" he asked, taking his wallet from his back pocket.

"Huh?" she said, turning away from him to see what he was pointing at. "Yeah. I think so. I don't really know."

"Are the current owners here?" he continued, counting out the bills.

Clearly annoyed at this point, she replied, "Does it look like they are here? I mean, why would they come to this dump?"

Cadmus looked at her in disbelief. In the handful of exchanges he had initiated over the years, this one was certainly the wild card.

"No offense, mister. I just work here." Cadmus nodded, taking the quarter that rolled down from the register to the change dish.

As Robert pulled his Mercedes away from the diner, Cadmus reflected on what his mother gave up in raising her children as Doyles, so engrossed in her marriage and children. It was not until after she died that Dear Ernestine confirmed the immense guilt Ilona carried for leaving his father that night, continuing to hold herself responsible for his death until it was her time. He did not realize her guilt overshadowed her anger over the affair. His mother had hopped right over that stage of the grieving process.

"She's free now, Caddie . . . she's free from it all . . . she's with your daddy now," he recalled Dear Ernestine weeping into his ear, squeezing him in a tight embrace at the funeral reception, both of them still in shock over her death, the visual image of her body splayed in the rose garden. Anchor, sanctuary, shackle: metaphors swirled through his mind regarding his mother and The Doyle House. She carried her suffering with grace and nobility for so much of her life. Waves of nausea rushed over him when he thought that he was the one who ultimately broke the fragile peace she had carefully assembled.

As they drove into Robert's world, billows of smoke from the refineries clouded the zinc-colored sky. Cadmus looked over at his husband, hair ruffling with eyes zeroed in on the freeway as they continued east.

ROBERT TAUGHT CADMUS A GREAT many things during their first nine years together: love, connection, the power of choice, fighting to create your own narrative, all tenets for a more fulfilling life. On a more superficial level, or not, Cadmus thanked Robert for the introduction to The Carlyle, a place that exuded the romance and elegance his parents had shared during their early days together.

Scoring the tickets to *Cats* was a feat in itself for Robert, considering its popularity. Cadmus remained somewhat befuddled even though he was familiar with the inspiration from T. S. Eliot, his attempts to envision humans in cat costumes traipsing the stage giving him pause.

"Hell, let's see what the hype is about," Robert shrugged as he sat at the library desk, phone in hand while he remained on hold with hotel reservations. "And at least we can count on Bobby Short as a sure thing."

And right he was about hearing Bobby play at The Carlyle—his belting of Cole Porter's songs swept Cadmus into a lovely nostalgia, with fashioned images of his parents tucked into a far corner, his father kissing his mother's hand. He did not remember his parents as having a happy marriage, and given Ilona's proclivity toward idealism, he wondered if times had ever been what she said they once were.

"We shared a beautiful romance, your father and I." Never including other details to substantiate her claim, she asserted this simple sentence, on occasion tacking on "at one time" a second or two later.

Cadmus knew that he and Robert shared the beautiful romance his mother said she once had. Not wanting the evening to end, they enjoyed another drink in The Gallery, the anonymity of the city affording them the luxury of sitting closer than they normally would in public.

"You can let us out here," Robert said to the cab driver the following evening, the traffic near the Winter Garden Theatre backing up several blocks.

"Well, based on the crowds, it must be something to see," Cadmus said as they headed down Broadway.

"What kind of gay man are you? Not liking musicals," Robert teased.

"Yes, right when the dialog gets going, everyone trumpets out snappy lyrics that rhyme. Who the hell talks like that?" Cadmus asked, defending his point.

"No one! It's called entertainment!"

The men inched their way through the throngs of people, balcony tickets granting prompt access once they made it to the door. Cadmus grabbed Robert's shoulder and pointed to the bar, knowing he would enjoy a drink before the show.

"Trust me, let's make it to our seats. You will be able to take it in from there," Robert assured.

The usher escorted them up the stairs, Cadmus wondering the reason

behind her enigmatic smile as she opened the curtain. He smiled and nodded as he entered and saw a bottle of champagne chilling next to their seats.
Robert turned to him, beaming.

"Another feat! How did you manage this one?" Cadmus asked.

"Everything has a price, Cadmus," Robert replied. "And I'm just happy
I'm equipped to pay it at this point in my life."

"I'M SORRY," ROBERT SAID AS they stepped out of the theatre. "If I
had known it would have such an effect on you . . ."

"You what? Wouldn't have suggested it?" Cadmus challenged, an unusual
move for the normally quiet soul. He knew the drinks at Bemelman's before
the show, coupled with the champagne, doused his sorrow. His ability to
make this distinction, however, failed to temper his anger in the moment. It
was as if the alcohol acted as grease to a fire, unleashing a rage.

"You will never understand the magnitude of what I did. If you did, you
would have seen this coming," he said as he walked ahead of Robert toward
Fifty-Second Street.

"Cadmus, you did not kill her!" Robert shouted, gaining the attention
of a few pockets, a group of young women raising their eyebrows as they
whispered into their huddle, one of the women turning back to give Cadmus
a once over.

"Don't you ever speak of it like that again!" Cadmus yelled, resuming his
walk and hailing a cab. "I need to be alone!"

"Yes, I think that is a helluva good idea!" Robert confirmed, turning to
walk in the opposite direction.

The irony was not lost on Cadmus as the cab sped toward uptown. A
part of him wanted to run back to his husband, to say he was sorry for
reacting to him in the same way he had reacted toward Ilona, the same way

his mother had acted toward his father on the night he died, but Cadmus' need for solitude remained. He wanted time to file through his memories. He periodically engaged in a chronological review of the collection, partly because he feared losing them over time.

The past nineteen years had not necessarily brought healing; the particles settled, but they became agitated from time to time. This evening, however, as he thought about the storyline, with the lyrics and melody from "Memory" circling through his mind, the usual undercurrent morphed into a riptide.

The cab dropped him off at the Madison Avenue door, and for a brief moment, he considered meandering the streets along the Upper East Side. The music beckoned him into the hotel, sending him a message that it was where he was meant to be.

He found one empty table in The Gallery and found himself ordering another martini, wanting to retain the fog. He thought about the cat Grizabella, how the others shunned her when she left the tribe, only to be chosen as the one to be reborn. Michael and Callista had certainly shunned Ilona, as did the women at Holy Family after she confronted their unkind remarks. While his grandparents and Arianna had not disowned her, he knew there was a strain because of her choice to marry his father, the differences like two diverging branches on a tree. They remained connected by their roots.

He spent vast amounts of time contemplating life after death, and while he missed parts of Catholicism, he left the religion shortly after Ilona's death. Aside from the teachings on homosexuality, Cadmus knowing without a doubt that a loving God would not punish him for being what He created, he could not reconcile the idea that choices stemming from free will could sentence someone to eternal damnation. He conceded that some choices are easier to judge, but the complexity behind the average person, the composite of the soul, coupled with life's circumstances beyond the individual's control, spoke to another truth, one that permitted essences to give life another whirl with lessons learned and lessons in need of a reteach.

As much as he wanted to see Ilona again, he believed more than not that this time would never come in the literal way for which he longed; that his father and mother were in the cycle of rebirth, in synchronization with the universe; and that the best possibility would be for him to cross paths with her soul, her essence, in one of his lifetimes. He just hoped he would recognize her.

As Cadmus made his way to the hotel room, the elevator operator nodded a *good evening*, reminding him of his days in the Esperson. He accepted it as a sign to extend his intention to cross paths with his father, as well. He knew Patrick was not in hell.

The hotel room door opened as he fumbled with the key. Robert stood with one hand on his hip, tension registered across his forehead.

"I'm sorry," Cadmus whispered.

"Good. And don't ever fuck with me like that again," Robert replied, opening the door wider for Cadmus to enter their room.

"I'LL BE BACK IN A few hours," Robert said.

"Where are you going?"

"Where am I going? Are you still drunk?"

"That's right," Cadmus muttered, raising his hand to his throbbing temple. "Your meeting. Good luck."

"Sleep it off. Before we met, I was often where you are now."

Cadmus sat up in bed, unable to fall back asleep, memories from the previous night acting as an encore. Rubbing his forehead, he struggled to understand how his father drank as often as he had. Cadmus pulled on his clothes from the previous night and headed across the street to Zitomer's pharmacy.

Ella Fitzgerald played softly from the dining room when he returned with the aspirin. He figured he did not look as bad as he felt, his expensive suit pants and jacket only slightly wrinkled. He stepped into the hotel restaurant for coffee, a white-jacketed attendant pulling out the table so he could sit on the sofa side. Aside from last night's debacle, Cadmus loved the hotel's charm that echoed elegance from long ago.

The storyline and that *damned song*, what he later dubbed the tune, would have taken him on a journey, but the alcohol had tilted the balance of his nostalgia into a haunting, a thin veil separating the two. Had he a stronger propensity for the drink, he would certainly have made a mess of his life after Ilona. It made him sympathetic toward his father, and he wondered how the affair plagued him in those dark moments, as Patrick's drinking had intensified in the months before his death.

As much as he wanted to stay, he headed to the room to sleep; he owed Robert a good recovery. They had dinner reservations at Tavern on the Green, and while Cadmus was eager to try it, a part of him did not want to leave the hotel. He would not mention this. He knew Robert wanted to dine there, and he owed him for ruining last evening.

Cadmus drifted off to sleep, sending a prayer that his mother had been reborn into a life that brought her happiness, a life that one day might intersect with his own.

DELPHINA

Autumn 1982

DELPHINA WONDERED WHY JESUS HAD to die for peoples' sins; the notion that original sin moored her to doom left her no less than baffled. During preparations for First Holy Communion, she was sickened to learn that she would consume the Body of Christ. She had always thought it was a symbol, and even after several Sundays of volleying questions at Mrs. White, her catechism teacher, she was no more convinced of transubstantiation than before.

The thought of consuming flesh further imbalanced the scales of her nocturnal anxieties, and not even the white frilly communion dress with a faux pearl necklace could soothe her anxiety at the thought of eating a body. She conceded that, if it were true, then she would crawl to the altar in absolute respect to receive the Body of Christ. Eyes widened, her momma ordered her to her room. She overheard her pick up the phone in a panic, punching the numbers on the receiver.

"I don't understand it, either, Mother. She is taking things too literally!"

It was unfathomable that they were not as bothered as she was.

Her momma did not have a response when Delphina referenced the choir ladies in her attempt to discredit the sanctity of the sacrament. The ladies smirked at Mrs. Martin, a recently divorced mother of three who unfortunately wore garish clothing as she embarked on her new single life.

Delphina studied Mrs. Martin's face over the years as Mrs. Martin sat in an adjacent pew, despondently staring forward at the altar, mechanically reciting responsorial psalms, and occasionally dabbing the corner of her eyes with tissue. She remembered Mr. Martin back when they were married and how he shared his wife's sadness, but his possessed an edge, as if he was one moment away from raging.

Delphina was too young to hypothesize much over the situation, but she knew enough to know there was a story. And she knew enough to know the other women were mean. Their lack of humility, their blasé walk to the front of the church for communion as they stared at Mrs. Martin, the overall implausibility of transubstantiation: She knew something was amiss. Delphina made the mistake of bringing up her latest revelations during catechism class. As one of the choir ladies, Delphina's teacher Mrs. White had had enough.

When Father Richard appeared at the classroom door the following Sunday, the students quieted down. When he asked Delphina to take a walk with him, she finally understood what it meant to hear a pin drop. Mrs. White offered Delphina a smug smile as she crossed the room, mouthing an exaggerated "thank you" to Father Richard as he closed the door behind them.

What Father Richard said she could not recall. She remembered him espousing the same basic tenets as Mrs. White, yet he did so with such conviction and displeasure. Coupled with the enormous, bloody crucifix mounted on the wall behind his desk, she struggled to find the ability to speak. Delphina simply nodded in agreement, especially at his conclusion that her disobedient nature would not be fully absolved until she made her First Confession next month. Through contrition, she would escape eternal damnation.

Eternal damnation. Late at night in her bed, Delphina played the odds of its existence in her mind. How could a God who created sand dollars and sea anemones damn her for asking questions? It still did not make sense, but the thought of hell, although remote, terrified her. It was out of this fear that Delphina played the part. She recited a near-perfect Act of Contrition in the confessional, and she placed a holy water receptacle next to her bedroom door, blessing herself with the sign of the cross before heading to school each morning. She welcomed the statues of Jesus and the Virgin Mary her godmother gave her as gifts to mark her First Communion.

The night after Delphina first received the Body of Christ, her momma smiled with relief as she rinsed the forks clean of the gritty icing remnants from the cake shaped like a cross. Delphina lay in bed tightly gripping the plastic Jesus, her eyes transfixed on His loving eyes with His right hand gently placed over His heart. She wished the answer was that black and white, but she knew in her heart that there was a bigger story, one that was known even to her goldfish, Cori.

CADMUS

Spring 1983

"THANKS FOR DROPPING BY TO see me."

"Our Boulevards are not far apart, at least not physically," he teased.

"The Boulevards are not far apart in many areas, including the most important, Cadmus," Margaret replied, uncharacteristically solemn. "We all face the same end."

"The azaleas are beautiful," he said, pushing her wheelchair through the grounds.

"Yes, it's amazing how much money the Azalea Trail raises these days," she said. "Speaking of tours, I do hope one day you will open your home to the Heights Home Tour."

He remained silent, which he figured reflected his unfavorable opinion of her suggestion. They continued their loop around the grounds, with Margaret motioning for her housekeeper as they approached the terrace.

"Annette dear, will you bring us some fresh lemonade?"

They made their way to a spot on the terrace, Cadmus adjusting the umbrella to shield her as she apologized, "I'm sorry I can't summon up a round of mimosas for us, but the medications refuse me even the slightest indulgence. Of course, I can certainly change *your* order with Annette."

"Aunt Margaret, you know that's not necessary."

"I know," she said as he took his seat. Annette came out with a tray of lemonade and petit fours. "I guess it helps remind me of better times. Not that I should complain given the life I've had."

"We do have a lot to be thankful for," he acknowledged, taking a sip of lemonade as he studied the grounds.

"Yes, my children are healthy and happy. Luke and Isabelle have one another in Dallas, so at least there are two strands of Genessees to make their mark, and I am thankful to have Gretchen and Phillip Junior here in Houston, and the grandchildren, of course."

Cadmus nodded in agreement.

"You know, Ilona and Patrick would both be so proud of you, Cadmus."

"Not so sure about my father," he countered.

"Look, I'm not saying it would have been all rainbows and sunshine, but I knew both of your parents very well," Margaret said. "I know Patrick's death showcased his demons, but we all have them. Your father was a good person, Cadmus."

"I realize there are many wonderful things about him that I will never know," Cadmus agreed. "But that does not necessarily equate to acceptance."

"It would have been very difficult for him, yes. But, he would have come around," Margaret defended. "And your mother, well, I have so many friends, but she was the truest."

"I'm thankful to have had such a wonderful mother," Cadmus said, looking down.

"Cadmus, I know what you carry with you, and I am not arrogant enough to believe these words from a dying woman right now will change your mind," Margaret began as Cadmus raised his gaze to meet hers. "But as I check off my to-do list in this final stretch, I need you to understand, my son, that you had nothing to do with her death."

Margaret tried to roll back her chair to move toward him, but her robe became caught in one of the wheels. Cadmus pushed his chair away from the table, circling over to her. She grabbed his hand, motioning him to kneel next to her.

Even without her makeup and diamonds, even though her body was riddled with cancer, she still looked radiant. Her wrinkles fell in all the right places, laugh lines a permanent mark despite her calm face.

"Cadmus," she said, cupping his face between her palms, "it was a total fluke that her aneurysm ruptured the day after your incident. It would have happened even if you had not argued."

"Aunt Margaret, you don't need to do this. You have other, more pressing matters, and I am not one of them."

"Yes, you are, Cadmus. Yes. You. Are," she enunciated, her blue eyes piercing into his. "Forgive yourself. Ilona forgave you long ago."

"Where do you believe our souls go, Aunt Margaret?"

"To find peace, to heal," she said, a gentle smile breaking across her face. "And I do believe your mother is finding it. And I look forward to joining her soon."

"YOU BUSY?"

"Just editing my piece for *The New Yorker*," Cadmus replied, leaning back in his office chair at Rice University.

"Can you break away to join me at the office?" Robert asked.

"Now?" Cadmus replied, checking his watch to confirm what he thought. It was a little after three in the afternoon on a Wednesday, a time Robert's office would be filled with people.

"We won. *I* won."

Cadmus knew it would happen. If any litigator could score the highest settlement in Houston history, it was Robert McClelland. Tears came to his eyes, full of pride and happiness for his husband.

"Congratulations, my love. It would be disingenuous to say I'm surprised."

"The judge rendered the decision not long ago, and all hell broke loose when Mr. MacDougall thrust open the liquor cabinet in the board room. Everyone is well on their way to getting shit-faced."

"And you're inviting me to join you?" Cadmus asked, knowing he had yet to attend an event at the firm.

"Yes, siree, I am. MacDougall slapped me on the back after the call, in awe of the God-almighty dollar signs headin' our way. You'd laugh your ass off if you coulda seen how he hemhawed, not knowin' how to say it," Robert continued, and Cadmus knew he had already enjoyed a few, his trailer park roots coming through with his loosened accent and tongue.

"MacDougall looked from side to side before he startin' whisperin' and shit, '*Um, please invite your friend. It's about time we met The Professor.*' Can you fuckin' believe it? After all this time?"

"I'm on my way," Cadmus replied, his heart full of excitement as he grabbed his sports coat and made his way from the office.

His desire to freshen up dissipated by the time he made his way to the car. Cadmus knew he was well dressed every single day, one of Harold's best customers long before Houston celebrities flocked to the store on Nineteenth Street. He gave thanks for the impromptu nature of the evening. Had he known he would meet Robert's colleagues, he would have spent the day preoccupied.

Cadmus walked confidently through the lobby. He knew this place, had breathed it as a child when he came here with his father. He smiled as he stepped into the elevator, pressing twenty-six and giving a slight bow to the ghosts of the operators from another time.

Champagne corks popped as the elevator doors opened, cheers and squeals wafting from the library and conference room. Cadmus stepped off the elevator, buttoning his sports coat as he cased the floor for his husband. A beautiful woman leaning against the interior staircase noted his arrival. He saw the look in her eye as she made her way toward him. *Lord, here we go again*, he thought to himself as she greeted him.

"Yes, I am looking for the man of the hour, Robert McClelland," Cadmus said with a wink, noting her disappointment as she gestured to the library.

He took a deep breath as he turned the corner into the grand room, his eyes searching for the Irishman who had stolen his heart. Robert met his gaze despite the crowd gathered around him, the new attorneys clamoring for one bit of what he had. His head nodded as Cadmus approached, and Robert placed his arm around his shoulders: Endearing but still casual, it exhibited the right dose of familiarity a gay man should when introducing his husband to others not accustomed to their world.

Robert's allure transferred to Cadmus. His colleagues wanted to know more about his work at Rice University and his publications in the works. Cadmus enjoyed the attention, his own reaction catching him by surprise given his private nature. Mr. MacDougall motioned Robert and Cadmus over to the lobby, and Cadmus wondered what might be next when he saw the gleam in his husband's eye. They followed him into MacDougall's office, where he poured them another glass of champagne.

"Okay, Mr. McClelland. Your wish is granted."

"As I suspected it should be, given today's accomplishment," Robert said with confidence.

Cadmus looked back and forth between both men as they eyed one another, their silent smile one of personal acknowledgment.

"You have fifteen minutes," MacDougall replied, pointing to the office door that now framed a building security guard.

Robert nodded his head toward the door, and Cadmus followed close behind. When he pressed the up button on the elevator, Cadmus realized the extent of the favor Robert had cashed.

Cadmus and his husband circled the cupola, champagne in hand as they took in a 360-degree view of the city.

"I couldn't have done this without you, Cadmus," Robert said.

"This achievement is yours alone, Robert," Cadmus demurred, placing his hand on Robert's arm as the security guard turned away to walk to the other side.

"No. I was shootin' in the dark before I met you, and I admit I had a pretty good aim," Robert acknowledged. "But you gave me purpose. You've shown me how to love." Knowing the security guard was out of sight, they embraced before indulging in a moment's kiss.

"And now for a photograph to rival Patrick and Ilona's!" Robert called as he made his way around the cupola to look for the security guard. "The view is damn pitiful now with all the buildings closing in against it, but I do think it still stands strong on its own."

The security guard took the camera, waiting out Robert's indecision on the angle.

"This is the place," Cadmus said, positioning himself at the northern end. "And please try to capture the University of Houston Downtown, even if it's just a smidge," he said, pointing to the right of the seventy-five-story skyscraper blocking the full view. He and his husband wrapped one arm around the other while toasting their champagne glasses.

As Robert thanked the security guard, Cadmus took a moment to look out on the city. He sent his love to his parents, wondering where their souls had gone.

DELPHINA

Autumn 1986

"PLEASE DON'T WAIT ON ME tonight, sweetheart. You go on over to Stacy's house right after school with the other girls. Bea's expecting you."

"Momma, I want to wait for you," Delphina said.

Patricia inched her car farther along the carpool queue, taking a deep breath and gripping the steering wheel. Delphina geared up for the lecture, staring intently out the window at the students loafing on the perimeter of the school yard and wondering when school had become a drag for so many—so much to learn and so little enthusiasm with which to learn it.

"Delphina, stop being so scared all the time! Nothing bad will happen!" Patricia shouted in frustration, pounding her right fist onto the seat.

"You don't know that!" Delphina yelled back, angry not only at the comment but at the timing.

Mornings marked an easier time of day, spent as she was from a night of tossing and turning, her anxiety hollowed to a shell. It filled again as the day passed, her energy restored and primed to stir the waves of trepidation. She was calm through her morning classes, but as students barreled down the breezeway to the cafeteria at lunchtime, anxiety took root again. And now today, thanks to her momma, her nerves awakened before the opening bell.

"Delphina, you need to live your life. Living in fear is not living at all!" Patricia pleaded as Delphina opened the car door.

"I'll live my life like I want to live it!" Delphina declared as she slammed the car door and ran down the sidewalk to the school.

Delphina rarely slept over at a friend's house, in part because she had few friends. Making her way into the school, she saw Stacy with the other favored girls at the entrance, their huddle cemented by shrill laughter, a cue for others to keep their distance. Just yesterday, Delphina stumbled upon one of them sobbing in the bathroom, lamenting that her friends back-stabbed her over the weekend. Delphina struggled to reconcile how or why that girl would reassume her position in the ring so soon after the drama.

Stacy saw Delphina from the corner of her eye and called out, "I'll see you tonight!" as her clique stared, stupefied by their leader's shout-out.

Delphina offered a tender smile to her secret friend, her beloved neighbor from across the street with whom she shared lazy summer days, stretched out in their backyards and running through the sprinklers to cool off, sipping Mellow Yellow, and reaching down into a bag of Funyuns that rested between their lawn chairs. Crushes, teachers, fashion, friends: Not one teenage topic remained uncovered, the difference between their daydreams and gossip being that they were examined through the lens of rapt, almost-dispassionate observers casing the events of the past school year, attempting to make sense of their middle school world in the hopes of a wiser start for the next. The chimes from the ice cream man's truck served as a subconscious signal that the time for daily philosophizing was drawing to a close, both girls belting out joy as they ran to the street, giddy while they waited behind the little ones, black exhaust from a dilapidated truck hollering at their shins.

Stacy's appreciation of Delphina's wisdom left her with open feelings of envy; she admitted to Delphina that she wished she did not care what people thought. Delphina stayed away when the other cheerleaders paid Stacy a visit during the summer, despite her friend's pleadings to "give them a chance, Deli, really. They will like you once they know you."

Stacy's countenance betrayed her words. They both knew Delphina would not be welcome, but they also both knew their seasonal friendship was more substantive than a school year of football games and passing period gossip. Inviting Delphina, the only one who did not own pom-poms, was a big step for Stacy, but it would be an act of courage for Delphina to leave her home for the night.

Delphina was the first to arrive in her English class, relieved to start the day in a place that gave her space to think. Reading and writing calmed her heart. Mr. Lopez opened the new short story unit with a warm-up: In one page, write a scene of a scary story. Delphina knew it was a good exercise, not only because Halloween was approaching, but also because it captured interest; everyone had a story to share. And although the topic came easily for her, she regretted it was assigned on this day, the already fragile day she had to keep together so she could be in good order for the party.

Ten minutes later, choruses of "Me! Me! Me!" filled the room, and once chosen, the students revealed images of monsters and murders and blood and guts. Mr. Lopez gave them healthy latitude, joining in the fits of laughter as each participant milked his or her story for all it was worth. At the end of the exercise, he paused, noting her in the back corner looking out the window at the sky.

"Delphina, will you share your piece?" he asked. She knew he could count on her to elevate the discourse and draw them back to the lesson.

"The white lights streaming from the windows beckoned me down the opaque, desolate street. The only sound I could hear? Shells crackling beneath my feet. Or were they bones? My feet crumbled the matter beneath me, the cartilage turning from powder to ash as it covered my bare feet.

The muffled shouts became louder as I approached the mansion, screams of terror and breaking glass filling the night air. My eyes raced, but there was not a soul to be found. I tried running to the front door, but the ashes acted as weight, and as I bent down to brush my feet clean, I noticed the particles in movement, swirling around like bugs, anchoring me to the ground.

I tried peering in the windows, but the radiating light blinded me. As my eyes came to, I saw the brown-eyed boy, eyes welled with tears as his arms stretched toward me, begging me to save him. I reached for him, but the ash beneath me turned to quicksand, engulfing me back to the earth as I joined the chorus of screams."

She looked into Mr. Lopez's eyes after reading the last word, his mouth open in surprise.

"Wow, Deli. Now that was even more amazing than I thought it would be!" he praised, the class bursting into a round of applause, the popular boy who never acknowledged her nodding his head in awe. Although the day had many other mishaps in store, she would look back on this experience as the day she earned her place as one of the smart ones, her fictional account a seventh-grade masterpiece. She dared not correct that it was a real nightmare and had been so since before she could remember.

Delphina went through the motions of school that day as she always did, attempting to focus on the tasks at hand to relieve her wandering mind. The 3:00 bell posed another round of challenges for her, because she needed to remain at school as long as she could, lest Bea and Stacy come across the street to look for her.

She nestled into the far corner of the library, ostensibly in the name of research for the history fair. The librarian shooed her out as the clock neared 4:00, leaving Delphina to walk through the halls to find something else to delay her walk home. Seeing the door open to the art room, her good fortune continued at the sight of her art teacher rinsing brushes. He welcomed her offer to help tidy the room.

At 4:30, Delphina began her walk home, estimating she could stretch it to thirty minutes if she took the long route. Her momma left work early on Fridays, and Delphina knew she would be home by the time she arrived. She would walk in the house to find her momma safe and then pack a few things before heading over to Stacy's. Taking a few deep breaths, she offered a prayer to St. Christopher for safe travel for her, her momma, and her daddy. She held doubts as to its effectiveness, but she surmised no harm could come from whispering but a few words to the heavens.

The late-day sun persisted, coloring the air with its autumn palette, knowing it was the penultimate day before the clocks painted early evenings in opacity. Delphina's mind swirled in veneration, giving thanks to the evening star and the pine trees scattered throughout the neighborhood. Her eyes searched for the patches of weeds sprouting from cracks in the road, murmuring, "Life finds a way" at each sighting. Her heart ironed out the wrinkles of anxiety, even more relief coming as she turned the corner onto her street, knowing that she would soon enter her house to see her momma home safe. She would do her best to stall until her daddy was home, but she knew that might be a tough one to manage, seeing that he often met his friends for a beer on Fridays after work.

The rolled newspaper at the foot of the driveway signaled something was amiss. Her watch marked her momma's standard arrival time as thirteen minutes prior, time enough for her to apply her formula: newspaper, mail, and 360-degree scan around the block to see if there was a neighbor to greet.

The equanimity of the walk dissipated as she picked up her gait, nearing the house to look for signs of her momma. Chants of the "Mighty Mustangs" thundered from across the street, prompting Delphina to look to the sky in gratitude that the group was ensconced in Stacy's backyard. She snapped up the stack of mail and newspaper before scurrying through the front door, the stale air inside still saturated with the scent of bacon from breakfast.

In the minute it took her to make it to the thermostat, Delphina's mind had spun an elaborate web of tragedy, from a mugging in the parking lot of the coffee plant to the misfortune of a flat tire during rush hour. She turned on the television, hoping to catch the local news in the event of an accident report on the east freeway. Murders, fires, rapes . . . the reported tragedies overwhelmed her. Her mind returned to her momma's comment from the morning, *Nothing bad will happen.*

"The hell it won't, Momma!" Delphina shouted to the empty house. Eyes filling with tears, she headed to the front window to peek through the curtains for any sight of her momma. She caught a glimpse of red and white pom-poms in Stacy's front yard and retreated to her room to wait.

Opening the door to her closet, she curled in the corner and wept. She wept for the murdered and the victims of arson and rape. She wept for the impending tragedy that would befall her family and for her complicity. Her unkind words to her momma and her slamming of the car door, the disappointment of being an odd daughter—certainly these thoughts were twisting through her momma's mind when the car veered off the road.

Delphina heard neither her momma enter the house nor the band of girls who followed, her sorrow acting as a cloak, isolating her from the world. She looked up when she heard the closet door opening, her body coiled in a blanket. Through her swollen eyes and matted hair, she counted six additional sets of bright eyes around her momma staring in bewilderment.

They held one another's gaze for only a moment, but during that time it was understood that it marked another episode of the hysteria that resulted when Delphina's fears took on a life of their own.

"You got your test back from Meany Feeney, didn't you?" Cheerleader #1 concluded, prompting Cheerleader #2 and #3 to nod in understanding.

Delphina had, indeed, received her math test from Mrs. Feeney. She scored a ninety-four, which still ticked her off, considering it was a trick question she got wrong. She took advantage of the assumption, milking it as her classmates had earlier that day in English.

"Yep. I have never scored so low! I don't know what happened!" she wailed, burying her head in her knees to stifle the laughter.

"I'm tellin' you, Mrs. Cizek, that woman is pure evil! The test was so unfair," moaned Cheerleader #2 as she pointed at herself while commiserating, "Fifty-two."

"I'm just lucky I could still attend the slumber party with my sixty-four," Cheerleader #3 lamented. "I begged my parents . . . told them I would study math all day Sunday."

"C'mon, Delphina. Forget about Meany Feeney! It's time to party!" Stacy cheered, holding out her hand to help her off the ground.

"I know you can't help yourself, Deli. This kinda stuff is way harder on you," Cheerleader #1 said as she patted her on the back. "You're one of the smart ones."

As the girls headed to the front door, Delphina and her momma shared a smile. Her momma gave her a hug at the front door and whispered in her ear, "I'll call the doctor on Monday."

DELPHINA DID NOT ENVISION HERSELF as a wife or mother. The other girls talked about who would make a good husband and how many children they wanted. Delphina played along and offered a few morsels on her crushes from over the years, but she only offered the names of boys that most girls found attractive.

The roles of wife and mother were fine in theory, but the subject left her wary. Her fears that something bad would happen to someone she loved made it easier to limit those close to her. Committing to a marriage was also a risk in other areas, whether it was unhappiness or divorce, and her parents did not make marriage seem worth it. Patricia and Benny were together, an accomplishment as compared to some parents, but a veil draped their relationship, as if they were two strangers in one house, both longing for different things in life.

Delphina burrowed in her sleeping bag in the early hours of the morning, reminiscing about a particular summer evening when she had been in elementary school. The streetlights had acted as a conductor calling attention to the league of cicadas, the intensity of their night song filling the darkening sky. This was her cue that it was time to head home, scraped bare feet, sticky hair, and all, signs of a well-lived day on the block.

As she opened the door, Lynn Anderson's "Rose Garden" played on the turntable, a far cry from the usual television that glowed in the dark, her daddy in his undershirt with a Lone Star in hand. She saw her parents smiling and laughing, hand in hand, as they tried to keep in step, dancing around the living room. She never realized her daddy's smile could illuminate his face so. Delphina stood on the perimeter, a smile creeping across her face. Their arms opened toward her when they noticed she was there, and she linked her hands with theirs to join the dance. Her parents joyfully belted out the lyrics as they let go of Delphina and wrapped one another in a full embrace. Delphina skipped around the room for the remainder of the A side of the album, retreating to her room at the start of "Sunday Morning Coming Down," giving a wink to her Jesus statue, tickled by her parents' new love of life.

The next day, things returned to normal: her daddy's dispassionate look as he cut his fried eggs with a fork, along with her momma thumbing through *Good Housekeeping* with hopeful eyes, as the green mud mask cracked on her face. Delphina regarded the night before as a loving memory, images of her parents laughing among images of roses, sunshine, and diamond rings.

But now she knew the truth. The irony of the song's lyrics profiled her parents' marriage and life in general, and she was not planning on replicating their mistake.

"TELL ME ABOUT SOMETHING YOU love to do, Delphina," Dr. Stilton asked as he tilted back in his office chair, creaks sounding from the floor in the other room indicating their session was winding down and the next patient was waiting.

"Write. Read and write," she replied, thinking back to the story she had worked on the night before, trying to make good use of the time insomnia attempted to steal.

"And tell me how you came to love it."

Delphina took him back to the summer before fourth grade, the summer she spent three days crouched behind her momma's desk at the coffee plant with a book in hand, three days spent on the receiving end of the boss' glares, because she had to join her momma while her babysitter recovered from an emergency appendectomy. She had caught a glimpse of her momma's workday, including her momma's fondness for spending her lunch break in her car in the parking lot, gazing at the east side of the Houston skyline, studying the intricacies of the buildings and contemplating stories of the inhabitants.

"I wonder what the offices look like in that one?" her momma said, pointing to the bronze building with columns circling the top. "I imagine heavy carpets and mahogany desks, with secretaries who wear the latest fashions from Foley's, with mod colors and delicate gold necklaces."

As they ate their olive loaf on white bread, Delphina offered her theory that the secretaries "drink coffee from a silver urn as they read *Vogue* in the lounge on their break."

Her momma had chuckled in approval, making Delphina feel guilty that she lifted the idea of the coffee urn from the mystery novel she was currently reading. She wondered if that was cheating.

As the thirty-minute lunch ended, they headed back into the factory, stopping by the break room for a free cup of Maxwell coffee, an employee perk. The harsh lights, Formica tables, and slightly overweight ladies wearing polyester knee skirts and rayon blouses offered a stark contrast to the imaginary world they had been a part of moments ago in the car. Delphina had never thought about creating a fictional world to escape her own; she had only looked to nature for comfort.

She returned to her spot behind the desk, excited at the thought of writing stories rather than just reading them. Her momma snuck her a few sheets of typing paper upon request, upon which she could write her idea for a creative story inspired by their lunchtime reveries.

Delphina resembled a medium communing with another world, her pencil spilling prose onto the paper, stories of the inhabitants of the bronze building filling two sheets, front and back. She reread the piece and, knowing her momma would be equally pleased, tapped on her leg as she lifted the story to her.

Her momma had looked down into her eyes with a wrinkled forehead, the spark of hope dashed, the one that was present at home after her drive or at lunch during downtime. Momma was mired in reality with a stack of typing against a five o'clock deadline. Delphina lowered her story, realizing that a secretary was a secretary, and it was irrelevant if the typewriter was in the coffee plant or the bronze building.

Dr. Stilton stared at Delphina a moment longer before jotting a few notes in her file and concluding, "I'd like you to bring in one of your stories next week."

Assuming her best game face, she rose and headed toward the office door for what was the most interesting part of each session: making eye contact with the next patient. It served as confirmation that she was not the only one who was crazy; other kids saw the psychiatrist, too.

She stepped into the waiting area, which at one time served as a living room. The apathetic expression Delphina worked so hard to conjure melted as soon as her hazel eyes met the red-rimmed ones of the little boy waiting. She offered a sympathetic smile of understanding, her heart resonating with his struggle.

"And how was it?" her momma asked once they were in the car, her shifting eyes revealing her nerves over her daughter's attempt to find peace.

"Please don't ask, Momma," Delphina said, admiring the houses along Heights Boulevard.

"Mind if we stop by Kaplan's?"

"Of course, not. I like it there," Delphina replied. And then quickly she added, "Just please don't tell the story again."

"Fair enough. I think I've already told everyone who works there anyway," her momma said with a giggle.

Patricia loved to regale the salesclerks with the story of the first time Delphina went to Kaplan's Ben Hur: "We entered over there on the Twenty-Second Street side. Delphina asks to go to the restroom not more than a step or two in the store. I ask her, 'Can't you wait for just a minute?' and she responds, 'But it is just around the corner there. I won't be long.' I asked her, 'How did you know that?' and she replies, 'Because I've been here lots of times.' Lots of times! Lord, she's my child! She has a sixth sense when it comes to shopping!"

Delphina and her momma parted ways in the store as they usually did, her momma heading to the crystal and china while she headed to the stationery and cards. She figured some of the sales ladies had to be in their seventies or eighties; their kind smiles and gentle greetings took her back to another time. She was certain at least one of them had been alive in 1913 when it was only a feed store.

Delphina's heart began to settle as she made her way through the store. With only three sessions under her belt, she could not say for certain if Dr. Stilton himself was the source. What she did know for sure was that she liked the experience of attending the sessions, starting with the drive from East Houston and the ramped excitement she felt when the University of Houston Downtown Building came into view, signaling they were crossing to the other side of the city. The building held fond memories for her from the day she awoke to it on their drive from Granger. She liked the symbolism of its location on the edge of downtown, as if dividing the east and west.

Her heart calmed as they made their way down Heights Boulevard, where enormous trees framed the street and esplanade. It amazed her how every house was unique, quite a difference from her street with her family's floor plan popping up multiple times on every block.

Victorian mansions and bungalows were interspersed with one another, the size in no way a prerequisite for charm. She wondered who lived in the houses, as well as who had once lived in the house that now served as Stilton,

Dean, and Associates, a dignified cover for a child psychiatry practice recommended by her pediatrician.

And then all she had to do was prattle on for an hour about her fears and worries, with her stories from the week's events at school and on the block working their way into the mix, as she answered the smattering of questions Dr. Stilton posed to keep her rolling. He scribbled a few notes before offering a parting smile, and then to top it off she scored a trip to Kaplan's, a store that ended up being a sanctuary for reflection. A part of her felt guilty for not outing herself to her momma. They could save a heck of a lot of money on Dr. Stilton and just drive to The Heights for free.

SHE HEARD HER DADDY MAKING his way to her room the next morning, which signaled that it was nearing half past six, the time he arrived home from the graveyard shift. He wrapped his hand around her doorknob, careful to turn it so he would not wake her from her sleep. He assumed it had been a usual restless night, but he did not realize she had not slept a wink.

Delphina feigned sleep while his eyes cased her body to make sure all was well. She felt his gaze bear on her closed eyelids, and giving into the desire to tease, she opened one eye and growled, "Arrr! Matey!"

Benny jumped back with a bellow, slapping his palm over his mouth so as not to wake Patricia. Delphina followed suit, burying her head in the covers in an effort to stifle her laughter from traveling through the thin wall that separated their rooms. It was Sunday morning, a time when the family could sleep late without the fuss of work, school, or appointments with Dr. Stilton.

"You were up all night, weren't you?" Benny asked as he took a seat on the edge of her bed, looking into her bloodshot eyes.

Delphina remained still for several seconds, weighing the benefits of a lie versus the truth.

"Yes. But I studied and made good headway on my research paper," Delphina replied, pointing to her desk covered in notecards and stacks of books.

"You seein' it again?" he asked, Delphina knowing his words referenced the mansion and the brown-eyed boy.

"Yes. Please don't tell Mom," Delphina pleaded, knowing her momma's limitations in dealing with her nightmares.

Benny nodded as the two settled into the silence in her room, Delphina placing her hand over his with a pat.

"You need to get some sleep, Daddy."

"I believe the same is true for you," he said, rising from the edge of her bed, baffled at how to help his only child find a peace she had yet to know. "Did you mention it to the doctor yesterday?"

"No, but I will next week," she assured, knowing it would come to light when she brought the warm-up piece she had written for Mr. Lopez. "Daddy?"

"Yep, Lil' D?" he said, holding the cracked door in his hand.

"I feel like there is a purpose to all this . . . just like Mr. Lopez talks about themes in literature. It's like I have a theme. I just need to figure it out."

"Got me a wise young lady here," he said as her eyes started to get heavy, her body knowing it was easier to sleep when both parents were safe under the roof. "I know you'll figure it out."

DELPHINA

Spring 1992

"WILL ANYONE TAKE A GUESS?"

A thick silence coated the room of second semester seniors. Delphina's eyes met those of her teacher, and just as her lips parted to begin, Mrs. Merriweather said with a wink, "Anyone other than Delphina, I should clarify."

Delphina retreated into her seat to study the sky as the other souls shifted in their desks, looking around the room and rummaging through their backpacks in an effort to avoid eye contact. She drowned Mrs. Merriweather's attempts to solicit any morsel of participation from the others, her mind wandering to the cerulean sky that hovered above the navy clouds.

"Even the most harrowing of storms will pass," she murmured without much care whether anyone heard. The rebuffs over the years had evolved into an unspoken respect. As one of the smart ones, her station as one of the quirky intellectuals had earned her a place at the table, albeit at the very end.

A splinter of lightning illuminated the sky. "One . . . two . . . three . . . four," she whispered until the thunder interrupted her count, reverberating through the desks and to the floor.

With less than a minute remaining, Mrs. Merriweather succumbed to the squeals of the class while managing a reminder, "Everyone needs to study for the final exam! Some of you are on the brink of not graduating, and even those of you who are could stand to finish strong."

"Everyone other than Delphina, I should clarify," Stacy said with a giggle as the bell rang.

"You know, it's not too late to join me in living the life of a nerd," Delphina replied.

"Well, it is far too late to do that here, but I do plan to channel you from my dorm in Nacogdoches."

"Fair enough. You know nerds enjoy happier adult lives," Delphina teased as they exited the classroom.

"It's not too late to join *me*, you know. I think it would serve you well to move away." Stacy said.

"I agree, but I'm already taking out a loan for school. I can't imagine it being any more than it already is. University of Houston will suit me just fine."

Delphina made her way to the library, waving to the assistant as she walked to her normal seat at the back window table that faced the courtyard. She took out her calculus homework and gave it a once over as she unwrapped her sandwich. It would not take her long, but she wanted to get it over with, knowing she would rather spend her evenings reading on her own.

She knew she should pay a visit to her school counselor, Mrs. Graf, but Delphina's agitation remained palpable. She should not have smarted off to her as she had, especially in light of the kindness Mrs. Graf had extended her over the years, Delphina's source of comfort away from Dr. Stilton, who was in the process of transferring her records to an adult psychiatrist—someone to monitor and adjust her medications as needed.

Delphina spent countless hours in Mrs. Graf's office, beginning her freshman year when she barely made it through the first day, overwhelmed by the exponentially rising number of decisions that came with growing up. The thought of transitioning between two floors every fifty minutes was only the beginning, and now lectures and advice on post-secondary plans monopolized her thoughts on how she should direct her life. And with her indecision came more waves of nervousness, feelings manifesting as portents for tragedy.

Delphina ate her sandwich, watching the torrent of rain pound the courtyard, waiting for the dark sky to lift and reveal the calm that rested overhead. She knew Mrs. Graf meant well when she used the word *hope*. "I hope you find the peace you are looking for, Deli," Mrs. Graf said. She did not know why the word *hope* struck a chord, but the one word that brought tremendous comfort to others gifted her with a visceral reaction.

"Hope is not a strategy, Mrs. Graf. It's a too damn passive approach to life," Delphina snapped as she grabbed her bag a little more forcefully than intended. As Delphina left the office, Mrs. Graf shook her head, weary of the recalcitrant nature she had tried to soften over the past four years.

On paper, Delphina looked forward to matriculating at the University of Houston. She looked forward to declaring an English major and to selecting her own classes. She looked forward to focusing on humanities, knowing that she would score high enough on her advanced placement exams to test out of the minimum mathematics and science credits she would need. She looked forward to the time between classes when she could do whatever the hell she wanted to do without someone asking for a hall pass or whether she had completed a ridiculous homework assignment that in no way made her a better thinker.

Taking a deep breath, Delphina attempted her assignment despite her mind wandering to the recurring dream from the night before: the mansion, sterile with light radiating from every window. The colors made it more vivid. It was night, yet the sky was bright blue while the house was shrouded in darkness. She surmised it was an extension of the surrealist movement she recently studied in art history, Rene Magritte's *Empire of Lights* seared in her mind from the moment her eyes rested on the work during a field trip to the Menil Museum.

Well after her classmates had meandered to the other rooms, Delphina stood in front of the painting, even taking a seat on the floor with tears in her eyes, reconciling the familiarity of the house with the one from her dreams. She begged her momma to drive her back to the Menil the weekend thereafter, Patricia well intentioned but puzzled at her daughter's fixation. Delphina remained silent on the ride home to East Houston, pondering her attraction while clutching the tube that carried the poster of the work.

Delphina made it through a few problems before the bell to sixth period sounded, prompting her to peer out the window and notice the clouds beginning to part, revealing exactly what she knew was there all along: a Magritte sky radiating peace for those who had the patience to wait.

CADMUS

Autumn 1992

ROBERT WALKED INTO THE HOUSE, sorting through the mail as he made his way down the hall.

"Another request for the home tour," he read.

Cadmus saw the Heights Association symbol on the letterhead as he carried a bottle of wine to the counter.

"Throw it away," Cadmus replied as Robert reached for two glasses high overhead in the cabinet.

"Maybe it's time to tell our story, your family's story," Robert suggested, resting the glasses on the counter.

Times were slowly changing, the evolution for gay rights afoot. It saddened Cadmus to think that his mother had not lived to see it, for he regarded her as the first progressive he knew.

He thought back to the call Mr. MacDougall had placed a few months ago regarding his granddaughter, who had applied to Rice University last year. MacDougall had remembered that Robert's "friend," the professor, taught at Rice University and hoped Cadmus could put in a good word or review her essay. Robert saw it as an opportunity to continue the merger of his worlds, happily making the introduction.

Cadmus had attended only a few events at Robert's firm since his remarkable victory years ago; the occasion of Robert's victory had resulted in a fleeting tolerance after the AIDS epidemic, people fearful of the "gay disease."

"No need to thank me. She is a remarkable young woman who no doubt would have matriculated without my thoughts on her essay," Cadmus had replied when Mr. MacDougall called to thank him the day she received her admissions letter.

The invitation to a dinner at his home came after fall midterms. "It has been too long since I last saw the incredible Dr. Doyle! Clementine loves his class; it's all she talks about," Mr. MacDougall said to Robert.

"It's easy to attack what you don't know," Robert defended when Cadmus was critical over the self-serving nature of the invitation. Now that Clementine admired Dr. Doyle, her grandfather followed suit.

Robert swirled his wine, continuing, "You hold tight to the wrong memories, Cadmus. You need to remember the joyous times with your mother, the ones that far eclipse your falling out. She knows you are sorry. Opening our home might be a way to heal."

"How do you know she's forgiven me? You don't. All I know is that my last words to her were 'leave me the fuck alone.' And she certainly has!" Cadmus replied, taking a deep breath as his agitation rose. "I won't open our house to the public. I can't. I can't write bit narratives for the docents about figurines and fixtures. I can't have them traipsing over hallowed ground where she died, ogling over the garden and the house."

"Isn't all ground hallowed?" Robert questioned, lawyering up. "What do you think was here on this land before 1904? You think it was all peace and happiness? Do you know how many trailers in my neighborhood rested their wheels on the earth, leaving stamps of pain and suffering before they headed to the next place? And long, long before the trailers, the place hosted the Battle of San Jacinto. Think of how many of our men and Santa Ana's men died a bloody death? Hell, Cadmus, who will be in this house in fifty years? One hundred years? They won't know she died here."

"Enough!" Cadmus shouted, his chair screeching back as he pushed away from the table. "We will not open our home to the tour, and that's final." Taking his wine glass, he headed out the back door for a walk in the garden.

He and Robert rarely fought, not necessarily because they always agreed, but rather because Cadmus never wanted to part ways angry, like they had in New York. Although he understood why his mother left his father at Shadyside that night, he knew it was a decision based on emotion, just as it was when he left her to die alone.

All these years later, he could not think about the words he shouted without closing his eyes to still his dizziness. He could count on one hand how many times in his life he had been profane. He had tried, especially when he had been a teenager in an attempt to appear tough, but it never took. That day with Ilona, however, his words were said with such conviction that it shook her to the core. She died thinking he hated her.

Before he met Robert, Cadmus spent the years following Ilona's death in isolation. Aside from the long delay in finishing his studies, teaching classes, and spending minimal time in his office at the University, he had preferred to remain at home, alone with his books and thoughts. The few dates he had were awkward. Cadmus, an old soul, did not have much in common with other men his age. Cadmus' Irish family had disowned him while leaving him wealth, but it was the wealth, alongside his sexuality, that distanced him from his Greek family. He was on his own.

He also had something most gay men did not: the fortunate, rare experience of a fully supportive parent, who created a nurturing environment for him for twenty-seven years. He never struggled to know who he was; he had known it since he was born. He conceded the fact that he did not know how he would have fared had his father lived, but he knew for certain that his mother had been a living example of unconditional love.

And then there was Dear Ernestine, another beautiful soul who had loved him unconditionally. He looked up to her old window of the garage apartment, feeling the occasional surprise that surfaced every now and then that she had passed from a heart attack nearly twenty years ago.

After his mother died, he drove Dear Ernestine to her sister's house so she could get a few things to prepare for the funeral reception. Before Ilona's death, she only stayed on the premises a couple of days during the week, not needing to reside permanently as she once had when the children were young.

He had sipped a cup of coffee in her sister's tiny kitchen, playing peeka-boo with the little ones peeking their heads around the corner and trying not to overhear their discussion in the next room, where Dear Ernestine was reprimanding her sister, "Leave my Caddie alone, Ethel! He knows what it's like to be black, black in his own way, trust me on that!"

On the drive home, Dear Ernestine, still agitated by the conversation with her sister, quickly admonished him when he referenced his mother's death.

"Now stop saying 'died'! We pass, Caddie, we pass to the next life," she said, shaking her head in frustration. He took a sip of wine and laughed to himself, raising his glass to her garage apartment. She was the first Buddhist he knew.

He made his way to the bench under the pecan tree, tracing his index finger along the crack where the paramedics split it in two. The stone company questioned his desire to cement it back together rather than buy a new one, but Cadmus remained firm.

The snap of the screen door prompted him to look up at the house, noting that Robert was walking across the grounds toward him, carrying a bottle of wine and his glass. He and his husband made a successful couple, beating the growing divorce rate for heterosexual couples and ascending in both of their given professions. The Doyle House may not have the legacy that Patrick Doyle, Sr. had once intended, but it had a legacy of love.

Robert refreshed his husband's glass and took a seat next to him, reaching for his hand.

"Okay," Cadmus replied, much to Robert's surprise. "Let's do it. But there's one thing . . . Can you imagine Callista's reaction?"

Robert burst into laughter, raising his eyebrows in agreement as they clinked glasses to the tour.

DELPHINA

Spring 1993

DELPHINA DID NOT REALIZE HER commute would be one of her favorite parts of college. Her high school classmates took great joy in thoughts of dorm life, and even though a part of her longed for that normalcy, she knew having a roommate would be miserable.

Her nightmares, her bouts of depression—as labeled by Dr. Stilton—and her restless nights would out her from the start. She knew many restless nights resulted from worrying over her daddy working the graveyard shift, but she figured the worry could even transfer to her roommate if they became true friends. And if they could put up with her eccentricities, they would no doubt reach that friendship status.

Delphina mentally scanned these reasons like a checklist to combat the tinges of jealousy that surfaced at the thought of college students on their own. Her new used car gave her a taste of that independence, which she would have soon enough.

She cherished the time spent nestled in her own world, listening to her music while thinking about her studies and the life she wanted to create. Driving west on I-10, she admired how the industrial part of the city gave way to downtown. She preferred her view of the skyline, the view from the east side, with older buildings acting as stepping-stones for the newer ones. She wondered about the Gulf Building, noting how it reminded her of a stack of golden Chinese boxes. She still did not know the name of the one that inspired her to write so long ago, the bronze anachronistic structure with columns placed so high that still made her wonder who, if anyone, had ever graced the top.

The times she and her momma drove home from The Galleria, she appreciated the view from the west: modern, glass skyscrapers that contrasted with the older ones on the east. It was as if they acted as a shield to the grittier part of the city. She knew the west view belonged to the wealthy.

Out of habit during her first year at college, she made the sign of the cross as she drove past Catholic churches, but she disregarded the gesture as she regained her sense of self when it came to organized religion. Life's purpose, God, her spiritual journey: These topics often surfaced during her drives. Even at age nineteen, she held firm to her childhood observations made at church all those years ago. During that first year of college, she returned home one autumn evening with confidence to follow her spiritual beliefs, believing in her heart that the truth had more to do with the sky and sea than it did with man's word. She picked up the statues she had kept in her room for so long, offering a final kiss to each one before placing them in a box under her bed.

"Are you ready, sweetheart?" her momma called from the kitchen, car keys in hand.

"Just another minute," Delphina called from her room as she stapled the cover page to her midterm essay that was due on Monday. She was looking forward to spending the day with her momma in The Heights. Although her new doctor was in another part of the city, The Heights had served as their sacred space since she was in seventh grade; it gifted her the purest sense of peace. They had a day planned starting at Kaplan's and ending after a walk on Nineteenth Street with sandwiches at Carter & Cooley.

"I don't mind driving, Momma," Delphina offered.

"Save your gas. And your focus needs to be on updating me about school," her momma replied, making her way to the garage.

Delphina found it easier to talk to her momma, or anyone for that matter, in a car. The windows offered places to rest her eyes, which it made it much easier than looking someone square in the face. She shared how much more she enjoyed her college studies. There were more opportunities to select unique classes, like the one she wanted to take the following year on world religions. She told her momma about a girl named Jane who was also majoring in English. She planned on attending law school, which prompted Delphina to question her decision to teach.

"Sweetheart, it's up to you, but I can't imagine you doing anything other than teaching. You are a beautiful thinker, Delphina."

"That might just be the nicest compliment I've ever received," she said, preferring that take on her propensity for intense reflection.

They parted ways as they usually did after entering the store, with Delphina heading to browse the stationery while her momma moved toward the home interiors section. She selected a box of paper with a light blue cursive *D* at the top. As a child, she found it frustrating that *Delphina* was never found on notepads, stickers, or cups from souvenir stands marking your travels. But with time came an acceptance of her unique name, and the simplicity of a cursive *D* that stood on its own proved quite appealing.

Delphina glanced down the aisle to her right to see a man studying her, the weight of his eyes having summoned her attention. He was older but quite handsome, his kind face drawing her interest. They stared at one another for several seconds, and despite its peculiarity, there was no awkwardness. Another man approached him, breaking the spell as the two headed to the other side of the store.

Stationery in hand, she meandered down the aisle in the hope of catching one more glimpse. He must have had the same urge, because he looked back and met her countenance again, his eyes widening in surprise that she reciprocated. Her momma waved her over from across the store, and Delphina was glad to have a reason to continue walking in his direction.

"Look at these beautiful flowers," Patricia said, her eyes captivated by the colored crystals that formed the petals.

"Amazing detail. I wonder how long it takes to make one?" Delphina asked.

"By the looks of the price tag, I imagine quite some time," her momma replied.

"Good point, indeed."

"I'm going to check out. Want anything else?"

"No, this is all," Delphina said, handing her momma the box of paper. "Don't forget the tickets to the home tour."

"Yes, and guess what? The big one is on it this year!" Patricia cheered.

"The big one?" Delphina questioned, glancing around for the man, who had vanished.

"The big house on Heights Boulevard, the one with the rose garden," Patricia said with excitement.

"Now there is some history there."

"Yes, and I bet it is decorated quite nicely. Can you imagine the furniture?"

"Can you imagine the stories?" Delphina playfully challenged.

As her momma checked out at the register, she turned back to the delicate glass flowers. The vase on display hosted an array of stems, each one combining to form a kaleidoscope of color that brought delight to her face. She noted the beauty of the iris, gingerly lifting it to examine the fine glass piping and the stark contrast of the yellow streaked along the violet petals.

"My mother liked irises."

She turned to see the man's deep brown eyes studying hers. His gaze was not flirtatious, but she was drawn to him in a way she struggled to understand.

"I like them, too," Delphina replied, carefully returning the iris to its rightful place in the vase.

"They represent the Greek goddess Iris. She helps guide souls from earth to heaven," he continued, their eyes locked. "Do you attend Rice? You look very familiar to me."

"No, I attend the University of Houston."

"Ah, and what is your course of study?" he asked, a gentle smile breaking across his face.

"English. I plan to teach."

"Another coincidence. I teach English at Rice. I know you from somewhere."

"I do visit this store often with my mother. Perhaps our paths have crossed here," she said.

"Delphina, let's go!" Patricia called.

"Delphina? Now that most certainly belongs to a Greek girl!" he replied with a laugh.

"Greek? No, sir. I'm Czech," she smiled. "It was nice to meet you . . ."

"Cadmus," he replied, shaking her hand.

"Perhaps our paths will cross again," Delphina said as she turned to catch up with her momma, resisting the urge to run back and embrace him, as ridiculous as it seemed.

THE WEATHER WAS UNSEASONABLY HUMID, perspiration forming a diadem of beads around Delphina's head that remained downcast. She closed her eyes for several seconds, attempting to use powers of the mind to still her heart as they waited in front of The Doyle House. She thought back to the man she had met at Kaplan's a few weeks ago and the feelings she had not been able to dismiss. He had an unusual name, and it irritated her that she could not remember it. Opening her eyes, she scanned the crowds hoping she would see him, his large brown eyes so full of warmth. She looked forward to the home tour, and she was upset that her anxieties were kicking into full gear.

Patricia was oblivious to her daughter's state, her head bent as her eyes anxiously scanned the article detailing the home. Delphina took a few deep breaths and looked over to the grounds. Counting offered a source of distraction . . . ten pristine white pickets lined and bound to make the front gate; three black birds perched on the home's tower watching all who entered; and forty-one people in line before them. At four or five people at a time, they were in for a wait.

"For thirty-two years, the lady of the house was Ilona Doyle," Patricia read from the brochure. "A Greek name like yours, but I must say I am partial to my Delphina," she said, briefly glancing at her with a grin.

"Rumor has it that she died in the house," offered a voice from a lady behind them.

"Really?" Patricia gasped.

"Yes, and her husband died years before that in a terrible auto accident. At least, this is what I recall from my grandmother's stories. She lived a block away on Harvard."

"How dreadful! The poor lady!" Patricia cried before returning to the article. "And now two men live here?"

"Yep. Her son and his partner. I think that's what they call it," the woman said, smug with her insider's knowledge tinged with judgment.

Patricia pursed her lips in surprise and turned to Delphina, who had raised her hands to her forehead. "What's wrong?"

"I don't feel well," Delphina whimpered. "Must be the heat."

"We need shade. Let's go over there by the pecan tree," Patricia ordered, wrapping her arm around her daughter to steady her walk. "Look! There is a bench."

A sign on the bench greeted them: Please do not sit.

"Well like hell we are!" Patricia said, shoving the sign aside.

Delphina tried to catch her breath as she lay on the bench, looking at the peak of The Doyle House's tower contrast against the Magritte sky. She looked at the windows that faced north and wondered how many faces since 1904 had looked out to the rose garden. She grew increasingly weak, the roses blurring to seas of red, pink, and white as she closed her eyes.

"We need water!" Patricia shouted over toward the people entering the house. "No, Deli! Stay awake!" she warned, fearing her daughter was losing consciousness.

Tears streamed from Delphina's eyes, gliding down the sides of her face as her head rocked from side to side.

"What is it?" Patricia shrieked.

"I'm so sad, Mom. So very, very sad," Delphina said, shaking her head and sobbing as her momma knelt beside the bench, pulling her into an embrace.

Patricia and Delphina never made it into The Doyle House. Patricia attributed it to heat exhaustion, and while Delphina knew it played a factor, she also knew that something else had also come over her. She stared out the window as her momma drove back to East Houston, weeping over an unknown sorrow and frustrated that years of therapy had not resolved her issues.

Patricia put her to bed, turning down the air conditioner and resting a pitcher of iced water on her nightstand. Delphina remembered her daddy checking on her throughout the night, placing his calloused hand on her forehead to feel for a temperature as if she were a small child again. She drifted in and out of sleep throughout the day and night, the recurring dream of the mansion coming into focus, clearer than it had ever been.

CADMUS

Spring 1993

CADMUS SPENT WEEKS DISTRACTED BY his conversation with Delphina. He could not brush off the unmistakable feeling that he knew her, as if she were a person dear to him. The image of her smiling at the glass iris bubbled in his mind, and several materializations later, he made a connection to Ilona's toothy smile.

He shook his head. "But they look nothing alike," he said aloud, causing Robert to ask from across the house if he was talking to him. He mouthed the name *Delphina*, wondering why a Czech woman would choose such a name. He made a weak attempt at convincing himself that it was the name that connected him to his mother, but he knew he felt a connection to this young woman before he knew her name, her large hazel eyes offering a beautiful balance to her light brown locks. And she was admiring an iris, which he found uncanny.

He looked to the plaque they received in the mail that day, a marker for their participation in the home tour. He knew their house was the gem, and it filled him with joy that he made it a tribute to Ilona, narrating her life and contributions to the home and to the Heights community, namely at Heights High School where he established a generous scholarship in her honor. Doyle Lumber was mentioned, but only as a reference to his grandfather who was thankful to Texas for helping his family realize their dreams.

He and Robert were not at home during the tour. The committee used docents and encouraged homeowners to leave, knowing that many visitors are just as critical as they are complimentary.

"No need for you to hear those things. Go enjoy a day out!" the head docent had told them.

After he and Robert had returned home, they'd been told about a woman who nearly fainted in the garden, very near where his mother had passed. No one caught her name, but he knew she was a young woman with her mother. The description prompted thoughts of Delphina, even though the odds of it being her were quite remote. He hoped she was well again.

"I don't believe I've properly thanked you for opening our home to the tour," Robert said that evening as they lay in bed reading. "I've never had much of a family until I met you. It made me damn proud to call this place my family's home. I love you."

"I love you, too," Cadmus said, pulling his husband into an embrace.

CALLISTA'S ATTEMPTS TO FIGHT THE cancer were met with defeat. She kept her illness from Cadmus during the battle, only deciding to share the news when she knew her time was limited. He remembered the call she made to him shortly after the home tour.

"What were you trying to do, kill me sooner?" she joked, referencing his and Robert's decision to "open your union to the world."

They left the wheelchair at the foot of the front porch stairs. Cadmus' hand brushed his niece's as they helped his sister up the steps, the moment's touch startling both of them, and they looked away, both uncomfortable at touching a close relative for the first time.

"I guess I should have come sooner," Callista said in a matter-of-fact tone as she gripped the railing.

"You were always welcome," Cadmus replied, steadying her as she made it up the stairs.

"Thank you, Grace," she said, turning to her daughter. "I'll call you when I'm ready."

Grace hugged her mother and gave her uncle a polite smile and nod before heading back to the car. He wished he knew her.

"What's changed up there?" she said, tilting her head toward the grand staircase.

"Not much, come to think of it. The third floor is Robert's art studio."

"Ah. Yes, I read about that in the home tour notes," she said as they made their way into the library. He walked her to a seat in the nook before turning back to pour two cups of tea.

Callista reached for his hand, and he accepted. They sat together in silence for several minutes, holding hands and sipping tea while staring out at the rose garden.

"I'm sorry I was not a better sister, Cadmus."

"I'm sorry I caused you pain," he replied after a minute.

"You didn't cause me pain," she said. And then looking over to him with a smile, she added, "I did a pretty good job of that on my own."

"But we all do, don't you think?" she probed a minute later.

"What do you mean?" Cadmus asked.

"Look at our father. He caused his own pain, his drinking and his affair. Look at our mother. If she just would have been stronger . . . had a stronger opinion about our place in the Doyle family and hadn't been so damn resentful of Uncle Michael . . . who knows what could have happened.

"And me, well, I regret our estrangement. My family does not know you, and you are truly one of the kindest people I know. You always have been, since you were a little boy. But then look at the choices *you* made, the choices you continue to make."

"You had me until that last remark," he said flatly.

"I did not come here to argue. I want to spend time with you, but I am not foolish enough to believe it will all be perfect. Certain topics are bound to surface."

"My sexuality is not a choice, Callista. Just as it was not a choice that you fell in love with William. It's a natural attraction," Cadmus defended.

"Well, marrying William was a choice, Cadmus. I wanted a better place at the table," she admitted and then softened. "I've come to love him very much. I'll miss him."

He remembered wanting to raise the subject of Uncle Michael and his choices, as well as her warped view of their mother, but he wanted peace at this moment more than he wanted reflective discussion on their family. It did not matter anymore. He had seen his uncle only one time since his mother's death, and he had not even attempted to disguise his disgust. He struggled to reconcile why his uncle continued to harbor resentment toward him. Michael had gotten everything he wanted, including a long life. He was eighty-five and still strong.

"So tell me about your writing," Callista said, staring into the garden as she took a sip of tea.

HE AND ROBERT WERE AMONG the last to arrive at Callista's funeral, ducking into the last pew at the back of the church. Cadmus could make out the backs of the heads of Grace, Lillian, and Timothy, all seated at the front with their respective spouses and children. William sat on the far left, staring at his wife's casket, cascading with roses and lilies. Heaviness filled Cadmus' heart as he looked at the family he would never know, countless birthdays and holidays spent in joyful union without giving him a passing thought.

A rattle from the door separating the nave from the narthex grabbed their attention, the person on the other side struggling. Robert rose to offer assistance, firmly pulling the door open.

"Robert? What are you doing here? I didn't know you knew my cousin," Benjamin said incredulously, looking over to his father, who was also entering the church. "Dad, Robert is one of the partners at Lehane and MacDougall. Dad? Dad, what's wrong?"

Uncle Michael stood in the aisle, staring at his nephew seated in the back pew. His shrunken frame bore little resemblance to the man who had so forcefully strong-armed him from the company when Cadmus was just five years old. It was as if Cadmus was staring at an image of his father had he lived to be an old man. Cadmus rose to meet them in the aisle, refusing to show the slightest hesitation.

"Truth be told, Ben, I never met Callista, but we are related," Robert said as Cadmus approached his side, placing his hand on his back. "I believe you know my husband, Cadmus Doyle?"

DELPHINA

Summer 1997

"IT COULDN'T BE MORE PERFECT for you," her momma said as she made her way into the kitchenette.

"Perfect? Too damn close to the street. Did you see that flimsy excuse for a gate?" Benny commented.

"I'm twenty-three years old, Daddy!"

"And you're still my baby girl, plain and simple," he replied.

"I have several more showings scheduled for today," the apartment manager said, clearly annoyed by Benny's assessment. "These vacancies do not last long. A lot of people prefer to live in an intimate complex on Heights Boulevard despite a few shortcomings."

"Give us a minute," he said, excusing his family to the courtyard.

Delphina looked at the eight doors framing the courtyard pond: old and shabby to some, but to her it was charming. Despite her anxious nature, she did not hesitate once when envisioning her future here. It excited her to think about walking along Heights Boulevard with her new messenger bag in tow, headed to Heights High School to teach.

"Daddy, please. I've always been afraid to be away from you and Momma, but this just feels right."

"I hear you, Deli, I do. And you know what? You don't need to listen to your daddy anymore. You're a grown woman, much as I hate to admit it. It sure makes me happy that you think you need my permission."

Delphina smiled. She knew the place was hers. He walked back into the unit, where the apartment manager was taking an exaggerated glance at her watch.

"She'll take it. And we are happy to pay the deposit and first couple months' rent."

"Really?" Delphina squealed, looking to both of her parents in astonishment.

"We are happy to do this for you, sweetheart. It's time for you to spread your wings," Patricia beamed.

IT DID NOT TAKE LONG for Delphina's idyllic vision of her life as a teacher to fracture. She knew reluctant learners were a given, but she woefully underestimated that the balance would be so far out of her favor. She also possessed too much optimism in her presumed ability to inspire, not realizing that many students viewed her as privileged, as someone who could not relate to their struggles.

"I could not afford college, either," she readily admitted to her second period class, the one that had the most students in need of winning over. "I'll be paying my loans back for years to come."

"You don't get it, Miss," Aurelio, one of her students, said. "My parents didn't finish high school. They need me to work, bring in money."

"Yes, and you can bring in more money with a degree," Delphina said in earnest.

"My father's in prison. No one's got time to wait when we need rent money now," he countered, with his head snaking from side to side to underscore his point as the other students nodded in agreement.

That first year, she could not count the number of times she walked Heights Boulevard in tears, wondering if it was too late to join Jane in law school. She knew in her heart that the legal field held little interest for her. Without the desire, she would not want to study.

One of her walks home the following October proved to be particularly bumpy with pecans crunching beneath her feet along Heights Boulevard. The symbolism annoyed her: bumps finding new ways to manifest. She picked a pecan up and placed it in her pocket, forgetting about it until it fell out when she changed into her nightgown later that evening. Delphina caressed its shell, noting the black markings on the casing. It swept her away to when she was a child, obsessed with all things in nature, in awe of divine proportion, of symmetry. Placing it on her nightstand as a reminder that she was part of something bigger than herself, she vowed to find a way to reach her students.

"SHIT!" DELPHINA YELPED, JERKING HER hand back from the copier to see how badly she had burned her fingers.

"Need help with that?"

She looked up at Mr. Jack Harris, the very attractive history teacher she had been eyeing.

"It's possessed," Delphina replied, trying to appear aloof.

"Hmmm. Let's see . . ." Jack began, kneeling next to her as he lifted and turned, raised and pulled. "If it is possessed, then following the diagrams should act as an exorcism." He yanked the crinkled paper a second after uttering the last word. "Voila!"

"Thanks. I should have more patience," she conceded.

"Yes, well, that is something hard to come by for us teachers. Too much to do."

"Tell me about it," Delphina said, nodding as she resumed copying.

"Still haven't returned the assignment, huh?" he said, inserting his original in the copier next to hers.

"How'd you know?" she asked, arms crossed and slightly annoyed.

"Students talk. I have many of your kids in my history class."

She looked away, feeling her face flush from embarrassment. They spoke of other teachers in her class, so of course they talked about her in other classes.

"Hey, it's a damn hard job, and it's your first year. Don't be so hard on yourself," he consoled, turning toward her as his copies filled the tray.

"How long have you taught?"

"Three years. And this is my last."

"Last? But the kids love you. You're good at what you do," she retorted, regretting the unintended accusatory tone that peppered her response.

"Yes, but it comes with a price. I make a pitiful sum, and the work is intense. I'd also like to provide a nice life for the wife I have yet to meet and the children I am expected to have," he said, Delphina absorbing his words. "And besides, there is no way my father will humor me much longer. He said it's time for me to join him at his firm."

"What are your plans?"

"Georgetown Law School next fall—the alma mater of my father, uncle, and grandfather. I'm the rebellious one, the one who was going to save the world before I join the practice."

"Wow. Congratulations," Delphina replied, the announcement pushing her to think of the next steps for the graduate degree she was thinking about pursuing.

"Hey, want to get together tonight and grade?"

"Get together and grade?" she teased.

"Well, excuse me. I guess you have more of a social life than I do," he replied, eyeing her out of the corner of his eye with a smile.

"Hardly," she giggled, excitement building that he was flirting with her. "It just caught me off guard. I'd love to."

"Andy's on Eleventh?" he said as he shuffled the copies into a neat stack. "They are open twenty-four hours, and I'm not ashamed to admit I can be found there in the middle of the night. Where else can you get a taco and coffee after midnight?"

"Good point."

"Seven?"

"See you there," Delphina said with a smile.

DELPHINA KNEW IT WAS A hike to Andy's from her apartment, but she knew the walk would serve her well. She had her fill of dalliances in college, but she always found a way to end them before it became too serious. They were not always sudden break-ups, and on more than one occasion she had been the one ultimately dumped. Once the newness of a relationship chipped away, bringing to light the reality of impermanence, Delphina picked fights and retreated to solitude. She surmised it was an easier route than to become attached to another person to shroud in worry.

Jack tempted her in a way she had yet experienced. His social consciousness and intelligence made his unconventional looks attractive, his confidence a seduction all its own. She knew money brought a level of assuredness, her friendship with Jane first bringing this realization. He was accustomed to life fanning in his favor, from the time he heralded to Houston from Connecticut to attend Rice University to his natural acceptance to law school with a job waiting. She wondered what it would be like to think of life as a giver of possibilities rather than a taker when you least expected it.

She saw Jack at a corner table before he saw her. He was retrieving a stack of papers from his messenger bag. It was as shame he was leaving for law school in the fall. She was thankful that she found a friend at work. At best, it might be something more, and if it ventured into that territory, then it was probably a good thing he was leaving. There was a natural end in sight rather than one of her maudlin fabrications.

He looked up to see her, waving to get the attention he did not know he already had. Delphina walked up to the table with a smile, and with a simple "hey" placed her bag down and took a seat.

"Good to see you! I need to delve right in to make a dent before my urge to grade passes."

"Good idea. I stare at the stack on my kitchen table for hours before I dare touch one," Delphina admitted, leaving out that her insomnia offered the blessing of time to grade at odd hours.

They graded and nibbled nachos over coffee, which she found to be an odd combination. She went with it, becoming accustomed to a bite of guacamole followed by a gulp of dark roast. While Jack's papers were easier to grade than an English teacher's, she remained impressed that he assigned open-ended assessments.

"Do you really spend that much time on one paper?" he asked, his question and the distraction from grading taking her a minute to absorb.

"Ummm . . . I don't really know? This isn't a paper. It's a daily grade," she replied, reaching for another chip.

"A daily grade? You have been on . . ." he began as he leaned his head over to read the heading, "Jocelyn's assignment for fifteen minutes."

"Your point?"

"How many students do you have?"

"One hundred and seventy-two."

"At fifteen minutes a paper, that brings your grading time to . . ." he paused, punching buttons on his calculator, "2,580 minutes, which equals . . . forty-three hours."

The waitress refilled their coffee cups, glancing at Delphina out of the corner of her eye as if in total agreement that he just checked her.

"They deserve good feedback, Jack. And you know not all of them take this long to grade. Some of them do not even turn one in at all."

"True, but you are still taking too long, Deli. And they deserve a teacher who is not overwhelmed all the time. This assignment is more like an assessment."

"Look, here, Jack . . ." she fired.

"Deli, I'm not trying to be an asshole," he interrupted, reaching for her forearm. "Hell, I did the same thing you are doing my first year. Honestly, I was a mess, and I can tell you that it is not sustainable."

Defensives settling, she asked, "Then what do you suggest I do?"

"For daily grades, I would assign a paragraph response to an open-ended question, or even just two to three sentences. I admire your desire for them to flesh out a thorough response, but one, it's too much work for a daily grade; two, they need help understanding the basic mechanics of sentences before they can compose properly; and three, your comments are not meaningful, because it takes too long to give them the feedback. Save assignments like this one for test grades."

She sipped her coffee, soaking in his advice and looking at the stack in front of her. It was true she found herself writing the same basic comments over and over, the only difference being that she personalized them by writing their name or a clever remark tailored to their interest.

"You mean well, Deli. If you channel your energy better, you will give them more of you in class. This is where you can spark their love for learning."

"Your students love you, Jack," she acquiesced.

"We have a relationship. They know my assignments are relevant."

"Food for thought," she said, scooping another nacho. "You know, I bet they won't have nachos like these at Georgetown."

"SO HOW DID YOU GET your name?" Jack asked as they lay in his bed eating pizza a few weeks later.

"St. Delphina. She took vows of poverty and chastity."

Jack's hearty burst of laughter caused him to choke momentarily on a pepperoni. He reached for his water to clear his throat before continuing his roar.

"Well, at least you're still committed to the poverty vow as a teacher!"

Delphina joined his laughter, not realizing the irony of her response until he reacted. The illuminated 11:18 on his nightstand clock reminded her it was time to head home. Noticing her gaze move toward her jeans at the foot of the bed, he darted in front of her to grab them first.

"Stay with me tonight," he teased, holding them out of reach.

"We need to teach tomorrow morning," she said, grabbing them back.

"So you'll stay next time if it's not a school night?" he said, winking at the last two words.

"We'll see," she said, slipping on her jeans and throwing on her top. "I'll see you tomorrow."

The drive back to The Heights was a short jaunt, but it was one Delphina came to appreciate as a means of transitioning back to her own world. Jack had been to her place a few times, but going to his place meant she could leave when she was ready, and this made all the difference when deciding to take the relationship further. She was secretly relieved the holidays would soon herald him to Connecticut, the growing intimacy lending its usual path to discomfort.

Without a car in sight at that hour, she barely touched the gas, allowing the darkness of the trees lining The Boulevard to envelop her in their slumber. She admired the houses, extending a moment's more attention to The Doyle House, regretting that she never made it inside the day she fell ill. She saw a light in the side bay window that faced the garden, and for a moment, she fancied knocking on the door to see if they would mind if she took a peek. She figured she would start walking on that side of the street when she walked to and from school in the hopes of catching a resident outside getting the paper or mail.

Delphina let herself in the courtyard gate of her apartment building to see the moon reflecting in the pond. Taking a seat on the patio chair, she gave thanks for her progress. The thought of spending a full night with Jack gave her room for pause, but she was starting to open to it as a possibility.

MR. HARRIS PROVED TO BE a professional godsend, as she started mirroring the long hours he put in after school, planning and tutoring students on campus. She could not make a heavy dent in the grading with her visitors, but the refined assignments made grading easier when they left for Andy's or one of their respective apartments. Although this took a sizeable chunk of time, her presence and consistency earned her credibility.

She remembered storming from school at the three o'clock bell when she had been a student, crowds forming waves rippling from the doors. Many of her students, however, did not want to go home. They did not want to be in class, either, but they preferred to spend idle time roaming the halls rather than returning to no air conditioning and babysitting.

Students began visiting; one by one they peeked their heads through the open door, first looking for food and then for company and eventually for help with English. She baked cookies for the students to eat after hours, and when the cookies proved insufficient, she brought snacks from the grocery store to fill her teacher cabinet.

Aurelio visited, as did others, and as they bonded over apples and chips, with Cheeto-stained fingers on many a rough draft, she finally came to terms with the fact that she had so much more growing up than many of her students did. Her marginalization centered on her anxiety, the part of her that lived in fear that something bad was on the horizon. Her conversations with the students after school helped her see the benefit of the unknown, the benefit of free will as a force for good, as a means to enact positive change in your life. And she was doing something very good with her life: She was trying to make a difference.

She surmised it also helped that Mr. Harris was her boyfriend, her coolness developing through osmosis. He put in an occasional appearance after school to grab a bag of chips before heading to his own room, the students teasing, "Here to see your girlfriend, Mister?" She felt her defenses rise when a student corrected, "Yeah, but last year it was Ms. Young." Her face blushed with embarrassment over the insinuation of a reputation. With her growing attachment to Jack came uneasiness, a worry broader than infidelity. She was scared something terrible would interfere with her happiness.

In late January, he began talking about a spring break trip to Mexico, a much-needed vacation, even more so because of his impending departure in June. Delphina paced the courtyard that evening, her desire to take the trip dampened by the fact that she had yet to spend a full night alone with him. Last week, he enjoyed a drunken weekend with a few college buddies in town for a visit. He finally picked up Sunday morning on her eleventh call, asking why in the hell she had called so many times now that he had gotten a good look at his caller ID. She impressed herself with the quick lie that her phone line had been acting up, disconnecting calls. She thought they were not going through to his line.

"Why don't we hang out at my place Friday night?" she whispered as they made their way down the hall early in the week. "I have a killer crepe recipe for breakfast."

His raised brows and smile reflected his approval, and as she turned right to take the stairs to the second floor, she realized there was no going back. She could not leave her own apartment.

DELPHINA MADE HER WAY DOWN The Boulevard, cursing her-
self for not leaving school sooner. She extended her vulnerability to include
an enchilada dinner, something she regretted suggesting a second after it
had escaped her lips when she remembered the preparation required for the
sauce, something that should be done hours in advance.

She kept her eyes downcast, walking down the uneven sidewalk, tree
roots angling the concrete slabs as much as forty-five degrees.

Nature finds a way, she thought to herself in an attempt to soothe her
nerves, moving her gaze up the majestic tree trunks responsible for the disarray.

A Metro bus barreled past her, the vibrations from its force snagging
her attention. Her stare landed on The Doyle House across the esplanade
and the silver-haired gentleman meandering through the grounds. Despite
the sizeable time she had spent in The Heights, it was the first time she had
seen who lived there. Distinguished in his bow tie and suit, she wondered if
she would ever enjoy a life so lovely, unwinding on a Friday without a care in
the world. She imagined that this well-put-together gentleman's wife would
undoubtedly soon join him, and Delphina was on her way to drink tequila.

While she enjoyed cooking, her real motive was using the drinks as a
way to kill time in the evening. After her advanced preparations, the plan
was to roll tortillas together as the clock ticked. Adding a boozy pitcher of
margaritas into the mix would hopefully result in an early, deep sleep for the
both of them. Her sleep, of course, would be helped even more so with a side
dose of antidepressant.

Jack arrived a little after seven, Don Julio in tow, while Delphina
squeezed fresh limes. They stuffed and rolled as they sipped margaritas,
Jack convincing her at one point to try a shot. Although the intended effect
proved appealing, she could not bear to make it two.

They ate by the moonlight, candles lit around the courtyard pond illuminating the buds, a symbol of the spring to come. He laughed at the seasonal

marker, his declaration that he would be wearing a sweater this time next year on the East Coast pricking her heart. Taking another salty sip, she tilted her head back to examine the night sky with the realization that she did not love him. She was attached and cared for him, which made her worry, but it was not love. It was a token for which she was thankful. She thought about the silver-haired man. In a house of that stature, surely he had someone to love.

A stack of books fell to the ground when she stumbled to her night-stand, the haze from the tequila putting her in slow motion. She saw Jack from the corner of her eye, smiling as he unbuttoned his shirt. As she knelt down to collect the books, she prayed for her mind and heart to still.

She gathered the books methodically, adjusting the book jackets to buy time to reset her thoughts. She had enough wits about her to know he would not last long given that the bottle of Don Julio housed barely a shot or two. As she gave the stack a final straightening on the carpet, she noticed a pecan peeking from the bed skirt, the one from her October walk home when her teaching career had seemed so bleak.

Thank you, she thought, grateful for the reminder from the universe that everything would be fine. She stacked the books on the nightstand, resting the pecan on top. Smiling, she turned to Jack; it was almost over.

He pulled her back toward him after the first time, nuzzling his face in her wavy brown hair.

"Again?" he kissed, which she accepted with the hope that another time after the tequila would put them both to sleep.

He held her afterward, full of love and care, telling her how much he already missed her and perhaps she could visit him Labor Day weekend, so many months away. She fought the urge to jerk away as he guided her temple to his chest. His heartbeat, the only sound in the room, echoed the irrevocable truth of life's impermanence. She rolled to the other side of the bed as soon as he passed out, weeping into the blanket while she waited for the sun to rise.

Dawn peered through the bedroom blinds, and with it came her recoil at his stroke to her back. He thought she was not fully awake, giving allowance that her action was mere reflex over intention. Exhausted from lack of sleep and temples throbbing from the tequila, she was spent from her restless night.

"What's wrong, Delphina?"

"Ummm . . . a hangover, Jack. What do you think it is?"

"Let me help you," he said, heading to the bathroom for aspirin and water. "I'll make the crepes," he called out.

"No. I'll throw up. I think I just need to sleep."

"Okay, well, they'll be there if you change your mind."

"You're not getting it," Delphina said, annoyed. "I need to be alone, Jack."

"You want me to leave?" he asked, coming back into the room with an aspirin bottle in hand and a baffled look in his eyes.

"Bingo!" she responded, pulling on her robe as he watched her, confused. "Quit looking at me like that!"

"Did I do something wrong?"

"Yes. You won't leave," she barked, throwing his clothes at him as she burst into tears.

"Wow. Was I wrong about you," he replied, shaking his head as he dressed and then headed out the door.

She knew her over-the-top reaction befuddled him, the tears that streamed down her face becoming more than a pretense. They were tears born from some inexplicable place within that left her doubting her ultimate sanity. The jilting came as a relief, as if a weight had been lifted. She expedited the inevitable hurt that would surface again had she let life's confluences take their own course.

As she slipped into a bath later that morning, she placed a hot hand towel over her head, counting the months she had to deal with having an ex-boyfriend at work. Delphina knew she was a fragile being, one who hoped to meet a man who would understand her fragility and ride out her tempestuousness, one who would embrace the thoughtfulness that accompanied it. But she had a lot of work ahead of her for that to ever become a possibility.

CADMUS

Autumn 1997

"SHE IS SO GODDAMN CALLOW."

"Ah, Mr. Phillips, two points of response. First, what does callow mean?" asked Cadmus.

"Foolish, immature."

"Not quite. It means immature, but that particular word is used to describe a youth. Our character must be around forty, given what we know."

Mr. Phillips nodded, his face blushing.

"Now, try again," Cadmus gestured, hands in pocket and gaze downcast as he began a stroll around the room. "Don't worry about the adjective just yet. What do you think of her?"

"I think she's immature to turn her back on her family."

"She has a family, a husband and four children of her own. They seem quite content."

"Yes, but she also has her own family, the one that raised her."

"And she's turning her back?" Cadmus asked.

Mr. Phillips nodded.

"Then what is a better word than *callow?*"

"Self-absorbed, selfish," Mr. Phillips responded with a truer confidence.

"Better," Cadmus smiled before looking to the whole room. "Now this announcement is for everyone! Work on using precise language. You can fancy it up later, but make sure you know the words you are using."

"Hey, Dr. Doyle?"

"Yes, sir?"

"You had two points. The second?"

"Ah, yes. The preceding profanity," Cadmus said in a playful tone.

"Dr. Doyle, come on," Mr. Phillips replied. "It's a compliment . . . a reflection of how much we can be ourselves in your class."

"Interesting point, and flattery affords forgiveness," Cadmus conceded. "And I do understand the need for colorful language from time to time, as a dear friend of mine shares your disposition."

"Who agrees with Mr. Phillips that she's so goddamn selfish?" Cadmus asked the group, causing a ripple of laughter from around the room.

"I disagree," came a voice from the back.

"Yes, Ms. Jackson. Please, tell us why."

"Her family verbally abused her for years," Ms. Jackson replied. "She's distancing herself for a good reason."

"But she knows they can't help it. She has a better sense of self and should be able to put it in perspective," Mr. Phillips countered.

"You mean she must continue to take it?" Ms. Jackson questioned.

Mr. Phillips paused, scanning all eyes on him as he doubled down. "Yes. Family is family. Dr. Doyle, you know what I mean."

"So the family you are born into is the one that deserves the most loyalty . . . regardless of what they do to you?" Cadmus asked with the usual cryptic smile he donned in class. "Think about it. And on that note, I will see you all on Thursday."

As Cadmus left the lecture hall, he overheard a student tell Mr. Phillips, "You do not know what you are talking about. You must come from a good family. Mine is absolutely nuts."

Cadmus laughed to himself, knowing that he and Robert's stories of familial dysfunction could rival them all. No one would ever guess it by looking at either of them, as educated and successful as they were.

He returned to his office to find a message from Agatha, an ominous sign. He surmised it was regarding her mother, considering she was eighty-eight and in poor health. He found it odd that tragedy often instigated contact. When severe illness or death was at the door, his family called, but only when it was too late to do anything other than an offer a last-minute apology or a prayer for the repose of the soul. He understood the need for resolution, but this was not it. It was a form of closure, but a real attempt to bridge the chasm should be made without the threat of death.

"Hello, Agatha. It's Cadmus."

"Hello, Cadmus. I'm sorry to bother you, but I thought you should know my mother died last night."

"I am so very sorry," he replied, surprised by the emotions that the news stirred, images of his mother and Arianna flitting through his mind.

"Thank you. She lived a very full life, so I know I shouldn't be too upset."

"Well, Arianna is your mother, and regardless of how old you are, it does feel melancholy to think you are an orphan in the world," he regretted his words, knowing after they escaped his mouth that he should have kept it simple.

"Yes, you know what it's like, cousin."

"Is there anything I can do?" Cadmus asked.

"No, we are planning the service. I'll let you know when the details are finalized in the event you want to come."

Cadmus noted her inflection. Robert was still not welcome, just as he was not at her father's funeral years back. Arianna's face had filled with horror the moment he and Robert entered the church. It had never occurred to her that Cadmus would have brought him to a family event even though Robert was his family.

"You are in my thoughts, as is Christos."

"Thank you. I'll pass your thoughts to my brother."

Cadmus made a mental note to compose a letter of sympathy to both of his cousins later that evening at home, and he would order a flower arrangement for the service. He looked out his office window and offered a prayer to Arianna, which he marked as the extent of his participation in her funeral.

DELPHINA

Autumn 2004

DELPHINA MET JANE FOR LUNCH at Neiman's, Jane's new position at a prominent law firm allowing her the continued option to take pleasure in such indulgences. As Delphina absentmindedly shuffled through the racks, she came across a beautiful dress, pale yellow with a wide collar that wrapped around the shoulders.

"Now you would make that dress look exquisite, like it was meant to look."

"I do believe the dress is exquisite enough on its own, and at five hundred dollars, it will need to make do without me."

"Delphina, you do not realize one of your gifts. You make inexpensive clothes look like designer duds. I, on the other hand, need to spend money on nice clothes, because they wear me and help me look like the highbrows with whom I must consort at work."

"That's even more of a reason for me not to buy it. Other than the fact that I cannot afford it, it certainly doesn't have a place in a teacher's closet."

Delphina's fingers caressed the fabric, so delicate and well made. It was the kind of dress her mother would have bought in an instant, whipping out a credit card and taking months to pay it off.

Later, when they sat down for lunch at Neiman's, Jane asked about the off-the-menu items, causing the waitress to hold her stare for a second more. The waitress looked at the numerous garment bags, smiled, and then turned to Delphina to detail the daily specials.

"Thank you for telling me about your fine offerings, but I do think it was my best friend who asked," she said, gesturing to Jane. "She's the one who has the money to shop here as a contrast to me, so I do think your attention is best directed to her, as misguided as your attention appears to be."

Jane looked at Delphina and winked, but the gesture could not conceal the effort it took to maintain her composure. This wasn't the first time something like this had happened, but it always left Delphina baffled. Jane's father was a renowned heart surgeon in the medical center; her mother was a professor at the University of Houston. People only saw Jane's skin color, despite her poise and intellect. Strangers presumed the worst while Delphina's hue gave her an aura that could not have been further from the truth of her background.

The friends nibbled over monkey bread, talking about the exciting times ahead for them both, especially since Jane and her husband would soon work on growing their family. Jane spent a shocking sum that afternoon, ready now to stroll into her new office at the Niels Esperson Building. She laughed when she signed the credit card receipt, saying even the building demanded a better wardrobe from her, as elegant and formidable as it was. When Jane excused herself to the ladies room, Delphina was left wondering whether she herself would ever marry. Next week marked her thirty-first birthday, and while she knew women could marry at any age, she also knew the expectations the South placed on having children at an early age.

"Good Lord, Jane, what more did you buy?" Delphina asked, seeing her friend strolling back to the table with another garment bag in tow.

"Delphina, this dress belongs to you. Happy birthday!" she cheered, wrapping her arms around her friend.

THE JITTERS STARTED WHEN IT was time to get ready for her birthday dinner. The warm lavender bath that she often found soothing left her even more anxious, her pounding heart prompting her to lie down on the bed with a towel draped over her body. She considered taking a Xanax, but she knew tonight would be a lively one, with wine and with Cistern's craft cocktails . . . *Have you had one?* Delphina could hear Jane and their college friend, Libby, in her head. Delphina dismissed the thought of taking just a chip of a pill to take the edge off, thinking back to the conversation with her psychiatrist about wanting to get off prescription drugs for good.

"Deli, your situation is different from that of your students. We are working through your anxiety," he had stated in a clinical tone.

"And we aren't making much progress now, are we?" she had responded in frustration.

Her jitters tonight felt different than usual, like she was on the precipice of something good, but it still left her unsettled. She made up her eyes with thick black eyeliner, looking like she was from another time. The pale yellow dress fit her perfectly, and although she was too humble to admit it, she carried herself with a regal quality, as if she were a lady of means, like someone from Jane's family. Perhaps the number of times her momma dragged her from East Houston to the fancy stores had paid off, as if the ether from the stores and its inhabitants rubbed off a bit. She grabbed her clutch and walked from her apartment on Heights Boulevard to Nineteenth Street.

Jane and Libby had a drink waiting for Delphina when she arrived at the bar, and it even had a sparkler poking up from the lime.

"Happy Birthday!" they screamed, after which the other patrons offered a round of applause.

Delphina made her way to the bar, smiling and nodding thanks to the other guests who offered drunken birthday wishes. After a few sips, she confirmed the cocktail was quite delicious, giggling at how the drink practically vanished. She intercepted Libby's attempt to refresh her glass, requesting a cabernet instead.

Her anticipation continued to build, leading her to wonder if the ladies had vetoed her request by arranging a surprise party instead. As she picked up the wine glass, Delphina turned her head to scan the restaurant for others who might be hiding in the corners. The alcohol loosened her arm to extend a bit too far, causing it to bump into a man walking past, the red wine splashing across her new dress.

Gasping in shock, she looked down at the red splotches covering the once pristine fabric. She glared at the man who ruined her dress, and as their eyes met, she instinctively uttered the words, "Where in the hell have you been?" in an accusatory tone. He grinned and held out his hand, "My name is Victor, and I am so sorry to have kept you waiting."

"HE TOOK YOU WHERE?" JANE ASKED IN a shrill voice, knowing full well she had understood her friend correctly the first time.

"Carter & Cooley, the sandwich shop on Nineteenth," Delphina snapped, a bit taken aback by her growing loyalty. "Fancy isn't always better, Jane. We were at Cistern the night before, for Christ's sake."

"Yes, where you met him by happenstance, Deli. He didn't plan it."

"Sometimes you just want to keep it real, you know?"

The conversation ended abruptly, Delphina sharing that she had to run, which was literally true. She tightened her laces, hit her classic country play-list, and started her run down the Heights Boulevard jogging trail, thankful that she did not share that she had also seen him on Sunday for green tea and veggie flatbread at the bungalow coffee shop on Heights Boulevard. It would not matter that it was three dates in three days. Jane would not be happy with his choice for date locations.

Victor joined her birthday celebration Friday, leaving his friends to dine on their own. They started as a party of four, with Jane and Libby egging on the duo, but as Victor and Delphina continued talking and Jane and Libby continued drinking, they coupled off, retreating to a quieter table at the corner of the bar.

Victor Walsh and his two business partners had recently founded their own architectural firm. They leased half a floor in the Niels Esperson Building, partially gutting the space while preserving the aesthetics of the old structure. The final masterpiece was stunning. "You really must come see it at our open house," he said, a testament that reflected the ingenuity of their work. This ingenuity, however, came with a steep price, and since he did not have a family of his own, he figured he might as well reside in a Heights garage apartment but a few blocks from The Boulevard. His partners urged him to rent a loft downtown, but he refused to leave The Heights, knowing this is where he belonged. "The history, the charm . . . not a place in Houston like it."

The following day at lunch, Delphina rattled on about her love for the area and how she understood his connection, for she felt the same. She knew she could teach anywhere, but she loved Heights High School and the fact that she walked to work every day down streets where no two houses looked the same. He asked her how she liked her egg salad, after which she surprised herself, by being so bold as to raise it to his mouth to try a bite. They walked down Nineteenth Street, iced teas in hand, as Victor pointed out various buildings and their histories that he had studied.

Delphina knew she was in trouble when he shared that he had a flight to Chicago the following evening for a conference and then a visit to an old college buddy, her heart sinking at the thought of not seeing him for the entire week. He must have felt it too, and by the time he had walked her to her apartment, they agreed to meet for lunch the following day. She pressed her palms to the door after he left, resting her forehead on the cool surface and smiling in the realization that she could envision herself marrying him, a desire she had never felt before.

As she rounded the esplanade to jog back to her apartment, she heard the ringing of her cell phone through Willie Nelson's oohs and ahhs. Victor's number flashed across her screen, causing Delphina's spirits to take a leap as she slowed to a walk.

"I have a bone to pick with you, Ms. Cizek."

She could not believe he would engage her again in a southern witticism challenge considering her victory on Sunday, but she admitted he had an awfully good twang when provoked.

"Well, butter my butt and call me a biscuit!" she exclaimed as she slapped her palm on her thigh, catching the attention of another jogger.

"Now don't you go pretendin' you don't know what I mean."

"What in tarnation? Okay, lay it on me," Delphina replied, curiosity piqued.

"I'm smitten, Ms. Cizek," Victor replied in a tone and accent more his own. "Can't get you off my mind."

"Well, now, that sounds pretty nice to me, especially considering I share your sentiment," Delphina replied, matching his more genteel disposition.

"Yes, I agree it is mighty nice, but not so much so when you are a thousand miles away. Which is why I am making plans for Saturday night."

"Saturday? I thought you were coming in on Sunday?" Delphina asked.

"Yes, well, I've decided to come home early. I still have Friday night to catch up with George."

"Wow."

"Wow? Now c'mon! You can't let me down with a response like that!"

"Mr. Walsh, you have made me blush, and this conversation is just between me, you, and the fencepost. Imagine what will happen when people see us together."

"And, yes, they will see us dance at the SPJST Lodge." Victor said.

"Dancing?"

"Yes, my grandparents danced there for many years, and I would very much like to twirl you around to the sounds of Texas Tea, one of my favorite bands."

Delphina's mind took her on a moment's journey to the Texas countryside, memories of her own grandparents two-stepping and waltzing at the Veteran's of Foreign War Hall, home to Vizcek weddings, family reunions, and funerals. Her momma had always looked forward to the visits home. She was all smiles in her new dresses from Joske's.

She remembered the family reunion when Patricia was giddy to meet her three-month old great niece. She practically skipped into the hall, a Kaplan's bag dangling from her wrist, a bag, her niece soon would learn, that contained a delicate sterling silver rattle, an expensive gift that left her family in wonder over its purpose. Her momma carried a three-layer coconut cake, her contribution to the potluck and an accidental match to her layered, white dress. It was a grand entrance for the Cizek family, one that elicited endless *bless your hearts* throughout the afternoon.

She remembered her daddy stationing himself in the VFW bar, where he had remained for most of the afternoon, the smell of booze and cigarette smoke peeling back the layers of distance and time so that all that remained was a group of good ole boys who forgave the one who had left for the big city. Delphina waltzed in the bar just once, her daddy seated in front of a bowl of fake red flowers. She jumped up to snatch one and placed it in her hair before tangoing across the bar with a ghost. It was the one time she made her daddy angry. He jumped off the stool and dragged her by the arm to the far corner.

"Delphina Ann Cizek, you listen here! This ain't no joke!" he reprimanded, yanking the poppy from the top of her ear. "This here was made by a GI, just like your Uncle Louis and Edward and your Cousin Joe. It's meant to be respected. Wear it with pride and not like a fool!"

That had been the last time she entered a VFW bar.

"I'll need to dust off my dancin' shoes, but I think that sounds quite nice," she responded in a way that conveyed the smile that spread across her face.

"There's a dress code, you know. You can wear that beautiful yellow dress."

"The one with the wine stains or the one without?"

"Pick you up at seven o'clock?"

"Yes, but that depends on your time with George on Friday, right? You certainly can't pick up your darlin' when you've been rode hard and put away wet."

VICTOR ARRIVED AT HER APARTMENT, beaming in an expensive navy suit with a box of flowers in hand. Delphina had only heard of such a delivery from her reading and vintage films. She accepted the long, white box with the satin ribbon, opening the lid slowly as the white petals peeked out from beneath the tissue. The early return to Houston, the flowers, the suit: While these things were impressive in their own right, what captured her attention was the enthusiasm in his eyes. She had never met someone who wanted to please her as much as he did.

He wrapped his arm around her as they made their way in the SPJST Lodge. Beckoned by the old country love songs, she broke away to the dance hall entrance as he paid for the tickets at the door. Twinkles of light bounced from the ceiling to the jewels, joining the momentum of a hundred souls two-stepping and twirling. The energy drew her into the scene like a magnet. She was part of the ether rather than a person standing in the doorway. It was her first time there, but it was a place she knew, a place that welcomed the Vizceks, Cizeks, Jilufkas and Havliks—with an affinity bound by laughter and a fair share of tears, one steeped in coffee and lime sherbet punch.

"Let's have a drink in the Blue Room," he whispered in her ear before kissing her cheek.

It was the first time she had a Tom Collins and learned the power of gin. She spoke more of the progress she had made toward her graduate degree, the thought of being referred to as a doctor humbling and rewarding. He teased about the challenges she would face when she married and whether she would keep her maiden name personally as well as professionally. She conceded the point but maintained, "It is important not to count chickens before they hatch." And the right man just might very well make her want to conform to the name change tradition that Southerners hold so dear.

He talked about his love for architecture and drive to "honor the old souls that once graced buildings while making room for the new ones." He was impressed with the renovation plans for Heights High School and was pleased that the school district took the pains necessary to preserve what they could. He held a fondness for Heights High, although he could not place the reason. He surmised it was because he loved the neighborhood, but he also appreciated that the campus was designed by renowned architect John Staub, who had also designed Rice University and multiple showcase homes in River Oaks and Shadyside.

"A Houston treasure, right in our neighborhood," he beamed. "And I hope my firm will make its own Houston treasures." He admitted he was open to school design, knowing that many schools were on the list for an update, including Lamar High School and Milby High School, the latter built just a year before Heights High. He held her hand and teased that she could be his inspiration, an inspiration for a twenty-first century school.

Delphina's ears perked with the first "hello" coming from the dance hall, Victor noting the light in her eyes.

"I was listening to "Hello Walls" when you called to ask me to the dance tonight."

"Then I think we better hurry and hit the dance floor."

"Yes, I do agree!" she cheered, rising from the table and slurping the last of her drink through the straw. She giggled to herself as they scooted out of the bar, hand-in-hand, Delphina a little more at ease thanks to the gin.

DELPHINA HELD OFF ON SLEEPING with him, so much so that he questioned whether she was truly interested in him at all. She was petrified for him to witness her anxiety that surfaced during intimacy, her struggle to lie affectionately with a man, to share the personal moments after the physical. As a testament to her growing vulnerability, she confessed her struggles to Victor one afternoon as they walked down Nineteenth Street, browsing in stores over ice cream.

"There's something I need to talk to you about."

"Okay," Victor replied, eyeing her cautiously as he took a lick of his butter pecan.

They stopped in front of the window of an antique store, Delphina looking at the display of bedroom furniture and lamps as she gathered the courage to continue.

"I've struggled with anxiety my entire life," she said, continuing her gaze into the display window. "It's been with me since I was a child. My earliest memories are rooted in fear that something will go wrong, that I will cause something to go wrong."

He stood next to her, placing his arm around her shoulders as she continued.

"It paralyzes me at times, Victor. Makes me afraid to commit. I . . . I am so scared of losing someone I love," she said, feeling tears coming to her eyes. "And, and . . . I . . . I . . ."

"I fell in love with you the first moment I saw you," Victor interrupted. "And I've spent my life as a pessimist when it comes to matters like these."

Delphina looked in the mirror of the art deco vanity to see their reflections, Victor's gentle eyes and patient smile already familiar. She held his gaze in the mirror, and although he was standing right behind her, the window and mirror acted as a buffer that gave her the courage to admit, "I love you, too, Victor. I feel like I've known you for a long, long time."

"I know," he replied, turning her to face him. "And we will take as long as you need, Delphina."

THE ENTHUSIASM JANE INITIALLY BESTOWED on Victor from the night at Cistern cooled, not only because of their dates' less-than-stellar locations, but also because he resided in a garage apartment.

"Deli, you are my dearest friend, so please forgive me. You are thirty-one, for Christ's sake. You deserve better than a man with a starter career."

Delphina knew her friend meant well, but she thought Jane's concerns were misplaced. She figured the best remedy for her friend's ailment rested in a natural unfolding rather than explaining that her boyfriend threw himself so much into work that he could not care less where he lived at this station in his life, something he said he was open to changing "when the right one comes along."

"Jane, please join me for Victor's open house. You need not stay long, just a quick hello will certainly compensate for the doubts you have raised."

"You're letting me off the hook rather easily, Deli. Thank you. You know my heart is in the right place."

"I know. Meet you at your office at six o'clock on Thursday?"

"Sure . . . You know, I can certainly find my own way and meet you there."

"No, it's a good excuse to see your new office. And . . . it's not that far away."

Delphina arrived at Jane's office a few minutes early and took a seat next to the receptionist. She knew Jane had a late meeting with her mentor, Mr. McClelland, the description ringing in her ears, "He can be such an asshole! Swears and constantly challenges me. And you know what? I adore him! If he wasn't so old and fond of men . . ." and she concluded with a burst of laughter, eyes full of light, revealing how much she had taken to him.

The older gentleman she deemed Mr. McClelland gave her a nod as he left Jane's office. Delphina conceded that he was alluring in a rugged kind of way. She found it hard to believe he was gay. What a lucky man, she said to herself, thinking about how Jane met his husband at the firm's holiday party last year.

"Come on in," Jane called, appearing at her office door.

Delphina walked in, placing her bag on a chair before heading to the window. "This is amazing. I can see the University of Houston Downtown from here."

"We're neighbors! I am glad you are teaching a class there this summer. I always thought you would make a good college professor," Jane said.

"It's funny how life finds ways to work itself out. It feels like a natural fit. So many of my students attend school there after Heights. Well, the ones who are fortunate enough," Delphina said as she turned back toward her friend. "I'm really proud of you, Jane."

"Thank you. I never would have thought I would work in a place like this," Jane admitted, raising her hands in the air. "This firm has been here since 1928, the year after the building opened. There are big shoes to fill."

"And you will bring your own shoes to fill . . . from Neiman's!" Delphina teased. "You ready?"

"Yes, I am ready. Ready for a drink," Jane replied, with her head buried in her handbag, looking for her lipstick. "Where are we heading? I don't mind driving."

"Sixteenth floor."

"Are you shittin' me?" Jane gasped, pausing with lipstick in hand.

"Please refrain from such vulgar language! We are, after all, in a fancy law office!"

"Yeah, but it belongs to an attorney who is the mentee of Mr. McClelland!"

The elevator doors opened ten floors below as if cuing the first scene of a performance. The elevator, elegant and old world, bore a sharp contrast to the neutral hues and modern fixtures of the redesign. Delphina and Jane stepped from the elevator, and Delphina watched Jane from the corner of her eye as Jane's gaze swept the room to get her bearings.

"Delphina!" Victor called from across the floor, waving in his smart designer jeans and crisp white shirt.

As he made his way through throngs of people, pats on the back, and attempts to engage him in conversation, Jane murmured, "Hmmm. I've been fooled."

He snatched two glasses of champagne from a server tightly gripping her tray of flutes, wary of the crowds rushing for more bubbly.

"I'm so glad you both could make it! Jane, I can't believe in a city this size that we work in the same building."

"This place is incredible, Victor," Jane said, her eyes scanning the room. "I knew someone was moving in on this floor, but I had no idea. Hey, there are a few partners from my firm."

"We wanted to extend the invitation to the tenants. This building is pretty special, you know? Like family," he replied before turning to Delphina. "Hey, Deli, I need to check something real quick, but then I want to introduce you to some people, okay?"

"Sounds good," Delphina replied, beaming at Victor as he walked to the other side of the room while stealing a few glances back at his admirer.

"He adores you," Jane said, eyes following Victor.

"Adores?" Delphina questioned.

"Yes. Adores. The way he looks at you," she replied, turning to her friend. "You may very well have found the one."

Jane excused herself upon Victor's return, chatting with her partners and weaving in that Victor Walsh was her best friend's boyfriend.

Had Delphina anticipated she would have spent the night by his side, her day would have been filled with anxiety, wondering how to be and what to say. Flocks of guests, from tenants to clients to colleagues in the industry, all clamored for a piece of Victor and his partners, offering congratulations and wanting to be part of new opportunities that knowing them might afford.

Delphina attempted to extricate herself on a few occasions when the conversation turned more serious, but Victor always pulled her back, at one point whispering, "I want to remember this moment with you," before kissing her on the cheek.

She met scores of people, and those who knew Victor well studied her with curiosity. Naming her profession as a teacher did not garner much interest other than a nod or the common, "I don't know how you do it. I could never be a teacher!" Given the event and her relationship, she did not utter her stock reply, "Then don't," but she managed to weave in that she not only planned to use her PhD in English for the advancement of secondary students but also for students matriculating to the University of Houston Downtown, a place that welcomes the inaugural collegiate experience for many families.

"As Thomas Jefferson asserted, 'An enlightened citizenry is indispensable for the proper functioning of a republic.'" A stupefied look usually followed this remark, garnering her much more adulation, which she accepted as an apology.

"Mr. Dunn, I'm so honored you made it tonight," Victor greeted the distinguished older man, extending his hand.

"The honor is mine. If only my grandfather could see what you've done to this floor!" he laughed, mouth open and head nodding as he surveyed the room.

"Mr. Dunn, I'd like you to meet Delphina. Deli, Mr. Dunn's family business has resided in the Niels Esperson since the building's inception in 1927."

"Well, it started out as Doyle Lumber way back then, but yes, we were here. What an unusual name. Lovely name. And are you in architecture, as well?"

"No, sir. I am a teacher," Delphina replied, waiting for the respectful nod of flat interest.

"Where do you teach?" he asked.

"Heights High School," Delphina said, tickled that someone showed a slight interest.

"My, my, it's a small world. My grandmother ... mind you, I don't remember her, died when I was not even a year old ... volunteered at Heights. She was very devoted to education. There is even a scholarship in her honor."

"Was your grandmother Ilona Doyle?"

"Yes! You are familiar with the award, then."

"Yes, I see it promoted every year."

"What is it they say . . . something about degrees of separation?" Mr. Dunn asked.

"Six. Six degrees of separation," Victor replied.

"Funny how that works, yes?" Mr. Dunn responded, laughing to himself.

The last guests left at half past midnight, leaving Victor's partners and their spouses, along with Delphina, to offer one final toast to the firm. When Delphina made her way to a back office to gather her handbag, she noted the abstract cutout of the walls made to expose the brick from the original construction. She placed her palms flat on the bricks' surface, wondering about the last soul from many moons ago who touched the same spot and wondering how often degrees spiral back in time, uniting people to one another's past and not just their present.

"Too much champagne?" Victor joked, raising his hands next to hers on the wall, pretending he needed the wall as support.

"Probably. But that's not why," she said, embarrassed. "Just thinking about the history of the building."

"A woman after my own heart." Victor pulled her closer to whisper, "Stay with me tonight. I've waited so long."

"It's only been a month," she teased, returning his kiss, feeling her resolve fade. She had discarded every other romantic relationship in her life, but this connection was the one she wanted to keep.

"Five weeks, and it feels like even longer. And that's a long time when you are in love."

That night, Victor proved to be the first man with whom she could sleep soundly through the night—her ear to his chest, the pulse of his heartbeat kissing her temple, reminding her of the fragility of life that she pushed to the back of her mind in order to function every day. She changed positions when her arm cramped, stretching out to the other side of the bed only to reach her left foot over to his, the warmth of his body a comfort to her restless soul.

CADMUS

Autumn 2007

CADMUS' HEART POUNDED WHEN HE saw the name of the sender in the upper left-hand corner: Genevieve Butler. The last time he had seen his great-niece was at Callista's funeral. He remembered the way she had looked back at him from the front of the church. He was amazed when her eyes found his own, her spot on the front pew quite a distance from his at the back. She was a child, and he remembered noting her countenance was on the cusp of transitioning to young adult. He wondered if she now assumed her mother and grandmother's aura.

The return address confirmed the rumor: She was a student at Harvard Law School. Ilona would be so proud of her accomplishment.

Dear Uncle Cadmus,

I know I am taking a chance not only with this letter but also with the liberal use of the word "uncle," seeing as we are connected in lineage and not relationship. Forgive me if my actions appear bold. It is an indicator of my desire to build the latter, if at all possible.

I grew up seeing the interlocking Ds throughout Houston, but my identity centered on one, Dunn. While I suppose it was a natural tendency given that it is my mother's maiden name, I have always been curious to know more about the Doyle side. Uncle Michael was always very kind to me, but he never wanted to talk much about Patrick, his brother and my great-grandfather, despite my repeated attempts to bait him in conversation. He talked about his father, my great-great grandfather, and the legacy he was proud to carry on in his honor.

I know even less about my great-grandmother. Since she passed away when my mother was barely two, she held no first-hand memories. Grandmother Callista was reluctant to speak much about her, I presume the reason nestled in shame or some other regret based on her tone and countenance when I asked, but I do not know for certain. She kept a photograph of my great-grandmother on her vanity, and more than once I stumbled in the room to see Grandmother Callista stroking her mother's face, a grainy black-and-white photograph of her standing on Main Street in front of the Merchants and Manufacturers Building. I do know she valued education and wanted to teach. This fact brings a smile to my face. I am certain she could not be more pleased of what came of the building, lumber from the Doyle family continuing to support the dreams of students in the University of Houston Downtown.

Perhaps we can visit the next time I am in Houston. I welcome you and your husband to visit me in Cambridge. I know a man of your intelligence would appreciate the culture of the city, and I would like nothing more than to take you both on a stroll throughout campus. We have so much to learn about one another, and I do hope God will grant us the time to do so.

In hopeful anticipation of your response,

Genevieve Butler

Cadmus made a beeline to the house. Placing the letter on his desk in the library, he reached for his fountain pen with one hand while the other reached for a sheet of heavy ivory stationery from the tray. Happy, overjoyed, excited—none of the adjectives seemed to fit. It took him a minute more to place his feeling: affirmed. Although he and Robert enjoyed a beautiful life together, her acceptance brought to light the depths of his void.

Glancing back to the envelope, he noticed a face peeking at him. He held the photograph of his great niece, and despite the exponential dose of Irish blood that ran through her veins, she clearly took after his mother. His eyes filled with tears as he wondered if Ilona and Callista were finally at peace.

DELPHINA

Autumn 2007

DELPHINA HAD NEVER SEEN HER daddy in a suit, much less a tuxedo. She did a double take when he stepped out from the town car, captivated by the image of how he may have looked had he been born into a different circumstance.

"Oh my, Daddy!" she gushed, making her way from Jane's house to the car. "You look so handsome!"

His eyes filled with tears, his lower lip curling in to fight a full-fledged flood.

"You're stunning, Lil' D," he whispered as he wrapped her in an embrace. "Guess you're not my Lil' D anymore."

"Daddy, I'll always be your Lil' D," she said, pulling back to face him, a tear sliding down her cheek. He wiped it away with his thumb, his rough hands marking a contrast to the well-dressed image he projected.

"Heavens, Benny! No more tears! We have perfect makeup here," her momma teased, bringing a needed moment of levity as they climbed into the car.

Delphina knew she would be on from the moment she stepped from the car, seeing the wedding was at Marmion Park on Heights Boulevard. No vestibule, no cry room to primp until the last second; she would step out to see Victor standing in the gazebo waiting for his bride. And there he was as the car pulled along the curb, surrounded by his friends, his smile visible from her seat.

"Delphina Ann, I do believe you made an excellent choice," her momma said as she looked out the window, prompting her to wonder if she were talking about her choice of husband or venue.

Victor and Delphina wanted a simple wedding, having lived through many southern productions, from elaborate receptions at country clubs to small town celebrations at halls across the Texas countryside. And although their friendships and families spanned both ends of the spectrum, those events held one thing in common: They were enormous undertakings. Nuptials under the gazebo at a Heights park, a reception at the old firehouse turned reception venue with friends and close family—they wanted a more intimate, simple affair to reflect their style. Their only indulgence was Texas Tea, the band, which the couple eagerly armed with an extensive playlist including their song, "Waltz Across Texas."

Delphina accepted her daddy's hand as she stepped from the car, the string quartet striking a chord the moment she placed her feet on the bumpy curbside flanked by pecan trees. As they made their stroll down the sidewalk, her eyes locked with Victor's. She gave thanks to the heavens above that she had fallen in love with a man who accepted her intensity, even embraced it. She thought of the nights she wept quietly in his arms, his palm stroking her head as he told her how much he loved that she felt life so deeply. He told her he knew she was connected to something greater; she was an old soul, as was he, and together they would channel their energies to create a beautiful life. In the silence of those nights, she knew he spoke the truth. His words echoed the same message etched in waves, pebbles, and vines that she had relied on as a young child to bring her peace.

Her daddy kissed her one last time on the cheek, as did her momma. She turned to Victor, and with joined hands they faced forward, life partners who gave one another the courage to commit in the face of impermanence.

DELPHINA

Spring 2010

"I HAVE PLENTY OF HAND-ME-DOWNS to give you. We will remain a family of four. Factory closed," Jane shared.

"And I have quite a few things left over, too," Libby added. "You are welcome to them."

"Your girl clothes outnumber the boy clothes by 3:1."

"Well, you might have a girl."

"No, it will not be a girl. I am more of a boy mom, I know it," Delphina confidently replied.

"What in the hell is that supposed to mean?" Jane said, slightly put off.

"Please don't take offense. You know what I mean."

"I know. It's fine," Jane said. "Pregnancy hormones are a bitch."

Delphina, however, did not know what she meant. She did not know how to explain that in her heart she felt more connected to the idea of a son. Having a daughter did not seem in the realm of possibility.

"Are you sure it's a girl?" Delphina asked the doctor later that week in a defiant tone, with Victor squeezing her hand to be quiet.

"I'm sorry, forgive me," she said before asking again, "You are certain?"

"As certain as we can be at this point, which is pretty certain," the doctor retorted.

The nurse gave Delphina and Victor a look of disapproval before returning to her notes, shaking her head. Delphina hoped anecdotal records were not a part of this process.

She made it to the restroom just in time, locking the door as she burst into tears, wondering why in the hell she was overwhelmed with sadness. The baby was healthy, and when she thought about it intellectually, she did not care whether she had a boy or a girl. But she could not shake the feeling that she was meant to have a son, and she struggled to reconcile this feeling with the reality that a little girl was on her way.

Delphina began a routine that night, rocking in the chair in the baby's room, palms open on her belly, the glow from the porch light making its way through the curtains. Variations of yellow paint samples dotted the walls: lemon meringue, morning sunshine, and number-two pencil. They had not planned on traditional gender colors, but she viewed the colors through the lens of a boy. She figured, perhaps, a son would follow in the next few years, a thought that already filled her with guilt, as if she were questioning the soul nestled within her body. Delphina spent the remaining months closing her eyes and summoning her connection; she knew enough to realize there was a pattern to her life, and with this acknowledgment she vowed to make an effort to put her thoughts of a son aside.

WITH AINSLEY MARIE CAME AN overwhelming love. The anxiety that haunted Delphina much of her life was countered by an impenetrable motherly love that made it all worth it, every ounce of worry dwarfed by a light that radiated from her heart, from a universal bond. As the doctor placed the baby on her chest after the birth, she kissed her head and whispered, "I'm so sorry I doubted you. This is how it is meant to be, my love."

Ainsley's perfect fingers and toes fed her reverence for divine order. She recalled the nights after she was born, gently rocking her as she slept, tracing her fingertip along her daughter's fingernail, moving over the fingerprint she knew was there and gliding along to her palm where tender wrinkles radiated into an asymmetrical web. She recalled not only waking, but enthusiastically waking, in the middle of the night to nurse her newborn daughter. Tenderly cradling the baby, she wondered how she could even call her Ainsley, the baby a splinter of the universe, the love and peace that emanated from this soul forcing Delphina to catch her breath. She silently shed tears during those moments, realizing that she had allowed her anxiety over the years to supersede the reverence. She vowed to follow her childhood instincts, wondering if the answer to her anxiety was simpler than she made it out to be.

Delphina cradled Ainsley's head on her shoulder, carrying her on a walking meditation through their home. She thought back to Victor's sentiments about creating a space that honored old souls while welcoming new ones. Their renovated 1935 bungalow certainly met his standard, the new addition and amenities tripling the square footage and welcoming the home to modern times. It was a place for the old and the new: She felt Ainsley's spirit energizing the home, the Walsh home. It would make a solid addition for a home tour one day.

Ainsley's November birthday gifted Delphina more time with her newborn, because the holidays did not count toward her leave. She had three months before returning to teach in the spring, time to study every movement and every breath, time to watch her daughter's eyes track the dancing moon and stars on the mobile, and time to realize that work would remove her connection to the divine she had created. Her return to work left her rattled, as if her absence placed her daughter in jeopardy.

Students noticed the difference in her demeanor. She appeared on edge, leaning in to what could be versus what was. Delphina stopped standing at her door in between passing periods, using the five minutes to shuffle at her desk and check her phone in the event Rosa tried to call. She stopped bringing snacks to school for her afternoon visitors, electing to stay only as long as she was required for tutorials, locking the door and scurrying down the hall to return to her daughter at home.

Dr. Walsh, I thought you were cool.

You need to chill, seriously.

My sister had hormone issues after her pregnancies, too, Mrs. It'll get better.

But Delphina knew it would not get better. She felt guilty for leaving Ainsley during the day. She now looked at her students through a mother's lens, and while this perspective could have served as a powerful connector to the lost souls that graced her classroom, it manifested too strong a bond in her heart and mind. Stories of abuse and neglect and of arguments in their homes that had captured her attention before left her physically sickened now. She wanted to serve them well, but the time and effort required to do it as she felt it needed to be done took her away from her own child. By the end of her first week back, she knew it would be her last year at Heights High.

"Dr. Walsh, thank you for writing that letter of recommendation. I received the scholarship!" Cecilia squealed.

"I am so very proud of you!" Delphina said, taking her in an embrace in the hallway. Cecilia was one of her favorite students from a time when she was a better teacher.

"I can't believe it. All my expenses are covered, including room and board . . . and to Rice University!"

"Now, that is incredible. I didn't realize it was so grand," Delphina remarked.

"It's usually not. It turns out that Ilona Doyle's son is a professor there. When he read my application and essay and knew I was already accepted, he said it was meant to be."

"And I'll be at awards night this year to see you receive it!" Delphina cheered. "The department chair is out of town, so I gladly stepped in to help. Perfect timing!"

Delphina lifted the hanger that held the yellow dress from Neiman's, brushing off the coat of dust and praying it would fit. She thought back to the night she met Victor, the night her dress had been ruined. Instead of bringing flowers to their first date, he brought a bag from Neiman's. He had bought her a new one, which left her speechless. She closed her eyes and took a deep breath as she pulled up the zipper.

"Yes!" she shouted in victory. "Goodbye baby weight!"

She walked into the living room to find Victor feeding Ainsley, her year-old eyes lighting up when her mother entered the room.

"You look beautiful," Victor said. "I mean really, really beautiful."

"Thank you. I feel beautiful. Tonight is a special one."

"It's not too late to stay on again for next year. I can't imagine you not working at Heights."

"I can return one day if I change my mind. There aren't many people gravitating to the profession."

Delphina kissed Ainsley and Victor as she headed out the door. She stopped at the white picket fence to admire her home, never imagining a million bucks could look so cozy. Giving thanks for the life she and Victor had created, she headed down the sidewalk, making her way to Heights Boulevard as the sun set.

She paused to take in a healthy view of the school as she strolled through the front entrance, committing it to memory. She knew that, when she left, the building would have a different air, the ebb and flow of new students and new faculty changing the energy.

Students and parents trickled down the hall, making their way to the auditorium doors. They wore smiles and freshly pressed clothes, and there were scents of perfume and flowers in the air. She saw Cecilia standing at the entrance, her hand waving wildly when she saw Delphina.

"Cecilia! And it's nice to see you, Mr. and Mrs. Cacique!" Delphina beamed, shaking their hands.

"It's so nice to see you again, Dr. Walsh! The teacher who inspired our daughter!" Mr. Cacique replied.

"Tonight is a special night, indeed." Delphina said as they walked into the auditorium.

"I'm disappointed that Dr. Doyle couldn't make it tonight," Cecilia said. "I wanted to thank him in person."

"Oh, well I am sure we can find another opportunity for you to meet him," Delphina encouraged.

"They said his husband had a heart attack. Say a prayer for him, will you?" Cecilia asked as they entered the auditorium.

Delphina headed to her seat on the stage along with the other department chairs. Mrs. Smith, the principal, headed over to her with a paper in hand.

"Dr. Walsh, thank you for stepping in tonight. I'm afraid I need to burden you once again. Dr. Doyle usually presents the scholarship, but he can't be with us tonight."

"Yes, I heard about the terrible news. I'm sorry."

"We all are. This is the first awards night he has missed since he founded the scholarship. I know he would be here if he could. Since you wrote Cecilia's letter, we figured it would be best if you presented the award in his absence."

"It would be an honor."

"Thank you. Here is the description for you to read on behalf of Dr. Doyle. It concludes with the letter you wrote, but feel free to add your own comments about Cecilia."

> The Ilona Doyle Scholarship was created in honor of my mother, an intelligent woman, a progressive for her time. Along with the example set through her kindness, compassion, and sacrifices made, she bestowed upon me a strong sense of self that allowed me to be the man I am today. A Heights resident for thirty-two years, she enjoyed her daily walks to Heights High School to tutor students in need. She was a firm believer in the value of education, and it is in this spirit that I enthusiastically present this award on her behalf.
>
> It is my sincerest pleasure to award this year's scholarship

to Cecilia Cacique, who will matriculate to my alma mater, Rice University. I look forward to welcoming her into my class this fall.

Delphina was overcome with emotion as she read his words, nose tingling as she imagined mother and son. This was exactly the type of mother she hoped to be for Ainsley.

CADMUS

Spring 2010

EVEN BEFORE THE DEMENTIA GAINED its footing, Cadmus visualized the memory process as a sieve sifting through sand, the largest particles remaining even though they were small in and of themselves. His memories of Robert had arranged themselves into their own score, vinyl spinning the sounds of Johnny Cash and Merle Haggard. Robert wanted the windows open on a smattering of humid nights, mosquitoes abounding and the pecan tree thirsting for a breeze. The mosquitoes left Robert be, as he deduced, "Because they know I'm a mean son-of-a-bitch." Cadmus had acquiesced, dousing himself in repellent after they had eaten supper and drank beer, their routine for those nights had Cadmus grading in the nook while Robert worked on briefs.

Robert had been in the kitchen grabbing another beer on one of those humid nights when he suddenly fell to the ground. Cadmus ran to his side to find him out of breath and reaching for his chest.

"Call an ambulance. And get the medical power of attorney," Robert gasped, Cadmus' fingers trembling as he dialed 9-1-1.

The paramedics arrived within minutes, freeing up Cadmus to run to the library for the documents. Robert kissed Cadmus as they lifted the gurney into the ambulance, and Cadmus followed along in his car. As he raced down Heights Boulevard, he begged God to spare him this loss, another loss that would be too much to bear. He offered his life in exchange, bargaining a higher power to allow him to pass first and let Robert live.

He knelt in the chapel, reverting to the prayers he had known as a child, the prayers to a God he no longer worshiped. The words comforted him even though he did not believe in a Savior; he felt the Savior was within everyone. He reached in his pocket for his mother's rosary, summoning all his energies to heal his husband.

"AND WHEN THE BIG ONE comes and takes me, just remember my son-of-bitch brothers will appear on the steps of The Doyle House with their hands out," Robert said as he lay in the hospital bed. He was feeling better.

"Robert, please don't talk like that. You need to cut back at the office, give more work to Jane."

Robert looked out the window, the sunlight that poured into the room revealing more wrinkles and spots. It was the first time Cadmus viewed him as an elderly man, the hospital gown dwarfing his frame.

"I've been thinking about it. I'll talk to her when I get out of here," he replied. "But I'm serious about my family, Cadmus. They have no use for a living gay brother, but a dead gay brother with a sizeable net worth? Well, trust me, I'll come in handy."

"Our papers are clear," Cadmus said, his discomfort growing. "But I may very well be the one to go first. And if I do, you will not need to worry. As beautiful as it is, no one in my family wants The Doyle House."

"You know, you can go to Heights tonight."

"I'm not leaving you."

"It's one of your favorite times of the year, Cadmus. Really, please go."

"No. Ilona would understand."

Cadmus longed to attend awards night despite his refusal to take his husband up on the offer. He wanted to meet Delphina Walsh, the teacher who composed the recommendation letter of the winning recipient. Reading the applicant's essay and knowing her enrollment to Rice would be derailed without financial assistance certainly helped her case. The lovely letter written by her teacher, Delphina, made it clear that he was meant to help Cecilia Cacique. He knew that Delphina must be the same soul he had seen at Kaplan's so long ago, questioning the odds over meeting more than one person with that name. He also recalled the young woman sharing that she studied English at the University of Houston.

He knew where to find her, though. She would be at Heights High School, and he could certainly find an excuse to visit and cross her path once Robert fully recovered.

DELPHINA

Autumn 2011

"DELI? DELI? ROSA'S HERE WITH Ainsley," Victor said, caressing her back as she lay in bed.

"I'll get up," she whispered. "I need to take care of her."

"No, please rest. I won't be long . . . just need to sign those papers at the office," Victor said, placing a kiss on her cheek. "Everything is going to be okay."

"I hope so," she replied. And then realizing the irony of her word choice, she added, "Maybe hope can be a strategy."

Delphina sat up in bed after Victor left the room, grogginess from the anesthesia lingering more than she thought it would. She wondered when to mark her baby's death, the day she learned there was no heartbeat during the sonogram or the day of the D&C. She knew the soul was taken long before the news was shared, and she hoped the being knew how much love she held for it during the brief time its spirit cradled in her womb. She wondered if it was the son she thought she was supposed to have.

She rose to take a shower, knowing she needed to spend time with her daughter, the one who was alive. Her parents would come by with lunch later. She longed for one of her daddy's hugs, to look in his eyes and know that they understood one another without having to say a word. He was not an educated man, but he was the wisest person she knew.

She wept in the shower, knowing that her nervous spirit made a firm return, an undercurrent throughout her life, but one that she managed as an adult. She could not allow it to take over the life she worked so purposefully to create.

Delphina did what she knew from years of self-care. She strapped Ainsley in her stroller and, telling Rosa she would be back in just a bit, she took a walk down Heights Boulevard to find evidence of the divine. She meandered along the pebbled trail, a slow pace as compared to the joggers who raced passed. She studied two butterflies as they danced in tandem into the gazebo, one butterfly not able to make its way from the lattice as it bumped the edges of the diamond-patterned wood. The escape was right in front of it, had it only taken a moment to notice its surroundings. After a few attempts, it joined its partner, flitting through the latticework and down the esplanade to the wildflowers sprouting along the curb.

A handful of leaves filled the bottom of the stroller on her return home. She held Ainsley as they rocked on the front porch, showing her daughter the veins of the leaves, guiding her index finger to trace along the pinnate and the palmate, sharing how the tender veins carry water to the blades.

"There is harmony to life, my love."

Ainsley grabbed the dried leaf, blades crumbling in the force of her tiny fingers. A few veins remained despite her daughter's impulse, prompting Delphina to realize the strength of the foundation. There was an order.

VICTOR WAS A PATIENT MAN. He held firm convictions but spoke with a soft voice. Delphina appreciated that his disposition balanced her unease. And this was why she knew, based on his countenance, that she was on borrowed time in rebounding. She knew he had something on his mind that he was hesitant to say.

"Let's go out tonight."

"I don't mind staying in, especially since Ainsley still has the sniffles."

"I already called Rosa. She'll be fine," he said, rising from the sofa and offering her a hand to help her up. "We can stay local . . . we haven't been to Cistern in a while."

Delphina smiled and agreed, "Yes, maybe a stroll on Nineteenth Street will serve us well."

After a round of cocktails and a bevy of tears, with oyster bacon potpie providing comfort, they vowed to resume date night with vigilance. After the shrimp and grits with Big Daddy's Hot Sauce and fried green tomatoes, alongside a most lovely bottle of chardonnay, they laughed, recalling times from the night he had ruined her dress at the bar to the wave of shock that overcame him when the sales lady at Neiman's disclosed the price the following day.

"I am proud to say I can easily afford that now and then some," he said, raising his glass in the air.

"And I am so proud of what you have accomplished. It's amazing, Victor, and I am sorry I do not say it as often as I should."

"I think we should talk about you, about what you are destined to accomplish," he said.

Delphina's heart sank. He was ready to say what was on his mind.

"Okay," she said, taking another sip of wine.

"I'm glad you are home with Ainsley, because it is what you wanted, and I am so damn proud I can provide a very nice life for us that allows you to do so," he started. "But I believe staying home is not the right path for you, Delphina. You were meant to teach."

"Victor, you saw how much life the job took from me! The summers off didn't matter . . . the work during the year was too grueling for me as a mother."

"Yes, the expectations of a public high school teacher are grueling for anyone, and the pay is lousy. I can't believe what society expects teachers to do with how little they are given."

Her heart settled, relieved that she would not be cornered to defend her decision.

"But that's not what I am getting at. I think you should teach, but at the university level. Even if you taught part-time, it would be something to fulfill you professionally and turn your attention to other things."

"And what about Ainsley? What 'other things' are more important than her?"

"Ainsley will be fine, because we are her parents, and you won't be working so much that it will be a bad situation for her. Delphina, you overthink things . . . your anxiety, your worry . . . you need more in life other than Ainsley."

Delphina stared out the window, unable to counter. She knew he was right. As much as she longed to be home with her daughter, she knew she had more to offer. She also began to fear her attention and focus could even be a detriment. There was something to be said about having something for yourself, and she knew her daughter would benefit from seeing her fulfilled through a vocation. The anxiety she held since her childhood acted as water, ready to fill any vessel. In this stage of her life, that vessel was Ainsley.

"I don't even know how to begin," she admitted.

"Well, I do. I have been thinking about this for quite some time, and just this week I thought about it again as I stared out my office window."

"And?"

"And my eyes were resting on the University of Houston Downtown. You taught a class there that summer, which gives you one foot in the door at UHD. The other foot is up to you," he replied as he tilted his head in a playful challenge.

DELPHINA FOLLOWED THE DEPARTMENT CHAIR, Mrs. Moore, down the long hallway, her excitement building as she saw the faculty names on the office doors. It had not occurred to her that she would have an office, seeing that she was slated to teach only two classes. She remembered the astonishment of a good number of Heights High teachers when she was given a classroom her first year. Most new teachers were relegated to the life of a floater. She had landed on her feet once again, other faculty members commenting they'd had a much harder time breaking into the system.

"Here you go, Dr. Walsh," Mrs. Moore said, opening the door to the tiny office at the end of the hall. "It's not very large, but the view is nice."

"Yes, it most certainly is," Delphina said, looking out the window. "Thank you."

Delphina rested her bags on the desk, her gaze fixed out the window at the east side of town. She looked over to see a trace of the Niels Esperson, and her heart filled with love for her husband. She felt her life coming together again just as it had at Heights High, and while she knew she had played an active role in creating it, she gave thanks to the fortuitous circumstances that continued to find their way to her.

"Dr. Walsh?" Startled from her reverie, she turned around to see Jasmine, one of her old students. She knew it was another echo that she was in the right place. "I had no idea you left Heights High!"

That greeting marked the beginning of a lovely hour of catching up on one another's lives, Delphina's first experience in cultivating a relationship with an adult student. Although Jasmine had only been fifteen when Delphina first met her, her street smarts dominated her book smarts at the time. Delphina's memory painted the relationship as more of a struggle, which was contrary to Jasmine's recollection: "You never gave up on trying to help me." Delphina's impact had not been tangible at the time, which made her wonder about the other times her hand would now be tipping the scales of their lives, so many years later.

"Let's go to the cafeteria for coffee . . . We can get there just in time before they close," Jasmine said.

"Sounds like just what I need," Delphina acknowledged, locking her office door as they returned to the lobby.

As Jasmine shared her journey after high school and her foray into retail, Delphina absorbed her surroundings, noting the windows and long hallways dividing the building. Although she had taught a summer class there many years ago, she had not paid much attention to the building. As they made their way to the elevators and then the lobby, Delphina noted a sprinkling of ornate remnants of days past scattered throughout the modern space.

"I was good at accounting in high school, not that you could tell by my grades since I didn't do much," Jasmine offered over a rueful laugh. "But I understood it. It came easily to me, and I liked how everything had its place."

"Yes, numbers do have black-and-white answers. Perhaps I should have taken to it more," Delphina acknowledged as she poured coffee into her cup. "Might have helped settle my heart!"

"Well, when my mother said her accounting office, she's a secretary there, was looking for a receptionist, I figured God was sending me a message."

Delphina raised her eyebrows in a question as they made their way to the lobby.

"I could work during the day and attend evening classes. It's a much better setup than the mall, especially with my baby, and it will be a better job in the end for all of us."

"I couldn't be happier for you, Jasmine," Delphina beamed. "I knew you had it in you."

"Yes, you did!" she affirmed. "And now I need to bring that *it* to my evening class. Mind if I stop by sometimes?"

"I'd be disappointed if you didn't," Delphina said as the two women hugged. "Enjoy class. I'm heading to the bookstore for a few things before I head back up."

COFFEE IN HAND, DELPHINA MADE her way around the lobby before taking the stairs to explore one floor at a time, meandering down the long hallways and envisioning what had once been. She knew very little of the building, other than that it was nearing ninety years old. A building of this scale could not have been intended as an educational institution given the time it was built and the size of the city at the time.

As she ascended to the fourth floor, the atmosphere thickened, enveloping her in silence as she traipsed down the long aisles, peeking into the handful of offices with open doors. She surmised the heaviness in her heart was due to her absence from Ainsley, knowing that her time would be better spent setting up her office and working on her syllabus rather than roaming the halls.

Delphina's mind drifted back to her thoughts from earlier and how her life's circumstances had come to be. For an anxious heart from East Houston, she had come a long way. She knew she still had a way to go, but she felt the pieces of her life settling almost in tandem with the steps she was taking around her new workplace.

Taking a sip of coffee, she remembered the first time she saw the UHD Building when her family first drove in from Granger. She remembered the days she spent with her momma at the coffee plant and the day she discovered her love of writing as she looked at the skyline and the bronze building, the one in which her future husband would pour his heart into redesigning. She offered thanks for her struggles, realizing that had she a calm heart she would have never met Dr. Stilton, the person who gave her the opportunity to spend time in The Heights. It was the location of her first and only home apart from her parents, her first job, and her meeting of her husband.

She recalled her social isolation as a child, and with it came another wave of gratitude: The moments she spent as an observer allowed her to appreciate interconnectedness from an early age. Interconnectedness was at work again today; Jasmine's unexpected visit had pulled her away from the grind, gifting a time for reflection that she would not have had otherwise.

By the time she made it to the sixth floor, her thoughts brought the realization that her anxiety was evolving to more of a restlessness, that perhaps each turn her life had taken was guiding her to what she was meant to do. The idea of looking ahead to the puzzle pieces left to fit in her lifetime brought more curiosity than unease, the balance on the former given the beauty of how her life continued to unfold. She paused at her office door; a sensation beckoned her to take a look around to see who was watching. The building felt like an old friend. Seeing an empty corridor, she continued through the door to begin the process of making the space her own.

DELPHINA SAT AT THE COMPUTER in her office, attempting to focus on grading midterm exams. Rosa was with Ainsley, which thankfully afforded her more time to work. Closing her eyes to still her mind, she looked out the window toward the east side of Houston. The late afternoons and evenings spent grading and planning in her office lulled her to another world, one where she heard the train whistles in concert with screeching of the rails. She fought off the urge to meander the halls with coffee as she did on so many nights, knowing she needed to focus on work rather than the musings of her mind.

"Of course, this place is haunted," a colleague replied when Delphina confided that she felt a little uneasy after hours on the tenth floor that first semester. "Three hundred and fifty Union soldiers were imprisoned here. You haven't read the history of this building?"

She asked Victor about it one night over supper.

"Architecturally, it was ahead of its time when it was constructed in 1930. Known as the Merchants and Manufacturers Building, it was meant to be a gem of the city, like a shopping mall of sorts with offices and industry," he replied.

"What happened?" Delphina asked.

"Great Depression, flooding on the bayou. Gave people a reason to look elsewhere. And you know how fast Houston changes . . . newer buildings were on the way when confidences rose."

Her initial unease evolved into feelings of warmth and comfort; Delphina was beginning to wonder if some part of her soul communed with the spirits in the building. She felt UHD was where she had belonged all along, a place where her responsibilities between home and work balanced, a place that allowed her to enjoy learning while helping students succeed. She poured love into her work, spending hours to create a flawless lesson that blended the art and science of teaching and discussions to ignite a passion in the students.

As the semester progressed, her late afternoons in the office turned to evenings, Delphina eventually taking the late classes for students who worked during the day. She had her mornings with Ainsley and time during the day to volunteer as a room parent. She was thankful for Victor's instinct, for the serendipity that came into play when his eyes rested on UHD from his office window as he reflected on how to support her.

She knew she needed to focus. She chastised herself for the poor use of time last week, too much time spent wandering the floors after hours with coffee in hand, imagining the people that once bustled through the halls and lobby. These sojourns throughout the building brought her comfort, but she knew she had indulged too much when even Rosa failed to make eye contact after her consecutive late arrivals home.

Closing her eyes, she summoned her focus and gave a slight bow to the spirits in the M&M. It was time to focus on her work.

CADMUS

Autumn 2013

ROBERT COULD HAVE EASILY SENT Jane to the client meeting in Boston, but he knew it offered a good reason to see Genevieve. They had met once when she was in town for the Christmas holiday, and although Cadmus' heart dipped when she confessed that her mother did not want to join her on the visit, he was pleased she remained undaunted in her decision to have dinner at their family's home on Heights Boulevard.

During that first visit in Houston, Cadmus shared his parents' love story as it had been told to him, but he also confided the affair and the most dreadful night at Shadyside. He told her about the letter he found from Maureen Sullivan after his mother died, as well as how Margaret filled out the rest of the sordid tale. He shared Michael's manipulation at the reading of the will, his intense jealousy of his father and of his parents' marriage. Cadmus spoke methodically, making every effort to convey the family history as factually as he could but admitting the bias of his own lens.

Robert served as a dutiful host of The Doyle House, refreshing glasses as the stories unfolded. Genevieve confided that she wanted to try her Greek cousins' newest place in town on her next visit. They joked at how the maître d' would react if they declared themselves as the long-lost Petrarkis relatives and, as such, deserved the best seat in the house. Cadmus shared that his mother's parents loved him as best they could, but his guilt over her death, as well as the fact their lives veered in differing directions, drove him to a life of seclusion.

Cadmus and Robert enjoyed their day meandering through South End, Beacon Hill, and Newberry Street, going in and out of stores and taking breaks over coffee and pastries. They would visit Cambridge with Genevieve the following day, and while Cadmus knew he would adore the university setting, he could not help but predict his favorite part of the visit would rest with their stroll down Commonwealth Avenue, the inspiration behind Heights Boulevard's esplanade, in place before The Doyle House existed.

They planned to enjoy a round of drinks on their own at The Last Hurrah before Genevieve arrived. He imagined his parents gracing the bar had they been alive, his father's eyes commanding attention while his mother maintained her powerful, understated presence. He beckoned back the waiter, deciding last-minute to change his usual drink order to a gimlet. He and Robert made a toast to their trip—the only trip they would ever take to see a family member.

Robert was taken aback by Genevieve's growing resemblance to Ilona, even though he only knew his mother-in-law through stories and photographs. Genevieve walked into the bar, unassuming yet full of confidence at the same time, her brown eyes full of life.

"I'm so glad to see you both!" she cheered, the strength of her embrace rattling Cadmus. Aside from Robert, Cadmus had last had a hug full of that much love only when his mother was alive. Genevieve went around the table to offer a hug to Robert, Cadmus rising to help her into her chair.

"And what are you having, Uncle Cadmus?" she asked, giving his drink a once-over.

"A gimlet, of course. In honor of your great-grandparents, what hell-raisers they were, enjoying gimlets during Prohibition!"

"Then that's what I'll have. Quite fitting for the news I have to share." Genevieve said as she licked her lips in anticipation. "*The Harvard Law Review* is publishing my article striking down the Defense of Marriage Act. We will see what the Supreme Court has to say soon enough!"

"Now that's an accomplishment, indeed!" Robert bellowed. "What a progressive you are!"

"Yes, my mother tells me I'm cut from the same cloth as my great-grandmother," she grinned, looking to Cadmus.

"Speaking of, I do have something for you," Cadmus responded, reaching into the interior breast pocket of his jacket. "This belonged to Ilona. I know she would be thrilled for you to have it."

Genevieve eyed the black velvet box for a moment before opening the lid, gasping when she saw the diamond bracelet Cadmus remembered his father buying the Christmas before he died.

"Uncle Cadmus, surely this should be given to someone else," She demurred as her fingers stroked the diamonds.

"No, my dear. It belongs to a hell-raiser, to a progressive," he replied, eyes twinkling as he sipped his gimlet. "Wear it, and think of Ilona."

CADMUS SPENT THE MORNING IN the rose garden, thoughts of his mother coming on stronger than normal in the month after their Boston trip. The September humidity glazed his forehead. He hoped autumn weather would make a mark this year. The phone was ringing when he entered the kitchen. By the time he arrived in the library, he was winded, falling heavily into the chair as he picked up the receiver.

"Cadmus! So glad you finally answered. Is everything okay?" a voice rang out.

"Evelyn? Why, of course!" he replied, bewildered by the call.

"Well, it's quite unusual for you to miss a class without calling. I can't recall such a time in the past twenty years I've known you."

"Missed a class? But it's Tuesday. My first class doesn't start until eleven thirty."

"Cadmus, it's Wednesday. Your first class was at nine o'clock."

He stared absently into space for several seconds before looking at his desk calendar.

"Oh, Good Lord, I don't know how that happened," he said, comparing the date on his watch. She was correct.

"Life happens. I'm just thankful you are okay."

He hung up the phone and headed to his room to get ready for his afternoon class, deciding that he would not share this detail with Robert, just another indicator of their growing concern over his memory struggles.

Fear set in as he drove to the University. He was only a few weeks into the fall semester, and he only taught two classes. As his teaching assistant, Clementine, planned to cover most of the grading, his workload was very simple, but he did not want to lose the dignity it brought.

The small lapses peppering the past year were easier to discard, simple things like forgetfulness over where he had placed his keys or whether he had finished grading a set of papers, things that were easily identified as "normal" with a seventy-seven-year-old mind. But this morning's episode supported a progression, as did his behavior at a dinner with a few of their friends, where he had struggled to follow the threads of conversation, unable to interject. He remembered the defensiveness that had crept over him on their drive home afterward, turning to Robert and saying, "I'm tired, that's all. I tossed and turned much of the night." He was not lying. He was very tired, fatigue becoming more of a daily companion.

"I am so glad you are here," he said to Clementine when he saw her seated at his desk.

"Of course, Dr. Doyle," she replied. He opted not to inquire about the concerned tone of her answer, which prompted him to wonder whether it was more than his forgetfulness over the morning class. He did not want to know.

"I'll attend the afternoon session with you," she said, moving from his desk to give him his seat.

"Thank you. And you know you are always welcome to chime in when

I'm at a loss for words!" he teased. "Sometimes my thoughts work faster than my tongue."

Her warm smile helped, but he saw that flash in her expression once more. Things were worse than he had thought.

"READY?" CADMUS ASKED, SWINGING ON his sports coat as he headed from the closet.

"Yes. I just need a minute," Robert replied, sitting on the ottoman at the foot of the bed with shoehorn in hand and staring at the floor.

"Are you okay?" Cadmus asked, taking a seat next to him.

"Yes. Just a little tired . . . slept like hell last night," Robert replied, wiggling his foot into his loafer.

"Yes, like me," Cadmus replied, a small feeling of vindication based on their conversation last week. "Perhaps you should consider cutting back at the office."

"Like hell I will! Three half-days a week? Lord help me if I can't manage that. Jane manages most of it. She's a smart one."

"Let's stay home today. You can paint, and I have reading to do."

"No. I know how much you want to see the Turrell exhibit. Closes tomorrow."

Robert handed Cadmus the keys to his car as he rose, and Cadmus later cursed himself for not demanding they stay home. Robert loved driving his convertible, knowing full well that at age seventy-nine his days were numbered.

They made their way down Montrose toward the art museum, Robert lovingly reaching his hand to rest on Cadmus' leg as they passed the block where Patrick died when he crashed the car the night of the Shadyside party. The tree stood firm as the victor, time healing the gash that had been left in the bark so long ago. Cadmus often wondered how the confluence of events may have shifted had his father not been able to get hold of a car to chase after his mother, screaming her name to come back. Cadmus looked over at Robert to offer a smile of appreciation for his remembrance, but Robert kept his gaze looking out to his right, as if he were searching for evidence of Patrick.

The line to the main exhibit measured at least fifty people deep. Robert pointed to a bench several yards behind the end of the line, and Cadmus nodded as he watched him walk over and take a seat.

A mother with twin toddler daughters stood in line in front of him, the mother trying her best to pass the time and distract them, but the little ones had grown weary of the rounds of I Spy. One daughter raised her index finger in the air, claiming that she needed a new princess Band-Aid. As the mother released the hand of the other daughter to rummage through her bag, the little one meandered away from the line, causing a moment's panic.

"Not to worry. I see her," Cadmus replied, walking over to the little girl, amazed that she had gotten so far. Bending down, he asked, "So, what's your name?"

"Sophia."

"My, what a beautiful name. Did you know it means wisdom?" he asked, pointing to her temple. "Let me take you back to your mother."

The little girl reached up to place her hand in his, beaming up at her new friend.

"What the hell is this?" Robert asked when they entered another room before the exhibit, Sophie still captivated by Cadmus as she moved forward in line.

"You can't wear shoes in the exhibit. We need to wear paper booties," Cadmus explained.

"Good God Almighty," Robert mumbled. "What ever happened to simply painting?"

"Trust me."

Robert and Cadmus slowly made their way up the stairs to the exhibit, taking sure-footed steps with a docent in tow. The dim light failed to conceal the uncertainty in Robert's eyes, the strong constitution Cadmus once knew fracturing. An audible sigh of relief marked their arrival to the top, where *Ends Around* came into full view, a haze of colors morphing from warms to colds, creating a heavenly ether that drew them into the space.

A docent raised her hand as they approached, "Be careful. There is no wall, only an eight-foot drop."

"Are you sure?" Robert questioned as he came to a standstill, staring forward in disbelief. "I see a wall."

"No, it's an illusion," the docent stated, accustomed to the questions from the spectators. "There is no end."

They stood there for several minutes, the light acting as a magnet holding them captive. Cadmus stood in one place, making a 360-degree turn to absorb the entirety while Robert remained fixated at the illusory wall.

"You would have made a good father," he said to Cadmus.

"What?"

"A good father," Robert repeated, turning his head to face his husband. "I saw you with the little girl. You would have made a good father."

Few words passed between them as they meandered through the remaining exhibits, the main exposition leaving them at a loss for words. *The Light Inside*, Turrell's illuminated tunnel that connected the two museum buildings, had less of an allure after traversing the special exhibits, but they still enjoyed the final sojourn as they returned to the exit nearer their car. Cadmus stopped at the men's room while Robert continued on his way up the stairs, sharing that he would be waiting when Cadmus was ready.

Only a handful of minutes passed before Cadmus headed back upstairs. He noted Robert seated in one of the lobby chairs with his eyes closed. As he neared, his smile faded with the observation that Robert was slightly slumped to the side. He placed his palm on Robert's cheek, and even though his flesh was still warm, he knew his husband was gone.

"I DON'T GIVE A RAT'S ass about the rainbow flags flyin' around town. A man can't marry a man," JD barked through the phone. "And Robert knows it, too, now that he's looked into the Good Lord's eyes."

"I have nothing to say to you," Cadmus retorted as he slammed down the receiver, an attempt to hide just how much the call rattled him.

Robert was right about the contact, but Cadmus was thankful no one had appeared at the door. He quickly placed a call to Jane, asking her to ward off the McClellands. The Doyles were not accepting, but at least they maintained decorum. He promised Robert he would keep his wishes and not give "the bastards" one dime, but he feared this might take more strength than he had.

Robert and Cadmus both wanted the same arrangements, a private service at the funeral home on Heights Boulevard with only a handful in attendance. Robert did not want his entire office there, only a few veteran partners, his assistant, and Jane, of course.

Cadmus understood. The last thing he wanted was a large number of faculty present. While his work was a part of him, it remained a private connection. He rarely graced faculty gatherings, only committing to the bare-bones obligations. Genevieve was the only Doyle family member invited, as well as Clementine, who Cadmus thought of fondly, beginning from when she had connected him to Robert's colleagues. With Robert gone, either of these ladies would take the helm for Cadmus' service. He had no one else.

He looked out to the rose garden and made his way outside for a walk, still haunted by the shocking images of the paramedics running into the museum, sirens and lights flashing from the vehicles stationed on the street outside. Cadmus stared at his husband's lifeless body as they lifted the gurney into the ambulance, and when they helped him into the back of the vehicle, he saw little Sophia studying him intently from the door to the museum, her mother's arm wrapped around her as she tried to absorb what was happening to her friend.

Genevieve meant well with her letters following Robert's death, and although they had created a beautiful relationship through the art of old-fashioned correspondence over the years, her most recent missives filled him with rage.

"How can she possibly understand?" He shouted at the library walls. She had some nerve in drawing a comparison from how she felt when Grandmother Callista died, a relationship so very different from his own. He resorted to tearing the letter into shreds, refusing to return that round.

Clementine dropped off meals twice per week and attempted to engage him in updates on the classes he relegated to her. On her most recent visit, he managed to hold his temper until her car pulled away from the curb. Then he threw the aluminum tins in the trash and screamed, "I am not a goddamn invalid!"

As he stormed through the garden, he cursed God for making him suffer another loss. "I didn't ask for much, damn you!" he shouted to the clouds. "I just wanted to go first! I needed to go first!"

Taking a seat on the bench, he counted three black birds on the roof of his home, their beaks revealing that their heads pointed in different directions, as if they were looking for someone. For the first time since Robert's death, Cadmus broke down into tears.

DELPHINA

Autumn 2013

DELPHINA DID NOT NEED TO look at the clock to know it was 2:19 a.m. or thereabouts. She did not need to hear the clock chime at a quarter past the hour to know it was time for what had, unfortunately, become an unintended ritual. She rose from bed, her care exercised from an intention to send warm thoughts of peace and relaxation to Victor as he lay next to her, serene and deeply nestled in sleep.

"Lucky soul," she whispered as she eyed him with jealousy. She began her count.

Eleven steps. One . . . two . . . three. Delphina counted the steps as she made her way to the alarm pad, a walking meditation, each foot placed solidly, deliberately, on the cool oak floor. She could easily extend her step to make it an even ten, but she liked the odd number, and eleven was the number first counted when the routine began.

Seventeen steps to the French door leading to the garden. She noticed the moonlight striking the bookcase, illuminating the shelves of books, each tome housing stories of lives led and interests pursued. The day following a night of fitful sleep, she fancied the idea of reading to nurse her insomnia, or if the time was right in the semester, there was grading to do. These sleepless moments, however, were always fraught with challenges, her fragmented mind struggling to comprehend text in the hours before dawn.

Delphina opened the door and made her way downstairs to the garden, the humidity enveloping her as she took a deep breath to acclimate to the nighttime air. As a train cried three long wails, she thought of the train lines that ran below UHD. She wished she could meander the UHD halls at that moment rather than her yard. Taking a full, deep breath, she began her walking meditation, intentionally grounding her feet on the cool, travertine stones lining the perimeter of the backyard.

After two revolutions, her meditation wandered to a reflection on her dreams of the mansion that had resumed with force, occurring almost nightly, a haunting in her mind. She attempted to reconstruct as many pieces of the dream as she could, pulling from previous dreams over the years. The house, a stately mansion resting on a simple lawn, faced a street lined with new oaks that ran perpendicular into a busier street. The street in front of the house ran east-west, but she could not explain why she knew this to be so. A brick wall bordered the busy street, and on the other side of the wall was a body of water with gentle currents. Perhaps it was a bay. A frequent image of black ripples, moonlight winking on the lapping water, made her more prone to connect the setting with night rather than with day. The dreams set at night often featured intense light radiating out of every window, offering a stark contrast to the blackness. Golden white poured from each frame, the intensity of it blocking the sight of anything on the inside.

Delphina had yet to make it inside the house, something she desperately wanted. In some dreams, she was a passenger in a car driving through the neighborhood; one particularly vivid dream had her on a thruway making a sharp curve. Yet on other sojourns, she hovered with a prime view, the home emanating a sterile feeling, as if it were frozen in time and deserted by the inhabitants.

Minutes before, Delphina had walked the perimeter of the grounds on an overcast day, captivated by scores of dead black birds covering the yard. The gruesome sight did not frighten her, but the birds strewn about the grounds gave her pause as she studied their contortions—a frail leg, twig like and bent in the opposite direction; a neck twisted in such a way that the black feathers parted to reveal gray, flaky flesh; a wing bent upward with a feather splayed like a Native American headdress. The images hollowed her stomach and brought a fantasy-like quality, much like dreams of flying or trying to run despite motionless feet. She remembered when a cousin had frightened her as a child, telling her that dreaming of snakes meant someone hated you. She feared snakes because of the anxiety that was triggered about who hated her, not so much because of their fangs and venom. This offered a good topic of study: birds as symbols. Perhaps she could find a pattern.

Delphina returned to her steps with greater mindfulness. Reflecting on the dream was a lapse in her focus, but now she was determined to stay in the present moment—the smooth texture of the stone, the water trickling down the obelisk fountain.

She still did not refer to herself as a Buddhist. It would be too much for her momma to accept. Any time she was critical of Catholicism, her momma raised her hands in the air to beg St. Delphina to forgive her daughter and not withhold blessings. Delphina often wondered why her momma, a woman hungry for glamour and elegance, chose as her namesake a saint regarded for piety and humility.

After circling the garden seven times, Delphina sat on the marble bench next to the fountain, continuing her attempt to settle her heart. A pecan from her neighbor's tree fell next to her foot, reminding her of the treasure she had found so long ago on the way home from Heights High. She picked up the gift, noting the irregular black markings on the shell, thumbing its length. She thought of the nut inside and its symmetrical composition before turning to her own life, to look for patterns she could see. She found it frustrating that the patterns in nature were simpler to discern. Animals instinctually know their purpose and function. A tree knows that it needs to grow, extend its roots, and in doing so contributes to the world, all without the interference of free will.

Delphina offered a slight bow to the pecan tree before returning to the house. After a gentle tug on the French door, she let out a shriek at the darkened figure standing in the hallway.

"Mommy?"

Adjusting to the nighttime shadows of the room, she offered a lopsided smile to the figure reaching toward her.

"You scared me, love!"

"It happened again, Mommy."

"Tell me about it, Lady Bug," Delphina scooped up her daughter and carried her back to bed.

"He was at my window, but I told him I did not want to go," Ainsley whimpered into her ear.

"And did he leave?"

"No. He giggled and said the Indian Princess wants to play with me."

"All is well, Ainsley. All is well. You are safe," Delphina murmured, trying to stifle a giggle at her daughter's fear of Peter Pan. She conceded that once you remove the knowledge of the well-loved fairy tale that has become an accepted part of children's culture, it was understandable to fear a boy in tights who flies to your room at night. Nuzzling her face into her daughter's neck, she breathed in her scent that was mingled with the faintest traces of cotton candy from the day's outing to the zoo.

One present moment topic she had mastered was showing her daughter affection, and Delphina acknowledged the irony that it had taken her position at UHD to help the cause. Victor was correct that she needed a professional outlet to channel her restless heart, which she knew was his euphemism for anxiety. Ainsley's enchantments intensified with every passing year, and with reverence she watched her daughter learn new words and connect life's dots, witnessing her journey in consummate adoration. If it was, indeed, true that you chose your parents, Delphina was over the moon to be chosen by this exquisite soul.

She could not help but give a rueful chuckle at what this round of choices beget. She remembered first noting the elaborate billboard with *Peter*

Pan emblazoned in the familiar script but with gold shimmering reflectors filling each letter, mirroring the late afternoon sun. Driving home from UHD later than normal, guilt nipped her for leaving her daughter with Rosa for so long, although Ainsley would not mind or notice.

The child loved Rosa to the point of anointing her with the endearment Abuelita, their time together often spent in the garden describing the treasures Ainsley found while combing through the yard: a hallowed snail shell, leaves from the boxwoods, a fragment from a bird's egg. Each object joined a narrative, woven in a blend of English and Spanish, as they thoughtfully constructed a village under the stairs leading to the porch, a hamlet that welcomed fairies at night to lull Ainsley to sleep as she dreamed of the enchanted world she created only steps from her bedroom bay window.

Leaving late from work led to taking an alternate route home to avoid traffic, which led to passing the infamous billboard that inspired Delphina's idea for a family theatre date to see *Peter Pan*, hence Ainsley's recurring nightmare of a boy in tights. Delphina was responsible for her daughter's nightmares.

Settling into bed with Ainsley, Delphina was full of hope at the thought of dreaming again. Wanting to make it inside the home this round, she tightly closed her eyes to force a return. It was doubtful she would make progress; she knew matters of the soul fail to surface on demand but often result from a peaceful mind. After several minutes, Delphina conceded it was a futile effort. She opened her eyes, and with that movement came the release of her facial and neck muscles, the physical intensity of her efforts having distanced herself from the dreamlike state to an even greater degree than she had realized.

Fully awake, she studied the distorted pattern of angles projected on the wall from her neighbor's porch light as it shone through the shutters. Resting her chin on Ainsley's head and feeling the tickles from her delicate strands of hair, she began counting the angles, one . . . two . . . three . . . four . . . as the clock struck a quarter to three.

CADMUS

Spring 2014

"DR. DOYLE, YOU NEED TO eat," Clementine pleaded after she returned to the library from the kitchen, noticing that the last meal she delivered had not been touched.

Cadmus sat in the nook, his books strewn about and hair disheveled.

"And I do think you would feel better if you had a bath."

"You're not going to bathe me!" he barked in astonishment.

"No, sir, I wasn't planning on it. I can call a nurse to assist you a few times a week."

Cadmus struggled to find the words to respond. He nodded his head without looking at her, grateful that she left the house without saying another word. He thought they had anticipated it all when it came to their end-of-life plans, mostly due to Robert's unwavering pragmatism to direct the course of their lives. All their papers were in order, everything taken care of to authorize one another to act as a spouse needs to act in the resolution of affairs. They had even talked about The Oaks, a luxury senior center, should the time come when their needs exceeded their desire to reside at home. They did not know how they would enter as a same-sex couple, the buzz that would certainly stir up the place. Robert's death had resolved that final loose thread.

In his heart, Cadmus thought he would be devastated if Robert predeceased him, but intellectually he recalled that he had spent his first thirty-seven years without a life partner. He figured he would find his solitary path once again, albeit in deep mourning. A part of him believed Robert's death would usher his own, so he would not have too long to suffer. What he did not anticipate were the waves of overwhelming agony he would feel after losing his soul mate or that time remained stagnant, that a day felt like a week.

He also did not realize that grieving would conjure more guilt over Ilona. Now that he knew the misery firsthand, he could not believe what his mother had endured for so many years after his father passed, and she had to look two children in the eye the entire time, two souls who carried her husband's life force. Contrary to what his sister believed, Ilona had not been weak. She held together as best she could, creating a stable place for her children with her volunteer work to keep her busy when they were at school. All the while, beneath her placid mien was a tormented soul, one whose actions led to the death of her husband. And then her support for her son correlated with an alienation from her daughter. Cadmus was amazed that, even at his age, life mercilessly continued to deepen his understanding of her suffering.

DELPHINA

Spring 2014

DELPHINA KNEW AINSLEY WOULD BE fast asleep by the time she arrived at their bungalow, buttered up with lemon and lavender lotion from the farmer's market. She opened the garage door leading to the house, preparing herself for Victor's questions. He did not understand why she spent so much time at work at night, and a hint of jealousy started to color his questions.

Hearing Patsy Cline's voice gave her confidence as she opened the screen door. Seated at the back porch table with a Lone Star, Victor's eyes squinted as he carefully cut another wing from the sheet of balsa wood.

"The plane is coming along well?" Delphina asked, making her way over to him.

"The novelty wore off with Ainsley after about . . . ummm . . . five minutes?" he replied, continuing with the X-Acto knife, not taking his eyes off the wing. "And that's a generous estimation."

"I'm slower than molasses tonight," she said with her best accent, hands rubbing the back of his shoulders. "Forgive me."

He laid down the knife and lowered his head.

"You been keepin' me so long, I think my pickle's been dilled."

"Your pickle? Hmmm . . . I think that crosses the line."

"What? My grandmother used to say it!"

"Even more troublesome."

Victor's snicker gave way to a hearty round of laughter, Delphina joining in. She took a seat next to him at the table, and placing her hands over his, she tried again, "I'm sorry I'm so late."

"I accept," he said before adding playfully, "and you can make it up to me by flipping the vinyl and bringing me another Lone Star."

Delphina returned after a few minutes, placing two beers on the table, much to his surprise.

"You're drinking one?"

"It's good to do new things. Dance with me," she replied, as Patsy sang about searching for love.

"You're not gonna tell the guys I drink this stuff, are you?" he asked, rising to lead her in a two-step around the porch.

"Hmmm . . . now I can't make any promises, Mr. Walsh."

"Now there's nothin' wrong wit a good ol' bottle of Lone Star," Victor teased in his grandfather's twang, lifting Delphina's arm to give her a twirl.

"Are you with me now? Or are you at your grandfather's ranch enjoyin' a bottle of Coca-Cola while he's sippin' a cold one?"

"Oh, I'm with you now, where I am meant to be," he said, drawing her in for a kiss.

THE MANSION WAS ILLUMINATED AGAINST the dark sky, but this time the front door remained wide open with shouts emanating from within. The boy appeared in one of the windows, with dark hair and wide brown eyes staring at her as she was seated in a car, his palms pressed flat against the upstairs window. Delphina bolted upright and noted it was just after two o'clock in the morning. She walked to the alarm pad and then to the living room, starting her routine to the garden.

She heard a thud at the front door that caused her body to jerk as a reflex. It took her eyes a moment to adjust to the reflection; it was times like these that she wished they had a solid door. Peering out the glass door, she noted an empty yard and street, but as she looked down at the porch, she noted two dead birds in front of the bay window. A small yellow-breasted bird lay cradled on its side facing a much larger black bird; the larger bird was resting flat on its back with its head facing the other one. The reason for the loud thud.

What an odd combination, Delphina thought as she opened the door and knelt, studying them with sympathy and fascination, the morbid curiosity of death hooking her attention with the unusual sight. They resembled a mother and child in their final rest. The likelihood of such an occurrence, especially at night, was difficult to fathom. She thought, perhaps, we all seek that in our moments of despair—to know that we are loved and that we are not alone—even if that love comes from a stranger in your moment of need. She thought back to a Buddhist writing about seeing your parents' face in everyone. There are no strangers, really. Then it occurred to her that she had never looked up the meaning of dead birds in dreams.

She returned to the house, tiptoeing into Ainsley's room to kiss her cheek. Her connection with her daughter pulsated through her being, and she felt guilty that she had once questioned if she could really love a girl child. It was as if they were meant to be a pair.

Delphina pecked away on her laptop, overwhelmed at the number of interpretations of black birds in dreams. Positive and negative; freedom and shackles: She could not discover much on her own other than that it might serve her well to seek guidance. And as much as she tried to disregard the advertisement for a psychic in the lower right-hand corner, it continued to appear throughout her research, despite her attempts to click it away from the screen.

DELPHINA WAS THANKFUL FOR THE drive through the hill country, the nightmare of the mansion robbing her of another night's sleep. Her heart longed to bring peace to the little boy who was appearing more and more often in her dreams, his face filled with pain and longing. Time in nature would serve her well.

She attempted to still her mind, taking in the wildflowers that draped the countryside with seas of color—vibrant yellow, fiery orange, and midnight blue flooding the landscape. It was only when people stopped to take the obligatory family photograph in a blanket of bluebonnets that they noticed the individuality of each stem. Each flower, unique and purposeful in its own way, joined the chorus of flowers that bloomed every spring.

"Look, let's head over there," Delphina gestured to Victor as he clumsily balanced Ainsley in his arms. Contriving a carefree child's pose in bluebonnets, as many Texan mothers know, can be quite difficult. The sea of blue that appears as delicate as a watercolor is only a sheer cover for the patches of stickers that serve as a haven for rattlesnakes. Quite a contrast from the idyllic street view, and it was one whose symbolism was not lost on Delphina. Battles, both large and small, are often waged under a calm countenance.

She carefully navigated her steps, pausing at what might be a contending area for the photograph, a small clearing about a foot and a half wide. Delphina laid her daughter's favorite baby blanket on the ground, a faded pink cotton that would blend in with her dress from afar. A good choice visually, but now as Ainsley whined about the stickers, Delphina realized that maybe the blanket would also offer a bit of solace, just enough to score a good photograph.

Victor lowered his daughter to the blanket, offering a kiss of encouragement for her to let go, but her arms remained locked, clinging stubbornly to his neck. Delphina swooped in to position her bow, offering animated reminders that the Blue Bell Creamery was a stone's throw away and that surely there was an ice cream with her name on it.

"Really? How do they know to put my name on it? How can they write on ice cream? With icing?" The comment did the trick. Ainsley released her grip and allowed her mother to position her on the blanket, captivated by the idea of personalized ice cream.

"It's a figure of speech. Your name will not literally be on it."

"C'mon, Ainsley. Deli, move to the side. Ready . . . Say mint chocolate chip!"

After a series of shots, interrupted by comments about ice cream flavors, how many samples are offered, and several readjustments to the pale pink hair bow, Victor eventually scanned the photographs and gave a thumb's up. It was time to get ice cream.

"Are you sure you captured some good ones? Let me look through the photos, just for a second. We're here, after all, and we can always squeeze in another round if need be." Delphina's attempts to sound casual fell flat.

"Nope, not this time. We have some good ones. Remember, it does not need to be perfect." He held her gaze for a few seconds before picking up Ainsley and abruptly turning toward the car.

As he tilted his head to follow Ainsley's finger that was pointing toward the sky, she caught a glimpse of his cheek. He was not as annoyed with her as she had incorrectly assumed. His dimples unapologetically revealed a good mood, betraying his attempt to feign frustration. Victor must have felt her gaze, because he turned back to offer a wink before mouthing the words, *Let's go.*

Delphina smiled and bent down to collect the blanket. Her eyes were distracted by an elderly couple slowly making their way across the field, arms linked in a sturdy embrace intended equally for affection and stability, with a twenty-something man leading closely in front, camera in tow. They wore smartly pressed, pastel yellow Oxford-style shirts, with a three-quarter inch sleeve and a strand of pearls on the lady that offered a subtle, feminine contrast. An anomaly in this crowd of young families, the wind tousled the woman's fine hair as she gingerly made each step on the uneven ground, offering furtive smiles as she spoke to the man who appeared to be her husband. The creases in the corners of his eyes indicated he was smiling broadly, although it was difficult to see with her windblown hair masking part of his face. Delphina wondered if she and Victor would one day resemble this couple— so seemingly content and peaceful in old age. They were a striking couple in the way that some elderly people are: silver hair, lean physique, wrinkles that reflected a lifetime more of delight than struggle. As much as Delphina loved Victor, she could not imagine growing old with him. She feared it was a sign that life planned to intervene and cut their time short.

As she bent down to shake out the blanket, Delphina's bracelet fell to the ground. Carefully kneeling to reach for it, she brushed up against a particularly full bluebonnet, standing proud with a slight lean to the left as if nodding in salutation to the sun. Its petals looked more periwinkle than the cobalt hue admired from a distance, and its symmetry was askew with fine, intricate petals missing on each level. Whether it was natural or the tromping of photography subjects that had caused the bloom's variation, she could not tell. What she did know, however, was that the intentional design was evident, a microcosmic blueprint of the universe.

"C'mon, Deli, let's go," Victor called as he opened the car door, breaking her reverie. "It's time for Blue Bell."

Delphina smiled to herself as she headed back to the car, reminded of her childhood fascination with nature that was more like a secret to which only she was privy. Amid the seemingly random conglomeration of life events, there is a foundation that is ever present to those who pause long enough to see it. The bluebonnet field emanated this message, but it was difficult to notice when competing with ice cream, perfectly pressed clothes, and the search for the quintessential photograph.

She approached the car and touched her daughter's face as it peered through the open window.

"Do you have any idea how much I love you, Ainsley?"

"Mommy, I have a question. Will your ice cream say *Delphina* or *Mommy?*"

CADMUS

Spring 2014

"HELLOOOO? DR. DOYLE?" THE NURSE called from the hallway.

"Yes, in here," Cadmus replied from the library nook.

"Thank heavens!" she exclaimed. "I've been calling for several minutes."

"I didn't hear you," he snapped. "Perhaps it would be a good idea if you called. I didn't expect you today."

"Dr. Doyle, I come every day," she replied, looking at the photo albums strewn about the room. "May I put these away? I'm afraid you might trip over them."

"Do not put them away; just stack them into piles," he barked, holding on to an open album, staring at family pictures.

"Was that your mother?" She asked, finger tapping one of the photographs.

"Was? This is my mother," he corrected. "She's looking for me."

The nurse stared at him, not knowing how to respond.

"She is the best person I know. And I treated her terribly that last day."

The nurse sat in the chair next to him, placing her hand on his forearm.

"I believe that she knows you love her and that you are sorry," she said with a quiet confidence.

With a furrowed brow, he nodded his head while keeping his eyes on the photograph, "I hope so. I plan to tell her myself when she finds me."

The nurse patted Cadmus' forearm, caressing it as he began to weep.

"Let me help you to bed, Doctor," she soothed.

A few tears fell on the photograph as he shook his head no. Using the sleeve of his pajamas, he wiped it dry.

"I do think you will feel better after a nap. Please let me help you."

"Leave me the fuck alone!" Cadmus screamed with wild eyes as he threw the photo album at her.

She hurried from the home and placed a call to Clementine. It was time for her to find another nurse.

HE CARRIED HIS HANDKERCHIEF, DABBING his eyes while he damned the Greek blood that ran through his veins. His grandparents had lived well into their eighties, staring through their window at Lawndale, keeping an eye out for their children who passed before them, Arianna the last child remaining.

"Your suite is the largest they offer, but it is not big enough to house everything. Choose carefully," Clementine said as they made their way through The Doyle House, Cadmus placing his hand on the pieces he wanted to take with him.

It took them most of the afternoon, Cadmus first selecting a table and lamp from the sitting room, as well as the loveseat upon which Dear Ernestine had stroked his mother's face when she arrived home that fateful night. She had not realized her husband was dead when he watched her from the staircase; her tears were a result of the exposed infidelity.

The library contained most of furnishings he wanted to keep, including his father's mahogany desk and the two chairs tucked in the nook, along with the liquor cabinet, sofa, and tables that marked the contents of a room that had served as the epicenter for generations of Doyles. He nodded at her mention of the rugs, and of course, he wanted his husband's paintings. The second and third floor held little interest for him, but he did take a few pieces here and there.

Cadmus returned to his place in the nook, looking at the roses swaying in the breeze. No one other than a Doyle had lived in this home since its creation. He did not know what to think of the realtor's sign in the yard, but he had enough wits about him to know it meant dollar signs. Dollar signs meant Ilona's legacy would continue. In addition to another scholarship, he pledged the money for a new, twenty-first century media center. The Doyle-McClelland Foundation would serve the students of Heights High for many generations to come.

DELPHINA

Summer 2014

GENTLE SCENTS OF OILS SURROUNDED Delphina as she entered the store. For a moment, she stood still, taking in the new environment that was in strong contrast to the noisy strip outside. It was a feast for the senses—a CD of waves crashing into the ocean and crystals in the window case reflecting the natural light, one in particular that claimed to foster creativity. For a moment, she considered purchasing it to help with her own writing. Perhaps the crystal would nudge her in the right direction. She laughed to herself at how seamless the transition from skeptic to participant was when hope could be made tangible with a crystal.

"May I help you?"

"No. I mean, yes." Delphina felt her face reddening. "Yes, please."

The woman smiled warmly, an authentic smile that was not often given, which made Delphina think there might be something to say about the power of crystals. This woman radiated a sense of peace, someone who would not scoff at wonderings of dead birds in dreams, someone who just might inherently understand her fascination with pattern, with purpose.

"I am interested in a book on dreams."

"Well, you have come to the right place," the lady said as she beckoned Delphina to the back of the store, her white gauzy skirt flowing around her feet as if she were floating. "Here are books on dream symbols, and here is another section on history and cultural meanings of dreams. Are you looking for general information, or do you have a specific question?"

Delphina's courage waned. She should have spent more time online rather than traipsing across town to a new age store. It seemed ridiculous to put into words why she was here: to look for a book to take her to a mansion by the sea. It made perfect sense in her head and in the drowsy hours of the night.

Noting hesitation, the clerk said, "I believe that dreams tell us stories of lives we've led, of lives we are living, and of lives we hope to live. Time really doesn't have a place in dreams."

Delphina remained silent, unsure how to respond.

"There are plenty of books for entertainment. I am happy to recommend lightweight books that are great for quick glimpses, but I also have recommendations if you want to delve a bit deeper. We have a little something for everyone."

The door chimes signaled the arrival of another customer. The saleslady excused herself for a moment to greet the newcomer, bringing Delphina a much-needed moment to gather her thoughts. She pinched the bridge her nose, hoping to quell the burning sensation that would soon lead to tears.

She saw the customer making her way up a back staircase as she apologized for running late for the appointment. The saleslady assured her not to worry and said something about "confluences of life come together at the right moment." Delphina wondered what kind of appointment she had in a place like this, perhaps a psychic or tarot card reader? Whatever it was, she figured that making an appointment took far more guts than buying a book on dreams.

The saleslady returned, smiling and wide-eyed, ready to help her.

With rising confidence, Delphina mustered her professorial tone and said, "I had a dream recently about dead birds. There were hundreds of them strewn across a lawn."

"What did the birds look like?"

"Black birds. Crows, I believe."

"Have you had this dream before?"

"Not with birds, but yes, I have dreamed about the location since I was a child, and it always fills me with anxiety. It's a mansion by the ocean. The water is calm, so maybe it is a bay, but I know the ocean is near. Well, on second thought, I don't know how I could know the ocean is near," Delphina said, eyes turning away as she second-guessed herself.

"And you say you have had this dream for years."

"Yes, for as long as I can remember, but it is occurring with greater frequency lately, and while I have never been in the house, I am getting closer. And there is a little boy . . . I feel very connected to the boy."

Delphina paused, gripping the bookcase with her right hand and catching her breath from her racing heartbeat. It did not take long for her initial hesitation over sharing the story to give way to an unforeseen outpouring of emotion. She was overcome by the revelation that her interest in the dream was just as she said, a deep-felt connection to the boy, to a son. She felt the saleslady's hand lightly touch her forearm. As she opened her eyes, she followed the gesture to sit on a reading sofa at the back of the store. Several minutes passed as the two sat in silence, the only sound a siren as an ambulance made its way down the street. Delphina felt the siren's vibrations in tandem with her heartbeat. Even if there was a recovery, the siren offered a blunt reminder of the fragility that holds our lives together.

"Birds can be used to send messages."

"Messages? What kind of messages? From whom?"

The clerk paused, her eyes focused but with a touch of hesitancy. Now she was the one who seemed unsure.

"From a soul you knew in a former life. I am sorry if this frightens you, but it sounds like you need resolution. We live in patterns—one lifetime's lessons and unresolved matters spiral into the next life."

Delphina noted how the concepts of patterns and order had continued to resurface throughout her life. And from a bird's-eye view, patterns could span vast reaches far beyond that of a strawberry or a bluebonnet.

"I have a book to recommend, as well as a contact to share," the saleslady said, making her way to the register.

Delphina took a deep breath as she watched the lady return with a knowing smile, book and business card in tow.

"This is the contact information for a regressionist."

"You mean a hypnotist?"

"Yes. It's someone who can help take you back a lifetime . . . or two . . . or more," she said with a laugh.

"PLEASE DON'T BRING THAT BOOK, for God's sake," Victor said as he opened the door to help Ainsley from her booster seat.

"But if the lines are long, it will be good to have something to look at," Delphina replied, her hand gripping the book on reincarnation.

"Why not look at us. Talk to us," Victor scolded.

She nodded in resignation, knowing she had to focus on the present moment. Her psychiatrist dismissed her inquiry about a past-life regression, maintaining that indulging in such a fantasy would take her down a rabbit hole far worse than what she was experiencing. He told her he wanted to see her weekly rather than monthly, especially in light of his renewed attempt to adjust her medication, hypothesizing that her insomnia and depression could very well be related to early premenopause. She left his office feeling crazy and old.

She nodded to Victor and left the book in the seat of the car, her mind focused on last night's dream. She was on the property, walking on the sidewalk to the front door, keeping an eye on the boy standing in the upstairs window. She looked away at the sound of a bird flapping its wings only to be startled that the boy was standing next to her when she turned back toward the house. She instinctively reached for his hand but screamed when she noticed it was covered in wrinkles and blue veins protruding like a constellation. She screamed in real life, startling Victor upright in bed. She was up for the rest of the night, walking the backyard and counting the hours until dawn.

As they stood in line to enter the zoo, Delphina made her best attempt to enjoy the moment. She left it to Victor and Ainsley to call to the animals, making funny noises they hoped would elicit a reaction. Always a few steps ahead or behind, she studied the patterns of fur, feathers, and skin. Looking into their black eyes, she thought back to every pet she had owned, knowing that they knew the secret for a calm heart—the secret she needed to know.

Victor grabbed her hand when they were in line to feed the giraffes, "Please be with us," he said, looking forlorn.

She nodded but turned away, understanding neither her overwhelming sensation to cry nor her continued desire to search.

They left the zoo and meandered to the reflection pool in front of Hermann Park. An ice cream truck pulled in to the roundabout, much to the delight of her daughter. Victor and Ainsley made their way to the truck while Delphina sat in front of the reflection pool, the slight breeze creating ripples on the water. It looked so deep, but she knew it was only a few inches, an illusion. Her heart picked up its beat, tears beginning to stream down her face.

"Mommy! Look what I got!" Ainsley screamed, running to her, waving a giant rainbow Popsicle in her right hand.

"Stop, Ainsley! Victor!" Delphina shouted as she saw the children's train making its way around the bend.

Ainsley skipped over the tracks to her, making her way to her mother with more than enough time, oblivious of her shouts.

"What in the hell are you doing, Victor? You need to hold her hand!" she yelled. "Something could've happened!"

Glances followed, trying to determine the cause for the commotion. Victor stood in front of her for almost a minute, allowing the train to pass behind him with the families on board waving to everyone along the way.

"This is ridiculous! You need to get it together, Delphina!" he shouted, much to her surprise. "You need time alone."

"No, Victor. I'm sorry, please, I'm fine," she replied, tears continuing down her face.

"You are not fine," he said, pulling her by the elbow farther away from Ainsley. "And it is not good for you to be around Ainsley when you are like this. What in the hell has happened?" he questioned as he looked over to his daughter sitting by the edge of the pool, blue and green juice dripping onto her hand.

"It's the nightmares. It's the boy," she wept.

"Walk around for a while . . . go to the Japanese Gardens," he commanded as she nodded quietly. "We will be by the swings. C'mon, Ainsley."

Ainsley walked over and gave her a kiss on the cheek as she grabbed Victor's hand.

"Salty," she said, smacking her lips from her mother's tears as they walked toward the playground.

Delphina put on her sunglasses, something she considered to be a good investment from a recent Neiman's excursion with Jane. She had been crying more and more lately. Wearing designer frames acted like a shield. She knew it was a false confidence, but it gave her fragile appearance more of an aloof, well-heeled effect. Better to be considered a snob than a basket case, she figured.

She took the long way to the playground along Main Street, walking parallel to the train tracks and wondering why she had decided to take that particular route. The train rattled by again, filled with children waving excitedly to her, the only soul on the odd path. Her eyes met the face of one of the mothers who had seen her having the moment with Victor earlier by the reflection pool, the woman offering a sympathetic smile and wave. She made a mental note to return the favor one day when she would witness a falling out between spouses, a better move than her usual one of turning away.

The breeze kicked up its force, the coolness tingling across her cheeks sticky from tears. A moment later, a cacophony of car horns came on the heels of a car screeching across the lanes of Main Street, prompting her to turn back to see if everyone was okay. As Delphina's eyes adjusted to the scene, her eyes landed on the brick wall that encased the exclusive pocket of homes tucked away just north of Rice University. She bolted across Fannin Street to Main and stood at the gate to the private road, seeing that on the other side of the brick wall was a large house shrouded in oak trees. And when she allowed her mind to peel back the years to a time when the trees were saplings and the grounds were simple, she realized she was looking at the house from her dreams.

"UNBELIEVABLE," SHE REPEATED, THE ONLY WORD she could say, craning her neck out the window as their car pulled back onto Main Street. "Drive by again."

"Love, if I drive by again, they will call the Houston Police Department," Victor said, offering a sarcastic wave to the security guard now standing in front of his car parked squarely in front of the gate, staring stone-faced at the suspect Audi on its seventh slow drive past the gate.

"Just once more, please," Delphina pleaded before glancing back at her daughter, asleep in the car seat with clothes soiled from the joys of that afternoon, completely oblivious to her mother's emotions.

Victor reluctantly made the U-turn, affording Delphina a few minutes to reflect on interconnectedness and impermanence, concepts that had appealed to her philosophically but were now ushered to the forefront of her reality. While she accepted theories of reincarnation, the idea of energy and vibrations finding like ones in the next cycle, she had never wondered about her own past lives. Her spirituality remained distant, disparate from the cycle.

"Do tell," Victor prompted, her familiar lip biting meaning her mind was racing.

"Tell? I've been dreaming of that house since I was a little girl. You know this!"

"Yeeessssss . . . but there's something more," he said with raised brows. "What else are you thinking?"

Delphina paused, looking ahead to see the house coming into view again.

"That the house just might hold the secret to cure my anxiety for good," she replied, her heart welling with hope at the thought of a remedy.

DELPHINA

Autumn 2014

"YOU ARE IN AN ELEVATOR. Select a floor."

Delphina obliged, imagining herself in an elevator, staring at the buttons. "Sixteen. I will go to the sixteenth floor."

She imagined the initial pull setting the lift in motion, the soft purr of the elevator making its climb. Her stomach gave a tingle when the sixteen lit up above the doors.

"As you exit the elevator, you will see a long hallway with doors on each side. Walk down the hallway, and select a door to open."

Delphina felt tears welling in her eyes. Rather than trying to hold them back, she allowed herself to weep softly as she made her way down the hall. She stopped at the second door on her left and opened it.

"I see two children, a girl and a boy," she said before whispering, "It's the boy. He's my boy . . . and he's with an older girl."

"What are they doing?"

"They are on a sofa, faces downcast. There is something wrong, but neither of them are speaking. The boy is resting his head on his sister's thigh, sucking his right thumb while pulling on the front of his hair with his left hand."

"What is the girl doing?"

"She's been crying. Her face is stained red. She has a sprinkling of freckles across her nose."

"What else do you see?"

"There is a circular table with a lamp, an old-fashioned lamp with a porcelain top. Next to the lamp is a pair of gold-rimmed eyeglasses. Small, circular frames. They are delicate and belong to my husband."

"How do you know?"

"I just do," Delphina replied with confidence.

"Do the children know you are there?"

"No. They will not look up."

"Is there anything else to note in this room?"

"Just the pain of the children. Something terrible happened." Tears cascaded from the corners of Delphina's eyes. She was overcome by the urge to wrap her arms around the children, to draw them close to her heart and become one again, but she began to feel the pull to return to the hallway and go to another room.

Delphina resumed her walk down the hallway, apprehensive about which door to select next. She paused, pressing her hand on the cold, brown paneling. She turned her head back toward the hallway and continued walking. She decided to try a door on the right side this time.

"I'm ready."

"Open the door. What do you see?"

Delphina opened the door to see two ladies in a powder room, a dark-haired woman looking at a blonde woman through the mirror. Delphina stood behind the blonde; it was a quick image of three women standing in a line facing the mirror, all looking at one another's reflections.

"It's an extravagant party. There are mostly men in the library, men who have been drinking quite a bit. It is smoky from cigars, and the men are very loud, laughing and drunk in their tuxedos.

"The dark-haired woman, wearing a silver-sequined gown and elegantly made-up face, appears at the door to the room. The other ladies in the hallway see her expression, and they whisper quietly before turning away. They feel sorry for her.

"She's staring at a man in a white jacket with gold-rimmed, circular eye-glasses. The glasses I saw in the previous room. A red-haired woman in an emerald-green dress is rubbing his shoulders."

"Who is the man?"

"The dark-haired woman's husband. He's my husband. I'm in the house by the water."

The tears that had been cascading slowly throughout the regression began streaming from her eyes. She did not hold back her tears this time, giving in to her emotions with full abandon.

"I turn to leave, but no one tries to stop me. The attention is on the fight with the red-haired woman's husband; people are trying to break it up but then get caught in middle. He's screaming my name."

"What's your name?"

"I can't make it out, but I know it is my name. I walk down the sidewalk leading from the front door to the street, where I see my driver waiting. The lights are streaming from the windows, and I can see people inside, but there is no evidence of the fight. The people are blocking the windows, watching the spectacle.

"We are turning along the roundabout in front of the Hermann Park reflection pool. I begin to weep. I miss him."

"Do you return to the party?"

"No. I am at home now sitting next to an African-American woman. She wraps me in her arms and shushes me like I'm a baby, rocking me back and forth and stroking my hair with tears in her own eyes.

I hear a knock at the door. She answers for me while I curl up on the love seat, heels kicked off and runs in my hose. The clock just struck a quarter after two in the morning minutes before. It's 2:19."

Delphina wailed, pounding her fists into the bed.

"What is it?"

"The police are at my house. My husband died. He crashed a car as he raced home to me."

A minute passed as Delphina continued to cry.

"I'm so sorry. So very, very sorry," Delphina mouthed.

"To whom?"

"My husband," she whispered before continuing. "And he said he's sorry, too."

Delphina absorbed the scene in silence. She sat with him on a bench resting under the swaying limbs of a pecan tree. He had a perfect face, one bearing neither bruise nor gash from the night, his eyes sending the message, *You will always be my love. It was never your fault. Our son needs you now.*

What about us? Delphina asked the man with the gold-rimmed eyeglasses. *We had our time and will have it again. Look for our son.*

Delphina came to with her face soaked in tears and sweat. She reached up to free her blouse, the perspiration clinging the cotton to her breasts as if she had been doused with a bucket of water. Opening her eyes, she looked around the modern office so far removed from the garden she had been in moments ago.

"I NEED YOU TO HELP me find my son."

Victor took a long breath as he poured Delphina a cup of coffee from the carafe the waitress had placed on the counter, eyes sweeping to see who was within earshot.

"I know how it sounds."

"You know how it sounds?" Victor retorted. "Let's review how it sounds . . . beginning with what I have accepted with respect to your anxiety since the day I fell in love with you. But now, I must accept you've connected with your former husband and that he's told you he loves you. And he's sorry for the torrid affair that resulted in his death and the subsequent guilt you've felt all your life for leaving him the night he died. And I must accept that you two will connect again one day and now you need to find your son?"

Delphina stared at Victor, uncomfortable at hearing her life, or former life, narrated aloud. It sounded more plausible in the recesses of the mind.

"Jesus Christ, Deli! How am I supposed to feel?" Delphina shifted in her seat as the family in the next booth shuffled to draw attention to the placemats for the children to color, attempting to distract them from the bickering couple.

She had yet to acknowledge the toll taken on Victor throughout the retracing of her soul's journey. Consumed by her own emotions, she gave little note to his feelings as a participant in the present moment, as if his current station rendered him less than his predecessors. He was her husband, the one she chose the very night they met, a subliminal knowing that they had crossed paths at another time. She reached for his hand, greying hair sprinkled along his arms signifying the fleeting time they shared. She was borrowing his time to compensate for another.

"I'm sorry, Victor. I can't explain it . . . the regression was like a cleansing . . . seeing the story and hearing his words . . ." she paused, lifting a fist to her mouth to choke back tears while casing the restaurant. "I know that he was the one responsible for his death, not me, and I do believe this is why I have felt anxious my entire life. Now that I know this, his absolution . . . his acknowledgment . . . it's like that part has been lifted. I can't explain the relief, but it's one that no psychiatrist has ever been able to give me."

Looking into her husband's eyes, she caught a glimpse of his soul, a spirit with a recollection of her musings, a spirit who had traversed many lifetimes and recognized her search. They held hands at the table, weighing the plausibility of the regression in silence, the theoretical spiritual belief they shared now applied to their actual lives.

"But now . . . now," she whispered, squeezing his hands. "I need to find my boy."

Victor nodded, a response to her and to the waitress who held herself at bay, sensing the gravity of the conversation.

"Have you made a decision?" the waitress asked after taking another minute to meander to their table.

"Yes," he replied as he cupped his wife's hands. "Yes, I think we are ready."

DELPHINA JOGGED ALONG THE TRAIL on Heights Boulevard, her mind considering where to start. Her research on Shadyside and its inhabitants had left her empty-handed, producing droves of threads but no particular strand helping her cause.

Arturo and Lucinda Medrano resided in the ten-million-dollar Shadyside home. Arturo was the son of an oilman, and he was the fourth owner of the home built in 1925.

Delphina felt a void reading the details of the Medrano family, nothing resonating in the scores of photos from society events. Her online research on Shadyside, on the Medranos, left her at a loss, desperate to connect dots not meant to connect. The Internet offered false hope, a belief that the truth was but a few clicks away.

Delphina took basically the same steps with the other three former owners: Fleming, Dubois, and Miller. Her only clue to the time was the car from her dream and the style of the partygoers, all of which spoke to her from the earlier days of the property. She surmised the original inhabitants, the Miller family, were the best people to research next.

The Millers built the home in 1925 and resided there until their deaths, his in 1970 and hers following many year later in 1982, when Delphina was nine. Aside from grandchildren and great-grandchildren, their only living child was now eighty-five. She wondered if he would know of any occurrences in the house from so many years ago but struggled to find a way to broach the subject with a stranger without appearing delusional.

Delphina stopped at an intersection to wait for the light to change, hopping in one place to keep her mind processing as she recounted the loose facts: dreams of the Shadyside house and her findings from the regression, which included herself in the house at a party, her husband's affair, his death, and his urging to find their son. With the changing of the light came the realization that using the term *loose facts* was an indulgent description. Narrating it aloud made her feel like a halfwit, as it had the previous day in the diner with Victor.

She thought back to the parting words of the regressionist: "Think of the people, places, and things throughout your life that have led to a visceral reaction, positive or negative. You are lucky . . . you are in the same city and within a close proximity of time."

Delphina took a seat on the bench in the esplanade, reflecting on the regressionist's advice. Her first words to Victor, "Where in the hell have you been?" made perfect sense to her now. They referenced her line throughout the years, one of them using the line as a go-to joke when the other person arrived late. He often attributed it to the alcohol from that night, but Delphina always knew that she was not all that woozy when she made the comment. She was tense and anxious, knowing that something was about to happen. It made for a funny detail, though, so she let this inaccuracy remain part of their story. She was meant to be with him in this lifetime even though she had not the faintest idea of who they were to one another before.

She rose and turned around to face the bench, raising her leg to the surface for a few stretches before resuming her run. As she lifted her head, her gaze fell to the home she had attempted to tour many moons ago with her mother, memories of her inexplicable malaise and subsequent breakdown in the garden bubbling to the forefront of her mind now. She remembered the brown-eyed man.

DELPHINA OPENED THE FRONT GATE, noting the line of workers entering the home with tools in tow. She knew the home had been for sale for close to two million dollars, Victor's words echoing, "And that does not even include renovations!" She still could not believe they ripped out part of the rose garden for a pool.

Her heart filled with anticipation as she stood in front of the home this time around, with no trace of anxiety to be found. Looking over to the garden, she recalled the immense sadness that overwhelmed her when she lay on the bench so long ago. She remembered feeling a physical pain in her heart, as if she had lost someone dear. Her momma dismissed it as heat exhaustion. Delphina had gone to bed that night not understanding why she could not shrug her weepiness and why her mind kept drifting to the older man she had met at Kaplan's a few weeks prior.

She thought about returning to the garden but then opted to enter the front door, the workers having left it wide open before trekking to the back of the house. As Delphina stepped into the grand hallway, she noticed the light pouring through the stained glass, colored beams revealing the particles suspended throughout the space, fragments from early last century stirring with fresh shavings whirling from the kitchen. Placing a hand on the staircase banister, she crept up to escape the bustle; there was not a soul to witness her arrival.

Delphina made her way down the second-floor hall, summoning each breath to detect the slightest note of familiarity. Plastic overlays draped the wood-paneled walls, their varnish remarkably fresh given the condition of the floors, which she surmised had been covered with rugs, imprints of faded rectangles remaining on the surface. Sliding her hands into an opening in the plastic curtain, she pressed her palms to the wood, attempting to connect with the energy of the house.

From downstairs came shouts, "Aqui! Aqui!" Her concentration fractured, she shook her head in frustration, wondering if her gander into the home had been a fool's errand.

An old bathtub rested lopsided in the hallway, one of its rusted feet bent inward. Scooting past it, Delphina made her way to one of the garden-facing bedrooms, where wallpaper embossed with faded pink and white bows was peeling from the wood. A delicate chandelier coated in dust adorned the ceiling, one relic she was certain would make the cut. Her fingers traced the scratches in the window as she looked out over the garden and neighboring unearthed soil intended to make room for the pool. Sooty fingerprints from over a hundred years marked the glass, creating a dreamlike haze that escorted her back in time.

She wondered if the room had once belonged to a little girl, and knowing her daughter's tendencies, she walked to the closet. Nestled in the grime of one of the shelves was an iridescent bead. Delphina rolled it between her fingers as she stepped into the closet to study the walls, her eyes scanning crown molding to base boards as she turned to study each wall. She knelt down to trace her fingers over the crayoned sunshine and stick figures before turning to notice another writing, *Callista Aislinn Doyle*, scribbled in brown crayon at the very bottom of the wall that framed the closet door.

"Callista Aislinn Doyle," Delphina enunciated aloud, her mind taking her back to the dissonance of males over females. She was certain her husband had been referring to a son, but now she found herself in doubt, recalling her former insistence that her daughter was destined to be a boy. "Aislinn . . . Ainsley."

She turned to the wall on the other side of the door, squinting at the faded scribbles—*Dad, Mom, Callista, Cadmus*—all with corresponding stick figures, a bow denoting the females.

"No deberías estar aquí!"

Delphina jumped, startled by the comment from the worker.

"I'm sorry."

"Afuera!" he shouted, pointing to the stairs and shaking his head.

Delphina scooted out of the bedroom and sprinted down the stairs, nodding to the man behind her as she walked out the front door. She took a few deliberate steps on the sidewalk before turning back. Noting his retreat, she turned to make her way around the perimeter, casing the area for hints of a possible past. The similarity between Aislinn and Ainsley was too uncanny to be a coincidence. She thought back to the man who had appeared to her during the regression, his handsome face tinged with a soft ruggedness. He was not someone she would have been physically attracted to in this lifetime, but the intimacy exchanged in that moment filled her with supreme love and interconnectedness. She knew his soul, and she knew he was correct about their son.

Sawdust sprinkled the back lawn of the house, a few men steadily cutting wood while the others went in and out of the back door, working on the kitchen renovation. An old stove held court in the driveway, and although it was past its prime, its enormity bore an almost regal quality, a weathered pride at having provided for the family that had once lived here. She remembered reading about The Doyle House in the neighborhood newsletter, the sale marking the end of an era with the transfer of ownership to a new family—only the second family to inhabit the home.

Looking through the lattice of workers, wood, and ladders, Delphina glimpsed the pecan tree and bench at the far end of the yard. As she made her way to the north side of the grounds, her soul's memory acted in tandem with her steps: first of her walking with him, hand-in-hand, an ivory stole draped over her shoulders; followed by another of her twirling in a wedding dress, sounds of cheers and laughter fueling the spin; and then by herself, alone and barefoot with a rosary dangling from her hands as she prayed in earnest to the morning sky.

Ease descended around her as she took a seat on the bench, the place where she sat with her husband but a few days ago in another plane. Delphina faced The Doyle House, the flush from her realization tempered by a gust of wind that consecrated the moment. She knew this had been her home.

AINSLEY WAS THE FIRST TO see Delphina walking on the sidewalk near the park, her entire arm waving a full 180 degrees from the swing, smile encapsulating her entire face. Ainsley's love was distinct, her desire to cuddle, kiss, and hold hands unwavering.

She recalled finding Ainsley in her closet at age three, weeping because she didn't want Delphina to die. "We have too much to do!" The feelings of guilt it once conjured for giving birth in her thirties now fell flat: She and her daughter shared unresolved business. And by the looks of their relationship, they were well on their way to resolution.

"How was your run?" Victor asked as he bent down to give her a kiss.

"Productive. Valuable." Delphina smiled, looking into his eyes with a newfound appreciation for the family they had created.

Victor turned away to give Ainsley another boost, her squeals of, "I am touching the sky!" permeating the late afternoon.

"You are closer to your son," he retorted, Delphina noticing the hesitancy in his countenance.

"I am. His name was Cadmus," she acknowledged, giving pause to mark this realization of her soul's journey. "But I am also closer to you and Ainsley."

CADMUS

Winter 2014

"THE DOCTORS BELIEVE HE SUFFERED another stroke recently."

"When?" Clementine questioned, cross that no one had called her.

"We don't know. Perhaps a few days ago."

"Has he spoken at all?"

"No, and he barely opens his eyes. He opens his mouth periodically as a reflex, so please do not be caught off guard when you see that."

Cadmus' closed eyelids did not shield her observation of his eyes' rapid movement, as if he was searching. His lips parted just as the nurse shared that they might; however, Clementine knew it was not a reflex. He was trying to communicate.

"The new owners welcomed me this afternoon," Clementine began. "They were grateful I brought the key to the attic . . . one less thing to worry about during the renovations."

He moistened his lips and, unbeknownst to Clementine, his eyes opened as they rested on the photographs of Ilona and Patrick on his nightstand.

"We trekked all the way up to the attic. I didn't know you could go higher than the third floor. It didn't contain much of anything, really, but we discovered this," she said, placing a doll dressed in Greek apparel, white lace contrasting against the blue.

Clementine placed her hand over his and offered a prayer for God to take him, adding a plea for Ilona to appear as a guide. Placing her mouth next to his ear, she whispered, "Dr. Doyle, you can go now. It's time to be with Robert, with your mother and father. It's time to go home."

DELPHINA

Winter 2014

BUILT IN 1904, THE DOYLE *House is known not only for its prominence on Heights Boulevard but also for the exquisite rose garden Houston lumber magnate Patrick Doyle planted for his wife, Hannah. Their descendants have called this George F. Barber mansion home for over a hundred years, with Rice University professor Dr. Cadmus Doyle at the helm of the estate, along with his husband, Robert McClelland, a partner with Lehane and MacDougall. This pristine, old-world Victorian mansion is the gem of The Heights, heralding the family's antiques, as well as Robert's art studio on the third floor. A must-see of the 1994 Home Tour!*

Delphina drew upon the strengths of silence and stillness, pillars of her daily readings, as she walked in her garden that night, embracing her mala with the mantra: *May all beings feel their love and interconnectedness.* The home tour description posted online acted as a loose thread, one pull and the fabric shrouding the mystery of her son's identity was but a remnant.

Cadmus Doyle was the son of Patrick and Ilona Doyle. His name surfaced on multiple Internet sites, including his affiliation with Rice University and his publications, an obituary for Callista Aislinn Doyle Dunn and another for Robert McClelland, as well as an article featuring his attendance at a Heights High School Award's Night, presenting the annual scholarship in his mother's name. Delphina recalled penning her name to Cecilia's recommendation letter, her heart struck in awe with the possibility that she had been Ilona and that Cadmus more than likely had read her letters, holding the paper upon which she had affixed her signature.

A photo of Cadmus and Robert at the Heights Candlelight Dinner, the year of their participation in the home tour, provided further attestation. She was all but certain he was the man from Kaplan's—his handsome, wide brown eyes exuding a warm countenance. Delphina did not recall the specifics of their conversation, but she remembered that her initial wondering of flirtation had further dissipated when he mentioned his mother. And to think his husband had been Jane's mentor.

Her mind dizzied with the flood of information. She took a deep breath: Her focus needed to be on finding Cadmus. His residence was nowhere to be found, and sans death certificate, Delphina assumed he was still alive.

While the discovery of Ilona's grandchildren, Grace Dunn McGee, Lillian Dunn Butler, and Timothy Dunn, offered a viable avenue for finding Cadmus, the marvel over her previous-life role as their grandmother left Delphina at a standstill. What would she say if she called them? Scores of photographs and society articles canvased their lives as the heirs to Doyle & Dunn, one of the most prominent construction companies in Texas.

Delphina closed her eyes and took several deep breaths. She felt a mild curiosity about Grace, Lillian, and Timothy; however, that connection paled in comparison to what she felt for Cadmus.

She rehearsed her story that she was a Rice University alum wishing to connect with her former professor. After several recitations, she reached into her pocket for her phone and hurriedly dialed the River Oaks home of Grace Dunn Butler before she could waiver. At the sound of the first ring, she knew the caller ID had revealed her number. The plausibility of her story would crumble with a hang-up or two.

"Mrs. Butler is away from home, but I am happy to take a message."

"Away?"

"Yes, she is away for the rest of the month in St. Kitts with the family, but they check in on occasion."

"Oh . . . um," Delphina stammered, not anticipating this response. "Yes, I am looking to get in touch with Mrs. Butler's uncle, Dr. Cadmus Doyle. He was one of my professors at Rice, and I am looking to reconnect."

"Hmmm," the housekeeper drew out with a long pause. "As I said before, I am happy to give her the message, but you might consider pursuing another option."

"Excuse me?" Delphina replied, taken aback by the brazen suggestion.

"Pardon me for speaking out of turn, ma'am, but I have worked for the Butlers and Dunns for a long, long time. Dr. Doyle has been estranged from his family ever since his mother died many years ago. Every family has their issues, you know? Even the very wealthy."

Delphina hung up the phone feeling an odd blend of outrage and sadness. How dare the housekeeper reveal such details about her family? She took a seat on the bench in her yard, placing her hands to her temples to focus her mind.

Were they her family? She did not know for certain, and she began to wonder what made a family in the first place. She certainly knew that it was far from compassionate to divulge such personal family information to a stranger. It made her even more determined to find her son, as she pieced together that he was very much alone.

She remembered how Jane had been overcome with emotion when she had received the invitation to Mr. McClelland's private funeral service, later sharing how his husband had told her how much Robert had enjoyed working with her. Perhaps Jane could help Delphina locate Cadmus, but she was currently traveling back from overseas. This topic needed to be raised in person.

SHE ASKED VICTOR ABOUT DOYLE & Dunn when he found her with heavy eyelids searching the Internet at two o'clock in the morning.

"They are the last of the original tenants, dating back to 1927. It was Doyle Lumber & Construction back then."

"Have you met Timothy Dunn?"

"Yes, and you did, too."

"When?" she gasped.

"At the firm's open house. Remember, he's the one with the Heights High connection."

"That night was a blur . . . so many people," Delphina muttered, retracing her memory with the parade of faces from the evening and glasses of champagne flowing to mark the new venture.

"Why are you asking?"

Delphina paused, and after a brief struggle with how to say it, she opted for a blunt approach.

"He's related to Cadmus."

Victor took a seat. Delphina thought his countenance bore the look of disbelief, but his words soon corrected her misconception.

"Deli, my firm hopes to work with Doyle & Dunn. Mr. Dunn was impressed with our plans for the new museum. I . . . I can't have this chance ruined!"

"I'm not going to waltz up and announce I'm his grandmother! Good Lord, Victor, please give me more credit than that!"

"His grandmother? Jesus Christ!" Victor said, jumping from his seat. "There is a way to find Cadmus, and it is not through Timothy Dunn."

"Victor! I am so close to unraveling this mystery!" Delphina pleaded. "You have always been open to reincarnation!"

"That's true, Deli, but it's been philosophical!" he shouted, turning away to leave the study. "This is nuts!"

Delphina agreed to stay away from the Dunns but for other reasons. As was the case with his sister, Timothy more than likely did not share a relationship with his uncle.

She returned her gaze to The Doyle House, her muse, her touchstone that initiated the nexus to her past. The listing from the realtors' association was still available online; it gave her glimpses of the interior of the home when it had still belonged to Cadmus. The house had served as a museum to the Doyle family, pristine antiques nestled on thick rugs, Robert's modern art flanking the walls with orchids abounding.

Although she sat by herself in the study, she felt far from alone. The uneasiness that had plagued her most of her life now had a form: the powers and limits of free will. Patrick absolving her from her involvement in his death had ushered a release of the anxiety she had suffered her entire life. His message to find Cadmus came with it the belief that she, perhaps, needed to extend a message to him.

She returned to the listing, noticing the realtor's name. She was surprised she had not noticed it when she first found the listing: Geoffrey Singleton. Victor was partnering with him on a project.

Geoffrey,

It was so good to see you last weekend at Cistern. Congratulations, again, on your new venture in EaDo! I know Victor is as excited about the opportunity as I am.

But on to my work . . . I have a favor to ask. I am working on a historical fiction piece on The Heights and am drafting a list of long-time residents I hope to interview. I recall that you recently sold The Doyle House. Any chance you can connect me with Dr. Cadmus Doyle?

Thanks so much . . . hope to see you soon.

Delphina

Delphina closed her laptop, quite proud of herself for drumming up a plausible white lie. It was nearing three o'clock in the morning, and she had to teach two classes the following day. Tiptoeing to Ainsley's room, she pushed open the cracked door to see her daughter fast asleep, right thumb in mouth and left hand embedded in her light brown curls, just like her vision of Cadmus as a boy. Curling up next to her, she stroked her daughter's back and kissed her forehead.

Delphina woke to her phone pinging that she had received a new message. Her heart picked up a beat as she reached into her robe pocket. It was a message from Geoffrey. She knew realtors worked odd hours, but this one surprised her.

Delphina!

What an exciting venture! I am more than happy to help with your novel. Our neighborhood holds many secrets . . . It will no doubt be a fascinating read. Scoring an interview with Dr. Doyle would be quite a feat, if only you can catch him in time. From what I understand, his health is quickly spiraling downward. He moved into The Oaks Retirement Community after the sale of his home.

Fingers crossed! Please send my best to Victor.

G

"AINSLEY HAS A FEVER," VICTOR REPORTED as he turned on the shower, waiting for the water to heat. "I have an eight o'clock status update on the new project that I cannot miss. You'll have to take this one, Deli."

"Today? You really can't help today? You know Rosa is at her mother's this morning."

"Yep," he replied, covering his face with a healthy dose of shaving cream.

"I had a breakthrough last night, Victor. I know where he lives."

"He's waited for you this long. He can wait another day," Victor replied, rinsing his razor.

"Victor, why are you doing this?"

"Your daughter needs you, Delphina. She needs her mother. I have helped as much as I could over these past several weeks. You know I have. But your family is suffering, and we are right here, loving you in this life-time." Delphina stood still, her heart torn between lives.

"Rosa will be here later this morning. You will still be able to teach at least one class today. And then . . . and then you can go to Cadmus."

"GOOD AFTERNOON, I AM HERE to see Dr. Cadmus Doyle," Delphina said, making sure to hold eye contact with her head held high.

The front desk attendant replied, "Of course, one moment, ma'am," before looking down at the keyboard for a few pecks.

"May I have your name, please?"

"Delphina Walsh."

The attendant nodded politely before returning to the screen.

"I'm sorry, Dr. Walsh, but Dr. Doyle does not receive visitors."

"No visitors? But he was my professor at Rice, one whom I would very much like to see again. He may not remember my name, but I know he will know my face." Delphina was proud of the partial truth behind her impromptu response. She knew her son would recognize her.

"I'm so very sorry. I am happy to leave a message with his next of kin in the event something changes."

"I don't think he has a next of kin. He's all alone!" Delphina protested, eliciting the attention of others in the lobby.

"He has a contact listed. I am happy to pass along your name and your interest."

"Yes, yes, please do so," Delphina replied, her voice trembling as she gave her phone number before heading back to her car and to her office.

Delphina was heading east on the freeway toward downtown when her phone rang. She had never been so excited to see an unknown number.

"Hello?"

"Hello, may I please speak with Delphina Walsh?"

"Speaking."

"Hi, Dr. Walsh. My name is Clementine MacDougall, and I am the personal contact for Dr. Cadmus Doyle."

"Yes, thank you so much for returning my call. I would very much like to visit Dr. Doyle, and I am hoping you can help me."

"Perhaps I can, but I think we should meet first."

"What? Why?" Delphina said, annoyance building. *Who in the hell is this Clementine? He's my goddamn son!*

"I'll tell you when we meet."

"When?"

"Are you free this afternoon?"

"Yes," Delphina said, not caring that she would miss another class. "Just tell me when and where."

DELPHINA ARRIVED AT THE CAFÉ on Heights Boulevard early, attempting to distract herself with grading. Victor's comments about her neglecting her family were also applicable to her work. The irony of discovering the literal interconnectedness of her life resulted in her failure to uphold her current obligations. She owed her students and her family an apology.

She heard the old wooden door to the bungalow open and looked up to see a woman approaching her with a cautious smile.

"Dr. Walsh?"

"Yes, how did you know?"

"I Googled you. I found your photograph on the University of Houston Downtown's website."

"Ah . . ." Delphina replied, motioning for Clementine to sit down. "And please call me Delphina. Let me pour you a cup of tea."

"Thank you. And thank you for meeting me."

Delphina nodded and took a sip of tea, waiting for Clementine to continue. Excitement and curiosity filled her heart at the thought of how close she was to meeting Cadmus. She knew she had to remain composed. Clementine was the only one who could help her.

"Dr. Doyle is very special to me. He was my favorite professor at Rice throughout my undergraduate and graduate studies, and I served as his teaching assistant for many years, even taking on his classes when he finally stepped away from teaching.

"My grandfather and his husband, Mr. McClelland, were partners at the same law firm for many years together. Dr. Doyle suffered many tragedies during his life, including his husband's death last year."

Delphina held her gaze, nodding and trying to understand why she was sharing this personal information.

"This is why I will not allow him to be hurt again."

"I don't want to hurt him!" Delphina protested. "I want to visit him."

"Why? The receptionist said you were a former student, but I know that is not true. Your name is nowhere in the records, and your bio on the UHD website in no way references Rice University."

Delphina's mind reeled. She had not anticipated such a confrontation.

"I'm sure you know Dr. Doyle is worth quite a bit of money. Aside from his own wealth, Mr. McClelland was one of the top litigators in the city. My father has made me keenly aware that people have tried to extort Dr. Doyle once he became a widower."

"I'm not interested in his money!" Delphina retorted.

"Please tell me why you want to see him," Clementine said, her voice softening.

Delphina bit her lip in a futile attempt to ward off tears.

"Why did you want to meet me? You could have done this over the phone," Delphina said.

"Because I believe he needs to see you. And obviously you need to see him. I just needed to meet you face-to-face first and see."

Delphina looked up at her, nodding but deficient in her attempt to find an opening to explain.

"He has an affinity for what was the Merchants and Manufacturers Building, which is now . . ."

"The University of Houston Downtown," Delphina finished.

"Yes, the place where you work. His father helped build it, and it is where his parents met."

Delphina caught her breath, tears coming to her eyes.

"His mother was a tutor at Heights High School, where you taught for many years, as I read in your bio."

Delphina nodded, Clementine's words making her story more plausible, her affection for the UHD and The Heights deeply, almost incomprehensively, engrained.

"He and his mother were very close, but they had a falling out the day before her unexpected death. He never shared the details other than that it was his greatest regret and that he longed to see her but once again.

"And then there is this," Clementine continued, reaching into her purse for a paper. As she slid it across the table, Delphina saw her name come into view on the title line.

DELPHINA PULLED ONTO THE BOULEVARD and in front of The Doyle House as the workers continued another day of transformation. The playlist shuffled to Lynn Anderson's "Rose Garden," and in a breath Delphina's mind shifted to her parents dancing so many years ago.

She thought about the anxiety she had wrestled her entire life, raw and innate as it was from her earliest memories. She thought about her natural love of The Heights and her emotional connection to UHD. There was a pattern, but she conceded that most people would not be able to discover theirs as she had hers. Before understanding her connection to Cadmus, she had held the opinion that past lives were more likely than not. She could not understand the concept of only having one lifetime to sort out issues, some struggles so extreme and so very far from control. One life, followed by an eternal sentence to heaven or hell: It had never made sense to her.

She wondered if there was a pattern as to why her daddy was reticent with an eye naturally cast for reflection, his responses calm and thoughtful when so many others gave way emotionally. Perhaps his wisdom came from being an old soul. She questioned if there was a pattern to her momma's naïve optimism and desire to be around all things elegant. Her last sojourn might have been in a much nicer setting.

She gave thanks for Victor, a man who continued to embody humility and confidence despite his growing success. His optimism, the peaceful way about him, he may very well be someone reaping the benefits of having learned many lessons. And then there was Ainsley, who could have very well been Aislinn. Delphina recalled Victor mentioning it as a possible name, one he liked. "Oh, my gosh! That's it! I love it," she remembered saying, never needing to thumb through the used baby name book Libby had lent her.

Delphina admired the roses that contrasted against the azure sky. One of the workers was watering the flowers spared from the new pool construction, the ones that had been there for over a hundred years as a gentle reminder of the divine to all who graced the garden.

She welcomed the reverence beginning to supplant her anxiety. She learned incarnation begets a composite of free will and interconnectedness, actions continually synergizing lessons and new patterns in an attempt to progress souls forward.

"We all spin a silk fiber for the web," she said aloud to the universe as she pulled her car away from the curb.

Her soul filled with gratitude over her struggles, knowing they made her more connected to others, including the child who still needed her. She was on her way to see her son.

DELPHINA SAT BY HER SON'S bedside, her hand placed gently over his as she kissed his forehead. His eyes remained closed as they had been for days and would remain through his final transition. She told him she loved him and that his father was waiting, full of love and eagerness to see him again.

She looked over to the photograph of Patrick on his nightstand, the man with whom she had reconnected several weeks ago. She looked into the eyes of her former self, smiling widely in front of the M&M, full of hope and life.

Pulling out Cadmus' poem from her pocket, she read aloud to him.

Delphina

swells nurse love and regret
once nourished in the collective womb that feeds us all
the record is found from the constellations to a drop of cerulean
a microcosmic blueprint of the Universe
east to west; the compass marks time
and if the needle intersects our sojourns but once more
a lattice of benediction, atonement

Agape

ACKNOWLEDGMENTS

BURTON, WITHOUT YOU, THIS BOOK literally would not have been written. Aside from your love and encouragement, you selflessly devoted your time so I could write. (And to all our friends, this is why you only saw Burton at children's birthday parties and play dates for the last few years!)

Caroline and Elizabeth, thank you for appreciating my passion and exploring it as a possibility of your own. I intentionally kept my printed rough drafts piled high so you would see how it looks to follow a passion, which is not always an easy path. You warm my heart when I see you curled up writing stories of your own. Your stories connect you to the world. Keep reflecting and writing, my loves.

Roger Leslie, thank you for serving as my first editor. Your feedback and encouragement gave me confidence to continue my journey.

Ellen Green, I appreciate your wit, humor, and southern sayings. You gave more color to Margaret. And we still need a NOD at Tony's.

Jano Nixon-Kelly, you were kind to indulge me and Burton in a private tour of the Niels Esperson Building. Walking the floors and hearing the stories provided context to the building I have admired since I was a child. Thank you for welcoming me into your fold.

My heart fills with gratitude for Greenleaf Book Group. The encouragement and support allowed me to take a big leap and share my thoughts with the world. In particular, I want to extend my appreciation to Daniel

Pederson, Lindsey Clark, Jen Glynn, Rachael Brandenburg, Scott James, Daniel Sandoval, Chelsea Richards, Elizabeth Chenette, and Tyler LeBleu.

I would be remiss not to express my deep love and gratitude for Houston. As a girl from the east side, I grew up absorbing my city's spirit through the smells of oil and industry, the sounds of trains continually underscoring its energy. My life is an example of the possibilities the city offers to anyone willing to work toward a dream.

QUESTIONS FOR DISCUSSION

Houston and its changing skyline are an important part of *Drops of Cerulean*. Discuss how location and architecture are central to the development of the plot of the novel.

What are the major themes in *Drops of Cerulean*? Discuss how these themes play out in the story (i.e., interconnectedness, free will, homosexuality, redemption, family).

Discuss Ilona and Patrick's relationship. Do you think Ilona would have been better off had she not met Patrick in the M&M building that fateful day?

The color blue comes up many times in the novel. Can you remember the different places in the story where it was mentioned? What is the significance of the color blue, and why is it meaningful?

Ilona's life could be described as tragic. What are the different tragedies that befall Ilona, and do you agree with the way that she handled them? Would you have liked her to handle things differently? Discuss what you think might be her greatest regret.

Do you believe that Ilona and Cadmus were finally able to forgive themselves? Were they able to let go of their guilt in the end? Why or why not? Do you believe they each achieved the redemption that they sought?

Spirituality and religion are a major part of this story. Discuss how the author may feel about organized religion versus spirituality based on what you have read in *Drops of Cerulean*.

Ilona was plagued with guilt over Patrick's death, but did Patrick get what he deserved?

Ilona's decision to sell Cadmus and Callista's part of Doyle Lumber & Construction was a difficult one for her to make. Do you think Ilona made the right decision? If so, why? If not, why not? Should she have told her children about this transaction sooner?

Cadmus and Robert were homosexuals in the south during the seventies, eighties, and nineties. Do you think they were somewhat protected from the prejudices of the time because of Robert's success and Cadmus' money? How might their lives have been different had they not had such advantages?

Had Patrick lived, do you think he would have accepted Cadmus for who he was? From what we know of Patrick's character, would he have embraced Cadmus, or would he have rejected him?

Discuss Cadmus' poem at the end of the book. What does this mean? Did Cadmus somehow know that Delphina was coming to him and was actually his mother?

AUTHOR Q&A

1. Can you share what inspired you to write *Drops of Cerulean*? Also, what are some of your favorite books?

   I remember reflecting about my soul when I was a child, perhaps as young as 5 years old. I struggled to reconcile the spirit inside my head and heart with my body. I recall wondering what was the real me—the stillness of my being or the body into which I was born. I could not state it like I am now, but the struggle to understand was very real. I believe this is where my initial appreciation of interconnectedness formed. I have always seen people as more alike than different, as spiritual beings manifested in physical form that search for many of the same things—primarily love, connection, and acceptance.

   My favorite book is The Alchemist *by Paulo Coelho. My copy, weathered after so many reads with layers of annotations and highlights, is never far from reach. Every reread brings a new lesson or a timely reinforcement of what I need to return to the forefront of my mind and heart.*

2. What is your writing process like? How do you get in the mood to write? Do you have any special or peculiar writing rituals? Is there anything in particular that helps you stay focused?

   Words and ideas come most easily when I am in the present moment, connected to the world around me. It helps when I am still, but awareness is key.

Phrases come to me while walking my dog in the neighborhood or walking the halls of school as I take in the world around me. People ask how I created this particular story and the characters. The best way I can describe is that they wrote themselves once I quieted my heart to let them speak.

3. What was your favorite chapter to write in *Drops of Cerulean* and why? And on the other side of the spectrum, were there any chapters that were particularly challenging for you to write? If so, can you share what it was about these parts of the story that challenged you?

   My favorite chapter was the first one I put to paper, the one that begins with "Delphina's love affair with the divine began when she noted the perfectly appointed seeds of a strawberry." I did not know where the narrative would lead, but I had the idea of a girl who took solace in the order of nature as an antidote to anxiety. Early on in the writing process, I was overwhelmed with how to capture the intersecting story lines of the characters. I was even questioning if I could write the book. I was teaching at the time, and I recall sitting on a school computer in the teacher's lounge working on a lesson. A former student from my early teaching years worked as a clerk on this campus. He took a seat next to me and wanted to talk. I remember thinking, I have so much to do! I don't have time! He asked if he could ask me a question. His question? "Have you ever noticed how strawberry seeds are perfectly positioned?" Needless to say, I accepted this random event as a sign to continue with my writing.

   The greatest challenge I faced was weaving the narratives of the three characters in a coherent timeline. I spent a great deal of time writing, deleting, and editing in an attempt to strike the right proportion of moving the story forward at a good pace without spiraling into too many details.

4. The ideas of free will and interconnectedness play a major role in the events of *Drops of Cerulean*. Can you talk a bit about how these themes play out in the novel?

The theme of interconnectedness and free will frame the piece. Ilona exemplifies the power of free will in her pivotal decision to marry Patrick and forge a new life of her own, a milestone decision I refer to as "Free Will." While it is a worthy theme to explore and is a result of its own confluence of events, Drops of Cerulean prompts reflection on "free will," which I believe is tempered by a heavier dose of subtlety and interconnectedness. Ilona's decision to delay confronting Patrick about his affair, her choice to leave him at the party, and Cadmus' regrettable words shouted in anger, all resemble everyday decisions that have the power to impact others significantly. This interplay of our thoughts, words, and actions beg the question: Is free will really free, and what responsibility do we have for the everyday acts that impact the world?

5. Do you have a favorite character in the story? If so, what is it about this character that you most appreciate?

   As a new writer, I did not anticipate the dear relationships I would form with the characters. I shared in their laughter, cried alongside their struggles, and rooted for their quests of peace and happiness. And while I see a part of myself in all of them, my real-life role as a mother draws me to Cadmus, especially since he is the one character we see literally from birth to death. My heart is heavy over the isolation and rejection, but I take comfort that he was able to assume a life true to his identity, which was quite an accomplishment for this time. I also longed for him to have peace with his mother. Creating an authentic reconciliation scene given the nature of the story was a challenge, but I appreciate the final words he heard, his own words, from Delphina.

6. Ilona is such a good-hearted character with nothing but the best intentions. Can you speak a bit about her misfortunes and why things turned out for her the way that they did?

Ilona's reticence, from her reluctance to confront Patrick early on in her suspicions, to her acceptance of Michael's influence over Callista and exclusion of Cadmus, and to her decision to keep the estate decision a secret, all resulted in tragic circumstances despite her good intentions. Ilona made these decisions, but the ramifications were also shaped by the other characters' thoughts, words, and actions. Callista's actions, in particular, fueled her mother's trajectory.

There were many times I wanted Ilona to take a more assertive approach to her life, but she wrote her own story, and I do believe many of us are impacted by our inactions rather than a grand stand for or against something. And while these times were pivotal in altering the course of her life, I find contentment in knowing she never waivered in her support of her son. I believe her greatest regret was breaking his trust, since she spent her life as a widow making decisions so he could live his fullest life.

7. Did Ilona and Cadmus achieve the redemption that they longed for?

Ilona and Cadmus allowed remorse to act as a prominent narrative in their lives. Ilona accepted her role as more of an observer of the joys of others rather than as an active participant in her own life. Cadmus' sexuality steered him to a more secluded existence, especially before he met Robert. When left alone to his own reflective nature, he naturally led the balance of this life in remorse at what his sexuality cost his family.

I do believe their souls found forgiveness in a lesson learned, but I do not believe they found it in the way most of us hope to find it for ourselves. Humans identify with ego over spirit. Many of us appreciate the idea of a soul, but we define it within the context of our current lifetime. There is the belief that I, Dawn, will always be Dawn, even after I pass into the next life. I believe parts of Dawn will remain, the lessons I learned and the ones still in need of tutorials. The labels I was born into will not continue with me.

Along this line, the concept of interconnectedness spans time; Ilona did not find redemption as Ilona, but her soul found it in its journey. It is open for interpretation on whether Cadmus heard Delphina's words. If he, indeed, heard her words, then perhaps he found redemption in the way we, as human beings moored to our identities, long to find it. If he was not cognizant, then his soul's next sojourn would continue to resolve the restlessness.

8. Houston and its evolving architecture play a major role in this story. Can you speak to the significance of the city and its buildings in *Drops of Cerulean?*

Houston embodies the mythical spirit of creation and possibility, a spirit that guided the course of Patrick and Ilona's lives. Although they believed that Houston was a place to forge unique pathways, even they would be humbled by how great the evolution manifested. The city was 72 square miles in 1930, the year the novel begins. Some people still think of Houston as a cowtown, but it is now 627 square miles, which nears the size of Oahu and includes multiple cosmopolitan centers.

The world caught a glimpse of Houston's can-do spirit in the aftermath of Hurricane Harvey, the devastation shining a spotlight on the cooperation and optimism endemic to Houston, the spirit present from the inception of the city. The historic buildings referenced in the novel exemplify this spirit. The Merchants and Manufactures Building, for example, harnessed the spirit of the railways on the ground floor, appealed to shoppers on the street level, while housing business interests on the upper floors. The Niels Esperson Building, commissioned by a widow and designed with features that continue to capture attention today, was the tallest structure in Texas when it was built in 1927. Mrs. Mellie Esperson certainly made her mark on the city with this feat. I think about the people who graced the original buildings, so full of hope for the future. The people who grace them now share the same hopes and dreams.

On a more literal level, I believe the city's evolution represents the absolute magnificence that resides in all of us. Patrick and Ilona focused on developing the downtown skyline, a notable and significant tribute to their city but an obvious choice. They did not appreciate the extent of development possible in the north, south, east, and west. They could not have known the extensive development of the tunnel system that threads underneath the current skyscrapers to span 95 city blocks, a labyrinth of restaurants, shops, and services that leads current visitors to wonder why the city streets are desolate during the work week. Just as redemption comes in forms we may not recognize, so does development. We must be open to what progress means and realize that our hopes may manifest in beautiful ways we may struggle to imagine.

Callista's desire to evolve with the new Houston could be viewed as her desire for newness, for development; however, it also reflects her desire to distance herself and not give reverence to parts of her past. As a contrast, Ilona chose to stay in The Heights after Patrick's death, as did Cadmus after her death. Their preference to remain in the same original blueprint of the city correlates to their reflective nature and tendency to cocoon rather than evolve.

9. Religion and spirituality also play major roles in the story, with a heavy emphasis on the idea of reincarnation. What inspired you to weave elements of Buddhism into the story?

To take a line from the book, I believe more than not in "another truth, one that permit[s] essences to give life another whirl with lessons learned and lessons in need of a reteach." I struggle to understand the belief that the composite of life's choices, a life with many circumstances out of a person's control, can result in eternal heaven or hell. On one hand, the basic concept of interconnectedness is simple, but when you mix in free will, our connections become a complex matrix that creates a rippling effect. While there were tragic ramifications from decisions made, I also firmly believe in our power to spread goodness and love. I believe we bear the divine within ourselves. I believe we can look for the divine in one another to accomplish beautiful things.

10. Do you have another book waiting in the wings? If so, can you tell us a bit about it?

My next book continues to explore interconnectedness but in a more light-hearted manner. With respect to the characters, my intention to is reflect the belief that people who are seemingly different can find common ground if given the right set of circumstances, which I find an important concept to reinforce given the current political climate. The piece also visits another Buddhist concept, that of impermanence. We know this life is temporary, yet we cling to form and identity. Even though we know this clinging is addictive and leads to suffering, it is a challenge not to indulge in the joys of incarnation when there are amazing sensory experiences to be had.

ABOUT THE AUTHOR

DAWN ADAMS COLE WAS BORN and raised in Houston. She received her BA from the University of St. Thomas and her MEd from Harvard University. Dawn wrote *Drops of Cerulean* while serving as a high school teacher and administrator. She hopes to create thought-provoking literary fiction that challenges readers to live deeply and appreciate interconnectedness. She lives in The Heights with her husband, Burton, and her daughters, Caroline and Elizabeth.